D0801636

Praise for Candice Proctor and her previous novel *Whispers of Heaven*

"Rich, unusual, and classic—*Whispers of Heaven* is like reading Woodiwiss again for the first time."
—JILL BARNETT
Author of *Sentimental Journey*

"There is great power in her writing and strong characterization; masterful storytelling and sensuality all add spice to her inborn talent."
—*Romantic Times*

"A wonderful novel rich in emotion . . . One of the best historical romances I have ever read."
—JILL MARIE LANDIS
Author of *Summer Moon*

"A winner . . . The tensions pervading this wonderful story make it impossible to put down. The characters are full of subtlety and a poignancy that makes them most appealing."
—*Rendezvous*

"Vividly drawn characters and a surprising denouement will ensure that this tale is well-received."
—*Publishers Weekly*

By Candice Proctor
Published by The Ballantine Publishing Group

NIGHT IN EDEN
THE BEQUEST
SEPTEMBER MOON
THE LAST KNIGHT
WHISPERS OF HEAVEN
MIDNIGHT CONFESSIONS

MIDNIGHT CONFESSIONS

Candice Proctor

IVY BOOKS • NEW YORK

An Ivy Book
Published by The Ballantine Publishing Group
Copyright © 2002 by Candice Proctor

Ivy Books and colophon are trademarks of Random House, Inc.

ISBN 0-7394-2621-4

Manufactured in the United States of America

For Tony, because, once . . .

CHAPTER
ONE

July 1862, Occupied New Orleans

It had been one of those hot, stifling New Orleans days when the air pressed down dense and breathless with the threat of a coming storm. Nightfall was still hours away, but already the sky hung gunmetal gray and ugly overhead, the peaked white roofs of the tombs glowing pale in the fading light of day. A jagged flash of lightning split the gloom, and Emmanuelle quickened her step, the black skirts of her widow's weeds swaying against the worn frock coat of the white-bearded old man whose arm she held as they hurried through the great, rusting black iron gates of St. Louis Cemetery.

"Perhaps we should not have come this year," Dr. Henri Santerre said as they turned down a weed-choked alley between the high peristyle tombs. About them, the hum of the locusts intensified until it was like a vibration in the thick, hot air. "Or at least we should have left the hospital sooner. There are too many soldiers on the streets tonight for my taste."

They spoke in French, as they always did, Emmanuelle's voice thick with emotion as she said, "I refuse to allow the presence of General Benjamin Butler and his vermin in blue to prevent me from visiting my parents' grave."

"Emmanuelle . . ." The old doctor touched her hand where it rested on his sleeve, his pace slowing. "Remember, my child: You can hate what a uniform stands for and what it does, without indiscriminately hating every man who wears it."

Emmanuelle pivoted to face him, the sweet scent of the jasmine sprays she carried wafting up to mingle with the odors of dampness and decay pressing in all around them. "Uniforms do not kill and maim and destroy. Men do."

"So do women, sometimes."

She gave a startled laugh and swung away from him. "Sometimes." Kneeling on the shallow granite steps leading up to the crypt beside her, she laid the flowers against the marble slab sealing the entrance to the Maret family tomb, and added more softly, "Only, not nearly as often."

He merely grunted, his gnarled, arthritic hand descending on her shoulder and gripping tightly for support as he eased himself down, his back to the tomb. He did not kneel, and she knew he would not pray, although he would sit beside her for as long as she did. Then they would visit his wife's grave, on the far side of this city of the dead.

Slipping her rosary from her pocket, Emmanuelle began, the smooth rosewood beads passing rapidly through her fingers. Normally, she would say the entire rosary, but when thunder rumbled ominously in the distance and the clouds dropped lower, stealing even more of the fading light, she felt an apprehensive shiver that seemed oddly out of place in the evening's heat. It wasn't like her, this sense of uneasiness, of lurking danger. Thunder rumbled again, closer, and after only two decades, Emmanuelle decided to stop.

"She would be proud of you if she could see you

today," Dr. Santerre said quietly when she raised her head. "Your mother, I mean. They both would."

Emmanuelle looked away, her throat suddenly tight. "Would they? I don't think so."

"That's because you've always been too hard on yourself."

She stood, shaking her head. She was stiff from kneeling, and when a sudden gust of hot wind caught her full black skirts and billowed them out around her, she staggered. Her heel slipped from the smooth stone base of the tomb, and she stumbled with a small cry that brought Dr. Santerre lurching to his feet. He reached for her just as she heard the whiz of something rushing past her.

Henri jerked backward as if he had been struck, his spine slamming against the door of the tomb behind him. She watched in numb horror as bright red blood soaked the old man's vest to bloom out in a flare around a small wooden projectile protruding from high in his torso. His pale gray eyes widening, he stared down at his chest, then at Emmanuelle.

"*Mon Dieu,*" she said in a strangled whisper, and stretched out her hand to him.

"Run," he said, blood bubbling up from his mouth as his legs slowly folded beneath him and his eyes rolled back in his head.

She felt the wrenching tear of conflicting compulsions, a scalp-tingling fear for her own life at war with a healer's instinct to help this man who had been like a father to her for so many years. But Emmanuelle knew death when she saw it. Picking up her skirts, she ran.

CHAPTER TWO

Major Zachary X. Cooper, U.S. Cavalry, leaned one shoulder against the frame of the French doors opening off the general's study and watched as the summer storm burst over the city of New Orleans. Rain poured from the darkening sky in windswept sheets that nearly obscured the faint glow of the gaslights lining the leafy street of tall mansions. There was something almost primeval about the way it could rain in this city, Zach thought as he watched the water rise in the gutters and spill in ever deepening ripples over the sidewalks; something at once elemental and decadent about the moist heat of the days and the soft velvet of the nights. It was like a dangerous woman, this city—as reckless and seductive as sin.

He could hear, behind him, the sounds of leave-taking as "Colonel" Andrew Butler wove his drunken steps toward the front of the house. Zach stayed where he was. The less he had to do with the general's opportunistic brother, the better for his career—and his temper.

"Thanks for waiting, Cooper. Here."

Zach turned to accept the crystal glass of French brandy held out to him by General Benjamin Butler, the so-called Beast of New Orleans and Zach's commanding officer. He was an almost comic-looking figure,

Butler, with his short, stout body, overly big head, and squinting, crossed eyes; comic-looking, shrewd, and dangerous—as the people of New Orleans had learned.

"I've had another communication from Washington," Butler said, his movements characteristically quick and nervous as he crossed the priceless Turkey carpet to send a sheet of elegant stationery bearing a familiar letterhead skittering across the leather top of his massive mahogany desk. The desk, like the Uptown house around them and the brandy in Zach's glass, had once belonged to a Confederate general. Butler might not have shown much talent in the field, but he had a real genius for making other people's property his own. Settling into the dead Confederate general's chair, Butler templed his fingers together and squinted at Zach over their tips. "It seems the Secretary of State has been forced to apologize to the Dutch for what he calls our 'unnecessary and rude' handling of their consul."

"Huh." Zach set the brandy to rocking in his glass, the heavy golden-brown liquid gleaming in the candlelight, the heady scent of expensive liquor filling the air. "If the Dutch consul didn't want to be stripped of everything but his socks, he shouldn't have refused to hand over his keys when I asked for them. What did the Secretary of State have to say about the eight hundred thousand dollars in Confederate silver we took from the consul's vault?"

Butler leaned back in his chair, his hands dropping. "Oh, Washington has every intention of keeping that. I'm simply supposed to order my provost marshal not to forcibly relieve any more foreign nationals of their drawers." His thin lips curved upward and parted to display an unusually fine set of even white teeth. The general's smile was his best feature; he knew it, and used it often. "So consider yourself warned."

Zach tasted the brandy in his glass. It was good, very good, but did little to calm the hum of anticipation and determination quickening his blood. "Actually, General," he said, deliberately keeping his voice casual, relaxed, "I've been wanting to speak to you about—"

"No."

"Sir?"

Butler smiled again. "No, I'm not sending you back to your old cavalry regiment. I need you here."

A gust of warm, moist wind caught one of the open doors, slamming it against the wall. Zach went to secure the latch. "Sir," he said, his grip on the latch tight, his grip on himself tighter. "This army needs trained cavalry officers. The Southerners have been riding circles around our troops since the war began."

It was true, all of it. But it wasn't the only reason, wasn't even the main reason Zach was so desperate to get back to his old regiment. Most men would consider it a gift—a blessing, even—this assignment as provost marshal, this easy, secure city life filled not with punishing marches and bloody cavalry charges but with brandy in crystal glasses and evenings spent at the theater or opera. But not Zach. He'd long ago come to terms with a soldier's fears, the fear of the kind of death and mutilation that could come in an instant with the slash of a saber, the whine of a bullet, the devastating impact of a cannonball. What Zach feared was something else entirely, and the longer he stayed in this city as provost marshal, the more inevitable it became that he was eventually going to have to face that fear, whether he wanted to or not.

"Our cavalry boys are getting better," Butler said now, his smile broadening at the expression on Zach's face as he swung back around. "I said they're getting better. I didn't say they are better."

"They could be. With the proper training."

Butler jerked forward. "Listen, Zach. I've no doubt you're a fine cavalry officer. But you're also a damned good provost marshal. I need you here, both to help control this city and to quiet the howling wolves in Washington who'd like nothing better than to get me out of here. However much they might object to your methods, you're a West Point man who spent years fighting on the frontier. They respect that." The general blinked. *And they know you're honest,* said those strange, mismatched eyes, although Butler would never admit, aloud, how important that was to his continued survival.

Like far too many generals in the Union army, Butler was one of Lincoln's political appointments, a lawyer who'd never seen a day of military action before Lincoln pinned the stars on his uniform and sent him out to do his best to get all the mothers' sons under his command killed. Only, Butler was too busy exploiting his despotic authority over the city of New Orleans to spend much time trying to carry the war up the Mississippi. The mothers' sons under Butler's command were growing rich on booty—like the general himself.

"With all due respect, sir, this was only supposed to be a temporary assignment while I recovered from my wound."

Butler smiled again, a purely spontaneous smile of amusement. "You think you're recovered now, do you?"

"Yes, sir."

"You might not think so after spending an eighteen-hour day in the saddle."

"I've been making it a point to ride every day, sir."

"And you rode particularly hard today, didn't you? Hell, even my wife could see the pain in your face when you limped into her dining room tonight."

"Sir—"

The general thrust up from his chair in one swift movement. "*Enough*, Major."

Zach set his jaw against a surge of angry disappointment so intense, he could taste it. "Yes, sir."

The two men eyed each other steadily for a moment. It was Butler who turned away. "Here. Have some more brandy."

"Thank you, sir, but I—" Zach broke off as a knock sounded.

The general raised his voice. "What is it?"

"Fletcher, sir. For Major Cooper." A tall, thickset captain with a flowing mane of fiery hair and a splendid pair of handlebar mustaches filled the doorway. Rain glistened on his full, florid cheeks, darkened the cloth of his cape, pooled on the hardwood floor around his polished black boots. His pale eyes darted across the room to Zach, and the mustaches twitched. Captain Hamish Fletcher knew why Zach was here. And he obviously knew, by whatever he could see in Zach's face, that Zach's request for a transfer had been refused. "There's been a murder."

The twist in Zach's gut was instantaneous and vicious. It was like a nightmarish echo from his past, a realization of what he had feared the most. *There's been a murder, sir. Another murder, sir, Another, another* . . . He felt the muscles in his throat tightening up, tighter and tighter. For one appalling moment, it was an effort even to draw breath, so that it was Butler who answered, his voice tinged with irritation.

"The riffraff of this city get themselves murdered at

the rate of something like four or five a month," he said, brandy bottle hovering in midair as he looked up. "Last week it was an Irishman. Next week it'll be an Italian . . . or a Negro, or a German, or a Pole. Do you propose to come running to Major Cooper with each one?"

"No, sir," said Hamish, his accent a peculiar combination of his parents' Scots and the New York City neighborhood where he'd grown up. "But this one is a wee bit out of the ordinary. It's a Creole." His gaze flicked back to meet Zach's. "A doctor."

"A Creole." Butler let out a derisory huff and sloshed a generous measure of brandy into his glass. "It's past time the Creoles of this city learned they're not nearly as important as they think they are."

Hamish's gaze held Zach's steadily as Zach tossed off the rest of his brandy and set the crystal glass aside. He had control of himself now, control of that sick, shameful fear. It was still there—he thought it would always be there—but he'd pushed it down where it wouldn't bother him, where he didn't need to deal with it. Butler was right: Men got themselves killed in this city all the time. There was no reason to think this murder would be any different, no reason to think it was the beginning of something ominous. Something that would happen again and again.

Something like what had happened before.

"I'll come," Zach said, reaching for his cape. "Where's the body?"

"St. Louis Cemetery. It's where he was killed," Hamish added when Zach swung around to stare at him.

"Convenient," Zach said, and buckled on his saber with hands that were utterly, convincingly steady.

• • •

It was still pouring when the hack let them out onto the rotting, broken wooden sidewalks of Basin Street.

"I left a couple of troopers here," said the captain, sounding very much like a policeman—but then, before the war, in New York, that's what Hamish Fletcher had been. It was something Zach could never understand, why any man would want to be a policeman, why he would deliberately put himself in the way of having to deal with the worst a city could spew out, every day, day after day, for a lifetime.

"We made a sweep of the graveyard," Hamish was saying, "but it didn't turn up anything. You've got to admit, it's a good place to hide and ambush someone. All these wee little templelike tombs jammed one up against the other."

Zach tipped back his head and scanned the cemetery's high, whitewashed walls and the slanting roofs of the tombs just visible beyond. Rain coursed over his cheeks and ran under his collar, and he swore. Settling his broad-brimmed hat lower on his forehead, he eyed the small lake that had accumulated in the cemetery's gateway, then plowed through it, rainwater gurgling and swelling about his black boots. With every step, white-hot pain shot up his left thigh, to his hip. The general was right: Zach had pushed himself too hard that day. Sometimes, it was like a live thing, the pain. But he still had his leg, which was more than most men who'd taken a minié ball midthigh could say. It was easier and quicker simply to cut off a man's leg—or his hand, or his arm—than it was to try to save it, and most army doctors tended to take the easy way out. After years of watching surgeons turn strong, hale men into cripples, Zach didn't have much use for the profession. He'd saved his own leg only by threatening to cut off the balls of anyone who tried to take a saw to him.

"What the hell was the good doctor doing out on a night like this, anyway?" he asked now, shouting to be heard over the roar of falling water.

Hamish laughed. "Visiting his wife's grave."

Zach swung to look at his friend's shining eyes and twitching mustaches, dripping with rain. "My God. You're actually enjoying this, aren't you?"

Hamish laughed again. "Some Irish immigrant getting his throat slit for a few dollars down on Gallatin Street, now, that might be sad, but it's still just routine. But this"—he rubbed his hands together—"*this* is going to be like a puzzle. This is the fun part of police work."

"I don't like puzzles," said Zach, his voice hardening. Once, he had liked puzzles. He'd even been a bit cocky about his ability to solve them . . . until two years ago, when someone had taken a fiendish delight in showing Zach he wasn't nearly as good at puzzles as he had thought, and a girl named Rachel who'd loved him had ended up dead because of it all. "Besides," he added dryly, "I'm a cavalry officer, not a policeman."

"Aren't you, then?" Hamish's broad hand slapped him on the back hard enough to make him stagger. "Look up *provost marshal* in the dictionary, lad."

Zach nodded to where the gatekeeper was hopping nervously from one foot to the other, his lantern swinging back and forth to cast eerie, erratic patterns of light and shadow across the surrounding tombs. "Did he see anything?"

Fletcher shrugged. "Who knows? The fella doesn't seem to understand more than ten words of English. You wouldn't happen to speak German, would you?"

"Speak it?" said Zach with a smile. "No."

"We'll have to get someone out in the morning who can talk to him."

Sloshing toward the immigrant, Zach lifted the lantern from the man's hand and sent him back to the gatehouse with a nod of his head and a shouted, *"Danke schön."*

Fletcher peered at him through the driving rain. "I thought you didn't speak German."

"I don't." Zach held the lantern aloft. They were surrounded by a seemingly endless expanse of marble crypts, small houses of the dead lined up one beside the other along crisscrossing avenues of rank grass and scattered broken stones. Water sluiced from the edges of the peaked roofs, beat against forlorn inscriptions. Here and there some of the older tombs had cracked and broken open, allowing shadowy glimpses of dull brass, splintered wood, and weathered bones. "So exactly who is this doctor?" he asked as they set off down the central alley.

"His name's Henri Santerre," said Fletcher, falling into step beside him. "Runs—or rather, used to run— the Hospital de Santerre on Bienville, in the old quarter. It's the only private hospital in the city that's managed to stay open through the war and occupation, which tells you something about him."

"Any family?"

"Not much. He's a widower. Lives with his sister Elise Santerre on Conti. There," said Fletcher suddenly, nodding toward two blue-coated soldiers huddled near the far wall, its stacks of small, brick-built, ovenlike crypts barely visible through the teeming rain. "Down that way."

They took off to the left. As they drew closer, Zach could see that beyond the soldiers stood a woman he supposed must be the dead man's sister. A small, fine-boned figure dressed all in black, her hair hanging in dark, wet hanks around a pale face, she had drawn off to one side and stood rigidly waiting, as if unwilling to remain too close to the men in blue. It didn't surprise him. Of all the people in this city, it was the women who had been the most open in expressing their hatred and contempt for the Union army. It was why Butler had promulgated his infamous Woman Order.

Zach barely glanced at her as he turned his attention to the white-headed body that lay sprawled awkwardly against the entrance to a crypt with the name MARET chiseled above the door. Rain washed over the old man's pale, wrinkled cheeks, soaked his short beard, pooled with the blood on his vest where a dark wooden shaft protruded from his chest.

The rain ran into Zach's eyes and he wiped it away, along with a film of cold sweat that had sprung up on his forehead. Stepping onto the base of the grave, he hunkered down beside the body and let the lantern light illuminate the still face. The scent of crushed jasmine came to him, mingling bizarrely with the smell of damp and decay and blood. The doctor's eyes were closed as if he were sleeping peacefully. Reaching out, Zach touched the man's still warm neck. "Are you certain he's dead?" Zach asked the trooper who had come to stand beside him.

"Wouldn't you be," said a young female voice lightly accented with French and husky with what sounded like hatred, "if someone shot a crossbow bolt straight through your heart?"

CHAPTER THREE

Zach glanced up at the woman in soaked black bombazine who stood beside him, her face pale and wet and young, her fine dark eyes unlined by age and snapping with blatant enmity. This was not Henri Santerre's sister.

She was exquisite in that way only the French can be, built long of neck and small of bone, with an impossibly tiny waist and high, round breasts and an aristocratic carriage that spoke of châteaux and salons and midnight flights from the guillotine. There clung to her an air of delicateness, of fragility, even, oddly belied by that fierce light shining from her eyes and the earthy fullness of her lips. Even with her hair plastered to her face and rain dripping from the tip of her small, upturned nose, she was both formidable, and stunning.

"I've seen men live an uncomfortably long time with some god-awful wounds," Zach said, straightening slowly.

"No doubt." Her gaze swept him to linger tellingly on his saber and Colt before returning to meet his eyes. "No doubt you have administered many of those wounds yourself."

Zach twisted around to stare at Fletcher. "What is she doing here?"

The majestic red mustaches twitched. "Allow me to present Madame de Beauvais. She was with the gentleman when he was killed."

Zach swung back to stare at the calm, unbelievably self-possessed woman before him. "You saw it happen?"

"Yes."

Most women who had witnessed a murder would have gone into hysterics, or fainted, or both. Not this one. He found himself impressed and intrigued and suspicious, all at the same time. "Couldn't you have chosen a more pleasant evening to pay a visit to the cemetery?"

She blinked against the rain. "Dr. Santerre's wife and my mother both died on the same day, in the yellow-fever epidemic of eighteen forty-nine. We come here every year, to pray, and to lay flowers at their graves." Her gaze fell to the crushed, bloodied jasmine sprays at their feet, but if she felt any emotion at all, it didn't show on her face.

God, Zach thought, but she was a cool one. "Did you see who did this?"

Instead of answering, she studied him through narrowed eyes. "Why is the army involved in this? Wouldn't it be better handled by the New Orleans police?"

Zach grunted. "There is no New Orleans police force. Not anymore."

"Because you've thrown most of them in prison!" she said, her coolness momentarily deserting her.

"Most of them," Zach agreed. He hooked his thumbs in his sword belt and leaned into her. "Now, are you going to tell me what happened, or not?"

Beside them, Hamish drew out a battered cloth-bound notebook and a pencil he held poised midair, ready to write. She glanced at the captain and his notebook, then away. "We always visit my mother's grave first," she said, staring into the rain-filled gloom of the night. "The Santerre crypt is farther down the row. Usually, I say an entire rosary. This time I didn't."

. The outward display of calm was illusory, Zach realized, studying her. There was a fine trembling going on inside her, although she was doing her best to control it. Control it, and hide it. Her need for self-protection was partially a reaction, he knew, to the color of his uniform; as far as she was concerned, he was her enemy, and one didn't willingly show weakness to an enemy. But he suspected it went beyond that. A woman like this would not willingly show any weakness. "Why did you stop?" he asked. "Did you see someone?"

"No. No one. I wanted to hurry because of the storm." Her slim throat worked as she swallowed. "I was just standing up when the crossbow bolt came from behind me."

"Crossbow bolt?" Zach repeated incredulously.

Again, that lifting of the chin, that flare of something much like contempt as she swung her head to study him again. "What do you think it is?"

The attempt to provoke him was both deliberate and damnably successful. Setting his teeth, Zach hunkered down on his heels and squinted at the shaft protruding from the doctor's chest. "Can't be. It's too small. And it's made of wood."

He expected her to make another one of those acerbic remarks of hers. When she didn't, he glanced up to find her staring off into the distance again. Rain fell about them, rushed in the stone-lined gutters at their feet, streamed down her stiff, pale cheeks. She suddenly looked wet and tired and quietly, profoundly shaken by grief and fear, and all the anger she'd aroused in him dissipated instantly.

"Here," he said, unclasping his cape as he stood. "Take this. You're soaked through. You'll become ill."

The blue cloth swirled between them. She jerked back as if it were poisoned, her eyes flashing fire, those magnificent lips curling in contempt, her voice hoarse with emotion. *"Never."*

They stared at each other through the rain-filled darkness. "All right. Don't take it." He let the cape settle back about his shoulders. "Where do you live?"

She hesitated, her jaw tight, then answered. "On the rue Dumaine, between Royal and Chartres."

"Captain Fletcher will escort you home."

"Thank you, but I have no need of an escort."

He allowed himself to smile, a fierce, tight smile that held no warmth. "I beg your pardon, madame, but at the moment I have only your word when it comes to who you say you are and where you live."

Her nostrils flared as she sucked in a quick, high breath. "I see. Very well."

The night about them was hot and silent except for the rain. Zach held her angry gaze for a long, significant moment. She was a young woman, he thought; a young woman recently widowed, judging from her deep mourning. She had come here to pray for her dead mother, and instead she had witnessed the brutal, violent murder of an old friend. She should have seemed vulnerable. She should have provoked in him nothing more than pity, and perhaps a chivalrous urge to protect the weak. Instead, she had deliberately antagonized him, and he found his reaction to her to be both violent and explicitly, damnably carnal.

Abruptly turning his back on her, he caught Fletcher's eye, and snapped, "Get her out of here."

· · ·

Henri Santerre's sister Elise was old, older even than the doctor, Zach thought, studying her as she sat in a wing chair to one side of an empty fireplace, her hands folded in her lap, her back held stiffly, determinedly straight. In the soft glow of the flickering light cast by a single candlestick, her hair shone white and thin against the pink of her scalp, the bones of her wrists and face looking fragile and painfully obvious beneath her aged, wrinkled flesh. But the intelligence in her pale gray eyes was still sharp and lively, and the only tremor in her voice was one of grief.

"It was kind of you to come, Major," she said now, her gaze steady as she returned his stare. "Thank you."

It wasn't true, of course, and they both knew it. He wasn't being kind, coming here, tonight, personally, to tell her of her brother's death. He was here because, whatever Butler might have said, the murder of a respected old doctor in a cemetery was hardly the kind of incident one could rely on simple soldiers to handle.

Zach glanced around the front room of the Santerre town house, where they sat, his gaze taking in the high plaster ceiling and formal, overstuffed furniture shrouded now with white cotton covers for the summer. Even the gilt gas jets had been covered with tulle to prevent fly specks, for in this climate, no one was willing to suffer their heat, whatever the inconvenience. From the distance came the sound of the cathedral bell, chiming the hour, the dull thud clanging on and on, and he leaned forward in his own chair and came to the point now as she'd known he would. "I'm sorry, but I need to ask if you have any idea who might have wanted your brother dead."

She sucked in a quick breath and sat, thoughtful and still for a moment, before shaking her head. "No. But

Emmanuelle could probably answer that question far better than I."

"Emmanuelle?"

"Emmanuelle de Beauvais."

"Ah." Zach shifted his attention to the black felt hat with its gold embroidered crossed cavalry swords that dangled idly from his fingers. The woman in mourning from the cemetery. Even the mention of her name was enough to awaken something within him—a quickening, an interest that had little to do with duty and murder. "And why is that?" he asked.

He looked up in time to see the aged skin at the corners of her eyes pucker in a way that left him wondering what she'd read in his face. "She has helped him, always, at the hospital." The soft, melodic French accent was similar to, and yet not quite the same as, that of Madame de Beauvais. "You see, the Hospital de Santerre was my brother's dream, but it was actually begun by the three of them together—Henri, Emmanuelle's father, Jacques Maret, and her husband, Philippe de Beauvais."

"Her father and husband are both doctors?" It would do much, Zach thought, to explain her calm demeanor in the presence of death.

"Were. Jacques Maret died in the great yellow-fever epidemic of eighteen fifty-three." She paused, her lips pressing together, and he knew she was going to make him ask for the rest of it.

"And Philippe de Beauvais?" he prompted, obliging her.

"Philippe was killed in the war. Two months ago."

Two months, Zach thought. It did much to explain the young widow's obvious hatred of his blue uniform, but he'd still swear there was more to her animosity than that.

"Emmanuelle always wanted to be a doctor herself, you know," Elise Santerre was saying. "But it's not allowed for women to become doctors." Something about the way she said it made Zach wonder if this old woman might not have had similar dreams herself, once; ambitions that society didn't allow someone of her sex to fulfill.

He asked more questions, about the hospital, and about the old man's acquaintances and habits, but it wasn't until sometime later, when he was leaving, that Elise Santerre said suddenly, as if she could hold it back no longer, "Is it possible Henri was killed by mistake?"

At the base of the steps Zach turned sharply, his head falling back as he stared up at her. "Why? Can you think of someone who might want Madame de Beauvais dead?"

"No. No, of course not," she said quickly.

But for the first time that evening, Zach had the feeling the elderly woman was being less than honest with him.

Emmanuelle stood in the doorway of her son's darkened bedroom and listened to the gentle rhythm of his breathing. "Dominic," she whispered, but quietly, because he was sleeping and she had no desire to disturb him. She only felt the need to say his name, just as she had felt the need to come here, to the door that communicated between her room and his, and assure herself that he was safe. Safe and alive.

He looked small in his big mahogany bed with its high footboard and mosquito net–draped half-tester. Odd, how long it had been since she had thought of him as young, for he was eleven now and growing rapidly toward manhood. But a child of eleven was still heart-stoppingly vulnerable. It was such a dangerous place, New Orleans. Even before the coming of the war and all its attendant miseries, life was precarious here, a constant battle against yellow fever and typhus and swamp sickness. Death could come too easily in this city, too quickly. Standing in the dark, watching her son sleep, Emmanuelle felt her heart fill with a love for him so deep and powerful that it seemed dangerous, and she found she had to curl her hands into fists and hold them clenched at her sides to keep from going to touch her fingertips to the reassuring warmth of his cheek, an action that would surely awaken him.

She turned, meaning to go back to bed. Instead, she went to sit beside one of the open French doors of her room overlooking the empty, rain-soaked paving stones of the rue Dumaine. She thought it must be late, for she could no longer hear the roar from the cabarets along the waterfront, only the endless rush of water, slapping into puddles and dripping from the eaves and running off the edges of the banquettes.

The breeze rustling the ferns and potted rosemary on the gallery felt warm and muggy against her face, but when she wrapped her arms across her chest she realized she was shaking, deep, soul-wracking tremors of horror and grief and fear. She kept seeing over and over again in her mind's eye the penetrating impact of the crossbow bolt striking deep into her old friend's chest, the bright spurting flow of his blood, the startlingly swift ebb of life and intelligence from those pale gray eyes.

Blood and death: frightening, even horrifying, sights to most people, but not, surely, to a woman like her, a woman who had devoted her life to healing and to the study of medicine. It was the suddenness, she decided, the violent deliberateness of Henri Santerre's killing, that had shaken her. That, and her own grief at his loss.

She kept thinking of things—like his study of native medicines, or the paper he'd been writing on the dangers of phlebotomy, and now would never finish. Or of his plans to open a ward devoted solely to maternity cases, once the war was over. She tried to tell herself it was better he had died, thus, in the fullness of a productive life, rather than wasting away at the end of a frustratingly debilitated old age. Yet the sense of the incompleteness of his dreams gnawed at her, perhaps because she knew how much it would have annoyed him.

And because she needed him so badly.

It shamed her to realize, deep down in what she felt to be the smallness of her soul, how much of her grief, like her fear, was for herself. She had lost, in one swift stroke, a dear friend, a respected mentor, and a badly needed business partner. Now, the burden of keeping the hospital open through the devastating hardships of war and occupation would fall to Emmanuelle alone.

"*Mon Dieu,*" said a scolding voice. "You'll catch your death, sitting in the night air like that, barefoot, and wearing nothing but that thin old nightdress." A shawl descended on Emmanuelle's shoulders, and she hugged it to her, turning with a low, shaky laugh.

"It's stinking hot, Rose."

"And you're as cold as ice." A warm, caramel-colored hand closed around Emmanuelle's. "Feel you. You've had a shock. You should be in bed. Everything always looks worse in the middle of the night than it will in the morning."

"This is bad, Rose."

Rose let out her breath in a long, mournful sigh and sank into a nearby straight-backed chair. "I know."

They sat together for a time in companionable silence, Emmanuelle and this woman who had once been her slave but was now simply servant, and friend.

"Why you think somebody killed that old man?" Rose asked, giving voice, finally, to the question that troubled them both.

Emmanuelle shook her head. "I don't know. I keep going over the people Henri knew—his patients, other doctors—but I can't think of anyone angry enough to kill him. And to kill him so deliberately, so coldly. . . ."

Only, it hadn't been cold, she thought, that rage she had sensed as she knelt in prayer. It had been fierce, passionate. Then she remembered that Henri hadn't wanted to go to the cemetery that night, and she found herself wondering if he had known something, if there had been some threat he hadn't told her about. Or maybe he had simply felt it, too, that sense of menace, of lurking danger.

She stared out at the rain, her heart heavy with grief and guilt. "I keep thinking, what if I hadn't insisted on going to the cemetery? Or what if we'd left sooner? What if—"

"That's a passel of silly questions you're asking," Rose said, interrupting her. "What happened, happened. And if you're trying to find some way to blame yourself, you can just stop right there."

"But I felt something, Rose. A kind of evil, or darkness. A . . ." She paused, struggling to put the unutterable into words.

"Well, what you expect?" said Rose brusquely. "Cutting up dead people by day, then wandering around graveyards when it's coming on to night?"

Emmanuelle let out a startled bark of laughter, quickly smothered. She glanced toward the half-opened door to the back bedroom, where Dominic slept the peaceful sleep of protected innocence. Fear for him rose up within her anew. Not just the fear that something might happen to him, but that age-old mother's fear:

What will become of my child if I should die? Death could strike so quickly, so unexpectedly. It could come out of the night with the poisonous touch of infected air, at the twang of a crossbow bolt, on the sharp edge of a swinging sword.

"You think it was supposed to be you who died tonight, don't you?" Rose said, giving solid form, finally, to what Emmanuelle had been groping toward but hadn't quite been able to bring herself to acknowledge.

"Oh, God, Rose." She brought up her hands to cover her face, her breath gusting out in a shuddering sigh. "That malice I sensed, just before Henri was hit? I don't think it was aimed at Henri, I think it was directed at me. And if I hadn't stumbled, if Henri hadn't moved to help me, that bolt would have killed me."

"The Yankee major you were telling me about—the provost marshal—does he know?"

Emmanuelle let her hands fall, clasped, to her lap, her gaze lifting to her friend's. "That I think Henri was killed by accident?" She shook her head. "He wouldn't believe me."

"He might. And if someone is trying to kill you—"

"What do you think the Yankees would do? Hmmm? Protect me?" Emmanuelle stood abruptly, her fingers clutching the shawl around her shoulders. "These people aren't policemen, Rose; they're *soldiers.* Enemy soldiers. They could arrest anyone—you, me, *anyone*—and have us executed after only a travesty of a trial. As far as that Yankee provost marshal is concerned, I'm probably his best suspect."

Rose sucked in a quick, worried gasp of air. "You? A suspect? But . . . why?"

"You should have seen the way he looked at me, Rose. As if he *knew* I had something to hide."

"But you don't."

"Don't I?" said Emmanuelle, her voice dropping when she heard the sounds of stirring from the back bedroom. It had been there in the man's eyes, she thought, when he'd looked at her; as if he'd somehow guessed all the dark and terrible secrets of her life. And she was afraid, so very afraid that, one by one, he was going to find out those secrets.

By dawn, the rain had stopped.

Gnawing absently at the heel of a loaf of French bread, Zach carried his coffee out onto the upstairs veranda that ran along the back of the Greek revival–style mansion General Butler had appropriated for the use of his staff officers. Beside him, water still dripped from the giant, moss-draped live oaks overhead to patter onto the tattered leaves of the banana trees and elephant ears and ferns in the garden below. In the heat of the early morning sun, the dark, wet earth steamed, filling the warm air with a lush odor of dampness and rot.

Looking out over that tangled mass of dark green vegetation, Zach found himself wondering exactly what it was about this city that stirred him so, that spoke to all that was sensual and dark within him. They were an old New England family, the Coopers of Rhode Island, self-disciplined and businesslike and maybe even a bit self-righteous. But Zach's mother had come from a different world, a Mediterranean-flavored world of hot nights and exotic flowers and the sultry, blood-stirring thrum of the guitar. Sometimes, she had taken him with her, back to that world. They'd never stayed long, but Zach had eventually come to understand that he was, in some vital way, more his mother's son than his father's, that the blood of Castile pumped potent and hot and reckless through his being. His father had known it, too, and had tried to beat it out of him, but it had never worked. That innate wildness was still there, and this city called to it—this city, and a dangerous, enigmatic woman in black named Emmanuelle de Beauvais. Together, they seemed to accentuate that part of him, the part that was dark and more than a bit wicked. And it occurred to him, as he looked out over the lush garden, that this murder might be more of a threat to him—to his equilibrium, to his career, to his entire future, even—than he'd first realized.

He was sitting in a wooden rocker at the edge of the veranda, his crossed boots propped up on the railing, when Hamish Fletcher found him. "So," said the captain, pulling a chair beside Zach's and lowering himself into it. "Did you learn anything from Henri Santerre's sister last night?"

Zach shook his head. "Not really. Only that Santerre's wife and Madame de Beauvais's mother died thirteen years ago yesterday. In a yellow-fever epidemic."

Hamish tugged at one end of his mustache. "Did you think she was lying?" There was no need to specify which "she" he was referring to. The memory of the petite Frenchwoman rode them both.

"I think Madame de Beauvais is more than capable of lying," Zach said. "She's more than capable of a lot of things."

The mustaches twitched. "You didn't like her much, did you?"

"She didn't exactly go out of her way to make us like her, now did she?"

Hamish threw back his head and laughed. "That she didn't. Refused to say a word to me the entire way to the rue Dumaine, then gave me a curt message and shut the door in my face when I was trying to be polite and say good night. It's no' going to be easy trying to get information out of these people. And as it stands, we don't have diddle to go on." He glanced sideways in an inquiring afterthought. "The sister had no ideas?"

"None. But we do have this." Reaching out, Zach plucked a small object from the tabletop beside him. "The army doctor sent it over. He thought it might be important."

"I'll be damned." Hamish's bushy red eyebrows drew together as he leaned forward to stare at the projectile in Zach's hand. "The lady was right. It is a crossbow bolt. Whoever heard of one that small?" He suddenly went quite still. "What kind of tip is that?"

"It's a silver alloy."

Fletcher sat back hard enough to make his chair creak. "My gawd. What are you suggesting? That someone saw the good doctor wandering around the cemetery last night and mistook him for a vampire?"

Zach shook his head. "It wasn't even dark yet, remember? But it is an interesting choice of weapon." He held the bolt up before him. "Why kill a man with a crossbow—or, more particularly, why *this* crossbow?"

"Well," said Hamish thoughtfully smoothing his mustaches with the thumb and forefinger of one hand. "It's silent."

"So's a knife."

"Aye. But you need to get close to stick a knife between a man's ribs. That's risky. And some people might balk at it—the thought of shoving cold steel into yielding flesh. I mean, it's no' very pleasant."

"All right. Silence and distance. No need to get blood on one's hands, no chance of being recognized, no chance of a struggle."

Hamish shook his head. "Santerre was an old man. He wouldn't have put up much of a fight."

"Not enough, perhaps, to worry a man who was healthy and strong." In the courtyard below, a plump black woman in a yellow tignon was hanging up wash. Zach watched her shake out one of the officers' shirts and pin it on the line. It bothered him, knowing the people who served him were slaves. Made him feel unclean, and tainted by an old, old sin that not even this war could wash away. "But for someone who was weak, or incapacitated in some way," he said, his gaze still on the woman, "a crossbow would be the perfect weapon."

Hamish grunted. "You mean, someone like one of the good doctor's patients?"

"Or a woman."

Hamish, too, had been watching the slave below. Now he swung his head to stare at Zach. "She was standing beside Santerre when he was hit." He paused. "Or at least that's what she says."

"Huh. Madame de Beauvais could slide a knife between a man's ribs without any problem at all." Zach brought his gaze back to the miniature bolt in his hand. Most quarrels were made of metal with a squared tip, but this shaft had been fashioned of wood, stained now with blood. "If she decided to use a crossbow, it was for a different reason altogether. One we haven't thought of yet." He tightened his grip on the bolt, then held it out. "The shaft has a name burned into it. DUFOUR ET FILS. See what you can find out about it. If we can track down who sold it, maybe we can find out who bought it."

Hamish took the slim, polished length of wood in his hand and frowned. "It's no' going to be easy."

"I suspect the widow could tell us something, if

she wanted to." Zach let his boots drop to the veranda floor, and stood. "After all, she knew exactly what it was, remember? She could very easily know who shot it."

Fletcher looked up at him. "You don't know that."

"No." Zach reached his arms over his head and stretched, drawing the warm, moist air deep into his lungs. It was already hot. By noon the heat and humidity would make it hard to breathe. "But I think I'll pay an early visit to the rue Dumaine."

"She won't be there." Fletcher sucked his upper lip between his teeth, the way he did when he was thoughtful. Or troubled. He dropped his gaze to the bloodstained bolt in his hands. "That was the only thing she said to me. She said if you was to be looking for her this morning, you'd find her at the Hospital de Santerre."

CHAPTER
FOUR

She'd known the Yankee provost marshal would come. She'd known it, and still she felt her stomach wrench when she caught sight of him from an open window on the hospital's second floor.

His name was Zachary Cooper, and he was almost as well-known—and feared—as his commanding officer, Beast Butler. Whenever Butler wanted a Rebel house seized, or an uncooperative newspaper editor thrown into prison, Cooper was the man who executed the orders. He was standing across the street, one hand resting casually on the cavalry saber at his side, his head thrown back and his eyes narrowed against the hot glare of the morning sun as he studied the old building's high facade. He was a tall man, tall and slim, much slimmer than the husky, red-haired Yankee who'd escorted her home last night. And younger, too, she realized now. Seeing the morning light fall on the major's smooth, tanned face, she realized he was probably no more than twenty-six or twenty-seven, although she'd thought him older last night. It should have reassured her, to realize how young he was, but it didn't.

Sunlight flashed on the steel hilt of his saber as he stepped from the brick banquette into the street, and she jerked, an unconscious reaction she regretted when the movement drew his eye to where she stood. Their gazes met and caught, and it was as if he had reached out and touched her, as if he held her transfixed by the intensity of his being and the powerful threat of his suspicions.

She held his gaze until he passed beneath the overhang of the gallery. Only then did she allow herself to turn from the window and move to the bedside of the man she had come to tend.

"How are you feeling this morning, Lieutenant?" she asked, carefully straightening the sheets he'd torn up in the course of a long and pain-wracked night.

The young man in the bed was thin and haggard, with labored breathing and a fatally grayish tinge to his complexion. But he managed to smile up at her and say jauntily enough, "Oh, I'll be out there drinking wine and eating five-course banquets soon enough."

"Huh. If you're not careful, I'll tell Mademoiselle La Touche you don't like the food she's been having prepared for you." He winced as she helped him sit up, and she said more seriously, "How is your shoulder?"

"The shoulder's fine. It's my right arm that's been keeping me awake." He laughed when he said it, for it was a kind of joke. The lieutenant had no right arm; the pains he felt were phantom.

"Let me take a look at it."

She was unrolling his bandages when she heard the click of boot heels on the bare stairs, followed by a firm tread with only a hint of hesitation in its stride as the major crossed the scrubbed floorboards behind her. She'd noticed his limp last night. Noticed, too, how hard he'd tried to hide it. She did not turn around.

"Dr. Santerre's office is on the first floor," she said, not glancing up. "Any of the nurses can show you where it is."

The footsteps stopped behind her. "Actually," said that deep, clipped New England voice she remembered from last night, "you're the one I wanted to see."

She dropped the scissors she'd been using to cut through the old bandage, and had to stoop to pick them up. "I'm sorry, Major, but I am busy."

"I'll wait."

A terrible stench filled the room, and she forced herself to concentrate as the last of the lieutenant's bandages fell away. He'd been a prisoner of war, Lieutenant Emile Rouant, his wound left untreated until he'd been paroled and brought to the Hospital de Santerre. They'd cut off as much of his arm as they could in a desperate attempt to save his life, although they'd all known, even then, that it was too late. He would be unlikely to live through another night.

Your heart's too soft, Philippe used to say to her, *but you're still tough.* She told herself that now: *You're tough. You know people die. People die all the time.* But he was so young, this lieutenant. So young and brave and determinedly cheerful. Emmanuelle felt a lump of sadness rise in her throat and forced it down so she could keep her voice steady when she said, "I think we'll put a wine compress on this, Lieutenant."

The man's remaining hand snaked out to close about her wrist, stopping her as she reached for her tray. "It's not good, is it?"

"No," she said quietly, meeting his gaze. "If there's someone you'd like to write—"

He nodded.

"I'll ask Mademoiselle La Touche to see you, when she comes in."

The young man lay back and closed his eyes as she went about the gruesome task of treating his stump. All the while she worked, she was aware of the powerful presence of the Yankee major behind her, although he said nothing. Once, she glanced back to find him leaning against the wall, his arms crossed at his chest, his hard, darkly handsome face intent as he watched her. She didn't look at him again.

"Why were you doing that?" he demanded, planting himself in front of her when she had finished and went to leave.

"Doing what?" she asked, moving around him.

He fell into step beside her as she crossed the room. "Bandaging that man's wound."

She stopped and swung to face him, one hand holding the tray balanced against her hip. "Why? Do you think I did a poor job of it?"

"You know you didn't. But I'm very familiar with the sort of tasks women normally perform in hospitals, and that isn't one of them."

She should be used to it by now, this attitude so many people had toward the idea of women in medicine, but it still riled her. Some people thought women too emotionally fragile to be exposed to the horrors of a hospital, while others thought them mentally incapable of the rigors of medical study. And almost everyone agreed there was something not quite proper about a woman—a *lady*—who was familiar with, and touched, men's bodies. "You've obviously never heard of Florence Nightingale," she said crisply as they passed through the doorway to the high-ceilinged, whitewashed stairwell. "Or the Sisters of Charity. Believe it or not, there are actually places—such as Paris, or even Philadelphia—where women are allowed to be doctors." She threw him a challenging look. "Does that shock you?"

He didn't look shocked. Instead, an unexpected gleam of amusement lit the depths of his eyes. He had unusually dark eyes for an American, almost black, she noticed; flashing Mediterranean eyes set deep beneath gently arched dark brows. With those high, wide cheekbones and his strong chin and darkly tanned skin, he reminded her of some lean, elegant Castilian swordsman . . . or a pirate, she thought, right off the Spanish Main.

"No," he said now, his lips curling into a half-smile, "it doesn't even surprise me. I have heard of Florence Nightingale. But this is neither the Crimea, nor Paris, nor even Philadelphia, and in my experience, the ladies who volunteer in hospitals might write letters, or hand out medicines, but they don't usually treat wounds. Or bandage them."

Emmanuelle paused with one hand gripping the banister, unsure of how to respond. She wondered what he would say—what he would do—if he knew it was Emmanuelle herself who had cut off Lieutenant Rouant's arm in the first place. She wasn't licensed—couldn't be licensed, as a woman—but since Philippe's death, she had been doing more and more of the surgery at the hospital. Henri Santerre had been a gifted doctor, but age had twisted his hands and left him clumsy. Lately, he had been content to let Emmanuelle be his hands.

"The lieutenant was uncomfortable," she said with deliberate casualness. "His shoulder needed to be dealt with. There was no one else to do it."

"Are you telling me Henri Santerre was the only doctor in this hospital?"

"No. But Dr. Yardley isn't exactly what you might call an early riser."

"Yardley?"

"Dr. Charles Yardley." They'd reached the bottom of

the steps. She swung to face him. "Shouldn't you have a little notebook or something you're writing all this down in?"

He gave her a slow, malignant smile that showed his teeth. "I leave that sort of thing to Captain Fletcher."

Turning on her heel, she walked with quick strides toward the back of the building.

"Elise Santerre told me your father was a doctor," he said, keeping pace with her easily, despite his limp.

"That's right." It disconcerted her to realize he'd been discussing her with Elise Santerre, to realize that he'd been asking questions about her, *learning* things about her, learning . . . what? With a clatter, she dumped the dirty tray on one of the long wooden shelves that ran along the wall between the office and the door that led to the courtyard and the service buildings beyond.

"She said your husband was a doctor, too."

She swung to face him. "Did she tell you how he died?"

"Yes." He stood before her, so tall that he seemed to loom over her. It made her uncomfortable, having him this close. She kept feeling as if she couldn't get enough air, as if his nearness were somehow making it difficult for her to breathe. "Tell me about Dr. Santerre," he said.

Emmanuelle jerked down the brass handle of the door beside them and pushed it open wide. "This was his office. Feel free to look around."

He didn't move, didn't even turn his head, but kept his gaze hard on her face. "When I asked Elise Santerre if she could think of anyone who might want her brother dead, she said to ask you. Why? Did he have enemies?"

Did he? Emmanuelle thought? *Did she?* "Everyone has enemies, monsieur," she said, not managing to keep her voice steady.

"Not everyone gets himself murdered."

She brushed past him into the office. It was a small room, lined with shelves filled with old leather-bound volumes and loose papers, stuffed here and there amongst the books in a system only Henri Santerre had understood. The desk near the window overlooking the rear courtyard was mahogany, but old and battered, the two green leather club chairs that faced it worn and cracked. In contrast to the scrupulous cleanliness that prevailed in the wards and private rooms, the atmosphere here was dusty and close. All of the old man's energy and most of his wealth had gone to the hospital itself.

Crossing to the window, she stared out at the leafy, brick-paved courtyard, where a tall, blond-headed boy laughed at the tumbling antics of a small gray kitten. Dominic, she realized with a start, wondering with all of a busy mother's guilt how long he had been waiting for her.

"Madame?" said the relentless man behind her.

She swung to face him. "Henri was passionate about his work," she said, picking her words carefully. "Passionate and opinionated, and at times brutally forthright. He made some people very angry."

"Angry enough to kill? Over a professional quarrel?"

"This city has two medical schools and two separate medical societies, one French, one American. At times the rivalry is intense."

He strolled over to scan the jumbled contents of the dead man's shelves. "I thought you were all Americans, and had been for more than fifty years."

"Technically, perhaps. But the differences persist. The French and Spanish doctors believe their role is to assist nature, not fight it. But the Americans, they practice what they like to call *heroic medicine*. They poison the body with massive doses of calomel and quinine, and then blister, purge, sweat, and bleed their patients until they lose consciousness. Dr. Santerre always said their patients recovered in spite of, rather than because of, what was done to them. And he was never the least bit hesitant when it came to calling another doctor a complete idiot."

Turning slowly, the Union major leaned his long, slim frame against the bookshelves behind him, one thumb hooking casually in his sword belt, an expression she couldn't read on his face as he studied her. "What about Santerre's patients? Did any of them threaten him? A soldier, perhaps? Someone who might have lost an arm or a leg on Santerre's operating table, and resented it."

She'd thought about such a possibility herself, but hearing this man say it, hearing the contempt in his voice, brought the heat of anger flooding to her face. "Henri Santerre was a fine doctor and a skilled surgeon."

"Perhaps. But I haven't met a doctor yet who wasn't too quick to use the saw."

It was an accusation as common as it was unfair. Most people simply didn't understand how close to impossible it was to control the onset of sepsis in a serious wound. "If a necessary amputation isn't performed within twenty-four hours, death is almost inevitable," she said, trying to keep her voice level, professional, but not quite succeeding.

"I'm still alive."

"You are more fortunate than you realize, Major.

The graveyards are full of men who threatened to shoot—or castrate—any surgeon who comes near them."

His laugh was both sudden and spontaneous, and unexpectedly, shamefully attractive. "How did you know?"

"You would not have kept your leg otherwise." She almost—*almost*—found herself warming to him, and had to force herself to say briskly, "But you're right. Men whose lives are saved at the cost of an arm or a leg do sometimes bear a grudge. So do the families of other patients. Men . . . women . . . children . . . they all die, and those who loved them often blame the doctor. If you like, I could provide you with a list of Dr. Santerre's patients for the last few years." It was a long list, maybe even long enough to keep this man busy—and away from them all—until the Confederates could recapture the city.

"I'll put some of my men on it," he said with a faint smile that told her he knew exactly what she was doing, and why. "Now, why don't you tell me who you really suspect?"

He was clever. Oh, very clever. She would have to be careful not to underestimate him again. He pushed away from the bookcases with one elegant thrust. "For example, who knew you would be at the cemetery last night?"

She shook her head. "If you think to narrow your list that way, monsieur, I'm sorry, but we go every year. The number of people who know that must be endless."

"All right, let's take a different track, then. Who owns the hospital now that Santerre is dead? You? Elise Santerre? Or this Dr. Yardley?"

It was the question she'd been dreading. "I do," she said, meeting his gaze squarely. "Dr. Yardley is a visiting doctor. He has his own practice elsewhere."

There was a short, dangerous pause. "I see."

"I doubt you do. Not if you think I've inherited a fortune. We have very few paying patients anymore, and now only one licensed doctor, while the building itself had to be mortgaged to pay the fine your General Butler imposed on everyone who supported the Confederacy. If I manage to keep this hospital open another month, I'll be surprised."

"Then why bother? Why not close it now?"

"Because the people of this city need us, desperately. Because Henri Santerre was my friend, and this hospital was his life's dream. I am not going to let whoever killed Henri kill this hospital, too. Not if I can help it."

Again, that flare of interest in the dark, intelligent eyes. "Perhaps that's why he was killed. To close the hospital."

She shook her head. "The war will close this hospital, monsieur. The war, and your occupation. The people of New Orleans no longer have the money to pay for such things as medical care."

She watched his face grow cold, hard. "They should have thought of that before they seceded," he said dryly.

They stared at each other, and it was as if the very air between them shimmered with antagonism and challenge and something else, something dangerous and shocking and very, very real.

A door opened in the distance. "Emmanuelle?" called a young woman's familiar, well-modulated voice. "*Où est-tu?* What is this I am hearing about Dr. Santerre? Are the Yankees—oh . . ." She appeared in the doorway, a slim, elegant woman with golden hair and a thin, elfin face, her words trailing away as she stared at the major.

"Mademoiselle La Touche is a volunteer at the hospital," Emmanuelle said, going to take her reticule and gloves from the drawer in the small table near Henri's desk, where she had always kept them. "She should be able to answer any further questions you have. Now you must excuse me, Major." Walking briskly toward the door, she lifted her black straw hat from its hook. "I promised to take my son to visit his grandparents, and we are already late."

"Of course, madame. We can continue our conversation later."

His words filled her with dismay; she didn't want to continue their conversation later. She never wanted to see him again. Automatically tying the frayed black satin ribbons of the hat beneath her chin, she said to Claire in rapid French, "If you have time, would you look in on Lieutenant Rouant? He would like to dicate a letter."

"How is he?" asked Claire, her soft gray eyes round with concern.

"Dying."

"*Mon Dieu.*"

Emmanuelle was in the hall, her hand on the door to the courtyard, when the major's voice stopped her. "One more thing, madame," he called after her.

She turned to find him beside the stairs, watching her. "Monsieur?"

"How did you know Dr. Santerre had been hit by a crossbow bolt?"

He said it casually, as if the question had only occurred to him, when she knew he must have been waiting for just this moment to spring it on her and disconcert her. Oh, he was good, she thought; very, very good. Her heart had begun to thump wildly, but she managed to say steadily enough, "I could think of nothing else it could be."

"And did you know it had a silver tip?"

For a moment, her voice deserted her completely as a wave of terror washed over her.

"Madame?" Those hard, knowing eyes narrowed as they studied her.

"No," she finally managed to say. "How could I? How . . . very odd." She glanced out the small panes of the French door. Dominic had found a bit of twine and was trailing it over the paving stones to the mock-ferocious delight of the kitten. "You must excuse me, monsieur," she said in a rush. "My son is waiting for me."

She pushed through the door without a backward glance or another word, but inside, she was screaming, *It can't be, it can't be . . . can it?*

"Maman!"

Dropping his end of the string, Dominic came running. She thought for a moment he would throw himself against her the way he used to do when he was younger. But he was eleven years old now, almost as tall as she, and he only skidded to a halt beside her. "There you are." His smile was wide and engaging. "I thought perhaps you'd forgotten we promised Papère we'd come today."

"No, of course not," she said, reaching out an unsteady hand to ruffle the curling blond hair that was so much like Philippe's. He pulled away and made a face, and she laughed. "We'll leave now. I just need to stop by our house on the way."

"Must you?" He turned around to dogtrot, backward,

ahead of her through the porte cochere. "We're already late. And you know Grand-mère doesn't like it when you're late."

"I'll only be a moment. There's something I need to check."

"What?"

"Never mind."

"Tell me," he demanded. "Do." But she only laughed and shook her head.

He continued to press her for an answer all the way home. But she never did tell him.

CHAPTER FIVE

The boy looked nothing like her, Zach thought, watching mother and son walk away. It wasn't only the curling blond hair, or the unusual height that promised to send the son soaring past his petite mother in a few years. The angles of his face were different, softer, the expression in his clear blue eyes dreamy.

"That Dominic, he looks more like Philippe every time I see him," said Mademoiselle Claire La Touche, coming to stand beside Zach, her French accent breathy and lilting.

Zach turned to find her gaze fixed not on the brick-walled courtyard, with its tubs of sweet olive and jasmine and the distant echoes of a child's laughter, but on him.

She was younger than the haughty, self-possessed widow, probably no more than eighteen, built tall and boyishly thin in her body, although there was nothing boyish about her softly pouting mouth, or the way she had of looking at a man. Nothing boyish at all. "You knew Philippe de Beauvais, did you?" he said.

"Of course I knew Philippe. We are distant cousins—or should I say, we *were* cousins," she corrected, her wide, dewy gray eyes clouding with a storm of emotions he couldn't begin to identify. "My mother is a de Beauvais."

He wasn't surprised. Zach hadn't been in New Orleans long, but it was long enough for him to have learned the importance here of family connections. And not just the father's family, either. If anything, it was often the mother's family with which the children tended to identify, for in many ways this was a matriarchal society in everything but name. "Is he the reason you volunteered to help here, at the hospital?"

A slow, delicious smile curled the pouting lips. "Ah, no. Antoine gets the blame for that." The smile told him the choice of words was deliberate. Blame, not credit.

"Antoine?"

"My brother. We were at a dinner party right after the war started—Antoine, Philippe, Emmanuelle, and I. Emmanuelle was talking about a group of wounded soldiers who'd been brought down by rail from Virginia, and I made the mistake of saying I wished I could do something like what she was doing, something beyond scraping lint and knitting socks. And Antoine, he said, 'So what's stopping you?' "

"In other words, you volunteered to help with the wounded because of a dare."

She gave a startled trill of laughter. "Yes, I suppose you could say that."

She pushed past him, through the door to the courtyard. He went with her to the two-story brick kitchen that ran along the hospital's rear property line, and stood watching as she spoke to the hospital's black cook and loaded a pitcher of cool lemon water and glasses on a tray. In some disturbing, elusive way, she reminded Zach of Rachel, in a way that went beyond the pretty blond looks and easy, arrogant self-assurance of old money. It was the second time he'd found himself thinking of Rachel in less than twenty-four hours, and the realization disturbed him. Because of him, Rachel had ended up dead.

"Are there other young women working as volunteers here at the hospital?" he asked, when Claire had finished.

"Hardly," she said with a smile, and hefted the heavy tray easily. She was stronger than she looked. "Most people find the idea of exposing refined, modest young ladies to the horrors of a hospital highly objectionable." She said it as if it were a quote, and he suspected it was.

He took the tray from her and carried it across the flagged courtyard. "Yet your parents don't object?"

She moved to open the door for him. "Oh, my mother objects."

"But it doesn't stop you."

She looked at him over her shoulder. "You think it should?"

It took an effort of will for him to enter the hospital again. The Hospital de Santerre was clean and bright and breezy, nothing like the dark, airless tent on the edge of a war-torn valley in Tennessee where Zach had spent countless weeks of agony. But the smells were the same—fainter, to be sure, but they were still there, along with that inescapable aura of suffering and fear that seemed to cling to the very walls. He really, really hated hospitals. At the entrance to the downstairs ward, he handed Claire La Touche back her tray and said, "Tell me about Henri Santerre."

She shrugged, the pout back on her lips. "What is there to tell? He was an old man."

And not one of Mademoiselle La Touche's admirers, Zach thought. "That's all you have to say about him? That he was old?"

Again, she shrugged. "The Santerres are a respectable

family. Not one of the better families," she added with all the unself-conscious pride of one who had grown up secure in the knowledge that her own family antecedents were among the best, "but old and respectable."

La famille again. Zach thought about that small, white tomb where Emmanuelle de Beauvais had gone to pray, the one with the name MARET chiseled deep above the entrance. There had been only two names carved in the slab that sealed the Maret crypt, no marble angel praying on the roof, no spiked wrought-iron gates barring the front. In a city where family was everything, where did the Marets fit?

He watched, one shoulder propped against the doorjamb, as Claire La Touche began to make the rounds of the ward, dispensing cool drinks, straightening beds, touching her soft lady's hand to fevered brows. The really heavy nursing—the changing of beds, the bathing of shattered bodies, the emptying of bedpans— was being done by the male nurses, a couple of black men and a young white boy with a thin face and a shock of light brown hair who leaned on a crutch as he moved slowly through the wards. But it wasn't an easy thing, this task performed by ladies such as Mademoiselle La Touche. Zach watched, his throat oddly thick, as she held a glass to the lips of a boy of no more than sixteen who'd lost both hands. She was wearing that pouty smile of hers, laughing at something he'd said as she touched his cheek in a fleeting caress. But when she left the boy's bedside, Zach could see the glitter of tears in her eyes, and he had to admire her. She might have begun working in the hospital on a dare, but it wasn't the reason she was still here, over a year later, enduring sights and sounds and smells that had been known to make battle-hardened men sick.

They were a breed unto themselves, these women of the South, Zach thought, watching her. All fluff and flutter on the outside and indomitable, stubborn willpower on the inside, like a drift of soft, sweetly scented wisteria blossoms hiding a bedrock of pure granite. And again he thought of Emmanuelle de Beauvais. She wasn't like that. She didn't hide either her strength, or her abilities and intelligence—didn't hide what she *was*—beneath an assumption of yielding softness. He thought she'd probably had a rough time of it, growing up around here.

"An affecting spectacle, is it not?" said a languid, cultured voice that spoke in English; not the English of the South, or even of the north Atlantic seaboard where Zach had grown up, but the Queen's English, the English of Eton and Oxford and Ascot. "Sweet maidenhood, ministering tenderly to the needs of a nation's wounded heroes."

Zach shifted to face the man who'd come in through the front door, left open to the hot, humid air and all the smells of a city built near the tropics. He was a slim man, probably in his early thirties, of no more than medium height; a man with an insolent way of walking as languid as his voice.

"You must be Dr. Yardley," said Zach, pushing away from the entrance of the ward and going to stand in the flagged hall.

"So the Yankees have decided to investigate our little murder, have they?" The man took off his broad-brimmed felt hat and swiped one forearm across his damp brow. He had straight, dark blond hair he wore long to frame his face. It was an unusual face, pale of skin and fine-boned, yet so sharply featured one could easily surmise the shape and appearance of the skull beneath. He studied Zach through badly bloodshot hazel

eyes shadowed by dark circles. Whatever this man had
spent last night doing, it hadn't involved much sleep. "I
need coffee," he said with a sigh. "I always require at
least three cups to get me going in the morning, and so
far I've only had two."

"And your patients?"

The man paused, his jaw hardening for a moment
before relaxing into a tight smile. "If I know our very
competent Madame de Beauvais, she has already seen
to my patients. She would have made a fine doctor . . .
if she'd been born a man, of course."

They sat at a rusting green wrought-iron table in the
shade of the big Chinaball tree that dominated the hospital's brick-walled courtyard, and drank rich dark coffee lightened with hot milk. Around them, chickens
scratched for grain among the moss-covered paving
stones, and linens hung limply in the sultry air.
"Madame de Beauvais tells me the hospital is failing,"
said Zach, the scent of chicory coffee warm and aromatic in his nostrils. "Is it?"

"Oh, yes. Badly." The Englishman took a swallow
of his coffee and grimaced. "Too few patients of the
paying variety. Santerre was always far too generous
with his talents and attentions, and Emmanuelle is no
better."

"He sounds like a good man."

"Oh, he was . . . if you consider being giving the def-
inition of good. He was also opinionated, irritable, and
proud."

"Know why anyone would want to kill him?"

Yardley leaned back in his chair in an arrogant pose.
"Really, Major. I thought I'd just saved you the trouble
of asking that question. Proud, opinionated, irritable
men do tend to rack up more than their share of enemies, don't they?"

Zach took a slow sip of his coffee. "Did he quarrel with anyone in particular recently?"

"Recently? As in the last two hours?" The Englishman gave him a broad smile. Santerre had been dead these sixteen hours or more. "Not to my knowledge."

"How well did you get along with him?"

Yardley's mug hit the rusty tabletop with a thump as he leaned forward to punch the air between them with one thin finger. "Oh, no. You're not pinning this one on me. I spent yesterday evening with an old, dear friend."

"Old, dear friends are often willing to lie for one another."

Again, that smile, the smile that meant nothing. "Yes, they are, aren't they? Isn't it convenient?"

From the street just visible through the arch of the carriageway came the rumble of a carrier's cart and the shrill chant of a hawker, crying, "I got ripe melons, uh-huh."

"So why did you leave England?" asked Zach.

The smile never slipped. "I didn't like the climate."

Zach nodded toward the giant green leaves of the elephant ears beside them, the rich humus beneath it steaming in the torrid heat. "You like this, do you?"

The Englishman laughed. This time, the amusement was real. "I grew up in India. The heat doesn't bother me."

"Still, one wouldn't expect to find you associated with a French hospital here."

"Ah, you've been talking to our dear Madame de Beauvais, who has little but contempt for any doctor not trained in Paris or Montpellier. As it happens, I'm not nearly as vigorous in my approach to treatment as most of your Yankee doctors. And Santerre wasn't as radical as our Emmanuelle. She thinks mercury is a

poison, and believes diseases are caused by these peculiar little organisms that are so tiny, no one can see
them."

"Animalcules," Zach said quietly.

"Good God." The Englishman sat forward, both
hands on his cup, his eyes opening wide in an exaggeration of astonishment. "What do you know about animalcules?"

"I'm provost marshal, remember? One of my jobs is
to try to keep this city from suffering its annual summer outbreak of yellow fever."

"And you think you can accomplish that by flushing
gutters and emptying privies, do you? Not that I'm
complaining, mind you. This city might be a lot less fun
since you Yankees set your righteous black boots to our
collective necks, but I must admit, it does smell considerably better."

Zach gave the English doctor a slow, tight smile.
"And there's been no outbreak of yellow fever."

Yardley waved one slim white hand through the air
in a dismissive gesture. "Coincidence. And luck, for
you. Only the hearty survive long enough to actually
settle in this city, and they still die at a rate of up to
twenty percent a year. How many of your boys in blue
do you think would make it through a full-blown
yellow-fever epidemic?"

"Unlike most of the other residents of this city, I'm
hoping I don't find out."

Yardley laughed. It was open knowledge that the
people of New Orleans were almost disappointed that
the nearly annual epidemic had failed to appear that
year. Everyone knew strangers always died in far
greater numbers than residents, and they'd been counting on the Yellow Jack to rid them of their unwanted

masters—or at least to make them suffer grievously for their conquest.

Zach ran his thumb and index finger up the sides of his mug, his attention seemingly centered on the movement of his hand. "So why out of all the hospitals that used to operate in this notoriously insalubrious city did you happen to end up with visiting privileges at this one?"

"Ah. That was because of Philippe. Philippe was"—Zach glanced up as the Englishman paused, the tip of his tongue pressed to his front teeth, his thoughts wandering where Zach couldn't begin to guess—"Philippe was a particular friend of mine."

"And Henri Santerre?"

Yardley met Zach's gaze, and held it. "We were colleagues, but not friends. I honestly don't know who would have wanted to kill him, or why. He seemed an open, straightforward sort of fellow. If he had secrets, they were well kept. I didn't know them."

Zach stood up, the metal legs of his chair scraping across the uneven paving stones. "And even if you did, you wouldn't tell me, would you?"

Yardley let his head fall back, his tongue, once again, tucking up by his teeth. "I think a man is entitled to his secrets. Don't you?"

"Not if it leads to murder."

Zach was turning away when the Englishman's voice stopped him. "What's it to you, anyway, Major Provost Marshal? With all you've got to do, why should you care if one old Creole doctor gets sent to his grave a year or two early?"

Zach paused to swing slowly back around. "It happened on my watch. That makes it my business."

The prominent bones in the Englishman's jaw

bunched beneath the skin in silent amusement. "But that's not what's making you *care,* Major."

Zach knew the Englishman didn't really expect an answer, and he made no attempt to give one as he turned to leave. But the sardonic tones of the other man's raised voice followed Zach through the dark musty brick tunnel of the carriageway. "It's a pity you met the good Dr. Santerre only after his death, Major. The two of you would have got on well together."

Emmanuelle stood just inside the door of what had been her husband's bedroom for the last ten years of their marriage.

She was in the *garçonnière,* that range of small rooms opening onto the gallery that ran along the second and third stories of the kitchen wing. In the tall, narrow house on the rue Dumaine, the kitchen wing had been built at the side of the lot line, rather than at the rear, and was separated from the main house by only a flight of steps. It was to these rooms that the sons of a family would be moved once they passed the age of thirteen or fourteen, so that they might come and go at night as they pleased. Most people thought Philippe had kept a room out here so that he wouldn't awaken Emmanuelle if he should happen to return late at night from visiting a sick patient. But the truth was, Philippe had slept here always—when he slept at home.

She had come into this room only once since Philippe's death, with Rose, to pack away those few things Emmanuelle specifically wished to save for Dominic. The rest of Philippe's possessions she had left as they were. Now she paused in the doorway, struck by how strong his presence here still was, his riding crop still lying where he'd tossed it carelessly on the bureau beside his pipe, a small, brown leather-bound book lying open on the floor beside his bed, his very scent hanging faint but distinguishable in the air, so that she had to wrap her arms around her waist and hug herself. Philippe might be dead, but it didn't lessen her sense that she was intruding. Although she was afraid not of what she might find, but of what might be missing.

She should have come last night, she thought, feeling her heart begin to thump hard and fast, her stomach roiling with a resurgence of fear. She'd known the truth even then, she realized, only she hadn't wanted to admit it. As if by not coming to look, she could somehow make it not true.

One arm still riding low at her waist, Emmanuelle forced herself to cross the short distance to the big old cedar armoire where she knew Philippe had kept his more personal possessions. This time, she didn't allow herself to hesitate, but grasped the key and turned it swiftly, the wide doors creaking on their hinges as they swung open toward her. His scent was stronger here, mingling with the pungent odor of hashish and vetiver and dust and other scents she didn't want to identify.

She knew exactly what she was looking for, for she had seen it on the cabinet's lower shelf when she'd gone through Philippe's things after his death. It was a box of burnished oak, some eighteen inches long and not quite as wide, that opened on brass hinges to reveal a vampire-killing kit, furnished with a vial of holy water, a wooden cross and stake, and a small crossbow complete with four miniature silver-tipped wooden bolts. It was the sort of bizarre curiosity that had always delighted Philippe, and had been given to him on his last birthday by Claire's brother, Antoine La Touche.

Now, only the faint outline of a rectangle impressed in the dust of the shelf showed where it had once rested.

CHAPTER
SIX

Her breath catching in her throat, Emmanuelle sank down onto the woven summer mat covering the room's cypress floorboards. For one, hideous moment, terror swamped her, beat against her ears like the roar of a deafening wind, drying her mouth and stealing her sense. She had sent Dominic on ahead to his grandparents' stately mansion on Esplanade Avenue; he was probably there already, she thought, waiting for her. She told herself she needed to move. And still she stayed, one clenched hand gripping the edge of the open armoire door.

The creak of boards on the gallery brought her head around. A shadow darkened the room's single, small window, then materialized at the open doorway. "Rose." Emmanuelle surged to her feet, her gaze locking with the black woman's. "You know it's gone?"

The other woman nodded. "I came up here looking for it, just as soon as I heard exactly what they took out of Dr. Santerre's chest."

Emmanuelle didn't bother asking how Rose had heard about the small, silver-tipped wooden crossbow bolt. This might be a city of almost 170,000 people, but it still functioned like a small town. Everyone knew everyone else's business, sometimes even before they knew it themselves.

"How many people you think know about that oak box, hmm?" Rose asked.

Emmanuelle brushed a stray wisp of hair off her hot, damp forehead, and realized with an odd sense of detachment that she was drenched with sweat. "Philippe was fascinated by it. He could have shown it to anyone." And anyone who knew Philippe well, she thought, would know where he kept that sort of thing.

The two women stared at each other, silently acknowledging all the horrible implications of their discovery. That whoever had lain in wait for Emmanuelle and Henri Santerre had been here, in this house, without their knowledge. That he had stolen his murder weapon from here. That he *knew* them—obviously knew them well.

"You got more trouble than you know," Rose said as Emmanuelle closed the armoire doors and drove the lock home with a click "There's a Yankee major standing across the street right now, studying this house like he knows we got something to hide."

Picking up her skirts, Emmanuelle ran along the open wooden gallery to the doors to Dominic's room, then quickly cut across it to her own room at the front of the house. The windows' heavy green velvet drapes had been taken down for the summer, leaving only long, flat panels of open lacework that Emmanuelle was careful not to disturb as she looked down at the rue Dumaine below.

Zachary Cooper stood on the brick banquette across the street, one shoulder propped against a post, his arms crossed at his chest, the brim of his black felt hat tipped low.

"*Mon Dieu*," she said under her breath, as if he could hear her from such a distance. "It's the one I told you about, the provost marshal."

Rose came to stand beside her. "Hmmm," said Rose, her gaze fixed on the man across the street. "He looks dangerous." She paused thoughtfully. "Attractive, but dangerous." She swung around as Emmanuelle turned from the window to snatch up her black widow's hat and gloves from where she'd tossed them on her daybed. "You going to tell him about Michie Philippe's vampire-killing kit?"

"Tell him what, exactly? That the murder weapon was a crossbow given by one of my dearest friends to my dead husband?" Emmanuelle eased the hat over the upswept knot of her hair, but she was careful this time not to tie the ribbons. Tying frayed them, and since the war, ribbons were hard to find, especially in black. "They'd hang both Antoine La Touche and me faster than you can say William Mumford."

Rose followed Emmanuelle out into the hall as she jerked on her gloves. "And did you never think," said the black woman, stopping at the head of the stairs, her elbows bent wide, her hands bracketing her slim hips in the posture she inevitably assumed when she was agitated, "that you might be wrong about that Yankee? That telling him what you know just might help him catch the one who *did* do the killing? Someone who must have been in this very house, maybe while you were sleeping in your bed, and that child of yours in his. You like thinking about that? What you going to do about that?"

Pausing at the base of the stairs, Emmanuelle met the woman's dark, worried gaze. "I'm going to lock the doors at night," she said, and let herself out into the hot, midday sun.

Zach stood where he was and let Madame de Beauvais walk up to him, the full black skirts of her widow's weeds swirling about her as she stopped abruptly in the flag-paved street before him, her head tipping back so that the harsh midday sun shone full on her face. She looked pale, her features pinched as if with fear, and that both surprised and intrigued him. She didn't scare easily, this petite woman with the fierce dark eyes and admirable sangfroid and a mysterious, dangerous allure.

"What are you doing here, at my house?" she demanded, staring at him.

He straightened slowly, letting a cold smile touch his lips, a smile that was a lie, because already he could feel his blood racing, burning; the effect this woman had on him was that powerful. Powerful and damnably unwanted. "I thought you said you were visiting your son's grandparents this afternoon."

"I am. And I'm already late."

"We can talk on the way." He stepped off the banquette, into the street beside her.

A cart with high wooden sides rattled past, wheels rumbling over the uneven stones. She continued staring at him for a moment, her breath coming hard and fast as she fought what she obviously knew was a useless urge to spit back at him, *But I have no desire to walk with you, monsieur.* It was a small, silent battle she waged within herself, and she won it, as he'd known she would. She was a woman of strong passions, Madame de Beauvais, and she worked very hard at keeping those passions under control. But sometimes . . . sometimes, he thought, those passions must run away with her.

Without another word, she turned to cross the street at an angle, toward the corner of Chartres, leaving him to follow or not, as he chose. In the distance, the cathedral bell began to toll the Angelus, a low, steady clang echoing out over the old city. "If you didn't expect to

find me at home," she asked, not even glancing sideways at him as he came abreast of her, "then why are
you here?"

"To talk to your servant."

Only the infinitesimal catch in her stride betrayed her
reaction, and she recovered quickly enough. "Rose is at
home now. Don't let me stop you from going to see
her."

He shook his head. "Later. You see, a few things
have been puzzling me, ever since I watched you at the
hospital."

"Such as?"

"Such as, why you left Henri Santerre when he was
wounded. With any other woman, I'd understand her
going to get help. But not you."

They were walking along Chartres now, toward Esplanade. Tall, narrow town houses rose up beside
them, faded stucco facades peeling in the hot, damp air.
From darkened, arched openings came the sounds and
smells of tradesmen at work, the hot starchiness of
pressed linen, the sweet, beckoning aroma of fresh pra-
lines, the sharp tanginess of ale from one of the
cabarets that could be found throughout the old city,
even on the best streets. Overhead, chair legs scraped
on gallery floors and shutters banged as housewives or
servants in the apartments above moved to shut out the
heat and glare of the encroaching sun.

Just when he'd decided she wasn't going to answer
him, the woman beside him said, her voice low, husky,
"He was within a breath of being dead. There was
nothing I could have done for him. He told me to run,
and I did. I was afraid. I'm not proud of it. I should
have stayed."

They paused at the corner as a carter swung in front
of them from Ursuline onto Chartres, the bay mule be-

tween the traces throwing up its head and neighing softly in exaggerated alarm at the sight of a tall black woman in gay yellow muslin, a basket full of greens balanced on her head. "Did it ever occur to you that Santerre might have been hit by mistake?" he asked almost casually as they stepped off the curb. "That the killer could have been aiming at you?"

She tripped on a broken section of the street where the previous night's rain had collected in a dirty puddle. He only just managed to catch her, his hand snaking out to close hard around her elbow, yanking her up short before she fell.

If she'd been pale before, she was white now, her eyes huge as she stared up at him. "I have no enemies, monsieur," she said in a broken whisper.

He held her gaze steadily. He'd thought her eyes were brown, but he realized now that they were actually green, the dark, mysterious green of a primeval forest, or a deep, shadowed ocean. "Everyone has enemies. You said so yourself."

Her chest lifted with a quick intake of breath. "I don't know of anyone who wants me dead, if that's what you mean."

He realized, suddenly, just how close they were standing. He dropped his hand from her arm and took a step away from her. "Someone obviously wanted one of you dead."

Yet even as Zach said it, he knew it might be untrue. Not all victims were familiar with their killers. Some people killed for twisted reasons of their own that had little to do with those who ended up dead at their hands, while others killed for the sheer, sadistic joy of it.

What's the matter, Captain? whispered a voice from the past. *Haven't you figured it out yet? Do you need another clue?*

"Monsieur?"

Zach heard her voice, as if from a distance, and looked up to find a hack driver shouting at them. *Alors! Qu'est-ce vous faites?* They started off again, silent now, heading toward the swath of green that was the sycamores and elms of the neutral ground on Esplanade Avenue.

They had gone another block or two when she stopped again, her attention caught by the death notice tacked to a nearby lamppost, one loose, black-banded edge fluttering in the river breeze. "You've released Henri Santerre's body," she said.

He paused beside her. "I didn't see a need to order anything more than a limited examination." Autopsies were a relatively new procedure, and one that didn't sit well with most people. "Especially with this heat."

She nodded, the hot breeze gusting up again to whip at the long black ribbons of her widow's bonnet. The heat was a problem, because Santerre's sister had wanted to hold a wake—that curious, old-world custom that had entrenched itself in this city, along with so much else that was strange, foreign, to those raised elsewhere in America.

He gazed down at the woman beside him, at the soft curve of her cheek and the seductive sweep of her long, thick lashes, and knew a rush of disquiet, deep within him. She was as alien to him as this steaming city around them, with its voodooiennes and quadroon balls and crumbling courtyard walls smothered in honeysuckle and ivy; this city of masked Mardi Gras balls and dueling oaks and a bloodcurdling death rate twice that of any other city in America. Like the city that was her home, Emmanuelle de Beauvais was beautiful, dark, and dangerous. He knew she was hiding things from him, knew she might even be responsible for the death of that white-haired old man Zach had found sprawled in a bloody heap on the steps of her family tomb. He knew all this, and still she fascinated him, still she drew him, still he felt the slow burn of unwilled desire.

Up ahead, the Esplanade mule car passed on its way to turn around at the river, and they started off again, her step quickening. "There is one more thing I'm curious about," he said abruptly as they came out of the narrow, closely built street into the relatively broad expanse of the avenue.

"What's that, monsieur?" She had her head turned away, her attention all for the mule car drawing away from the built-up area of the river levee.

"If you were as fond of Henri Santerre as you'd like me to believe, then why won't you help me find the man who killed him?"

She paused on the grassy neutral ground, the long, loose black ribbons of her hat fluttering out to brush against his arm as she swung to meet his hard gaze. She made no attempt to deny the accusation, to claim she was cooperating with him, but then, he'd known she wouldn't. "If Henri had been shot by a Yankee sniper while helping tend the wounded on a battlefield, you wouldn't be giving his death a second thought. Yet he would have been just as dead, and his killing just as deliberate and untimely."

Zach set his jaw. "But not as senseless."

She shook her head, her nostrils flaring as she sucked in a quick, deep breath. "War is senseless. Senseless, barbaric, and cruel. This war and all others."

"I don't agree."

"No, you wouldn't, would you?"

She made as if to turn away again, but he caught her arm, stopping her. "You didn't answer my question."

Her gaze dropped, pointedly, to where his hand

rested on her sleeve, but he didn't remove it. "Make no mistake about this, Major Cooper," she said, her eyes glittering with an enemy's hatred as she looked up at him again. "Henri Santerre was like a second father to me. But another innocent man hanging from a Federal gallows won't bring him back to life."

He let her go. "What makes you so sure the man we'd hang would be innocent?"

"You haven't exactly earned a reputation for legality and due process of law since you seized this city," she said, and although she meant *you, the Yankees,* rather than *you, personally,* it still stung, particularly because he knew it was true.

The mule car jingled to a stop beside them and she moved quickly, grasping the railing to climb up onto the high platform before he could make a move to help her. Before he could touch her again.

One hand resting on his saber, Zach took a step back from the curb. She stared down at him, relief mingling with wariness when she realized he meant to accompany her no farther. "You're going back to talk to Rose," she said.

He gave her a slow, mean smile. "Yes."

"You're wasting your time. She won't tell you anything."

He shook his head. "People always tell you things, even when they don't mean to." He took another step back, his boots sinking into the damp ground, the smell of wet grass heavy in the air. "I'll see you at the wake, madame."

The mule car jerked forward, but not before he saw the flare of surprise and consternation in those dark green eyes.

CHAPTER
SEVEN

The woman, Rose, took her time answering the door, and then she let it swing inward no more than eight inches before stopping it with her shoulder.

She was a tall woman, tall and thin, with a long neck and sloping shoulders and an innately regal carriage. The pale, café au lait tone of her skin proclaimed her mixed parentage, but the features of her face were all African, the nose broad and flat, the lips full, the cheekbones high and wide. "Miss Emmanuelle's gone out, and you know it," she said, her mouth held in a tight, hostile line. "What you doing back here?"

Her accent surprised him, although it occurred to him he should have been expecting it. He'd become familiar with the upcountry blacks pouring into the camps in the city; American Negroes, who spoke English with broad tones and a diction all their own. But this woman was a Creole black, her English even more disdainful and heavily inflected with French than that of her mistress.

Beast Butler would probably have ordered the woman arrested for that kind of insolence. Zach took off his hat and said, "I'd like to ask you a few questions."

She hesitated, but no one in this city, man or woman, black, colored, or white, could afford to say no to a blue uniform. Shrugging, she stepped back and let the door swing wide. "I've things to do. You want to talk to me, you talk while I work."

She led the way down a cool, flagged passage to an inner courtyard filled with potted laurels and mock orange, and a charcoal brazier topped by a copper pot that bubbled soapy steam into the hot air. "I don't know what you'd be wanting to talk to me for," she said, going to stir the wash in the copper with a long wooden paddle. "I didn't know Michie Henri."

"You know Madame de Beauvais." An arched niche tangled with ivy and Carolina jessamine half-hid a gray, weathered bench, and he went to sit on it, disturbing a mockingbird that fluttered up to the second floor gallery and fussed at him. "She wasn't born here, was she?"

The woman, Rose, glanced over at him, her eyes narrowing with suspicion. But she evidently could see no harm in answering, because she said, grudgingly, "They came here from France, her Maman and Papa. Fourteen years ago now."

Eighteen forty-eight, Zach thought, counting backward. It had been a year of revolution all over Europe. He didn't think it could be a coincidence that the Marets had chosen to leave France that year. Aloud, he said, "How long have you been with her?"

"I was the first thing they bought, just as soon as they stepped off that ship. I was sixteen, same as Miss Emmanuelle." Rose tapped the three-legged paddle against the edge of the copper pot. "And I've been with her ever since."

Zach fought hard to tamp down a spurt of irritation. If he got anything useful out of this woman, he'd be surprised. He would never understand it, this misplaced loyalty, even affection, so many slaves maintained for the people who owned them. And he knew a moment of vague self-disgust at the realization that he had actually found himself aroused by and attracted to a woman who kept another human being in bondage, like so much chattel. "Dr. Maret gave you to her, did he?" he said dryly.

The paddle hit the flagstones with a clatter as Rose swung to face him, her hands on her hips. "What you think? You think I'm a slave? Well, let me tell you, I'm as free as you are. Oh, I belonged to an old colored man, once. He used to beat me something awful, just to show as how he was better than me. He was lighting into me with his cane, down on the wharves, the day the Marets came off that ship from France. They bought me from him right there, on the waterfront, but they set me free just as soon as they could. And I paid them back every cent they spent on me out of my wages."

Bending over, she picked up the paddle in one graceful motion and went to stir the washing again. "You don't know Miss Emmanuelle," she said, not looking at him, "if you think she'd ever own a slave. That was the one thing she and Michie Philippe agreed on—that, and the medicine. They both thought slavery was wrong, wrong, wrong."

"You say that as if they didn't agree on much."

She glanced up quickly, then away, her lips pressing into a thin, tight line. "I didn't say that."

Zach knew he wasn't going to get anything more out of her on that subject. Sighing, he propped one boot up on the other knee and said, "Tell me about Jacques Maret and his wife."

"I want you to look into everyone associated with that hospital," Zach told Hamish as they grabbed a quick lunch at the small Italian café near headquarters.

Hamish looked up from his plate of spaghetti, his eyes owlish. "Everybody?"

"That's right. Send a couple of men to look over their patient files. I want the families of every patient who died or suffered an amputation there in the last year investigated."

"You think that's who we're looking for?" Hamish asked, fumbling in his pocket for his notebook. "A patient with a grudge?"

"No. But I want to look into it, just to be sure. I want you to concentrate on the people Santerre worked with. Like this Englishman, Yardley. See what you can dig up about him. He claims he was with a friend last night. Find out who the friend is, and see if you can get someone else to verify that they were together. He says he had no quarrel with Santerre, but I have a feeling he's hiding something, and I'd like to know what."

Nodding, Hamish flicked open his clothbound notebook and began making a list with a dull, stubby pencil.

"Then there's this young woman, this Claire La Touche," Zach said. "She's a volunteer, but I don't think she got on well with Santerre. See if you can find out why."

Hamish looked up, his pencil poised in midair. "And Madame de Beauvais?"

"I'll take care of her."

Hamish's mustaches swept back and forth as he gnawed at his lower lip. "You can't suspect her."

Zach reached to break off a chunk of the café's heavy Italian bread. "Why not?"

"Because she's . . . well, she's a woman, for one thing."

"Huh. You telling me New York women don't commit murder?"

Hamish shook his head. "Not women like her."

"Like what? I don't think we have the least idea what Madame de Beauvais is really like." Zach pushed back his chair and stood up. "I want someone at this wake tonight from the time it starts. I want to know who comes—and who doesn't come that people think should have." He had a meeting scheduled with Butler that evening that was liable to run late, very late, for Butler had ambitious plans to turn over the area's confiscated sugar plantations—and their black workers—to Northern profiteers.

Hamish nodded. "I'll be there myself." He patted his notebook. "I'll get it all down, don't worry." Zach smiled, and the big New Yorker's eyebrows drew together in a suspicious frown. "What's so funny?"

But Zach only laughed and turned away.

"Now perhaps you will see some sense," said Marie Thérèse de Beauvais, one pale, blue-veined hand moving languidly as she settled back in her chair and waved a palmetto fan to and fro through the still, hot midday air. "Dominic must come with us, to Beau Lac. At least for the next few months."

They were on the rear gallery of the de Beauvais Greek Revival–style city residence, Emmanuelle and the mother of her dead husband. From here, they could watch Dominic and his grandfather, Jean-Lambert, playing horseshoes on the small strip of side lawn. Jean-Lambert might be seventy-six years old, thin and white-haired and dragging one leg since his stroke last May, but he still played a mean game of horseshoes.

Once, the family's town house had been on Ursuline, in the old quarter. But with the expansion of the city and the steady influx of new, poor immigrants, they had moved here, to Esplanade Avenue, on the ridge of

high land running northwest from the Vieux Carré to
Bayou St. John. The de Beauvaises were one of New
Orleans's oldest families, and one of the most respected
and wealthiest, for they had somehow managed for
generations to avoid most of the vices that had brought
ruin to so many of the original Creole families, the
gambling and drinking, the dueling and overindulgence
in that peculiar institution known as *plaçage*—colored
women kept as mistresses in respectable cottages by
rich white men. The center of the de Beauvais wealth
was still the vast sugar plantation known as Beau Lac,
on the Bayou Crevé, but the family had long ago di-
versified into shipping and banking, manufacturing and
real estate. The occupation of the city by Union troops
in May had been costly, but it hadn't yet brought complete ruin to the de Beauvais family, the way it had to
so many in this city. Old Jean-Lambert might hate the
Yankees, but when it came to business, he never let his
heart rule his head.

Standing at the gallery's cast-iron railing, Emmanuelle smiled while she watched her son go suddenly, intensely still in concentration as he prepared for
his next toss. But the smile faded when she turned to
meet the fierce stare of her son's grandmother. "It's too
dangerous. Some of what we hear about these Yankee
patrols is exaggerated, but not all, I'm afraid. I'd feel
better with him here, safe, in the city."

"Safe? Here?" Marie Thérèse's brows drew together
in a frown that might have been either concern or an-
noyance. She was younger than her husband by some
dozen years or more, a tall, attractive, silver-haired
woman with a proud, erect carriage and flashing gray
eyes. "And when the yellow fever strikes? Will he be
safe then, hmm?"

Normally, everyone who could afford it would have left the city by now, fleeing to their country estates to escape the epidemics that raged so often through the hot summer months. Only, this year, the presence of undisciplined Yankee troops and Confederate guerrillas made the countryside even more dangerous than the city. And the dreaded fever had not arrived. Emmanuelle shook her head. "I don't think it will come this year."

The older woman expelled her breath in a disdainful, very Gallic sound. "*Pppuhhh*. Because of a few flushed canals and drained gutters? As if that has anything to do with it."

Emmanuelle curled her hands around the railing at her side and somehow managed to keep quiet, for they'd had this argument more times than she could remember, and Marie Thérèse never changed her mind. About anything.

"It's pure self-interest, of course," Marie Thérèse was saying, "this campaign of the Yankees to clean up the city. They know they would be the first to die."

Emmanuelle pushed away from the rail. "The first, but not the only ones."

Marie Thérèse lifted one thin shoulder in an elegant shrug. "The weak die."

It seemed a cold, calloused thing to say to a young woman who had watched first her mother, then her father die in separate epidemics less than five years apart. But then, Marie Thérèse had lost two of her own sons to the Yellow Jack, and a third to swamp fever.

"Not only the weak," said Emmanuelle, her voice husky with emotion.

The game of horseshoes must be over. Dominic had run off, laughing, toward the stables behind the house, while Jean-Lambert was making his slow, careful way up the stairs to the gallery, his weight leaning heavily on the arm of his big mulatto slave, Baptiste.

Marie Thérèse set aside the fan, the gold rings on her fingers clanging against the table's iron rim. "Is it true," she said, "what Dominic has been telling us? That you've had Yankees at the Hospital de Santerre because of this unpleasantness?"

This unpleasantness. It took Emmanuelle a moment to realize that Marie Thérèse was referring to Henri Santerre's murder. "One Yankee," Emmanuelle said as Jean-Lambert reached the top of the steps. "General Butler's provost marshal."

"It's unlikely he'll trouble you again," said Jean-Lambert, his voice shaky as he paused to catch his breath. "What's another dead Southerner to Ben Butler and his band of murderers and thieves?" With the big black man's help, he eased down into one of the gallery's whitewashed plantation rockers, only the quick spasm of his features betraying his pain. "Thank you, Baptiste," he said quietly. Baptiste nodded, and moved off.

"I don't think this Major Cooper intends to let the matter slide," said Emmanuelle, her voice oddly tight.

With the slow deliberation that characterized his movements these days, the old man hooked his silver-headed cane over the rocker's arm and fumbled in his pockets for his pipe and leather pouch. "Sees it as a matter of pride, does he?"

Emmanuelle shook her head. "Not if you mean pride in the sense of vanity."

Jean-Lambert looked up from tamping the tobacco in his pipe, his startlingly blue eyes narrowing in quick understanding and what might have been amusement. Philippe had had eyes like that. So did Dominic. *Viking eyes,* Jean-Lambert liked to call them. "Ah. So he's a man of honor, is he? He sees catching this killer as a matter of duty. Well, well, well." He stuck the pipe in his mouth and clamped down on it with his teeth. "Interesting."

Emmanuelle said nothing, although she was beginning to think that Zach Cooper's determination to catch this murderer went beyond the ordinary concept of duty. After all, the man was Butler's provost marshal, which meant he was responsible not only for keeping the peace but also for overseeing everything from the confiscation and disposal of Rebel property to the cleaning of the streets and the feeding and housing of thousands of displaced Negroes and the city's own growing population of poor. That he had come to the cemetery last night was understandable. That he was personally taking a part in the investigation of Henri Santerre's death, was not.

"Duty and honor?" scoffed Marie Thérèse. "A Yankee? I doubt it. If Henri hadn't found such a ridiculously sensational way of getting himself murdered, no one would be giving the incident a second thought."

Jean-Lambert struck a match, but paused to eye his wife with the civil hostility that had characterized their partnership for as long as Emmanuelle had known them. "The man can hardly be held responsible for the manner of his death."

Marie Thérèse returned the cold stare. "Of course he can. The life he led, the people he knew—something he'd done must have contributed to what happened, to the way it happened."

Jean-Lambert sucked on his pipe, and said nothing.

Marie Thérèse swung about in her chair to look up at Emmanuelle and say briskly, "You'll be closing the hospital now, of course."

Emmanuelle shook her head. "No. As long as I can, I'll keep it open."

Jean-Lambert nodded in quiet understanding, but Marie Thérèse let out her breath in another of those explosive, very French *pppuhhhs*. It had never sat well with her notions of propriety and respectability, for the wife of a de Beauvais to be working in a hospital. To be working outside the home at all.

"I'm having another sewing meeting on Tuesday," Marie Thérèse said now, her gaze still hard on Emmanuelle's face, "to sew shirts for the Confederate prisoners being held on Ship Island. Will you be attending?"

Every month, Marie Thérèse hosted one of these sewing get-togethers. Every month she invited Emmanuelle, and every month, Emmanuelle knew the harassed feeling that comes from disappointing the expectations of others. She swallowed a sigh. "I'll try," she said. "But with Henri gone, the work at the hospital is likely to become overwhelming."

"Then close it," said Marie Thérèse.

Emmanuelle set her jaw, and said nothing. Again.

Jean-Lambert cleared his throat, filling the awkward silence. "The wake is tonight; had you heard?" He had his head bowed, his attention seemingly all for his pipe. "Will he be there, do you think? This Union major you were telling us about?"

"Surely not," said Marie Thérèse quickly. "To impose himself on mourners at such a time? Even a Yankee must have more manners than that."

Emmanuelle stared off across the garden, toward the stables, where high white clouds were beginning to gather in the pale blue afternoon sky. "He'll be there."

• • •

The daylight was fading fast by the time Emmanuelle turned into the rue Conti, the hum of locusts in the hidden, high-walled gardens loud and ringing in the hot, still air. The afternoon rainstorm had swept in early, drenching the city not long after she left the house on Esplanade Avenue and returned to the hospital. Now, the skies had cleared again, so that a nearly full moon shone pale as a white disk from out of the dusky sky.

Already she could hear the distant roar from the cabarets along the waterfront, for it was Saturday night and not even the war and occupation were enough to quiet the billiard halls and taverns and brothels of the Quarter. But the houses here on the rue Conti were quiet, the air filled with the scent of garlic sizzling in olive oil and the gentle clink of china as tables were set for supper, movements hushed behind shuttered windows. She had a sudden sense of how alone she was on this deserted street, and for a moment she felt a childlike fear of the dark creep up on her, a fear that made her feel contemptibly weak and vulnerable, and that persisted despite her efforts to brush it off. It was with relief that she reached the corner of Burgundy Street and saw the town house Henri Santerre had shared with his sister, Elise.

It was a tall, narrow building, its living quarters on the second and third floors reached through the lamplit darkness of an arched carriageway and up a gracefully curving flight of stone steps. Inside, Emmanuelle found the rooms already crowded with whispering groups of shadowy men and women, the gaslights unlit because of the heat, the mirrors shrouded in black, the air hot and hazy with smoke from the crepe-draped branches of candles that flickered near the dead man's head. She had to force herself to walk across the mat-covered floorboards to stand beside the cold still figure of Henri Santerre. She might be familiar with death, but being familiar with death and being familiar with murder were, she realized, two very different things.

Henri Santerre had been laid out, as was the custom, on a black-draped table placed near the front parlor windows, his hands folded above the heart. Yet as she stared down at him, the sweet scent of jasmine and carnations rose up to envelop her, and Emmanuelle knew a peculiar, scalp-tingling timeslip. Henri's chest was as motionless as the table beneath him, the linen of his shirt faultlessly white and freshly pressed, the black silk of his vest untorn and whole. And yet there was something about that frozen posture that echoed, horribly, terrifyingly, those last hideous moments in the cemetery, the bloodied bolt buried deep in his chest, Henri's hands lifting in confused pain.

Sucking in a quick breath, Emmanuelle jerked her gaze away from those folded hands to her old friend's familiar face. The wrinkled cheeks were relaxed now and at peace, the white beard soft and immaculately groomed as it never was in life, the unseeing eyes shielded by closed lids. And she had a most peculiar thought. *This is Henri, and yet it isn't.* It was as if she were viewing a familiar and yet strangely empty husk, nothing but the shell that had once contained the essence of her friend. And she knew a quick upsurge of fear that nearly swamped her, a fear that shamed her because when she should have been mourning her dead friend she found herself thinking, instead, This could have been me. And she squeezed her eyes shut, her mind whispering into the void of eternity, *Oh, God, Henri. I'm so sorry. Was it supposed to be me?*

She opened her eyes and became aware, suddenly, of

the line forming at the prie-dieu, of a man coming up hat in hand as her world enlarged once again to include the black-hung parlor with its stopped clocks and quietly conversing mourners. She saw Elise Santerre, her face gray with grief, her spine characteristically straight and her head held determinedly high, and went to touch the elderly woman's cold, arthritic hand and brush her dry cheek and murmur all the heartfelt but useless phrases one always said at such times. *He was a wonderful man. If there's anything I can do . . .*

It was such a familiar occurrence in this city, death; so familiar that its forms and rituals had become an important part of life here. All about her, food was eaten, sherry sipped from fine crystal glasses, relationships reaffirmed as aunts and uncles and cousins who hadn't seen one another since the last wake or christening met, and spoke. Funerals and wakes were like weddings and christenings and first communions: they set the pattern, provided the framework of life in New Orleans.

Normally, conversation at wakes was respectful and yet spontaneous and free-flowing, but not tonight. Tonight, voices were hushed, speech stilted as nervous sideways glances were cast at the blue-uniformed man who stood in one corner, his arms crossed at his broad chest, his golden red hair worn in long, flowing magnificence about his thickset shoulders, his pale eyes narrowed and watchful in an expressionless face. Fletcher, his name was, Emmanuelle remembered. She had expected to see Major Cooper here, and knew a profound moment of disquiet when she found herself disappointed by his absence.

"*Alors,* what does he think then?" drawled a familiar French voice behind her. "That the murderer is among us even now, and will betray himself by a fortuitously nervous tic? Or perhaps the guilty one will be so overwhelmed by remorse at the sight of his victim that he'll fall to his knees in tearful confession."

"Antoine." She turned to the man who stood behind her. Antoine La Touche was a tall, lean man, darker than his sister Claire and older, much older, more than thirty-five now, although it was pain rather than age that had dug the deep lines around his aquiline nose and thin mouth, and etched twin grooves between his light brown eyes. He wore a swallow-tailed evening coat with a satin waistcoat and dress tie, yet everything about him proclaimed the planter: the patrician air, the faintly illusive scent of expensive tobacco, the flawless shine on his leather boots—or rather, boot, for Antoine's left leg ended midthigh. He had served in the Confederate cavalry for less than a year before he'd caught a minié ball in his knee at Pea Ridge. They'd fought hard to save his leg, Philippe and Henry and Emmanuelle, and still in the end they'd had to cut most of it off. But it was the bayonet wound he'd received in his gut that would eventually kill him. He might live another two years, maybe five, but Antoine La Touche would not make an old man.

"Antoine," she said again, her hand closing perhaps too tightly about his left arm just below where it rested idly on the top of his crutch. "I must speak with you."

She saw a flicker of surprise in his light brown eyes before they narrowed shrewdly. "*Mais oui, ma chère.*" He threw a glance at Fletcher, busy scribbling in his notebook. "Although if it's that important, perhaps we'd do better to step outside."

They passed silently through the knots of men and women in the dining room and out onto the rear gallery. The sky was black now with the night, the air heavy with the scents of jasmine and honeysuckle, sweet olive and angels' trumpet rising up from the darkness of the garden below.

He took a cheroot from his pocket and lit it, while Emmanuelle went to wrap her hands around the iron railing and stare down at the faint glow of white flowers unfurling toward the moonlight. "Are you all right, Emmanuelle?" he asked quietly, coming to stand beside her. "Even with all you've seen, this can't have been easy for you."

She felt his concern like a gentle blanket cast tenderly about her shoulders, and turned her head to smile thankfully up at him. "I'm all right." Of all of Philippe's friends, she had always liked Antoine the best, perhaps because she sensed that the wildness that drove him came not so much from innate vice as from boredom. He was an only son, well-educated, yet raised to do nothing except someday take over the plantation that was still firmly under his father's control.

"Something's wrong," Antoine said, studying her face.

She nodded. "Has the Yankee provost marshal been to see you?"

"No. Why would he? Unless"—he narrowed his eyes, the tip of his cheroot glowing red in the darkness—"so it's true, is it? They dug a miniature crossbow bolt out of Henri's chest? A bolt with a silver point? *Mon Dieu*." He took a quick step away, the tips of his crutches thumping awkwardly on the wooden floorboards as he swung to face her again. "Do they know?"

"About the vampire-killing set you gave Philippe? I don't think so. But, Antoine—" She broke off, her head turning at the sound of approaching voices and the echo of footsteps in the carriageway below.

He reached out to touch his fingers, briefly, to her lips in warning. "We shouldn't speak of it here."

She nodded. "Can you come to the hospital tomorrow morning?"

"Yes. Of course."

She glanced beyond him, to the crowded rooms inside. "I don't see Claire. Is she here?"

He shook his head. "You know how she is." In the flickering gaslight from the gallery's high lamp, his face looked pale, tight. "Why?"

"She was at the hospital this morning, when the provost marshal came. She might have said something."

"I doubt it." Antoine gripped the end of his cheroot with his teeth, his lips curling back. "He's an interesting man, this provost marshal. Different from Butler and the rest of that gang of lawyers and politicians."

"Different?" Emmanuelle rested her back against the cool iron of the gallery's railing, her hands gripping her elbows at her sides. "How?"

Antoine let out his breath in a slow hiss of tobacco-scented smoke. "He's a career cavalry officer, for one thing—a West Point graduate. He's only been sidelined here because of some injury."

Emmanuelle nodded. "His leg. He limps," she added by way of explanation when Antoine's eyebrows went up. "I shouldn't think he'd have much experience with this sort of thing."

"Oh, but I'm afraid he does."

She shook her head. "How can he?"

"There was a string of sensational killings at a fort he was posted to out West. Fort McKenna, or some such place. He's the one who finally caught the killer. It was in all the papers a few years back."

In the distance, the cathedral bells began to chime,

tolling the hour. "I never heard of it," she said, her voice coming out oddly hollow.

Antoine's pinched features relaxed into a smile. "That's because you rarely pay attention to anything that doesn't involve medicine, *ma chère*."

The rosary began some half an hour later.

In life, Henri Santerre might have been born a Catholic, but whatever faith he'd once had in a Christian God had died years ago. Her beads passing smoothly through her fingers, Emmanuelle smiled at the thought of what Henri would say if he could see them now, murmuring ancient prayers over his candlelit corpse. But then she decided he'd understand. Funeral rites had always been more about comforting the living than helping the dead.

It wasn't until they were finishing the last decade that she heard an uneven tread upon the stairs, saw a tall, blue-uniformed figure appear in the doorway, then move out onto the gallery in private conversation with the big, redheaded New Yorker.

So he has come, she thought, and felt her breath quicken with anticipation and what might have been fear, but wasn't. And then she thought, *This man, this man* . . . He was her enemy, the enemy of her nation. He suspected her of complicity in murder and could have her condemned without trial or recourse, if he wished. He was a threat to her in ways she wouldn't admit even to her closest confidant. And yet all she felt at his arrival was a sense of waiting fulfilled, a surge of excitement that was both cerebral and undeniably, damnably sensual in origin.

CHAPTER EIGHT

"The gatekeeper at the St. Louis Cemetery didn't see anyone," Zach said, the evening breeze warm against his cheek, the low murmur of voices from the wake inside barely audible above the hum of the locusts and the splash of the fountain in the darkened courtyard below.

From where they stood on the back gallery of Henri Santerre's town house, Zach could see the dimly lit interior of the dining room and the front parlor beyond. You could tell there was a war on, he thought, just by looking at the people gathered here tonight. There were somberly clad women of every age, but noticeably few men, and those who had come were either old, or crippled, or very young. Some cast angry glances toward the gallery, but most were doing their best to ignore the two officers in blue uniforms who stood there.

Hamish bit the tip off a cigar and stuck it between his teeth. "Found someone who could speak German, did you?"

Zach nodded, his gaze narrowing as he watched a tall, gaunt man on crutches lean forward to whisper something in the ear of a striking, dusky haired woman with an elegant, diminutive figure and a mouth that was too big, too provocatively sensual for her aristocratic, fine-boned face. Madame de Beauvais. "The gatekeeper's name is Kessler," Zach said, his gaze fixed on the woman. "He came here two years ago from Prussia, and he's as efficient as a German can be. He says the only people through those gates in the three hours before Santerre and Madame de Beauvais were a couple of old black men come to make repairs on their master's family crypt, and I think he knows what he's talking about."

Hamish grunted, and patted his uniform in search of a light. "Our friend with the crossbow must have climbed over the wall. So much for the theory that he used a crossbow because of some physical weakness."

Zach fished a container of safety matches from his coat and lit one. "Find out anything about that silver-tipped bolt?"

"Not a blessed thing." Hamish puffed on his cigar, one hand coming up to shield the flame from the breeze. The aromatic smoke billowed around them. "But I am learning enough about this city to make it hard for me to believe it was ever a part of the United States. All that voodoo and hoodoo, gris-gris and ju ju and love beads . . . makes me glad I'm a good Presbyterian, so I don't take any stock in that shit."

Zach stared thoughtfully into the night. He'd felt it himself, the strangeness of this city full of sights and smells and traditions at once foreign and evocative, but he found it seductive, not repellent. "No vampire killers?"

"Nope. I've got some men looking into the people from the hospital, but they haven't turned up much yet, either."

Zach nodded toward the dining room. "Who's the man on crutches?"

Hamish swung about to follow Zach's gaze. "Ah. That's the neighborhood war hero." Hamish fished out his notebook and flipped it open. "Antoine La Touche. He lost the leg after Pea Ridge. It's his sister who volunteers at the Hospital de Santerre."

"Claire La Touche." Zach's eyes narrowed as he searched the still crowded rooms within. "She's not here?"

"They say she's no' very fond of wakes." Hamish grinned. "Which I can understand, mind you, except that if I were her, I think I'd come anyway, just to keep the others from talking about me. They do love to talk about one another, don't they?"

A mosquito whined near Zach's ear, and he batted at it absently with one hand. "I don't see Dr. Yardley, either."

"The Englishman?" Hamish's teeth tightened their grip on his cigar. "He was here, but not for long. After he left, they talked about him, too. For at least twenty minutes."

Zach shifted so he could see his friend's face more clearly. "And?"

Hamish's mustaches twitched. "It seems he doesn't care for women, if you get the drift of what I'm saying? Or at least, that's what they all think. But then, they don't like the English much, around here. Or the Scots, for that matter," he added, his voice turning disgruntled.

Zach ducked his head to hide a smile that faded all too quickly. She was laughing now, Madame de Beauvais. Discreetly, of course, but in obviously easy camaraderie with the one-legged man beside her. "What do they say about her?" Zach asked suddenly. "About Madame de Beauvais?"

Hamish scrubbed one hand across his face. "Not a lot. I think they're a bit afraid of her, actually. Don't know what to make of her. As if she weren't really one of them."

"She's not."

"Huh?" Hamish's face went blank with a lack of comprehension. "She's *French.*"

"That's right." Straightening, Zach pushed away from the railing, toward the open doors to the dining room. Inside, Madame de Beauvais paused beside the table, one hand arrested in the act of bringing a sherry glass to her lips. Across the distance that separated them, her gaze met his, and he wasn't surprised to see the edges of her lips lift in a slow, taunting smile that seemed to say, *Come catch me, if you can.* He knew she was afraid of what he might learn about her, but she wasn't afraid of *him.* What she played with him was a sophisticated kind of game, cerebral, sensual, and dangerous. "She's French, all right," he said absently. "But they're not. Not anymore. They haven't been for almost sixty years now. Even if they don't like to admit it."

"You still think she's involved in all this in some way?"

Zach nodded. "I know it. And I'm going to prove it."

"It's not healthy," she said to him, her eyes sparkling with a hostile challenge as he walked up to her. "This habit you men have, of smoking cigars and pipes and cheroots. It can kill you as surely as any bullet or sword."

"Are you concerned about my health, madame?" He paused beside her, close enough that the tip of his saber thrust against her full black skirts. "I'm flattered."

Her lips were still smiling, sultry and faintly

contemptuous, but he could see that her breathing had quickened, the rise and fall of her high, rounded breasts fluttering the narrow line of black lace on the bodice of her mourning gown. "Have you ever seen the lungs of a man who smokes?" she asked. "A healthy lung is pink with blood. Plump. Moist. But your friend's lungs, now, they'd be brown and shriveled and dry, if you were to cut him open and look at him. After he was dead, of course."

The image she conjured up was both startling and slightly nauseous, but he managed to dredge up a smile every bit as nasty as her own. "That a fact? No wonder he can't run more than half a block without puffing like a steam engine."

She surprised him by laughing, a short, quick laugh of genuine amusement that lit up her face and gave him, briefly, a beguiling glimpse at another side of this intriguing woman, a side he hadn't seen before.

"You do it deliberately, don't you," he said suddenly.

"Do what, monsieur?"

"Keep people at a distance. Make them think you're strange."

All trace of laughter drained from her face. She looked both more vulnerable and less sure of herself than he'd ever seen her, although no less attractive. "I am strange."

He shook his head. "You're different. That doesn't make you strange."

"It does to most people." Their gazes met and held, and the moment became something intimate and personal and vaguely disturbing. He didn't want this between them, this silent understanding, this startling recognition of affinity and innate connection.

He looked away first, nodding to where Antoine La Touche now sat in quiet conversation with Henri Santerre's sister, Miss Elise. "I'm told they're an old family, the La Touches. Old and respected. But neither as old nor as wealthy as the de Beauvaises."

"You've been asking questions about us, monsieur."

"I've had a busy afternoon."

"And what have you learned?"

"Well, let's see. I've learned that Dr. Jacques Maret arrived in New Orleans from France in eighteen forty-eight." A gaunt black man, stoop-shouldered with age, walked past, carrying a tray of sherry glasses. Zach snagged one with a murmur of thanks. "The date is significant," he continued, "it being the year of abortive revolutions all over Europe."

She lifted her glass as if in a toast. "Echoes of *liberté, égalité,* and *fraternité.*"

"It must have been an interesting marriage, your parents'," he said, raising his own glass. The sherry was cool and dry and easy going down. "Interesting, and unusual—a Parisian revolutionary and the grand-daughter of a Burgundian count who lost his head on the guillotine."

She sipped her sherry, her gaze showing him only mild inquiry.

"And which are you, madame," he asked, when she said nothing, "the aristocrat, or the revolutionary?"

The wine had wet her lips, making them look even fuller, softer. In the dim light, her eyes were huge. "I am both. And neither." She turned to set aside her glass. "And what does any of this have to do with Henri Santerre's murder?" She glanced up, sideways, at him. "Hmm, monsieur?"

He met the challenge in her eyes and threw it right back at her. "I also looked into those medical schools you were telling me about—the French and the American. Most of the doctors who used to be associated with them have joined the Confederate medical corps, but the few I could find didn't seem to be aware of any significant quarrels between Dr. Santerre and his colleagues."

She raised her eyebrows in an exaggerated show of surprise. "Did you really expect them to tell you?"

"Maybe. What exactly was Santerre working on when he died?"

She gave a slow shrug that looked casual, but wasn't. "He's been writing papers against phlebotomy—the practice of bleeding—for years now. But with the shortage of medicines caused by your blockade of our ports, he was spending more and more of his time investigating the curative properties of local plants."

"Local plants?"

"That's right. There's an old African who lives out in the swamps, a man they call Papa John. Most people know him as a voodoo king, but he has also made quite a study of native medicines. Henri used to visit him."

Zach took a long, slow sip of his sherry, his gaze fixed on her beautiful face, so calm, so deceitful. "Why are you telling me this?"

Again, that shrug. "I thought it might help."

He shook his head. "You don't want to help me. You want me to go away and leave you alone. What are you hoping? That this Papa John will—how do you say it?—put the gris-gris on me?"

She gave a low laugh. "Perhaps." The smile faded. "They say he can read minds. And foresee the future."

"Have you ever been to him?"

Her hand crept up to touch the widow's brooch she wore at her neck, then fluttered away, as if the gesture had been unconscious and she'd only just realized what she had done. "I don't want to know my future," she said, her cheekbones standing out stark in the delicate, flawless beauty of her face. "No one could ever foresee the whole, and to know only a part . . . that could be a dangerous thing."

"He must not have told Henri Santerre his future. Or didn't Santerre believe in it?"

"He believed," she said softly. "Henri didn't believe in much, but he believed in Papa John."

"I can stay longer, if you think it necessary," Hamish offered as they left the wake together some fifteen minutes later.

Zach shook his head. "I think we've learned everything we're going to learn here. Besides . . ." They passed through the town house's tunnel-like carriageway, their footsteps echoing queerly, then paused for a moment on the brick banquette. The moist heat of the night enveloped them with the mingling scents of the city, sweet magnolia and jasmine overlaying the subtle odors of decay and stagnant water and damp, fecund earth. "We need to give them a chance to talk about us."

Hamish's laugh rang out in the dark street as he turned away, up Burgundy Street toward Canal and the mansions Uptown, where they all, like their general, lived in confiscated luxury. But Zach continued on, toward the river with its groggeries and pool halls and brothels, where men of all colors and nations congregated and drank, and information was plentiful, and cheap.

The worst of the drinking holes were on the waterfront, but there were taverns and licensed gambling dens scattered throughout the old quarter, particularly on the streets running parallel to the river, streets like Bourbon and Royal, where the business establishments tended to be concentrated. He had just crossed the rue

Dauphine when he saw a knot of some five or six soldiers clustered near the banquette about halfway down
the block, their blue uniforms looking almost black in
the lamplight, their voices loud and movements clumsy
with alcohol. As he drew nearer, he realized they had
formed a ring around a man, a middle-aged colored
man dressed in the neat, single-breasted suit and
stovepipe hat of a successful businessman.

One of the soldiers—a big, burly sergeant with a
flowing blond beard and a broad Ohio accent—
thumped the colored man on the shoulder hard enough
to make him stagger. "You think you're as good as a
white man, do you, boy?" said the soldier, leaning in
close, "jist because some massa set your grandmammy
free after gettin' one of his bastards on her? You think
that gives you the right to dress in these fancy clothes,
just like a white man? You think that gives you the
right to walk on the sidewalk like a white man, and not
even bother to get outta the way when a real white
man's trying to get past you?"

The colored man held himself very still, his face dark
and impassive in the dim light. There were more than
eleven thousand of them in this city, the *gens de couleur
libres*—free people of color, many of whom had been
free for generations. They tended to be both educated
and skilled, accomplished tradesmen, or landholders
with plantations and slaves of their own.

The sergeant gave the man another shove. "I'm
talkin' to you, darky."

"*Je suis désolé, monsieur,*" said the colored man, his
voice deep and educated, his Parisian accent flawless.
"*Je ne comprends pas.*"

"Let him go," Zach said, his voice ringing out loud
and sharp in the otherwise empty street, his hand on his
saber.

The soldiers swung about, their faces slack and flushed with drink. "Well, look what we got us here," said the sergeant. The others dropped back as he took a step forward, swaggering with his insolence. "A nigger-lovin' officer."

A mean smile pulled at the sergeant's mouth. Zach could hear the man's heavy breathing, smell the stink of alcohol and sweat and hate rolling off him. He saw the man's fists clench, but he didn't really expect him to throw a punch. Not at an officer.

The attack when it came was slow and clumsy. Zach blocked the wide right hook easily with his left arm, his own right fist curling up to smash, hard, into the sergeant's nose. Bone and cartilage crumpled, spewing blood over the man's chin and chest. Howling with pain, the big man stumbled back, both hands flying up to his bloodied face. For one, tense instant, the soldiers with him stood as if frozen. Then they threw themselves at Zach.

Two of them, Zach figured, he could have fought off with his fists and his feet—maybe even three. But there were six of them. And when he considered that a soldier could be executed for attacking an officer, he suspected they weren't likely to let him live to see them court-martialed.

A swift kick caught one of the men in the face and sent him staggering back into another, which bought Zach enough time to bring his saber singing from its scabbard. He thought they'd run then, but they were too drunk, or too stupid, to realize that the confrontation had just turned against them.

The man Zach had kicked rushed back at him with a snarl, spewing bloody spittle and scrabbling for the Colt at his belt. Zach's saber caught him in the neck, half-taking the man's head off, and got a second in the gut on the backswing, opening up a killing gash that sent blood spraying through the air.

Their eyes wide with shock and fear, three of the remaining men turned to run. A sound from behind brought Zach whirling around, and he jerked his blade from the dying soldier's body just as the sergeant lunged forward again, lamplight flashing on the blade of the bowie knife clutched in his fist. Over the pounding of his own blood, loud in his ears, Zach could hear the sound of running feet. Hamish, he thought absently. But the big New Yorker was still too far away. His teeth bared in a grim smile, Zach took a step back, his arm coming up to send the curving edge of his sword singing through the air at the blond sergeant's face. But the ballast-paved street was slick with blood, and as his foot came down, Zach felt his boot heel slip sideways, throwing him off balance.

He caught himself almost at once, but not before he felt the man's knife slice through the flesh of his side, cutting deep. Swearing, Zach thrust his saber forward like a bayonet, swift and hard enough to send the tip of his blade clean through the other man's chest and out his back.

"Shit," Zach said, and jerked his saber from the dead man's body.

"Gawd." Hamish turned in a slow circle, his head shaking as he took in the crumpled bodies, the blood splashed from the flagged street up onto the brick banquette and beyond, to the stucco walls of the nearest houses. "I leave you alone for two minutes and you turn the neighborhood into an abattoir."

Zach leaned over to wipe his bloodstained blade on one of the dead men's uniforms. "You took your own sweet time getting here."

"Your estimate was too generous," said a woman's calm, familiar voice. "He can't run even half a block."

Zach straightened. The colored man the soldiers had been harassing had disappeared. The good people who lived in the tall, narrow town houses rising up from the brick banquettes on either side of the rue Conti had peeked through their shuttered windows, seen the carnage taking place in their normally quiet street, and withdrawn with hushed whispers to their back rooms. But Madame de Beauvais, on her way to check on some patient at the hospital, he supposed, had heard the fight and run toward it, not away.

He shoved his saber into its scabbard with a quiet hiss of well-tended metal and swung to face her. "You shouldn't be out here alone."

She was moving from one still body to the next, checking them with quiet efficiency. "Was it necessary to kill them all?"

It wasn't pretty, what his sword had done to those men. He wished she didn't need to see it. But then, if she'd tended men wounded in battle, he'd no doubt she'd seen worse. "I didn't kill all of them," he said, still breathing heavily. "Three of them ran away."

"They won't get far," growled Hamish, his face dark with anger.

"They're gunners, probably all from the same outfit. It shouldn't be hard to trace them." His side felt oddly cold. Glancing down, he was surprised to find his uniform dark and wet.

"Easy lad," said Hamish, starting forward. "You're bleeding like a leaking levee there."

But it was the widow who reached him first, one arm coming around his waist to catch his weight on her surprisingly strong shoulders. "I thought you'd been hurt."

"It's nothing," he said, his hand closing tight about her upper arm, her flesh feeling warm and solid through the cloth of her mourning gown.

"Nothing, of course," she said dryly. "That's why your entire side is wet with blood. Here." She handed him something rolled into a tight wad that she pressed against his cut, something he realized must be her cloth handbag. "Hold this tightly against the wound. It will help stop the bleeding until we get to the hospital."

He looked down into her upturned face, glowing pale and smooth in the lamplight. He expected to find both hostility and contempt there, but was surprised to see only a frown of gentle concern he found disconcerting. "It's not deep," he said gruffly. "I can see to it later."

"Don't be a fool. The Hospital de Santerre is just around the corner."

"Go on, lad," said Hamish, squatting down beside one of the dead soldiers. "I can manage better here if I don't need to worry about you bleeding to death on me."

She tilted her head, that challenging smile Zach knew so well playing about her lips as she stared up at him. "Or don't you think me capable of dealing with this?"

And so of course he went with her, her arm still about his waist, the sweet scent of her mingling in his head with the smell of jasmine and warm night air and freshly spilled blood.

CHAPTER
NINE

Emmanuelle turned their steps toward the rue Bienville, her arm around the Union major's waist as she held the makeshift pad to his wound, his weight resting lightly on her shoulders. The evening breeze rattled the banana fronds in a nearby walled garden and brought her the murmur of distant voices and the splash of an unseen fountain. Such familiar sounds, she thought, and yet there was nothing familiar about this moment at all.

"Why?" he said at last, as they turned the corner and a large, three-story Spanish-style house finally hid from view the carnage he had wrought. "Why are you doing this?"

She kept her gaze fixed straight ahead. "Because I know how quickly even the simplest of wounds can fester in this climate. And because I also know how careless—and stupid—men can be when they think they're not seriously injured."

"And you would care? I'm flattered."

"Don't be. I've also been known to tend mangy dogs and a lame skunk I once found in the street." She felt the quiver of silent laughter that ran through him, and knew an unwanted and frighteningly powerful response that quickened within her. She was suddenly, acutely aware of his nearness, of the beat of his heart and the intake of his breath and the strength of his body, so hard and vitally male beneath the fine cloth of his hated blue uniform. That she should react in such a way to any man appalled her. That she should respond, thus, to the nearness of *this* man filled her with shame, and fear.

"It was an admirable thing you did back there," she said after a moment. "Rescuing that colored man from those soldiers."

"Why? Because he's a Negro?"

"That's not what I meant and you know it. Those Yankee soldiers you fought, they obviously can't accept the idea of an educated, affluent man with dark skin. They'd probably never even seen one before. But here in New Orleans, there are almost as many *gens de couleur libres* as there are black slaves."

"And they're still not allowed to vote."

"I am not allowed to vote," she said softly.

"I don't think that's right, either."

It was so simply said, it took her utterly by surprise. Most men—most *people*—laughed at the suggestion of extending the right to vote to women. But not this man.

It had been a mistake, she thought, her arm still tight around his warm man's body. It had been a mistake to offer to help him, to touch him like this, to hold him close to her, to walk with him, talking, through the gently scented night as if they were lovers instead of enemies.

"You enjoy it, don't you?" she said suddenly. "Killing, I mean."

He was silent for so long, she didn't think he was going to answer her. His sigh, when it came, surprised her, for there could be no mistaking the weariness and regret it echoed. "No, I don't enjoy it."

Her mind resurrected for her an image of him

surrounded by that pack of men, his teeth bared in a frightful smile, the bloodied steel of his saber slashing, and slashing, and slashing. Not even Henri Santerre's murder, with its terrorizing suddenness and haunting anonymity, had prepared her for the cold savagery of those few deadly moments in the rue Conti. She might have seen the results of such carnage in the past, but she had never actually witnessed its creation. "You were smiling."

"I was angry. I don't like people who try to kill me."

She glanced up at his dark profile, silhouetted against the dim light spilling out through a nearby shuttered window. "That's what war is about, isn't it? Killing."

"This wasn't war. This was just men being stupid."

"So you only enjoy war?"

"I didn't say that."

They had reached the front steps of the Hospital de Santerre. Stretching out her free hand, Emmanuelle gave the bell a hard yank that set it to clanging violently. "You must enjoy it. You made it your career."

He let his arm drop from her shoulders and turned to face her. "You wanted to become a doctor. Does that mean you enjoy death?"

She stared back at him, but the gas lamp mounted beside the hospital's wide entrance threw only shadow across his features. She could see nothing but the sharp angle of his cheekbone and the powerful, hard line of his jaw.

With a sudden creaking of hinges, the massive door beside them swung inward. *"Lieber Gott,"* said the tall, lanky young man who stood there, his dark brown eyes widening in surprise at the sight of the bloodied, blue-uniformed man before him. He was just nineteen, Hans, and he'd come to America less than five years before with his mother and four brothers, all trying to avoid being caught up in the wars of unification sweeping Germany. Only, instead of fighting the French, Hans had simply ended up losing part of his foot—and very nearly his life—in a bloody little engagement with a Yankee patrol in the back swamps of the Bayou Crevé.

"Do you need me to help you with him?" Hans asked, although with his accent it came out sounding like *vith him.*

Emmanuelle struck a match to light one of the lanterns that stood in a row on the long table just inside the door. "I can manage, thanks. But I could use some hot water from the kitchen."

"I'll get it."

"Who's he?" said the major, his gaze following the young German as he swung away with an awkward maneuver of his crutch.

"Hans?" She turned, the lantern in hand, to lead the way down the hall. "He does light nursing work around the hospital, and keeps an eye on the patients at night."

"On a crutch?"

"Where else is he likely to find work—on a crutch?" She pushed open the door to the sparsely furnished, well-scrubbed room across from the office. "You'll need to take off your jacket and shirt." She found she couldn't look at him as she said it, as if she were suddenly shy or embarrassed, as if she had never before seen a man's naked flesh. "And your saber, of course."

The scabbard rattled as he unbuckled its belt and turned in a slow circle, his gaze studying the high-ceilinged, bare-floored room with its unadorned, white-washed walls and stone-topped table and curtainless windows showing only the black of the night beyond. "This is where you do your surgery?"

She hung the lamp from the hook beside the table, then quickly stripped off her hat and gloves and laid them aside. "What do you think we do here? Dissections?"

"If that's meant to scare me," he said, his fingers going to work on the brass buttons of his uniform, "then you've succeeded."

He had fine-boned hands, long-fingered and elegant, and she found herself watching them, watching him as he eased open the last button of his coat and began to peel it off. She thought of those hands, tightly gripped around the pommel of his sword. Maiming. Killing. "Try to keep the pad pressed against your wound," she said, and swung away to go wash her own hands at the sink in the corner.

"Has he been here long?"

"Who?" she said, busy with the pump.

"Hans."

"Almost three years. He worked as a nurse before he was wounded."

"Which was when?"

"May." She took a cloth from the stack kept wrapped up, clean, on a shelf near the sink. "I want to wash that wound before I bandage it. You may have bits of thread from your uniform caught in it. . . ." Her voice trailed off as she turned to face him again.

He stood at his ease with one hip hitched on the edge of the table, an outstretched arm braced at his side, the other hand holding the blood-soaked, makeshift pad pressed to his ribs. He was built long and lean, with sinewy arms and shoulders and an exquisitely molded chest that gleamed golden and naked in the soft lamplight, and the sight of him, the sheer beauty of him, momentarily took her breath. Around them, the night seemed strangely still, the soft rustle of the breeze

through the leaves of the Chinaball tree in the courtyard outside an intrusion.

"Your water, madame," said Hans from the doorway.

She jerked away to take the white enamel basin of
hot water and close the door behind him with a murmured thanks. Then she stood for a moment, one hand
splayed against the door panel, the other holding the
basin of water against her hip as she asked herself what
was *wrong* with her. She was as familiar with men's
bodies as any *fille de joie* out of a riverfront bordello.
There was no excuse for her reaction to this man, no
excuse for her exquisite sensitivity to his nearness,
no excuse for her unprofessional awareness of his half-
naked body. It must be the strain of these last few days,
she decided—the fear and uncertainty. It was making
her act like some bizarre cross between a shivering
coward and a love-struck schoolgirl.

"I don't smoke," said the man behind her.

She spun about fast enough to send the water sloshing over the cobalt rim of the basin, wetting the bodice
of her gown. "Monsieur?" She met his dark eyes to find
them gleaming with amusement and something else,
something he hid with a downward sweep of those impossibly long lashes.

"In case you should be tempted to take a peek at my
lungs."

"Humph." She pushed away from the door and went
to set the basin on the table beside him with a clatter.
"I generally don't kill my own cadavers."

"Now that's reassuring."

She pushed away the hand holding the blood-soaked
pad to his wound. "Let me see this."

The knife had caught him high in the side to slice
through flesh and sinewy muscle in a long, ugly gash

that oozed fresh blood as soon as the pressure of the cloth was removed. "You've lost a fair amount of blood," she said, "but it looks as if your ribs kept the blade from cutting deep enough to do any real damage." She put her hand on his side, just above the wound. His flesh felt warm and smooth to the touch, the muscle beneath it hard, powerful. She heard his breath catch. "Does it hurt?"

He gave a low, hoarse laugh. "Not really."

"It will." Reaching out, she dipped the cloth into the water and, wringing it out only slightly, began carefully to clean the edges of the cut. She was aware, once again, of the silence of the night around them, of the trickle of water in the basin when she rinsed the cloth, of the sound of his breathing, and hers.

"Where did you learn to do all this?" he asked, breaking the tense intimacy of the moment.

She went to get a bottle of alcohol from the cupboard near the door. "Do what?"

"This," he said when she bent over his wound again. "Those two medical schools you were telling me about? I checked. Neither of them admits women."

"Of course not." Grimly, she pressed a pad soaked in the alcohol to his wound. The sting of it in the open flesh brought the breath hissing out of him. "Why would they, when a woman can only be licensed as a midwife?"

"So where did you study? Paris?"

She straightened sharply and swung away again. "I always planned to go back to Paris to study," she said, replacing the alcohol and gathering the bandages and curving needle she would use to suture the wound.

"But you didn't?"

"No."

"Why not?"

Dumping the bandages on the table, she stood before him, the silk-threaded needle in one hand, the other fisted on her hip. "I really don't see how that is any of your business, Major."

Hard and compelling, his gaze met hers. "Henri Santerre's murder is my business. And you were with him the night he was killed."

She bent over his wound again to draw the edges together with her free hand. "That makes me your business, does it, monsieur?"

"Yes."

Without warning, she thrust the needle through his skin, and was feeling mean enough to smile when he flinched.

"I think you're enjoying this," he said. "And you didn't answer my question."

"Which one?" She drove the needle, again, through first one side, then the other of the cut flesh. As she worked, her hip pressed against the hard muscle of his thigh. She could feel the strength of him, the heat of him, through the blue cloth of his uniform, distracting her, disconcerting her, so that she had to force herself to focus. It was rather like sewing a seam, this suturing of wounds. She wasn't particularly clever with a needle, not compared with most women. But her sutures had always been much neater than either Henri's or Philippe's. "You've asked a great many questions."

"Where did you learn medicine?"

She shrugged. "Officially, enrollment in the medical schools here is limited to men only. But anyone willing to pay the professors twenty dollars a course can attend their lectures." She worked a small knot into her thread, and cut it. "Even women." She reached for the clean bandages. "Although I learned far more from my father and Henri Santerre than I ever learned in those lecture halls."

"And from your husband."

"Hold that," she said briskly, and pressed a clean pad against his wound.

"It's unusual, isn't it," he said, reaching up to hold the pad in place with the splayed fingers of his right hand, "for the only son of such a wealthy family to become a doctor?"

"Not so unusual." She began to wrap the bandages around his ribs. "There are other planters who are also doctors."

"The de Beauvaises aren't just planters."

She shrugged. "Philippe was the fourth son. He never expected to inherit everything." She tied off the ends of the bandage and straightened. "As it turned out, of course, he never did."

Against his flesh, the bandage shone startlingly white, for his skin was the deep warm golden color usually seen only in those of Mediterranean blood. He sat very still on the edge of the table, his arms hanging loosely at his sides, his bare chest lifting slightly with each indrawn breath. And she was aware of it again, of the intimacy of being here with him, of the strange, forbidden pull of his naked body, of her dangerous fascination with this hard, frightening man.

"Who do you know who uses a crossbow?" he asked quietly.

The suddenness, the complete unexpectedness of the question caught her by surprise, so that she took a step back, her lips parting as she sucked in a quick gasp of air. "Monsieur?"

"It's an uncommon weapon," he said, his eyes bright with a calculated gleam. "Yet you're familiar enough with it to recognize a bolt when you see one. Even an unusually small, silver-tipped bolt."

Impossible to deny any real knowledge of the weapon, Emmanuelle thought; impossible, too, to admit the truth—or at least all of it. She watched him reach for his shirt and wince as he began to pull it on. His movements were slow and awkward, for if his wound hadn't been hurting him before, it would be now. If he'd been any other man, she would have helped him dress. She didn't move.

"Philippe," she said at last, her hands fisting in her black skirts. "Philippe often hunted with a crossbow. It . . . intrigued him." Many things intrigued Philippe, the more unusual and bizarre, the better, but she didn't say that.

She saw his brows draw together in a frown. "Your husband?"

"Yes."

He finished buttoning his coat and straightened slowly. "Are you sure he's dead?"

It was a simple, chance question, but the effect on her was like a physical blow, bringing with it a blinding flash of possibility and fear. All day, she had been asking herself, over and over again, just one question: *Who?* If Henri had, in fact, been hit by mistake, then the question became, not who had wanted to kill Henri, but who wanted to kill Emmanuelle? And it occurred to her now, as the seconds stretched out silent and damning, that Philippe . . . Philippe might have believed he had a reason to kill her.

But Philippe was dead.

Her gaze fell to where the Yankee's cavalry scabbard rested, shining and deadly. She bent swiftly to pick it up. "If you're asking did I see his body, then the answer is no. No, I didn't. You'll need to talk to the Yankees

on the Bayou Crevé. They're the ones who killed him."
She thrust the saber into his arms. Her gaze met his,
and she let all of her loathing, all of her contempt for
this man and his uniform and his violent ways leach
into her eyes and into her voice. "They killed him," she
said again. "And they buried him."

CHAPTER
TEN

She didn't start to shake until Hans was outside helping the major into a hack.

She was on her way up to the second floor to look in on Emile Rouant, the young Confederate lieutenant. It was, after all, why she'd been on her way to the hospital when she'd come across that violent scene in the rue Conti. But she'd only made it halfway up the stairs when she felt herself begin to tremble so hard, she had to press her back against the wall and close her eyes and admit to herself—finally, honestly—that it wasn't just some vague fear. That she actually *knew*, deep down in the fundamental core of her being, that Henri Santerre had died in her place, that someone—*someone*—wanted her dead. Someone who not only knew how to shoot a crossbow, but who had also known exactly where to find a crossbow that was small and easy to notch and reliably lethal.

She could think of only two men who fit that description: Antoine La Touche, who had hunted the swamps and bayous of Beau Lac with his cousin Philippe as a child, and who had given Philippe the vampire-killing set in the first place, and Philippe himself. But Antoine had no *reason* to want to kill her, and Philippe . . .

No, she thought, pushing away from the wall and

continuing up the stairs, angry with herself for her suspicions as much as for the humiliating moment of weakness and terror. Antoine would be as incapable of murder as Philippe. And Philippe was dead.

She found Lieutenant Rouant wracked with fever and begging deliriously for someone to do something, anything, to make the pain in his nonexistent arm go away. They worked for hours, she and Hans, bathing the lieutenant's hot body with vinegar water and dosing him with opium. Just after four o'clock, Rudolph, the big Senegalese who had worked as a nurse at the hospital for ten years or more, arrived to take over, and Emmanuelle dragged herself the few blocks to the house on the rue Dumaine for a couple of hours sleep and a quick breakfast with Dominic. She made it back to the hospital again by ten o'clock, just after Henri's funeral mass, but by then Rouant had slipped into a deep sleep that wasn't really sleep at all. He would not live to see another dawn, and she knew it.

She was sitting in Henri's worn old leather desk chair, her hands lying limply in her lap, her gaze fixed unseeingly on the exuberantly lush growth of the banana trees and elephants ears and ginger lilies that half-obscured the high brick walls of the courtyard, when a voice behind her said, "Sleep is not an indulgence, *ma chère*. And you look as if you've been depriving yourself."

She brought her head around. "Antoine," she said, and rose quickly to take his hands in hers and kiss his cheek, as was the French custom among friends. She'd never understood the Americans, who stiffly shook hands with strangers, and then never hugged or kissed or touched their friends in any way. "Thank you for coming."

He cocked his head to look down at her. His mouth was smiling, but his eyes were narrowed with a concern that shamed her, when she remembered how she had actually, for one brief moment, let herself suspect him of having tried to kill her. "What's wrong? What's happened now?"

She let out her breath in a tired sigh. "One of the wounded men in the hospital. He's dying."

"Ah." He let go of her hands to flick her cheek with his fingertips. "You must learn not to take each death so hard, *bébé*. There are too many of them."

She searched his thin, aquiline face. "Did you speak to Claire?"

Two tight white lines appeared to bracket his mouth. They were not close, Antoine and his younger sister. "She won't tell your provost marshal about Philippe's vampire-killing kit, if that's what you're worried about. Not that I think it need concern us too much, anyway. The crossbow might be unusual, Emmanuelle, but I doubt it's unique. There must be others like it." He paused, then gave a sharp laugh. "Well, obviously there must be at least one more like it, since one was used to kill Henri Santerre."

Emmanuelle shook her head, a sick feeling gripping her stomach. "The set you gave Philippe is missing, Antoine. Someone has taken it."

"*Mon Dieu.*" He went to stand at the window, one arm draped over the brace of his crutch, the other bent elbow propped high against the frame as he tapped his teeth thoughtfully with one knuckle. "No wonder you don't want the Yankees to learn of it."

"Where did you get it?" She saw the glitter of wicked amusement in his eyes when he swung his head to look at her over his shoulder, and said quickly, "*Eh bien,* you don't need to tell me. Only, did they know who you are? I mean, would they tell?"

"I'm not sure. You probably know him better than I do."

Emmanuelle shook her head in confusion. "Who?"

"Papa John."

For a long, agonizing moment, Emmanuelle simply stared at him, the blood thundering abnormally loud in her ears.

"What is it?" said Antoine, taking an awkward step toward her.

Emmanuelle put up a splayed hand to press her fingers to her lips. "Last night, I told the provost marshal about Henri's visits to the swamps."

"You *what*?"

"I didn't know that's where the crossbow had come from. I only wanted to give the Yankees something else to focus on besides the hospital." Something else besides her. "I never imagined . . ."

"Don't worry." Antoine reached out to grip her hand, tightly, in reassurance. "Papa John must know the darkest secrets of half the people in this city. He won't tell." His brows twitched together in a worried frown. "Will he?"

Zach was sitting at a small round table at the Café del Aquila on the corner of St. Anne and Chartres, sipping chicory-flavored coffee and idly watching two elderly Creoles playing dominoes at a nearby table, when a booming New York voice oddly tinged with a bit of Scots said, "And did no one ever tell you, lad, that you're supposed to rest when you've been wounded?"

"I am resting." Zach gave his friend a slow smile. "Besides, I'm scratched, not wounded."

"Scratched, is it?" Hamish pulled out the metal chair beside him and sat down with a stifled groan that spoke of heat and exhaustion and sore feet. "I know three lads from Ohio who're wishing that's all it was."

"You found them?"

"Aye." Hamish took off his hat and used it to fan his damp red face. The day had turned sultry and overcast, although the light was still bright enough to hurt the eyes. "I also talked to your Englishman's *particular friend*. Turns out he's a flashy gambler who used to spend most of his time riding the paddle wheelers up and downriver. Swears Yardley spent the evening with him, although there's no one to back up the tale."

Zach turned to signal the waiter for two more coffees. "Could Yardley be in debt?"

"I'm looking into that. He runs in rough company for a doctor, that's for sure. And from what I hear, Santerre wasn't too pleased about it."

"Yardley says he was also a *particular friend* of Philippe de Beauvais." Zach paused while the waiter set their coffees on the table with a discreet thump of indignation. They weren't good for business, Yankee uniforms, but no establishment in New Orleans would dare refuse to serve one. A month or so ago, when a shoe store owner had refused to sell a Union soldier a pair of boots, General Butler had ordered the man's store confiscated and his entire stock auctioned off.

Hamish leaned forward. "What do you think that means?"

"I'm not sure. But I have another name you can add to your list." He paused while Hamish pulled out his notebook. "A young German named Hans who works at the Hospital de Santerre as a nurse. According to Madame de Beauvais, he was wounded last May, presumably in the war. See what you can find out about him."

Hamish nodded, then looked up, his eyes shining. "You havena asked about that wee crossbow bolt."

Zach took a slow sip of his coffee. "My, you have been busy this morning."

"Aye. I've found a gentleman by the name of La Barre who says he used to own a brass-trimmed oak box fitted out as what he calls a vampire-killing kit."

"A vampire-killing kit?"

"That's right." Hamish's heat-limp red mustaches twitched. "Everything a body could need to kill a vampire, should he happen to meet one: a wooden stake, a cross, a vial of holy water, and a miniature crossbow with four silver-tipped wooden bolts."

"So what happened to it?"

"He claims he gave it to some voodoo king as payment for a love charm. Last spring."

"Did the charm work?"

Hamish grunted. "He dinna say. But he did tell me the name of the voodoo king he claims he gave it to. An old black man who lives in the swamps out toward Bayou Sauvage. A man they call Papa John." He reached for his coffee and shook his head. "I've heard of voodoo queens and voodooiennes, but I sure never heard of any voodoo king."

"I've heard of this one," said Zach, his gaze lifting to the iron-fenced square across the street. A Greek in a fez had set up a stall and was selling ice cream between a blanket-wrapped Choctaw hawking blowguns and a mulatress in a red tignon who thumped the side of her wooden tub and shouted, "*Bière douce.* Ginger beer, cold."

"He came here from the revolts in Saint-Dominque."

Hamish rubbed a beefy hand across his face. "The slave revolts? I don't think I like the sound of this."

Zach shook his head. "It didn't start as a slave revolt. It started with the coloreds fighting the whites, when the *gens de couleur libres* on the island discovered that the French Revolutionaries weren't as genuinely attached to the principles of *liberté* and *égalité* as they liked to pretend."

Hamish grunted. "All I know is that by the end of it, there was hardly a white man, woman, or child left alive on that island." The big New Yorker took a long, noisy sip of his coffee and slowly raised his gaze to Zach's face. "Exactly how'd you come to know so much about this Papa John, anyway?"

"According to Madame de Beauvais, Henri Santerre used to visit him."

"She told you that? A voodoo king? What would our good doctor have to do with a voodoo king?"

Zach dropped a few coins on the table and stood up. "It seems they shared an interest in native plants and old Indian cures."

Hamish cast a desperate glance at the sky. "We won't get there and back before dark."

Zach smiled. "There'll be a full moon."

Hamish pushed back his chair with a loud scraping of metal over flagstones. "Oh, now that's reassuring. We're going out to some alligator-infested swamp, in the dark, to talk to a murderous ex-slave who collects the dirt off dead children's graves and mixes it with the blood of virgins, and I'm supposed to be thankful for a full moon?"

The sun was sliding inexorably toward the west by the time they left the neatly tended gardens, raised cottages, and Greek Revival–style mansions of Esplanade

Ridge behind and struck out into the wilder, wetter land beyond, a land of cypress swamps and black bayou waters and the furtive rustlings of unseen creatures. At first, the land was still fairly settled, with tumbledown huts perched on stilts and cows grazing in fields and swishing unconcernedly at flies with their tails, while boys fishing for their supper stared silently at the two Union officers riding past.

This was country, a far different world from the city of New Orleans with its theaters and tightly packed town houses and delicately scented ladies with parasols and Paris gowns. Gradually, even the shanties with their plank walls and smoking cook fires grew more scattered, the rutted dirt road turned into a track, and then the track became a path half-obscured by gloomy thickets of cypress and pale green willows trailing wispy branches that stirred sluggishly in the muggy breeze.

"I knew I shoulda waited until tomorrow to talk to you about voodoo kings," Hamish said, then swore as his horse shied violently at the rusting remains of an old indigo vat thrusting up through the canebrakes beside them. Something slithered through the reeds up ahead to disappear into the black water with a splash that had Hamish's horse shying again, and the air suddenly seemed filled with the whirling chirrup of insects and the hoarse calls of ducks and geese and the swift black shadows of what looked like bats, although it was too early, surely, for bats?

"He'll be expecting us today," Zach said.

"Expecting us? How in the name of all that's holy—or unholy—could he be expecting us?"

Zach grinned. "If you know about him, he knows you know about him."

"Huh," Hamish said, then swore once more when

the hoot of an owl set his horse to cavorting nervously again. "At least we've finally got ourselves a good solid suspect."

Zach tilted back his head, his gaze drawn to the giant dragonflies—mosquito hawks, they called them here— swooping through the air. "I'm not so sure about that."

"*What?*" Hamish slewed around awkwardly in his saddle to stare back at Zach. "But . . . he has the cross- bow."

"Yeah. Which is why I can't see him committing murder with the one weapon sure to lead us to him. Jamestown weed or crushed love beads would be more his style."

"And that *wouldn't* lead us back to him?"

"Not in a place like New Orleans." Zach drew rein sharply as a peculiar, mushroomlike structure material- ized out of the shadows before them.

He wasn't sure what he'd been expecting—some squatter's shack, perhaps, built of scrap lumber and bits of tar paper, such as one might find lining the batture between the levee and the river; something crude, predictable, familiar. Well, there was nothing crude or familiar about this strangely elegant hut of peeled cypress logs and reeds that rose high on stilts in the center of a clearing ringed by ancient cypress trees. Built in the round, with a steeply pitched, conical thatched roof, it looked for all the world as if it had been plucked up from the jungles of Africa only to be dropped down here, whole, in the swamps of southern Louisiana.

"I don't think I got it quite right," said the tall, bone- thin black man who stood in the open doorway at the top of a set of steps that was really more like a slanted ladder fashioned of peeled saplings tied together with some kind of reed. "But it's close."

"How old were you when you left?" Zach asked, nudging his reluctant horse forward.

The old man's eyes gleamed. "Twelve. Or thereabouts."

"What are you two talking about?" Hamish demanded, looking from one to the other.

"The house," said Zach, swinging out of the saddle. "And Africa." He tilted back his head to stare up at the old man. "Are you going to climb down, or shall we come up?"

"Please," Papa John said, stepping back. "Come up." Hamish made a kind of strangling noise, deep in his throat, but Zach pushed him up the ladder. The old man smiled, showing large, even teeth yellowed by age.

His skin was the dark ebony of a pure African, his age-lined face marked with a zigzag pattern of tribal tattoos at once hideous and oddly beautiful. The contrast between that dark, savagely marked flesh and the snowy white frills of the dress shirt he wore was startling. He must be eighty years of age, at least, Zach figured, from what he'd been told. And yet the big man still held himself proudly erect, with only a faint shimmer of silver showing in the black of his close-cropped, woolly hair as it caught the fading daylight streaming in the openings that served as windows.

Inside, the house was essentially one large room, scrupulously clean and simply furnished with a cot, table, and chairs made of the same logs as the hut, and a small, curiously carved chest that stood beside the cot. Bunches of dried plants dangled from the exposed rafters, their pungent aroma mingling with a medley of other scents, the dampness of the swamp and the tang of the freshly peeled logs and the warmth of kerosene from the lamp that had been lit against the gloom. No smoking tallow candles here.

Except for the herbs and other plants overhead, there was little in the room to suggest the occupation of its inhabitant. But a red cloth had been suspended from the ceiling to curtain off one side of the hut, and it was to this that Hamish went at once, jerking it back to reveal row after row of shelves cleverly fitted into the curving recesses of the walls and filled with everything from bundles of blackened Spanish moss to mysterious blue glass vials with white porcelain tops and crudely hollowed-out wooden bowls overflowing with cowry shells.

Hamish had leaped back, leery of the snake voodoo practitioners were said to keep, but the only identifiable creature Zach could see was a large white cat stretched out motionless along one shelf. It lay so still that at first Zach thought it must be dead. Then its head swung around to stare at them through wide, unblinking green eyes, and Zach thought, if Papa John keeps a snake, it can't be here.

"No, I don't have a snake," said the tall black man in a slightly amused voice. He still stood near the doorway, his hands dangling loosely at his sides. "And what you're looking for is not here, either."

"How do you know what we're looking for?" demanded Hamish, his voice belligerent, his manner every inch that of the New York City policeman.

The black man's lips parted in a slow, malignant smile. "You mean, besides the dirt of children's graves and the blood of virgins?"

Hamish was a good enough policeman to keep most of the effect those words had on him from showing on his face. But he couldn't stop his eyes from widening, or the drops of sweat that were rolling down his flushed cheeks despite the breezy coolness of the hut. "Where is it, then?"

The old man lifted one shoulder in a careless, dismissive shrug. "What use have I for a vampire-killing kit? That's white men's foolishness." Even after sixty years or more, the lyrical French of the islands still accented his English, still influenced every gesture. "I sold it, last spring."

"That a fact?" said Hamish, his arms linked across his beefy chest. "Who'd you sell it to?"

From its perch on the shelf, the white cat suddenly stood up, stretching, then jumped down to pad across the floor to the man beside the door. Papa John stooped to scratch its ears, his attention seemingly all for the cat. "He didn't tell me his name, and I didn't ask. I'd never seen him before."

Hamish sucked in a quick, impatient breath that deepened the florid color in his cheeks. "So what did he look like?"

Again, that shrug of the shoulders. "He was a white man. All white men look pretty much alike." He made a curious clucking sound with his tongue, and the cat leaped up into his arms.

Zach wondered if Hamish realized he was wasting his time, that the old man would tell them nothing he didn't want them to know. Tipping back his head, Zach studied the bunches of dried plants overhead. Some, such as the foxglove and marshmallow, he recognized. Others were utterly unfamiliar. "They say you can read men's minds," he said suddenly, his gaze falling to where the voodoo king now stood, the white cat draped loosely about his neck.

"Read men's minds? I don't know about that." His lower lip pushed out as he glanced at Hamish. "Fear's not hard to smell." He brought his gaze back to Zach's face. "Or guilt to sense."

Zach didn't even blink. "They also say you can foresee the future."

"People say lots of things."

"They say Henri Santerre respected you, and that you were friends of a sort." Zach went to lean one shoulder against the hut's massive center pole, his eyes narrowing as he stared at the man with the cat. "So did you warn him of what you'd seen in his future?"

Long and bony and yellowed with age, the voodoo king's fingers moved back and forth in the cat's fur. "Henri was an old man. He didn't need me to warn him to prepare to meet death."

"A warning from you might have helped him to avoid it."

"You can't avoid death." The cat still around his neck, Papa John walked to stand in the open doorway again, his back to the room, his gaze on the black waters of the bayou just visible through a break in the cypress thicket. "It's arrogance, thinking you can change what's meant to be. I learned that a long time ago." Slowly, he turned his head to look over his shoulder at Zach. "It's a lesson you still must learn."

Zach shook his head. "I don't believe in fate. We all make our own lives."

"The conscious decisions, oh, yes." His eyebrows rose as if in inquiry. "But who's responsible for all the little accidents that can trip us up and alter the course of our lives, or even kill us? Hmmm?"

Outside the hut, the day was fading fast. They seemed suddenly, oddly isolated from the world, the three of them, caught together in the flickering golden light of the single kerosene lamp. "And if you had destroyed that vampire set," Zach said softly, "instead of selling it?"

The old man kept his gaze fixed on Zach's face. "Men are easy to kill. So are women . . . as you should know, Captain."

Behind him, Zach heard Hamish draw in his breath as if in a gasp, but Zach's own voice was level, controlled, as he said, "I'm a major now."

"Yes. Of course. My apologies." Papa John moved away from the door. "I'm being remiss in my duties as a host. Would you like something to drink? Some *bière douce*, perhaps?"

Zach shook his head. "We need to get back."

He'd expected Hamish to object to leaving with nothing, maybe even want to ransack the place just to make sure the crossbow wasn't here. But the big New Yorker evidently had had enough of Papa John's silken voice and eerily pointed comments. At one nod from Zach, Hamish was out the door, his boots clumping on the rungs of the ladderlike stairs.

Zach started to follow, but at the top of the steps he paused to look back at the man who stood, unmoving, near the homemade table. "Not being told the name of a man you've never seen before is not at all the same as being unaware of who he is."

Amusement, and something else, flickered in the dark depths of the old man's eyes. "True. But a little bit of knowledge can be a dangerous thing, Major. The man who bought that fateful little oak box? He didn't buy it for himself. He bought it as a gift for a friend."

It was the first real piece of information Papa John had given them, and he'd given it freely. Zach held himself quite still. "Did he tell you the name of this friend?"

Papa John shook his head. "There was no need. Such was his friend's interest in both vampires and crossbows, that the set might have been made for him."

From the edge of the swamp came the hoot of an owl, low and mournful. It was almost dark now, the horses below mere shadows in the moonlight. *Do you*

need another clue, Captain? whispered the voice from
Zach's past. *How about another corpse?*

"It's Philippe, isn't it?" Zach said. "The set was a gift
for Philippe de Beauvais."

His face impassive, the black man simply stared at
him.

"But Philippe is dead," said Zach.

"So they say."

"So did you."

The other man's eyes widened in delighted surprise.
"Did I?"

"You said, Such *was* his interest, not, Such *is* his interest."

"So I did. Careless of me, wasn't it?"

From below came Hamish's low hiss, and the chink
of a bit as one of the horses shook its head. "I don't
think you've ever been careless in your life," said Zach.

"Oh yes I have." The black man stepped forward so
that the dying light caught the white frills of his shirt in
a way that made him seem almost to glow. "At times,
we are all careless, Major. Because we're all human."

"I want you to find out everything you can about
Philippe de Beauvais," Zach said as he and Hamish
turned their horses' heads toward the city. "What he
was like when he was alive, and exactly how he died."

"Aye." Hamish threw him a closed, troubled look. "I
hope this means you're finally planning to rest that
wound of yours, lad. This ride can't have been good
for it."

Zach smiled into the warm velvet night. "As a matter of fact, I'm thinking of paying a visit to the Hospital de Santerre. Madame de Beauvais has some
explaining to do."

CHAPTER ELEVEN

Zach found her in the small, semiprivate room on the hospital's second floor.

A lamp on the painted table against the far wall lit the room with a pale glow. She was standing alone in the middle of the scrubbed bare floor—just standing there, her cupped hands holding her elbows tight against her sides, her back straight and rigid. She was turned away from him, so he couldn't see her face, but he knew she must have heard him, must have heard his uneven footsteps echoing hollowly as he limped into the room.

The doors and windows had all been thrown open to the night breeze blowing in warm and sweetly scented by the gardenias and honeysuckle and sweet olive of the courtyard below. The room's four cots all stood empty except for one, where an ominously still form lay beneath a crisp white sheet near the far window. The face was covered, but Zach knew who the man was—or rather, who he had been. Lieutenant Emile Rouant.

"Please go away," she said, not turning, not looking at him, her voice cracking as she spoke. "Please just . . . go away."

He put his hand on her shoulder and swung her around. Her eyes glittered brightly, but she wasn't crying, for all that her face was ravaged with grief and anger. "He lived longer than you expected."

She drew in a quick breath that shuddered her thin frame, but her gaze stayed fixed somewhere in the vicinity of the third button of his coat. "And yet he still died."

Zach kept his hand on her shoulder. "It was inevitable. You always knew that."

She raised her head to look at him then, and he saw the anger in her flare up wild and bright. "Inevitable? It shouldn't be inevitable. We are so *ignorant*. How can we save a man's life if we don't really understand what's killing him?"

"You will understand someday," he said softly.

He stared down into her beautiful face and watched the anger drain out of her, watched the tears she'd been trying to hold back well up hot and unstoppable, watched her full lips tremble, watched her self-control break.

He had come here to accuse her of knowing far more about the murder of Henri Santerre than she'd been willing to admit—maybe even to try to scare her into telling him some of the things he knew she'd been hiding from him. Instead, he found his palm shifting to enfold the back of her head as he drew her close.

She resisted, but only for a moment. He heard her breath catch in her throat. Her hands came up to his chest, her fingers clenching at the dark blue cloth of his uniform. A sob shook her, then another. She smelled sweetly of lilac water and the night air and herself, and he breathed her in as he drew her closer and she buried her face against his shoulder and wept.

She wept, and he held her, warm and pliant against him. Just held her.

•   •   •

Afterward, he walked beside her through a sleepy city lit only by flickering lamp shine and the pale glow of the full moon, and cooled by the breeze from the river.

They walked in silence, their footsteps echoing in the Sunday-quiet streets as they turned toward the rue Dumaine. There was an edginess between them that he could feel, an edginess that came from those moments at the hospital when he had held her in his arms and she had found comfort in his warmth and his nearness. Except that it wasn't the physical intimacy of that incident that was causing this profound, mutual disquiet; it was the emotional intimacy, that underscoring of the indefinable, inescapable connection between them that she didn't want . . . that he didn't want, any more than he wanted the slow burn of desire that was always there between them, too, simmering along with the animosity and the mistrust.

Finally, as if she could bear the silence and suspense no longer, she said, "You've been to see Papa John."

He could hear the wary defiance in her voice. Throwing back his head, he stared up at the sprinkling of stars overhead. Usually they were obscured by the heat haze that hung over the city, but tonight they were brilliant in their clarity. "Why didn't you simply tell me about Philippe's vampire-killing set yourself? Why send me out toward the bayous?"

"I didn't know until this afternoon where it had originally come from."

"Ah." He didn't believe much that she told him, but he believed that. "So the trip to the swamps was meant to be a distraction, was it? How unfortunate for you that it turned out to be informative, instead."

"Yes, it was, wasn't it?"

"Are you going to tell me where it is now?"

"The set?" From the tavern beside them came a spill

of light and the twang of banjo strings, underscored by a man's voice raised in laughter. She shook her head. "I don't know. I saw it in the cabinet in Philippe's room, shortly after he was killed. But it's no longer there."

In Philippe's room. Zach gazed at the woman beside him, at the regal curve of her cheek and the pale glow of her skin in the soft moonlight. She was so cool, he thought; so cool and controlled on the outside, so seething with vital passion beneath. Yet she and her husband had kept separate rooms. "I could have your house searched, you know. And the hospital."

She turned her head to meet his gaze steadily. "And you know that if I still had that crossbow, it wouldn't be in my house. Or the hospital."

"You have no idea who could have taken it?"

"You think I wouldn't tell you, if I did?"

"As a matter of fact, yes." The stone bulk of the Cabildo rose up beside them, its massive, Spanish-built walls dark and somber. From here, he could see the dark shapes of the elms and sycamores in the square and, just visible beyond the levee, the silhouettes of the tall masts of the ships tied up at the wharves. "It's a peculiar collection of interests," he said. "Vampires and crossbows."

"Philippe was fascinated by death, by its legends and rituals, by its"—she paused, her face intent as she searched for the right word—"nature." She let out her breath in a sigh of sadness and weariness tinged, perhaps, with regret. "I used to think it was half the reason he became a doctor—not so much to save lives as to beat death."

"He sounds a very different man from Henri Santerre."

"He was." The breeze was stronger here, lifting the long, loose ribbons of her mourning bonnet and ruffling the black lace that edged her slim white throat. "But don't misunderstand me," she said, "Philippe was a brilliant doctor. Knowledgeable, skilled, dedicated—"

"And utterly self-obsessed," he finished for her.

She shrugged. "Most brilliant people are."

"And Henri Santerre? What had he to do with vampires and crossbows?"

"Nothing. He thought Philippe's interests bizarre but essentially harmless—as long as they didn't interfere with his work."

"Did they?"

He saw something leap in her eyes, something dark and quickly hidden as she turned her face away. "Not those."

He put his hand on her arm, swinging her around to face him. "So why was Philippe's crossbow used to kill Henri Santerre?"

She backed away from him, into the shadow of a massive stone pillar of the building looming behind her. "How would I know?" she said, her voice husky with what he knew now was fear, fear of what was happening around her, and fear of him.

He took a step toward her, trapping her against the pillar and holding her there with the powerful threat of his size and his maleness and the authority of the blue uniform he wore and she hated. "I think you know far more than what you've let on."

She shook her head slowly from side to side, her neck arching back so that she could stare up at him. She was such a tiny thing, he thought; so delicate and small that a man would need to lift her up onto her tiptoes just to kiss her.

"No," she said.

He pressed his hands flat against the smooth stone

on either side of her, his body almost but not quite touching hers. There was a fine trembling going on inside her, a trembling of fear, and something else, too. "What is it you want me to believe? That you've told me everything you know about Henri Santerre and the people who might have wanted him dead? *Goddamn it,*" he swore, leaning into his spread hands. "When will you understand that I'm not your enemy?"

Her gaze swept him, taking in the blue uniform he wore and the saber with which he killed. He saw her eyes darken with emotion, the muscles in her throat working hard as she swallowed. "You are my enemy."

He bracketed her face with one hand, his thumb curving beneath her chin, forcing her to look at him when she would have turned away. "Not in this. Not unless you know the killer and you're deliberately protecting him."

He saw the flare of surprise in her eyes. "I was under the impression you suspected me of killing Henri."

Beneath his touch, her skin felt as soft and warm as the seductive Southern night around them. He shook his head. "Crossbow bolts flying out of the night aren't your style."

"So you do believe I could kill."

"You could kill," he said, his fingers moving across her cheek in a whisper of a caress. "But not in an act of cold calculation. If you killed, it would be in the heat of the moment. A crime of passion."

She stared at him, her lips parted, her breath coming hard and fast. "I'm not a woman of passion."

"Aren't you?"

He had been wanting to kiss this woman since that first night he had seen her wet with the rain, her features glowing pale in quick flashes of lightning. She was a woman only recently widowed, a Confederate sympathizer and a suspect in a brutal murder. And yet when he held her close and looked at her mouth, none of that seemed to matter anymore. It wasn't that he forgot, only that those things suddenly ceased to be of such all-consuming importance.

She knew he wanted her. The awareness was there, in each shuddering breath, in the quiet stillness of her eyes as she stared up at him. If she had said anything, made any move to put some distance between them, he wouldn't have done it. But she only looked at him, and the night hushed with expectancy and want and the high, wild rush of the dangerous and the forbidden. Keeping his gaze still locked with hers, he tipped his head and covered her mouth with his.

He heard her moan, a woman's low murmur of want and surrender as her eyelids slid shut and her arms crept up to circle his neck and pull his head down to her. He felt her lips move beneath his, open to him, and he lost himself in her, in the taste of her mouth and the scent of her flesh and the warm, giving softness of her woman's body.

With a groan, he crushed her up against the length of him, his hands sweeping down the narrow curve of her back to grip her hips. She was hunger and heat, damnation and redemption, and he wanted her with a reckless need that subsumed all logic and sense, a wild sweet yearning that thrummed in his blood and dimmed his sight and swept away all trappings of civilization and civility. And if he didn't put her away from him, now, he would take her, right here, in the moonlit street, whether she wanted him to or not.

He tore his mouth from hers, his hands tightening on her shoulders. Yet before he could thrust her from him she wrenched from his grasp, as if she, too, realized how near they had come to disaster.

"That shouldn't have happened," she said, backing away from him, her eyes wild, her body shuddering with a passion and reaction that matched his own.

He brought up one hand to touch her, then let it fall to his side again, once he realized what he was doing. "No. But we've both known it was going to happen, sooner or later."

She shook her head, not to deny the truth of it, but to deny the rightness of it. "I am less than three months widowed."

He took a step toward her, then stopped. "And for how many years before that did your husband keep his own room?"

She hugged herself, her hands gripping her arms so tightly, he could see her fingers digging into the stiff bombazine sleeves of the mourning gown she wore. "That has nothing to do with it."

"No. No, it doesn't," he said, although he wasn't sure they were talking about the same thing.

They stared at each other. The wind blew warm and heavy with damp around them, fluttered the fine curls at her forehead, and it was all he could do not to reach out to her, to touch her face and let his hand slip behind her head and draw her to him again.

He swung away, his chest lifting with a quickly in-drawn breath, his vision a blur of somber stone walls and lacy ironwork and star-spangled night sky as his head fell back and he eased his eyes shut against the rage of desire pulsing through him.

"I can see myself home from here," she said.

"No. I'll see you home," he said. But he didn't touch her. And as soon as she reached her doorway he left her there, and he didn't look back.

CHAPTER
TWELVE

Two days later, Zach was riding through the old quarter, on his way from the mint out to the New Basin Canal, when he heard the lilting, taunting refrain of "The Bonny Blue Flag" being sung by a voice so sweet and clear that it might have belonged to an angel—if that angel were a partisan of the rebellious Confederate States of America.

They were always doing it—the schoolboys and the women of New Orleans—singing patriotic Confederate songs and setting up a cheer for the Confederate president. It seemed to Zach a harmless enough venting of the local population's feelings of frustration and rebelliousness. But lately Ben Butler had been coming down hard on such expressions of native discontent and disloyalty. He'd even gone so far as to levy fines on schools whose pupils were caught doodling pictures of the Confederate flag in their copybooks.

"Where the devil is that coming from?" demanded Zach's sergeant, slewing around in his saddle, his narrowed, angry gaze searching the brick facades of the deserted, boarded-up warehouses lining that part of the street.

A tousled, curly blond head peeking around a pile of half-broken barrels caught Zach's attention. "Ride on ahead with the men, Sergeant," he said. "I'll take care of it."

It was an easy enough thing, to ride in a wide arc and come up behind the barrels. The boy, perched precariously near the top of the pile, had his attention fixed on the small troop of Union soldiers passing in the street ahead of him. He was a tall lad, although not all that old, Zach decided, judging from that choirboy voice. His knickerbockers and jacket looked worn but of good quality and, beneath the smudges he'd doubtless acquired that morning, clean. This was no street urchin.

"I could send you to prison for singing that song," said Zach, reining in behind the boy. "You know that, don't you?"

The boy swung around, vivid blue eyes going wide, his small Adam's apple bobbing as he swallowed convulsively. "I'm not afraid of you," said Dominic de Beauvais.

"Then why are you thinking about running?" Zach asked when the boy's eyes slid sideways, as if evaluating the distance to the ground and the time it would take him to make it to the nearest corner.

Dominic's gaze flew back to Zach's face. "When I grow up, I'm going to go off to war and kill lots and lots of Yankees," the boy said, his nostrils flaring wide with fear and determined bravado.

Zach laid one forearm along his pommel and leaned into it. "I don't think your mama would like that."

A muscle jumped along the boy's tightly clenched jaw. "You think my *maman* doesn't hate Yankees? She does. They killed my papa."

"I think your *maman* doesn't like killing."

"She makes an exception for Yankees."

Zach thought about the strain on the young widow's

face as she went from one dead Union soldier to the next on the rue Conti. "I don't think so," he said slowly.

The boy's chin jerked up. "You going to put me in prison?"

"Well . . ." Zach's horse moved restlessly beneath him as he visibly took his time thinking about it. "I'll let you go this time," he said at last. "But I'd better not hear you singing that song again."

"Hurrah for Jeff Davis and Beauregard!" shouted Emmanuelle de Beauvais's son, and he leaped from his barrel to land crouched on the flagstones below. Coming up with a bound, he took off running toward the mouth of a narrow, garbage-strewn alley.

Zach watched him go, then turned the bay's head toward the New Basin Canal.

Emmanuelle studied her son's tight, strained face as he dipped his spoon in his gumbo and brought it with studied care to his mouth.

"I hear you had a run-in with a Yankee officer this morning," she said after watching him for a few minutes. "Down near the wharves." She'd heard the story from the old Italian man who pushed his cart of fresh fruits through the streets of the Quarter every day. She didn't know all the details, but what she'd heard had been enough to make her stomach clench with dread.

Dominic looked up, his eyebrows twitching together more out of resignation than surprise. People were always carrying tales of his activities to his mother. That was life in the Quarter. "I was singing 'The Bonny Blue Flag,' " he said, his chin coming up.

"Oh, Dominic. Be careful."

Dominic's spoon hit the edge of his bowl with a clatter. "You think that Yankee scared me? He didn't. I hate the Yankees. Every last one. They're murdering, thieving scum."

"Dominic," said Emmanuelle, leaning forward, her own meal forgotten. "Listen to me. You can't make assumptions about a man's character—you can't *hate* him—just because of the color of the coat he wears."

Dominic stared at her with wide, accusing eyes. "You hate the Yankees. When that woman from Baton Rouge was telling you about how a Union patrol smashed her furniture and ripped up her clothes and stole her silver, you said the Yankees were hateful, despicable monsters. You said you wished the earth would open up and swallow every bluecoat in the South."

Emmanuelle sat very still. "I didn't know you heard me say those things." She wondered what else Dominic had heard, if he'd also heard the woman crying about her fifteen-year-old daughter, who'd been raped so brutally and repeatedly by those same Union soldiers that she hadn't spoken a coherent sentence since then. "I was angry, Dominic. Sometimes people say things in anger they don't really mean. Things they shouldn't."

Dominic stared at her long and hard. "You mean you don't hate the Yankees?"

It would have been easy enough to simply say no. But she had always tried very, very hard not to lie to her son. "It's wrong to hate someone you don't know," she said, choosing her words carefully. "Wrong to jump to conclusions about who and what they are, based only on something like the color of their uniform. It's like making assumptions about people based on the color of their skin, or what church they go to, or whether they're a man or a woman."

Dominic looked at her with wide, troubled blue eyes.

"But it's wrong, isn't it, what the Yankees are doing to us?"

"Yes. I think it is."

"Then they're bad people, aren't they?"

Emmanuelle let out her breath in a long sigh. "I wish it were that simple." She started to take another mouthful of gumbo, then changed her mind. "If you're finished, go wash your face and get your hat. Your *grand-mère* is expecting me, and I don't want to be late."

Dominic pushed back his chair and hopped up. "Can I take my blowgun?"

"Yes, yes. Just hurry."

Its nose twitching in nervous excitement, the squirrel crept down the trunk of one of a line of pecan trees fronting the fence of an old raised cottage on Esplanade Avenue. Halfway down the trunk, the squirrel stopped, its ears back, its head turning as it anxiously scanned the sun-warmed expanse of grass below. It was young yet, that squirrel, Emmanuelle thought, smiling to herself as she watched it; too young and inexperienced to know that danger can come not only on four feline paws. Danger can also come in the form of little boys with hollowed pipes of bamboo and pockets full of Chinaball berries.

"You aim that blowgun at anything other than that fence, *mon fils,*" she said softly, "and you'll spend next week painting the railings on every gallery around the courtyard."

"Ah, Maman," whined Dominic, but he subtly shifted his aim so that the dried little berry smacked into a knot in the fence post with an accuracy that sent Dominic war-whooping up the wide, tree-lined avenue, and the chattering squirrel bounding back into the leafy branches overhead.

Walking up the banquette after her son, Emmanuelle knew a moment of disquiet. They were common enough boyhood toys, blowguns, fashioned after the Choctaw furze guns still sold around Jackson Square for a picayune apiece by half-naked, bronze-skinned men wrapped in blankets. And like all things associated with growing up male in southern Louisiana, they had been embraced by Dominic with an enthusiasm that disturbed his mother.

"It's who he is," Philippe had said to her once, not long before he died, when she was complaining about Dominic's passion for what she called blood sports. "Hunting, fishing, riding—that's what life is about down here. Especially for a planter. He needs to learn to love it."

"He already loves it."

"And you think that's bad?" Philippe had asked, a deep line of concern appearing between his vivid, handsome eyes as he'd frowned. "Dominic may not be precisely who you dreamed he would be, but he's who *he* wants to be." He took Emmanuelle's hand in his, something he rarely did anymore, and squeezed it once, almost apologetically, before letting it go again. "You and I have never fit in our worlds, Emmanuelle, and it has brought us nothing but grief. But by some alchemy of genetics, Dominic *does* fit. Effortlessly. Joyously. Let him have that joy."

She'd smiled at him, feeling both humbled and a bit sad for all that had been lost between them. "Wise Philippe," she'd said.

And so she had left her son his rifle and his bowie knife and his blowgun. But she adamantly refused to allow him to shoot at anything he didn't intend to eat.

He might never become a scholar or a doctor, but that didn't mean he couldn't grow up with a profound respect for life.

"Maman," he called now, one arm wrapping around the gate post guarding the entrance to the de Beauvaises' stately drive as he swung to face her. "We're late. *Again.* There's *beaucoup* people here already."

It was the day of Marie Thérèse's sewing meeting, and for some reason Emmanuelle couldn't begin to define, she had decided to attend to help sew shirts and knit socks for the prisoners of war, just like the dutiful daughter-in-law and proper widow she was not. Oh, no; the woman Emmanuelle was had walked through the warm, jasmine-scented night with a man who was her enemy, who was the enemy of her nation. She had pressed herself against that man's body and lost herself in the hungry heat of his kiss. And even now, when she thought about it, she felt not guilt, but a shameless, breath-stealing desire for more.

"Maman," called Dominic.

"I'm coming," she called, and quickened her step.

Less than an hour later, Emmanuelle found herself heartily regretting her uncharacteristic decision to attend. Sitting beside Claire La Touche on the linen-covered sofa between the tall guillotine windows of Marie Thérèse's drawing room, Emmanuelle swore softly to herself as she struggled to fit together the pieces of the shirt she'd been allocated to sew.

"Bah," she said under her breath, then threw a quick glance across the room to where Marie Thérèse was blessedly busy supervising two middle-aged women scraping lint. "Something's not right."

"*Alors.*" Claire leaned forward to peer suspiciously at the half-sewn shirt in Emmanuelle's lap. "Look what you're doing, Emmanuelle. You're putting the placket in backward."

Emmanuelle sat back in disgust. "I knew there was a reason I never came to these things before."

Laughing softly, Claire lifted the half-sewn shirt from Emmanuelle's slack grasp. "So why did you come?" She, too, glanced toward Marie Thérèse. "It won't make her like you any better, you know, even if you were as good at sewing as you are at doctoring. Which," she added as she frowned down at the mess Emmanuelle had made, "you are not."

"I came because . . ." She broke off, finding it impossible to explain to Claire, of all people, how lonely she'd been lately. Although perhaps *lonely* wasn't quite the right word, she decided; what she felt was isolated and dangerously disconnected from what should have been her life. "I suppose I came because I never have." She looked around the room at the score or more women who filled Marie Thérèse's large drawing room. At least half wore some form of mourning, if not for a husband or son, then for a brother, or father, or cousin. "It didn't seem right."

"You do enough already," Claire said, her head bowed as she concentrated on ripping out Emmanuelle's mistake.

"So do you."

Claire glanced up, the pupils of her soft gray eyes dilated unnaturally, almost frighteningly wide. "But for a different reason, mmmm?" she said.

"Claire—" Emmanuelle began, just as a stocky, crisply uniformed maid carrying a coffee service entered the room, followed by Baptiste bearing a heavy silver tray loaded with sandwiches and small cakes.

"*Eh, bien.*" Marie Thérèse clapped her hands as if

she were a director on a stage set. "Emmanuelle? You will pour. And Claire will assist you. Hmmm?"

Some five minutes later, Emmanuelle was still pouring coffee when Claire dropped the plate she'd been holding, and started to scream.

Zach was on the banks of the New Basin Canal dealing with a confiscated load of smuggled salt that had been headed toward Confederate troops across the lake, when a young corporal, red in the face and dripping with sweat, ran up to him and saluted sharply. "Major Cooper, sir?"

Zach looked at the corporal over the pink, sweating bald head of the barge's indignant owner, who was hopping from one foot to the other and screeching, over and over again, "You can't do this! I have a permit signed by General Butler himself!"

"What is it, soldier?"

"A message from Captain Fletcher, sir," said the corporal, gasping for breath. He was very young, this corporal, young enough that his voice hadn't finished changing yet, and only a few stray wisps of downy soft ash blond hair adorned his unshaven red cheeks. "He says to tell you there's been another murder, sir."

"Can't he deal with it himself?"

The corporal shook his head vehemently, his slightly protuberant pale eyes bulging out even farther. "No, sir. He said you'd want to be there. He said to tell you it's a woman this time, sir. A young Creole woman."

Emmanuelle. Oh, God, not Emmanuelle. A gut-wrenching surge of horror and fury and guilt tore through Zach's being. It shouldn't have happened again. He shouldn't have *let* it happen again. He could feel the sun bearing down blazing and white hot on his shoulders, feel the heat sucking the air from his lungs so that he found it impossible to breathe. There was a roaring in his ears, a burning in his chest. Then he breathed again and heard his own voice saying, hoarsely, and as if from a great distance, "Her name. What's her name?"

"Claire, sir. The captain said to tell you the woman's name is Claire La Touche. He thinks she's been poisoned, sir. He's there now."

Zach found he had to put out one hand to grip the side of the barge and steady himself. "Where?"

"Some big house on Esplanade Avenue, sir. Belongs to one of those old Frenchie families with the fancy names. De . . . de . . ." The boy looked stricken. "De something." He shook his head hopelessly. "Captain Fletcher said you'd know it, sir."

"De Beauvais," said Zach, his gaze fixed on the egret rising slow and pristine white from the murky green waters of the canal.

"That's it, sir. De Beauvais."

CHAPTER THIRTEEN

Emmanuelle stood alone on the rear gallery of the house on Esplanade Avenue, her hands gripping the railing, her gaze fixed on the garden awash now in the golden light of coming evening. A pair of blue jays flitted playfully through the lower branches of the big water oak near the kitchen. She listened to the sound of their chirruping, so sweet and bright and misplaced, and realized she was more deeply, profoundly afraid than she had ever been in her life.

She could not begin to understand what was happening, who was doing this to the people she loved. But there could be no doubt, she knew, that Claire's death was linked to that dark night of terror in St. Louis Cemetery. And she knew, too, that it wasn't over.

Zach gazed down at the golden-haired woman lying on a linen-covered sofa between two tall guillotine windows on the street side of Marie Thérèse de Beauvais's front parlor. Both windows had been thrown open, but even this late in the day the air was hot, the lace curtains hanging limp and motionless. The atmosphere was so close, he found it hard to breathe, so that he was painfully aware of the lifting of his chest, drawing each breath deep into his lungs.

She shouldn't have died. She'd been a vital, caring

young woman, and she shouldn't have had to die like this, in a frothing, screaming agony. He felt a dangerous rage burning within him. Rage and guilt and fear, because he knew—he knew that if he couldn't find this killer and stop him, it was going to happen again. And again, and again.

"What time?" he asked, not looking up when Hamish came to stand beside him.

The big New Yorker let out his breath in a long sigh. "A couple of hours ago, according to Emmanuelle de Beauvais."

Zach brought his head around to stare at the captain. "She's here?"

Hamish was looking hot and sweaty and troubled. "Out the back. She was with the lady when she died."

Zach let his gaze drift around the parlor, with its piles of half-sewn shirts strewn in hastily discarded heaps amid abandoned coffee cups and half-eaten slices of ginger cake. "Looks like there were a lot of people here."

"It was a sewing meeting. The old lady holds one every month, to sew shirts and scrape lint for the boys in gray on Ship Island." Hamish paused, his chin flattening against his chest as he gazed down at the dead woman's face. "It's no' looking good, I can tell you. I don't like it when the bodies start to pile up. You keep glancing around, wondering who's going to be next."

"Not much fun anymore, is it?" Zach hunkered down on his heels beside the dead woman. "What makes you think it's poison?"

Hamish scrubbed a hand across his face. "That would be Madame de Beauvais's diagnosis."

"Get her."

Zach was standing by the open pocket doors to the back parlor when she came in, alone. She looked pale and shaken but admirably, unbelievably composed. What did it take, he wondered, all his old doubts and suspicions flowing back; what did it take to rattle this woman?

Something of his thoughts must have shown in his expression, for she met his hard stare without flinching and threw it right back at him. "Don't say it."

He strolled toward her, his gaze fixed on the delicate features of her face. He knew an overwhelming need to put some distance between them, to distance this death-haunted parlor from that dangerous, disastrous moment in the shadows of the Cabildo. "Don't say what?" He paused in front of her, his thumbs hooking in his sword belt. "That you seem to make it a habit of being in the wrong place at the wrong time? Or that an uncomfortable number of your friends are turning up dead?"

Her chest jerked as she sucked in a quick breath of air, and he found himself almost—almost—regretting the harshness of his words. "Tell me what happened," he said.

He watched as she laced the fingers of her hands together and let them fall against her skirts, stark black framing pale, soft flesh that beckoned him to touch, to offer comfort he couldn't give. "We were helping with the refreshments when Claire . . ." Her voice broke, so that she had to swallow, hard. "She went into convulsions. I tried to help her upstairs, but it was too late. I think her heart stopped."

He glanced around at the litter of cups and plates. "No one else became ill?"

"No."

He brought his gaze back to her face. "You were the one handing out the food and drink, were you?"

Her nostrils flared on a quickly indrawn breath. "I

know what you're thinking, but you're wrong. If Claire was poisoned, it wasn't anything she ate here."

"How can you be so sure?"

"When we were sitting together earlier, on the sofa, I noticed her eyes. The pupils were dilated."

He walked over to stare down at Claire's still, pale face. Someone had closed her eyes. "Did anyone else notice?"

"No. But an autopsy would show it. Poisons often take several hours before they start to work, but then they can kill quite quickly." She hesitated. "I think it might be tansy."

He looked up. "Tansy?"

"It's a plant that grows wild around here. The leaves and stem contain an oil that is used to kill intestinal worms, or to . . ." She hesitated, and he knew by the way her gaze drifted away from him that she was amending what she'd been about to say. "To help with certain women's problems."

"So why is she dead?"

"Small doses can be helpful, but more will kill. It doesn't take much. Even seven or eight drops of the concentrated oil can bring on convulsions." She paused. "It's possible she took it deliberately, and simply took too much."

Zach met her narrow, worried gaze. "You don't believe that any more than I do."

The sound of loud voices in the hall brought them both around. There was a scuffle of feet, then a youthful voice with a Boston twang sang out, "Here now, you can't go in there. Captain Fletcher! Sir, you can't go in there—"

Antoine La Touche appeared in the arched entrance from the hall, a tall, gaunt figure gripping the braces of his crutches so tightly that the knuckles of his hands showed white as he went suddenly, painfully still. Behind him, a wide-eyed private threw a questioning look at Zach, but Zach only shook his head.

"*Mon Dieu.* Antoine." She crossed the room, the silk of her mourning gown swishing faintly as she went to touch the man's cheek and bury her face against his chest in a giving and taking of comfort that flicked Zach—unexpectedly, inexcusably—on the raw.

La Touche brought one arm around her, his hand splaying against her shoulder, gripping her tightly as he sucked in a deep breath that shuddered his entire frame. "*Alors,*" he whispered. "It's true." He held her for a moment, his eyes squeezing shut. Then with slow, awkward steps, the tips of his crutches thumping hollowly across the floor, he went to stand beside the sofa, his chin against his chest as he stared down at his sister.

"I want to take her home," he said after a moment. "Now."

"I'm afraid you can't do that, sir," said Hamish, appearing in the entrance from the hall, the scared-looking private hard at his heels. "Not just yet."

La Touche swung around, one crutch flinging out wildly to catch his weight. "She's my *sister,* you bastard."

"I'm sorry, sir, but we'll be needing to do a full postmortem on the body."

A bead of sweat formed on the Creole's temple to roll slowly down his pale, tight cheek. "*A what?*" he demanded, his nostrils flaring wide.

It was Madame de Beauvais who stepped forward to lay a gentle hand on his sleeve. "It's a medical examination, Antoine. It's needed to understand exactly what killed her."

Antoine looked wildly from the widow, to Hamish,

to Zach. "No." His head shook from side to side. "You're not cutting her, if that's what you mean."

"I'm sorry," said Hamish. "But under the circumstances, there's no choice."

"If it would make you feel better," said the widow, her hand still on the Creole's arm, "I can go to the army hospital and stay with her while it's done."

"Oh no you can't," said Zach.

She swung to face him. "If it's because I'm a woman, I assure you, you needn't worry. I've attended autopsies before."

Zach stared down at the petite, incredibly capable and fiercely determined woman before him. Just the thought of watching a postmortem made him feel slightly nauseous, yet he knew she'd not only watched them before, she'd *performed* them. "No," he said, "it's not because you're a woman."

"Then why?" she demanded, her eyes wide and accusing in a way that made the sharp bones of her face stand out stark, beautiful.

He had to force himself to look away from her, to where what was left of Claire La Touche lay on Marie Thérèse de Beauvais's summer dressed sofa. "Because you're a suspect."

By seven o'clock the next morning, the sun was already so hot, Zach could feel his shirt sticking to his back when he turned off Basin Street and passed through the open gates of St. Louis Cemetery. The German gatekeeper, Kessler, waved and shouted, *Guten Morgen.* Zach nodded, and kept walking.

The Santerre family crypt was at the far end of the allée in which Henri Santerre had been killed by a crossbow bolt less than a week ago. The pile of flowers left by his mourners made a bright splash of discordant color against the stark, sun-drenched white of the line of tombs and the rusting black iron of their gates. But as he drew nearer, Zach could see that most of the blooms had already been ruined by the heat, faded yellow and red petals shriveling into brown.

He stood before the tomb, hat in hand, and let his gaze drift down the row of crypts and along the high, whitewashed cemetery wall. He kept having this feeling that he was missing something, something that might have prevented Claire La Touche from being given enough poison to steal her life. Two deaths so close together, yet with such different ways of killing and such very different victims: an old man, a doctor, shot through the heart with a miniature crossbow bolt designed to kill vampires, and a beautiful young aristocratic woman, who died in agony.

What's the matter, Captain? At a loss? Have your precious logic and fine mind failed you again?

Zach spun about in a circle, the vivid blue of the Southern sky swirling with sepulchral white, his fingers tightening hard enough to crush the black felt in his hands. Two years ago, at an army fort on the edge of nowhere, someone had started killing. The victims had ranged in age from the very old to the heartrendingly young, their ways of death varied and unrelated. He hadn't been a provost marshal then, only a cocky young cavalry captain, fascinated by puzzles and perhaps a bit proud of his ability to solve them. The murders hadn't been his responsibility, but they had intrigued him, and so he had looked for a link, sifted through the clues, never realizing until it was too late— too late for Rachel, too late for all the others—that the victims and their ways of death had been deliberately chosen at random to confuse him, to toy with him, to punish him.

But this was different. He told himself this was different. These killings weren't random. He eased his hat back on his head, the brim pulled low against the glare of the sun, and turned to leave. Claire La Touche and Henri Santerre did have something in common. Two things, that he could see: the Hospital de Santerre, and a close association with Emmanuelle de Beauvais. And maybe something else that he was missing.

He arrived at the Hospital de Santerre to find the entrance crowded with howling children and hot, ragged women who glared at him in sweaty, stony-faced silence.

"Remember," Madame de Beauvais was saying to a sad-eyed woman in black who balanced a pale girl of five or six on one hip. "She needs greens—even young dandelion leaves, if that's all you can find. And eat some yourself."

His spurs scraped the flagging of the entry, and Madame de Beauvais looked up, her gaze meeting his. He saw her breath catch, her eyes widening with some emotion he could not name before narrowing down in a wary hostility that was both unmistakable and fierce.

"Now is not a good time, Major," she said, and would have turned away if he hadn't stopped her by saying, "Now."

A towheaded little boy wearing a long shirt and nothing else wrapped his arms around Zach's leg and began to wail. "Two questions," Zach said, reaching down to peel the baby off his leg. He handed the screaming child to a tall, impossibly thin woman with faded, copper-colored hair and a careworn face who looked as if she'd set him on fire with the loathing in her eyes, if she could. "Two questions. That's all."

Except for the screaming baby, an unnatural silence

had fallen over the room. They were all staring at him, women and children alike, their hatred of him and his uniform a palpable thing in the air. They all knew he had no need to ask; the authority of the Union army in this city was as absolute as the despotic reign of any tyrant. He waited.

Emmanuelle de Beauvais gazed at him a moment longer, then swung about to lead him past Henri Santerre's old office to the courtyard beyond. "Ask," she said, going to stand behind the rusting iron table, her hands gripping her elbows close to her midriff, her face set in hard lines.

The atmosphere in the shady green courtyard was cool and sweet, a calm oasis in a city of sweltering heat and noise. He shut the door against the renewed uproar behind him. "Who are all those people?"

"Every Tuesday and Thursday, we offer free consultations to the families of men away at war. And to their widows and orphans."

"We?" He leaned his shoulder blades against the door behind him, one hand resting by habit on the hilt of his sword in a way that drew her attention. "I didn't see Yardley."

She brought her gaze back to his face. "He'll be here. He does far more than he would like you to think."

"Why?"

"Why does he do it, or why does he like to act as if he doesn't?"

"Of course I can understand why he does it," Zach said, pushing away from the door.

"Can you?" She flattened her palms on the table in front of her and leaned into them, her gaze on him narrowed and hostile. "Did you recognize the tall, red-headed woman with the little boy?"

"No. Should I have?"

"Her name is Mary Anne Cahill. She had an eighteen-year-old son who was taken prisoner and froze to death last winter at Camp Douglas in Chicago. But her husband, Paddy, is still alive, with the army in Virginia, and because of him, your General Ben Butler confiscated her house and put it up for auction. It wasn't much, just a little shotgun on Annunciation, but it was hers. The man who bought it offered to rent it back to her, but of course she couldn't afford what he was asking, so he threw her and her baby out into the street. His name was Butler, too. Andrew Butler. And the men who threw her out were sent by the provost marshal. You."

Zach tightened his jaw. Even before Lincoln's Confiscation Act, Butler had been seizing the property and possessions of the people of New Orleans. Now that his actions had official sanction, his rapacity knew almost no bounds. Lately, he'd helped himself to so much old family silver that people had taken to calling him "Spoons" Butler.

"Do you never think what becomes of them," said Madame de Beauvais, her features pinched with emotion, "the women and children you throw out in the streets? Some have families that take them in, but others, like Mary Cahill, are sleeping in the parks and other public places. I don't know what they'll do when winter comes. I offered her one of the rooms in the *garçonnière*, but she's a proud woman, and she refused to take it."

He went to stand beside the fountain in the center of the courtyard, his gaze on the quick flickers of gold weaving in and out among the lilies. He hated the Confiscation Act, hated what it did to families, hated what it made him do. It was alien to everything he believed in, alien to everything he was fighting for, alien to everything he'd always thought his country stood for. But there was good being done here, too. He kept telling himself that the good outweighed the bad, even if it didn't justify it. "Rose told me you think slavery is wrong," he said, looking over his shoulder at her.

Her throaty voice quivered with passion. "It's worse than wrong. It's an abomination."

"Then if you feel that way, how can you support the Confederacy?"

She pushed away from the table and came around to stand before him, a strong, vital woman so tiny, she had to tip back her head to look up at him. "In New England," she said, her eyes narrowing as she searched his face, "children as young as five work in factories for twelve hours a day, six and a half days a week, for pennies. *Pennies.* Yet you support the United States government that allows that."

"It's not the same. Those children aren't slaves."

"No, they're not. But the industrial economy of the North depends upon their cheap labor, just as the agrarian economy of the South depends on slaves. Both are wrong. Yet you are fighting to end one abuse while ignoring the other."

He thought about the grim brick buildings that had stood—that still stood—on the outskirts of the Rhode Island town where he'd grown up, and the children, hollow-eyed with exhaustion and pale from lack of sunlight, who disappeared into them every day, before dawn. They didn't normally live long, those factory children. The few who did survive long enough to breed inevitably ended up sending their own children, in time, to tend the machines that spewed out the goods that made the wealthy of the town wealthier. Yet it was their choice . . . in a sense.

"There is more to slavery than the exploitation of labor," he said softly, "and you know it."

"Yes," she said, her gaze still locked with his.

"And yet you don't think the dignity of millions of human beings worth fighting for?"

"Worth *striving* for, always. But worth killing for? No. I don't think anything justifies war." She drew her open hand through the air in a wide arc. "Look around you. Look at that room in there, full of crying children and grieving women. Go upstairs and look at the shattered and maimed bodies of their men. Look in any cemetery across the South—and the North. War doesn't solve problems, monsieur, it creates them."

"So you would have slavery continue? Simply to avoid the cost of a war to end it?"

She shook her head. "This war isn't about slavery and you know it. If it were, your President Lincoln would have issued a proclamation freeing all the slaves as soon as the war broke out. Yet we've been at war for well over a year now, and it still hasn't happened."

"It will."

She suddenly looked very, very tired. "It would have happened, anyway," she said, the anger draining from her voice. "In five years, maybe ten. Slavery is a dying institution the world over. One nation after another has outlawed it, without war. But this war . . . the anger, and resentment, and hatred it has spawned will last a hundred years or more into the future."

A silence stretched out between them, a silence filled with the melodic trickling of the fountain and the thrumming awareness of the depth and power of the emotion running between them. In the distance, a sick child began to wail, and she turned her head toward the sound. "You must excuse me, Major," she said, her chest lifting as she sucked in a quick, deep breath. "I have work to do."

She would have pushed past him then, to the door, but he stopped her by saying, "You haven't answered my questions yet."

CHAPTER
FOURTEEN

She swung slowly to face him again. "What questions, Major?"

"That night in the cemetery, when Henri Santerre was shot, did you see anyone else there?"

"You already asked me that. I told you, I saw no one."

"According to the gatekeeper, two black men were tending their master's family crypt in the cemetery that night. You didn't see them?"

She shook her head. "No. But it's a large cemetery, and the tombs are high enough to hide a man even one row over." She gripped her elbows in her hands, hugging them close. "That's one question, monsieur. What's the other?"

A breeze stirred up, rustling the leaves of the Chinaball tree overhead with enough force to loosen a bunch of the tree's green berries and send them tumbling to the paving stones below. He stooped to pick them up; small and hard, they lay in his palm. They were poisonous, the berries of the Chinaball tree, as poisonous as the oil of common tansy.

"I wanted to know if you could think of anything," he said, "anything at all that Claire La Touche and Henri Santerre had in common with each other besides this hospital. It doesn't need to make any sense. It could be something as obscure as an interest in the opera, or being born on the same day."

She didn't answer him right away. A small crease appeared between her brows as she thought, but in the end, she only shook her head again, her gaze coming back to his face. "No. I'm sorry. I can't think of anything. Have you spoken to her parents?"

"Last night." He bounced the Chinaball berries up and down in his palm, then closed his fist over them. "Did you know her mother blames you for Claire's death?"

"Me?"

"She thinks that if it hadn't been for you, Claire never would have volunteered at the hospital."

She brought up one hand to rub her forehead in a telling gesture of exhaustion. She was driving herself too hard, and it was starting to show. "Madame La Touche didn't know her daughter well."

"Did you?"

"I understood how she thought. I understood her anger and frustration."

"Anger and frustration? With what?"

"With society's expectations and prejudices." She paused. "Do you even know what I'm talking about?"

"I have read Mary Wollstonecraft and John Stuart Mill." He smiled at the startled widening of her eyes. "That surprises you, doesn't it?" he said, leaning into her. "And did you ever think that perhaps you have a few prejudices of your own, Madame de Beauvais?"

"Against men who wear uniforms, you mean? Especially blue uniforms?"

"Against men, period."

She stared at him without blinking, the black lace at her throat shuddering as she drew a quick, high breath.

He thought she meant to deny it, but all she did was say, her voice crisp, "Has your army doctor finished the postmortem?"

Zach shook his head. The baby inside was crying again. "Not yet. But I promised the La Touche family I'd try to have the body released in time for them to be able to hold a wake tomorrow night." It would need to be a closed coffin, of course. They hadn't liked that, the La Touche family.

"Will you tell me the results, when you receive them?" She paused. "Or does my status as a suspect preclude that?"

"I'll tell you." He realized he still held the Chinaball berries in his hand, and looked down at them before tossing them away. "You know, Claire La Touche and Henri Santerre did have one other connection besides this hospital that you didn't mention."

She shook her head. "What's that?"

"Philippe. Philippe de Beauvais. And you."

That evening, after an endless, numbing day spent treating malnourished children and scurvy-wracked, hollow-eyed women, Emmanuelle took Dominic and one of his friends uptown on the Carrollton steam train. There, while the two boys raced across the grassy flat below, their young voices raised in excited laughter, Dominic's bright red kite climbing higher and higher into the pale blue sky, Emmanuelle walked to the top of the levee, where she could look out across the drift-wood houses lining the batture, to the surging gray-brown expanse of the river.

A cool wind buffeted her face, blowing away the driving anger that had kept her going all day. Trouble was, beneath the anger lurked a grief and fear so profound, she knew herself to be hollowed out by it and left dangerously fragile. A gust of wind tugged at the brim of her hat and she brought up one hand to hold it down, her eyes narrowing against the dazzle of sunlight reflecting off the swift-moving waters of the river. She sucked in a deep breath, drawing it all in, the sound of the children's laughter and the warmth of the sun on her shoulders and the majestic beauty of the river, and then felt a warning sting of tears in her eyes when she thought of how fleeting it all was, how quickly it could all be lost, how quickly it had been lost, first to Philippe, then to Henri, and now to Claire. She tightened her grip on her hat, her other hand fisting in her skirts as she fought the urge to run down the levee and sweep her son up into her arms and hold him safe and alive against her. Hold herself safe for him.

She became aware of a man riding toward her, a tall man in a blue officer's uniform, his seat on his horse as graceful and effortless as that of any Louisiana planter. She turned her back to the river breeze and watched as he kneed his big cavalry mount at an angle up the slope of the levee, toward her. He was her enemy, the enemy of her people, a part of the terrible things that were being done to them every day. And yet, just the sight of him was enough to set her heart to beating hard and fast.

"How did you know where to find me?" she asked when he drew nearer, her head tipping back, her hand shifting to grasp the ribbons of her bonnet as the wind caught at it again.

"I stopped by the rue Dumaine," he said, and swung out of the saddle beside her.

They turned and walked together along the shell-strewn path at the crest of the levee, his big bay ambling along behind them. She could see Dominic, below, sprawled on the grass as he worked at untangling a snarl in his kite string. "You have the results of the autopsy," she said quietly, when the man beside her didn't speak.

"Yes."

She threw a quick look sideways at him. "And what did your Yankee doctor find?"

He had his gaze fixed straight ahead, his profile hard and handsome and utterly unreadable. "You were right. It was tansy." He drew the length of his reins through his other hand, dark leather against pale gauntlets. "I asked the army doctor what sort of 'women's problems' it's used to treat. He said women take it to bring on their monthly flow." He looked at her. "Which is a fuzzy way of saying it's used to get rid of an unwanted child."

Emmanuelle felt an aching sensation in her chest, as if a hole had suddenly opened up in her heart. "And was she with child?"

"No. Although she was no innocent maiden, either." He searched her face, his eyes narrowed, fierce. "But then, you knew that, didn't you?"

She made no attempt to deny it, only swung away from him to look out over the shantytown on the batture below. This stretch of willow and weeds between the levee and the riverbank was public land, a part of the river, really. Those who squatted here lived a precarious existence, their houses perched on stilts high above the level of the yearly floodwaters, their chickens and pigs running free and vulnerable beneath the feathery branches of the willows. But she'd always thought the view of the ever-rolling river from those rickety porches must be magnificent.

"Do you know the name of the man she was seeing?" he asked.

"We didn't discuss such things." It wasn't exactly a

lie, although it hid a shameful truth she had no intention of revealing. She turned to walk on, the shells crunching beneath her feet, her face lifted toward the golden light of the lowering sun. The wind was almost cold, this close to the river. It always surprised her, how cold the wind on the levee could be.

"So of course you don't know who might have wanted Miss La Touche dead?" he said, keeping pace beside her.

"No."

"When I talked to her family last night, they described their daughter as innocent. Untouched. Which means either they didn't know the truth, or they were too ashamed to admit it. Or too afraid."

"Afraid?" She swung to face him, her head tilting to one side as she studied his set features. "What are you suggesting? That they killed Claire because she was no longer a virgin?"

"It's been known to happen, when a young woman threatens to bring disgrace to her family—to her old, proud, oh-so-respectable family. It seems Miss La Touche was rather daring in her sexual activities. According to the doctor who did the autopsy, some of the things she did were . . . well, let's put it this way, a man would need to pay extra for that kind of fun, in the bordellos along the waterfront."

She felt her cheeks flame with understanding. "I'm not an innocent, Major. I can guess what you're talking about."

Something glittered in the depths of his dangerously dark eyes, something he hid with a downward sweep of his lashes. "For some people—say, for instance, a proud father, or an outraged brother—it might be reason enough to kill."

"No. Not for Antoine," she said hastily, too hastily,

she thought, when she saw the flicker of interest that crossed his features.

"How close was she to Henri Santerre?"

"You can't think Henri." She shook her head in vehement denial. "No. Henri would never."

"What makes you so certain?"

"*Mon Dieu.* He was an old man!"

He glanced sideways at her, a hard smile curling his lips. "It's been known to happen before."

"No. Henri was an honorable man. He would never have seduced a woman young enough to be his granddaughter."

"Perhaps he was the one seduced. Claire La Touche was a very beautiful young woman. Beautiful and bold and knowing."

"No," she said again. "You don't understand. There was only one woman in Henri's life. His wife might have been dead thirteen years, but he was still devoted to her. Besides . . ." The snapping of a line made her look up, her gaze narrowing as she saw Dominic's red kite climb, leaping and dipping, into the cornflower blue sky again. "Henri didn't even *like* Claire. I mean, he appreciated what she did for the men in the hospital, but he"—she hesitated, looking for the right word—"disapproved of her."

"Did he know she took laudanum?"

She threw him a quick glance of surprise.

"According to the army doctor, she was a regular user. And don't try to tell me you had no idea, because you'd have known. Someone like you would have noticed the signs."

"I wouldn't say she took it regularly, but she took it more than was prudent, yes. Most people don't understand how addictive it can be. I tried to warn her, but she only laughed at me."

"Do you know where she got it?"

Emmanuelle shook her head. "Before the war made opium scarce, you could get it anywhere. But that's not true anymore." In the shade of one of the driftwood porches below, a mulatto man was weaving a wicker chair from the batture's willows. Emmanuelle stood very still, watching his hands flash in and out as he worked. "It's still possible Claire's death was an accident, isn't it?" she said slowly. "I mean, she could have thought she was with child, and taken the tansy to get rid of it." Yet even as she said it, Emmanuelle knew it could never have happened that way. No matter how desperate she might have imagined herself to be, Claire would never have taken such a harsh purgative in the afternoon, when she was going out. She would have waited for the long, secret hours of the night.

"It was no accident," he said. "The tansy was in her laudanum. Fletcher found the bottle in a search of her room—a search your friend Antoine did his best to prevent, by the way."

"In the laudanum? But . . . is that possible? It's sweet, laudanum, but surely not sweet enough to completely mask the bitterness of the tansy."

He shook his head. "It was a new bottle. Even if she did notice a different taste, she probably just thought it was a bad mix. After all, she wouldn't be likely to think someone was trying to poison her, would she?"

A strange sound escaped Emmanuelle's lips before she could stop it. He took a step toward her, his hand closing on her upper arm to bring her around to face him when she would have turned away. "Listen to me," he said, holding both her arms now in a fierce grip that pulled her to him. "Something ugly is going on here, something ugly and dangerous, and you know a hell of a lot more about it than you've admitted so far. Can't you see that you're in danger? Don't you even care?"

She stared up into his fierce, hard face, and found herself caught by the turbulent darkness of his eyes. "Do you think I'm not afraid? I have a son who lost his father less than three months ago. Do you think I don't worry about what will become of him if something were to happen to me?"

"Then why the hell won't you tell me the truth?"

They were too close, and the emotions raging through her were all too linked, too entwined, fear and excitement, passion and hate. She felt her heart thundering hard and fast within her. Saw his features sharpen with an intense, almost predatory sexuality as his head dipped, his gaze fixed on her mouth. "Monsieur . . . ," she whispered. "My son . . . his friend . . ."

He flung up his head, a quick breath shuddering his chest, his hands lifting from her shoulders. She spun away from him, but he made no move to touch her again.

"How many more people are going to have to die?" he said, standing suddenly, frighteningly still. "How many people are going to die before you overcome your prejudices against my uniform and my sword enough to tell me what is going on?"

She shook her head slowly from side to side, her fingers twisting in the heavy folds of her black mourning gown. "That has nothing to do with it."

She could hear Dominic's voice calling in the distance. "Maman, Maman." Turning her head, she watched him race up the levee toward her, his kite soaring. "Maman, look how high!"

"It has everything to do with it," the man beside her said and, gathering his horse's reins, he swung into his

saddle and rode away, a solitary figure in blue silhouetted against a fading Southern sky.

That night, sometime in the still hours around midnight, Emmanuelle jerked awake, her heart pounding.
She sat up in bed, her ears straining to catch an echo of
whatever had awakened her. But the silence in the
house was a ringing, tangible thing, as heavy and impenetrable as the darkness.

Shivering with fear, she got up and crept to the doorway of Dominic's room, but he slept peacefully, his
breathing a gentle sound on the quiet night. And so she
forced herself to venture farther, across the room and
out into the hall, the night air warm against her goose-
fleshed skin, her bare feet moving noiselessly over the
bare floorboards. She felt terrified and vaguely foolish.
Before going to bed she'd checked all the long windows
facing the street herself, and had slid home the bolt on
the front door. No one could be in the house. Yet her
fear remained, and when a stair tread creaked beneath
her foot, her stomach seemed to leap up into her
throat, so that her breath was coming in gasping pants.

She checked the French windows of the parlor, but
both were closed and securely locked. And so she continued down, to the entryway. She wondered, one hand
clutching tightly to the banister, what she would do if
she were to find someone there. But the hall was empty,
the door safely closed against the dangers of the night.
Closed, but no longer barred.

And she knew, then, that someone had been in the
house, that what she had heard in her sleep had been
the sound of that someone pulling back the bar to let
himself out, and then carefully closing the door behind
him. ·

CHAPTER
FIFTEEN

Early the next morning, Emmanuelle borrowed a neat little gray mare from one of her neighbors and rode out of the city, toward the swamps to the east and the peculiar, mushroomed-shaped hut of the black man who lived there and was said to be able to foresee the future.

She hadn't been raised with horses, like Philippe. But in that heady first year of their marriage he had taken her down to Beau Lac and taught her to ride, the way he had taught her so many things. And so she supposed it was natural that she should find her thoughts drifting to him as fields of sugarcane replaced the tight rows of houses, and city gave way to country.

Last night, after discovering the front door closed but unbolted, she'd gone to check on Rose and found the colored woman safely asleep in her bed. "But how?" Rose had asked, her eyes widening with fear when Emmanuelle told her. She sat up, her arms hugging her bent knees to her chest. "How could anyone have got in?" Her eyes grew even wider. "And what was he doing here?"

They'd checked the house then, the two of them together, searching for some sign of the intruder. But they hadn't found anything.

"There's only one explanation that makes sense,"

Emmanuelle said later, as they sat beside the kitchen hearth and drank hot chicory coffee from thick mugs. "Whoever it was must have come in and hidden some-place during the day, when the door wasn't locked, and then waited until we were all asleep to do whatever it was he came to do."

"I tell you what," Rose said, her gaze dropping with sudden suspicion to the coffee in her hands. "From now on, I'm keeping that door locked all day long. And come morning, I'm throwing out every lick of food in this house. One thing you can be sure of, whoever he was, he was up to no good, sneaking around in the dead of the night like that."

Emmanuelle kept her peace, but she didn't believe their intruder had come to poison them. Anyone want-ing them dead could simply have murdered them all in their beds. "Have you heard any talk in the market, Rose? Any ideas about who's been doing these killings, or why?" They were a well-known and valuable source of information, the servants of this city, both slave and free. People said that was where the voodoo practi-tioners learned so many of the secrets they used to daz-zle their credulous customers.

"Oh, there's lots of talk," Rose said airily. Too airily. "But nobody really knows anything."

"What kind of talk?"

Rose's gaze slid away. "Foolish talk."

Emmanuelle leaned forward, her mug clutched in both hands. "Tell me, Rose."

Rose brought her gaze back to Emmanuelle's face, and let out her breath in a long sigh. "All right. Some are saying it's Michie Philippe. That he didn't die down on the bayous like the Yankees think. That he got away, only he's not quite right in the head anymore and so he's killing everybody he knows."

Emmanuelle's hands tightened so hard around her mug, she wondered it didn't crack. "What else?"

Rose shrugged. "That's about it. Oh, some are saying no, it's that English doctor, or the German boy who lost his foot, but that's just prejudice against people who talk funny and got different ways."

Emmanuelle nodded, but already an idea was forming in her head, an idea that wouldn't go away. She wasn't sure at what point during the long, sleepless night that followed that she gave in to it and decided to come here, to the edges of the Bayou Sauvage. She still felt foolish to be doing it, for while she had the utmost respect for Papa John's knowledge of healing herbs and potions, she'd never really believed in his famous readings, in his guiding deity and his supposed ability to tap into the so-called collective unconscious. But Henri had believed. As she neared the small clearing, she told herself she had come because people did tell the old black man things, so many things, secrets and suspicions and fears. Yet she also knew it wasn't the only reason she was here, and she found herself thinking about what Philippe would say, if he were to see her, now. Philippe hadn't believed in Papa John, either.

He was sitting at a small table covered with a white cloth in the clearing in front of his house, when she rode up. An empty stool stood across from him, and the table was bare except for a crudely hollowed-out wooden cup filled with cowry shells.

"You're going to tell me you were expecting me, right?" she said, reining in.

He threw back his head and laughed, a deep, rich laugh of genuine amusement. "Miss Emmanuelle. Ever the skeptic."

"I'm here, aren't I?" she said, and swung out of the saddle.

He laughed again. "Because you think I might have heard something."

She tied the gray to the low branch of a nearby cypress and walked toward him. "Have you?" she asked, stopping just short of the table.

"Nothing that's true."

"How do you know what's true?"

"I only know what I'm told."

She hesitated a moment, then went to sit on the far side of the table from him. "All right." She spread her hands on the clean white cloth; white, the color of purity and protection. "Do it. Shake your cowry shells and invoke your goddess and tell me who's doing this."

"It's not that easy."

She caught his gaze, and held it. "Isn't it?"

He handed her the wooden cup of shells. "Hold this in both your hands. Clear your mind of everything but what you want to know."

She took the cup in her palms, feeling both ridiculous and vaguely hopeful at the same time. It was smooth and surprisingly cool, and vibrating with a strange kind of energy that came near to frightening her.

"Now close your eyes and shake the shells, and ask your question."

She did as she was told, her eyes opening as she felt him lift the cup from her grasp. He shook it himself then, intoning a chant in the language of his youth, a chant that, according to Henri, addressed the four corners and invoked Papa John's own patron deity but also called on the Almighty Father, for it was a peculiar spiritual mixture, voodoo, combining memories of ancient African religions with the mystical Catholicism of Saint-Dominque, that dark island of the Caribbean where Papa John had once been a slave before the horrors there had brought him and so many like him to New Orleans.

As she watched, he began to sway back and forth, the muscles of his face going peculiarly slack, his eyes rolling back in his head as he cast himself into a trance. When he suddenly spilled the shells across the table-cloth, she was so startled, she jumped.

It looked like a simple random scattering of shells to Emmanuelle, but Papa John studied them intently, his features no longer slack, but concentrated now, sharp.

"Hmmm," he murmured, leaning over the shells, his forehead creasing as he stared down at them. "Some-one is being moved by a dangerous combination of fierce passions. Hatred, but even more so, rage. A dark, burning rage."

"I could have told you that," Emmanuelle said.

He looked up at her, the corners of his eyes crinkling in amusement. "Really? How?"

She felt herself flush, aware suddenly of the contra-diction, that she should believe so intensely in the ac-curacy of her own indefinable perceptions, and at the same time doubt his. "I sensed it. That night in the cemetery."

"Directed at you?"

"Yes."

He turned his attention back to the shells. "Mmmm," he murmured again after a long, anxiety-filled moment.

"What is it?" she demanded when he said nothing.

He pointed to some of the shells, which she saw now had fallen in such a way that two lines seemed to run side by side. "I see a double threat. One directed at you, but a second, as well, that will endanger someone you love."

"*Dominic.*" She leaned forward, her voice sharp

with near panic. "Oh, God. It's not Dominic, is it?" She had totally forgotten she didn't believe any of this.

Papa John shook his head. "I don't know."

She stood up so quickly, the crude stool tipped over behind her in the grass. "What do you mean, you don't know? Who is doing this to us? Why won't you give me a name?"

He sat back, his hand sweeping in a grand gesture over the cloth. "Do you see a name written here?"

She gripped the edge of the table and leaned into it. "I only see shells. But you see something. They mean something to you."

"They don't tell me everything." His voice was quiet, gentle, as he stared up at her. "I used to wish they did, but now I've learned to be thankful that they don't." He paused, as if reconsidering. "Most of the time."

She straightened slowly, ashamed of herself, ashamed of both her panic and her rudeness. "I'm sorry. You tried to help me, and all I did was scream at you." She took from her reticule the prime Cuban tobacco she had brought him as a gift, and laid it on the table beside him.

He kept his gaze on her face. "Sometimes we all need to scream."

She gave a shaky half-laugh. "Thank you," she said again, and went to untie her horse. "Aren't you going to tell me to be careful?" she asked, leading the mare to a stump so she could mount.

He walked up beside her, his head falling back as he stared up at her. "You're already being careful. Just . . ." He paused.

She looked up from adjusting her skirts over the sidesaddle. "Just, what?"

"Just . . ." He paused again, and gave the mare's neck a gentle, farewell pat. "Be careful, hmmm?"

• • •

"Is there something I should maybe know about?" Hamish asked.

They were sitting at the Morning Call, the remnants of a couple orders of doughnuts and café au lait littering the table in front of them. The breeze off the river was cool this morning, bringing them the shouts of luggers tying up at the wharves and the voices of women on their way to market, baskets on their heads, their hips swaying with an innate grace. The air was filled with the smell of olive oil and malt and roasting coffee, and that elusive scent that was unidentifiable and yet purely, distinctively New Orleans.

"Like, maybe what's going on between you and that Frenchie widow whose friends seem to have a bad habit of turning up dead," Hamish was saying.

Zach turned his head to look at him.

"And don't try raising your eyebrows and looking arrogant at me," continued Hamish, shaking a big, fat finger at him, "because I watched you with her the other day, and I watched her, and even if I'd have been blind, I'd still have known there was something going on just by the way the air was crackling between the two of you."

Zach let out a soft laugh that had a catch in it and swung his head away again, to stare out over the square with its wrought-iron fence and swaying sycamore trees and equestrian statue of Andrew Jackson, where a workman under the direction of General "Spoons" Butler was busy carving a new inscription on the base: THE UNION MUST AND SHALL BE PRESERVED.

"Christalmighty, she's a *suspect*," Hamish said, leaning forward.

"I'm not so sure she is."

"You were before."

Zach shrugged. "I think she knows more than what she's telling us, but that's to be expected, isn't it? We're not exactly popular around here."

"You can say that again."

Zach leaned back in his seat, his gaze still caught by the workman in the square. "I want you to set some troopers to scouring that cemetery. Have them write down the names of any tombs that show signs of recent repairs, and then go talk to the families involved. We need to find the two black men that German gatekeeper was telling me about. They could have seen something."

Hamish pulled out his notebook and scribbled for a moment, then looked up, thoughtful. "You remember how you asked me to see what I could find out about Philippe de Beauvais?"

"Yes," said Zach slowly, watching the big New Yorker rub his hand against the back of his neck and screw up his face in a grimace.

"At first, I thought he must have enrolled in the Confederate medical corps and been killed that way, but he hadn't. Seems he volunteered to smuggle some Confederate gold out through the bayous, not long after we took the city. He didn't make it."

"A hero's death," Zach said softly.

"Aye. Although from what I hear, it's no' what one would have expected of him."

"Meaning?"

"Meaning that pretty little French widow's husband had a dark side to him."

"Don't most people?"

Hamish shook his head. "Not this dark. We're talking absinthe houses and high-stakes faro and the nastiest kind of brothels—like that one down on Old Levee Street that sells very young girls—and boys—to very twisted rich men. And I don't think I'm being told the half of it."

Near the iron fence of the square, an old Indian woman was spreading dried plants out on a blanket to sell. Zach watched her thoughtfully. "Sounds like the kind of man someone might be tempted to aim a cross-bow at. Or poison. If he were our victim, this whole mess might begin to make some sense."

"Yeah? Well, get this: de Beauvais's little smuggling expedition through the Bayou Crevé? We didn't just discover it by accident. Someone informed on him."

The sun was climbing higher, heating the air, stealing the coolness from the morning, heating the bricks of the banquette and the paving stones in the street. "You going to tell me who?"

"I don't know yet," said Hamish, the metal legs of his chair screeching as he pushed it back. "But the way I'm looking at it, we're not dealing with two murders here. Right now, the score is three and counting. And I'm thinking that Hospital de Santerre is a mighty un-healthy place to be associated with. Unhealthy, and dangerous—like Madame de Beauvais."

Zach spent what was left of the morning, and most of the afternoon, overseeing the distribution of food to the city's poor. But something kept nagging at him, like an old tune he couldn't quite recall, or a half-remembered dream that hovered just beyond con-sciousness.

In the end, he left one of his lieutenants to finish up, and went in search of Antoine La Touche.

He wasn't an easy man to locate. Zach finally ran him to ground in a seedy cabaret on Old Levee Street. He was sitting in a dark, smoky corner at a round table covered by a dirty cloth, although Zach noticed that the bottle of cognac at the man's elbow was one of the best. He was by himself. The wall behind him had at one time been papered with a pale sprigged pattern, but the colors had long ago almost disappeared beneath the grime, and the paper had started to peel. Someone had tried to cover up the worst patches with cheap reproductions of holy pictures. Only in New Orleans, Zach thought.

As he watched, La Touche drained his glass and reached an unsteady hand for the bottle. At the sight of Zach, he paused, then his hand tightened around the neck of the cognac, and he smiled. "Well. To what do I owe the privilege of a visit from our local provost marshal?"

The air in the dive was hot and muggy and smelled strongly of beer and whiskey and sweat. "I want to talk to you."

"Really?" The other man waved his hand through the air in a languid gesture that sent cognac sloshing up the sides of the bottle. "Talk."

It was early yet, but the bar was already full of half-drunk Irishmen and Italians and, here and there, the odd man of color. "Considering the topic, I think you might prefer a more private place."

La Touche ran the back of one hand across the small beads of perspiration on his forehead. His silk neck-cloth was askew, the collar of his fine linen shirt limp and yellow with sweat. "Ah. Claire." His breath came out in a sigh, his gaze dropping to the bottle in his hand. "You're right. This isn't the place."

He took the bottle with him. Outside, the sun was still baking the tops of the buildings, but compared with the atmosphere in the bar, the air on Old Levee Street smelled sweet and fresh. Pausing on the banquette, one arm draped over the support of his solitary crutch, La Touche squinted up at the fading blue sky streaked with thick, high clouds. "It's earlier than I expected."

"How long have you been drinking?"

"How long?" The man shrugged. "I don't know."

"You and your sister must have been close."

"No, we weren't." La Touche gave a low, mirthless laugh. "You might think that's why I'm drinking, but you'd be wrong. Regret is such a pathetic, self-indulgent emotion, don't you agree, Major?"

"It can be."

They turned toward the river, where the stalls in the French Market were closing for the day, the seagulls overhead wheeling and screeching. "Why, Major," the Creole said, staggering slightly on his crutch as he turned to look at Zach. "I do believe I've hit a nerve."

"How well did you know your sister?" Zach asked.

La Touche brought the bottle to his lips again. "I thought we'd already established the answer to that."

"Did you know she was intimately involved with a man?"

He had his head thrown back, his throat rippling as he swallowed. At Zach's words, he choked. "How delicately phrased, Major." He brought the bottle down. "Are you being sensitive, I wonder, or are you simply afraid I might take offense and challenge you to a duel? I can still shoot, you know, even if I can no longer fence."

Zach waited, and after a moment, the other man said, "My sister Claire has been—was—*intimately involved* with men since the age of fifteen. The first was a strapping, handsome young Irish laborer hired to repair the paving in the courtyard. The last was anyone's guess."

"Do you know if she was involved with someone at the hospital?"

"I thought so, at first—altruism not being one of Claire's more distinguishing characteristics. But in the end, I decided I'd underestimated her." La Touche leaned his back against one of the market's massive pillars, the bottle dangling limply by his side, his eyes sliding half-shut. "In the end," he repeated softly.

"Did your parents know?"

He swung his head to look at Zach. "Know what? That their daughter had decided she had as much right to sexual freedom as any son? I don't think so. Although I could be wrong. Perhaps they simply didn't want to know."

"Why didn't they marry her off?"

"Oh, they tried. She refused. She used to say that as long as a husband in America has essentially as much authority over his wife as a master over his slaves, then she would never marry. Never give a man that kind of power over her." A wry smile twisted his pain-thinned lips. "Of course, for Claire, *never* didn't last very long, did it? And the slaves will soon be free, even if the women aren't." He took another drink of cognac and eyed Zach over the bottle's rim. "What do you think? Hmmm? That we killed her because she was a disgrace to the family?" He gave a short, harsh laugh. "She was never half the disgrace I was."

"You're not female."

La Touche swung the bottle through the air in a grand gesture. "No, of course. A family's honor lies between the legs of its women, doesn't it?" He laughed again. "Am I supposed to have shot old Santerre as well? Whatever for?" His eyes suddenly went wide. "You don't think—" This time, his laughter echoed with real amusement, quickly cut off. "Oh, Major. I'm afraid not. Claire had highly refined, rather esthetically inclined tastes. She liked her men at least reasonably young and handsome, and visibly virile."

The sun was sinking low in the sky, the light growing weak and faintly pink, the bustle in the streets lessening as people hurried home for their evening meal. Zach watched a shoemaker close the shutters on the storefront across the street, then brought his gaze back to the Creole's thin, pain-nipped face. "What do you know about the death of Philippe de Beauvais?"

"Philippe?" La Touche frowned, the bottle coming up to his lips again, the shift in subject visibly confusing him. "You killed Philippe—you Yankees. They say he died instantly. Shot right through the head."

"Did you know someone had betrayed his mission?"

Perhaps the Creole wasn't as drunk as Zach had thought. He went quite still, his shattered body drawing up, tensing. It was a moment before he spoke. "No, I didn't know." He took another long, deep swallow. "Interesting."

Darkness was falling quickly now. Too quickly. Glancing up, Zach realized the sky was filling with clouds blowing in fast. He could feel the wind, smell the promise of rain in its coolness. "You're going to be late for your sister's wake," Zach said, bringing his gaze back to the Creole's flushed face.

He shook his head. "Claire always hated wakes." He gave a mirthless laugh, then said, "It's funny, isn't it? How life can change. How the things that once seemed so terribly important to us can in a very short space of time come to mean nothing at all." He started to bring the bottle up to his lips again, then stopped, his cognac-scented breath gusting out in a weary sigh. "Last spring, at the hospital, there was some big blowup. I don't know what it was about, but I do know it involved Claire and that English doctor, Yardley." He rolled his head to look sideways at Zach. "It also involved *beaucoup* shouting and pushing. If you'd known Claire, you wouldn't have any difficulty imagining it. Philippe got dragged into it somehow, and then Santerre, who finally managed to break it up. That German boy—the one who lost his foot—he was there, as well. Ask him about it."

"Hans Spears?"

"*Oui*. Hans. Did you know he was with Philippe at Bayou Crevé? That's how he was wounded."

Zach shook his head. "Why are you telling me this?"

La Touche let out a low half-laugh. "Oh, Major. Have we been so terribly uncooperative that when one of us decides to open up a bit, you don't trust us?" Shifting his shoulders against the pillar behind him, he hitched himself up straighter on his crutch. "You might think I'm telling you because of Claire, and in a sense, you wouldn't be wrong."

"It's because of Madame de Beauvais, isn't it?" Zach said softly. "Was she there, at this argument?"

"Not at first. But she was there."

Zach felt the blood flow slow and cold through his veins. He heard his own voice, speaking as if from a long ways off. "Do you think she could be the one behind the killings?"

"Emmanuelle?" The Creole's laughter this time was loud and ringing. "You really don't understand, do you, Major? If I thought that, I never would have mentioned any of this to you." The laughter died as quickly as it had come, his face growing earnest, strained. "I told you because I'm afraid she might be next."

• • •

Night was falling by the time Zach reached the Hospital de Santerre. The upper floor lay dark, deserted, but he could see light leaching out through the slats of the shutters on some of the lower floor's windows. Finding the door unlocked, he let himself in and followed the light to a small room near the stairs, where Dr. Charles Yardley sat in a straight-backed chair beside the bed of a sleeping black child. At the sound of Zach's footsteps, the man looked up, and stiffened.

"I didn't expect to find you here," Zach said, pausing in the doorway.

Yardley blew out his breath in a tired sigh. "Typhus. This place is starting to resemble Charity Hospital. The mother died an hour ago, but I'm actually beginning to think the boy might make it." He scrubbed one hand across his eyes, then stood up and came forward to where Zach stood in the doorway. "She's not here, if you're looking for Madame de Beauvais."

"As a matter of fact, I was looking for Hans Spears."

"It's his night off. You can probably find him home with his Mutter and four brothers, if you're desperate to talk to him. He's not much for socializing. What little free time he has he seems to devote to that church the German immigrants are building Uptown."

"I'll talk to you, then. If you have a minute."

"Dear me. This sounds ominous." The Englishman glanced back at the sleeping child. "I suppose I could use a break. Although I really don't know much about all this, believe me."

"You might know why a German emigrant who makes his living as a nurse would decide to take part in a desperate attempt to smuggle Confederate gold out of New Orleans."

"Why?" The Englishman curled his tongue against

his upper teeth and screwed up his face, as if thinking. "Well, let's see. How about a yearning for adventure? Or, no—let's make it a desire to get away from Mutter and the boys." He showed his teeth in a wide smile. "Am I being any help?" Walking over to the pitcher of water that rested on the shelf near the office, he poured himself a drink and threw it down. "Actually," he said over his shoulder, "I don't think *desperate* is quite the right word. Philippe grew up on Bayou Crevé. He should have made it to the Gulf Coast and Mobile easily." His bony white fingers tightened around the glass, then pushed it away. "It was sheer bad luck some Union patrol stumbled across them."

"Not luck."

The Englishman swung around quickly, his eyebrows arching in surprise. "Really?"

"Know who might have hated Philippe enough to want to see him dead?"

"See Philippe dead? Well, that's rather a stretch, isn't it? Especially when you're dealing with money. Where did it go, all that Confederate gold? If you think it went to Washington, you're even more naive than I'd realized."

"Were you involved with Claire La Touche?"

Yardley let out a quick laugh. "Me? You must be joking," he said, then tilted his head in an exaggerated show of reappraisal as he searched Zach's hard face. "But no. You don't joke much, do you, Major?"

"Not about a young woman's murder."

"Perhaps that's because you didn't know the woman in question." Again, the smile. "Oh, dear, under the circumstances that was probably a rather unwise thing to say, wasn't it?"

"I understand you had a spectacular argument with her, last spring."

"Now where did you hear that, I wonder?"

Zach shook his head and let a tight smile curve his own lips. "What did you quarrel about?"

Yardley leaned his shoulders against the wall behind him. "You mean your informant didn't tell you?"

"I'll ask you one more time," Zach said, keeping his voice low and even. "Were you involved with Claire La Touche?"

A muscle ticked in the other man's suddenly tight jaw. "If your informant told you that, Major, then I'm afraid he—or she—was sadly mistaken."

"But you know who Miss La Touche was seeing."

The Englishman pushed away from the wall. "I don't know if *seeing* is the right word."

"What word would you use?"

Yardley's eyebrows rose in that way he had. "You did have a thorough postmortem performed, didn't you? It's rather difficult to establish eye contact in that position," he said, and started to turn away.

Zach's hand caught him by the shoulder and swung him around to slam him back, hard, against the wall. "Who," Zach said, his lips pulling away from his teeth as he shoved his forearm up under the other man's chin, "who was the man?"

The Englishman's smile never slipped, but something flashed in his eyes, something that spoke of a deep and powerful anger. "You really haven't figured it out yet, have you, Major? You want a name? How's this one: Philippe. Philippe de Beauvais."

Zach let the man go and took a quick step back. He could be lying, of course. Hamish would probably assume the man was lying. But Zach knew, deep in his gut, that he was hearing the truth. "Did she know? Madame de Beauvais. Did she know?"

Yardley smoothed his coat and swept his long,

straight hair back from his face before answering. "That her good friend was fucking her husband?" He gave his lapels another twitch. "Not before Claire and I had our little shouting match."

"But she found out?"

"Oh, yes. She found out. And then she went at Philippe with a scalpel." The gray eyes widened as if in innocent amazement. "Didn't your informant tell you that?"

CHAPTER
SIXTEEN

"Why are they even having this wake?" Hamish demanded as he and Zach made their way through the narrow, lamplit streets of the old quarter, toward Esplanade Avenue and the mule car that would take them out to the La Touche city residence. "They must know she hated wakes. Even I know Claire La Touche hated wakes."

"It's their custom." Zach glanced up at the black sky. It was too dark now to see the clouds, but he could feel them there, hanging thick and heavy and threatening above the city.

"And a mighty havey-cavey custom it is, too, if you ask me. Eating and drinking when a body's not even decently laid in its grave."

Zach ducked his head to hide a smile. "Any luck finding those two black men from the cemetery?"

Hamish made a rude noise. "Do you have any idea how many crypts there are in that cemetery? We don't even know what kind of work those men were doing. For all we know, they could have been there simply to sweep the steps and change the flowers."

Zach shook his head. "That wouldn't have taken long. According to Kessler, they arrived at least two hours before Santerre. And they must have left during all the commotion that followed his killing, because the gatekeeper can't remember them leaving."

"Yeah? Even if they did see something, they wouldn't tell. Slavery seems to hone the practice of being unco-operative down to a fine art." They had reached Es-planade Avenue by now. Hamish's eyes narrowed down to slits as he squinted toward the levee, where the mule car was just pulling out. "The way I figure it, the widow is starting to look more and more like our best suspect. She gets rid of her unfaithful husband by be-traying him to the Yanks—us. And then she poisons his mistress."

Zach bit down hard on a dangerous and unprofes-sional upsurge of anger. "It would help if we knew who actually did betray Philippe," he said, watching the lantern-lit mule car rattle toward them, and somehow managing to keep his voice even.

Hamish sniffed. "I'm working on it."

"Besides," said Zach, his breath coming easier now, his gaze still carefully fixed on the mule car's bobbing lantern, "Emmanuelle de Beauvais had no reason kill Santerre."

"Didn't she? Think about it: Three men start a hos-pital together. Now they're all dead, and the little lady is the new owner."

Zach shook his head. "She was telling the truth when she said the Hospital de Santerre is about to go under. I checked. The building is mortgaged, and she's been having trouble making the note."

"Weeell . . ." Hamish smoothed his mustaches with a spread hand, his neck stretching as he lifted his chin. "I suppose it could have been Yardley. His debts don't seem to be overwhelming, but they're still bad. And from what I hear, he and Santerre had a few set-tos after de Beauvais got himself killed. It was Philippe de Beauvais who brought Yardley into the hospital in the first place, right? All that gambling and drinking and opium eating probably didn't sit too well with the old man." The mule snorted to a halt in front of them. "The way I see it," said Hamish, dropping his voice as they boarded the car and took seats by themselves in the rear, "the crossbow and the poison are the keys. Yardley and Madame de Beauvais were both in a position to know about Philippe de Beauvais's nasty little vampire-killing kit, and they both know enough about poisons to kill anyone off."

"So does Papa John."

"Yeah. But he's got no motive that I can see." Hamish pulled out his notebook and flipped through the pages. "I've also got this La Touche on my list. Antoine. He might not have much knowledge of poisons himself, but he could have got the tansy from Papa John, and it'd be easy for a brother to slip poison into his sister's laudanum. The way I see it, he could have killed Claire for betraying the family honor, and Philippe de Beauvais for seducing her."

Zach stared out the open window at moss-draped live oaks and rusting iron fences and high, double gallery houses looming white and elegant out of the storm-charged darkness. "And Santerre?"

"The old man let it all happen, didn't he? Right there under his nose, at the hospital." Hamish leaned forward, his voice dropping even lower. "And another thing: La Touche would have had a reason to use a crossbow—I mean, he's crippled, right? And get this— he lost his leg at the Hospital de Santerre." Hamish paused, his brows drawing together, his voice losing some of its enthusiasm. "The problem is, of course, how did he get over the cemetery wall with only one leg?"

"We don't know the murderer came over the wall."

Hamish let out a snort. "And how else do you think he got there? Just walked through the front gates as invisible as a ghost?"

Zach leaned back in his seat, his arms coming up to cross at his chest. "If this is a list of suspects, you're leaving out Hans Spears. He lost his foot because of what happened on the Bayou Crevé, remember? If it was Claire who betrayed Philippe, Hans would have a good reason to blame her for his being crippled, wouldn't he?"

Hamish stared at him. "And Santerre?"

"Maybe he wasn't aiming at Santerre. Maybe he meant to kill Emmanuelle de Beauvais and hit Santerre by accident. Maybe he didn't know which of the two women had betrayed the mission, so he decided to kill them both."

There was a long pause. Then Hamish said, "You're laughing at me. I'm trying to come up with plausible scenarios here, and you're laughing at me."

Zach did laugh then, but sobered all too quickly. "You do realize there is one person we haven't considered."

"Who's that?"

"Philippe."

Hamish stared at him through wide, startled, golden brown eyes. "But . . . he's dead."

"So everyone keeps saying." Zach sat forward, his legs spread against the jolting rattle of the car, his hands clasped loosely between his knees. The motion of the car was stirring up a faint breeze that came through the open window beside him, but it was still hot. "Think about this," he said quietly. "Crossbows aren't easy weapons to use—not with any real accuracy. Philippe is the one person we know who had experience with them. As a doctor, he'd know exactly how much tansy was needed to kill a woman and, as Claire's lover, he'd know she was a habitual laudanum user, and he'd be likely to know her usual supplier, too. Remember, it was a new bottle you found. The poison was probably in it when she bought it."

"But again," said Hamish, reaching up to pull the cord, "if it was Philippe, why kill Santerre?"

"Maybe he wasn't aiming at Santerre. Maybe he was aiming at his wife."

"You keep circling around to that, don't you?" said Hamish, lurching to his feet as the car swayed to a halt. "Are you sure it isn't because you don't want to come up with a real reason for Santerre's murder, a reason that might point to Madame de Beauvais as the killer?"

Zach stood slowly. He could feel the big Scotsman's gaze on him, but he simply turned and made his way to the back platform. The street wasn't paved here, its surface rutted, its gutter still dark and a bit slimy from the last rain. Zach leaped the distance to the boardwalk, then swore softly when he came down on his bad leg and felt the ripple of the impact all the way up to his bandaged side.

"Hurt, did it?" said Hamish, landing heavily beside him.

"You don't need to sound so damn gleeful about it."

"I told you you needed to take a few days off and rest that wound."

Zach paused on the wooden sidewalk, Hamish falling silent beside him as he stared up at the crepe-draped, white facade of the neo-Grecian house before them. The La Touche house, like that of the de Beauvaises' farther up the street, had been built high on piers that raised it above the ravages of insects and floods, and coaxed the cooling breezes from the distant river through its ten-foot-high guillotine windows and French doors. But unlike the de Beauvais family, the La Touches were obviously feeling the economic crunch of the war, Zach thought, as he took in the paint beginning to peel off the tall green shutters, the bushes looming overgrown and in need of a trim near the front gate.

"It looks even worse in daylight," said a tall, thin man leaning on crutches, who emerged from the shadows of the porch to thump his way slowly, painfully down the steps toward them. "But perhaps we should be grateful for our poverty." La Touche paused to rest halfway down the walk. "I've noticed old 'Spoons' Butler only requisitions houses that are in the best of repair."

"I didn't expect to find you here," said Zach, his hand on the gate.

The other man shrugged. He had shaved, Zach noticed, and cleaned up considerably. But he was still half-drunk. "I came for my mother."

"Then what are you doing lurking around outside?" said Hamish with something like a growl.

The Creole glanced at him, once, then brought his gaze back to Zach's face. "I was hoping you'd come."

"Why?" said Zach. "What's wrong?"

"It's Emmanuelle—Madame de Beauvais. She's gone to tend some sick old man on the rue Poulet, in the Faubourg Marigny, and if I know Emmanuelle, she'll walk home. Alone."

Zach kept his gaze on the other man's face. "You could have gone with her."

"I offered. She insisted my place was here, at Claire's wake. I sent her in our carriage and told her to have the man wait, but she sent him back. Said she'd be too long and she was worried about the horses." He let out a low laugh. "The horses."

Zach turned in a slow circle, taking in the dark, deserted street, the lowering clouds, the distant rumble of thunder. "Where's the best place to find a hack at this time of night?"

"You're not going after her?" said Hamish, the ends of his mustaches twitching as he scowled up at the wind-tossed sky above them. "It's fixing to rain like the bejesus."

"It's always raining around here," Zach said just as the first drops began to hit the leaves of the oak tree overhead.

A soft, fragrant rain was falling by the time Emmanuelle left the small cottage in the Faubourg Marigny and headed back toward the Vieux Carré. Lifting her face to stare up at the wind-tossed clouds, she considered, for a moment, trying to find a hack. But the streets were still far from deserted, and the family of the old man to whose sickbed she had been called had been unable to repay her with anything more than profound gratitude. She kept walking.

She had covered some two blocks when the sky opened up and the rain came down harder, sluicing off the ends of the eaves and gurgling in the cisterns. She eyed the muddy water rushing in the gutters and beginning to spill up onto the rotting gunwale sidewalks, and sighed. Leaning against the iron fence of the house beside her, she stripped off her ankle boots and stockings. New shoes, like hacks, were a luxury she couldn't afford.

By the time she neared the canal that had been dug on the outskirts of the old city, the rain was a roaring curtain of water that bounced off the slanting roofs of the houses and pounded the sluggish channel into a froth. She became aware, suddenly, that the downpour had driven everyone else off the streets. She was alone with the wind and the rain and the darkness of the night, and at the thought, she felt a prickle of fear creep stealthily up her spine. She'd been a fool to send back Antoine's carriage, she decided. There was a fine line between bravery and frugality, and stupidity, and she'd just crossed it.

The sight of a black hack, its bay mule struggling head down and miserable toward her through the mud, made her pause, her breath coming in little pants as rain trickled down her face and into her mouth. The carriage drew opposite her and stopped. Blinking water from her eyes, she watched the door swing open and a man jump down, a familiar man in a dark blue uniform with a cape that swirled in the wind and cavalry boots that sent thick mud flying into the air as he hit the street.

"Get in, quickly," said Major Zachary Cooper. He held out his hand as if to help her to the granite carriage block that rose above the rain-filled street, but his face was hard, his eyes hidden behind the lowered brim of his officer's hat.

Emmanuelle stared at him, her arms tightening around the boots she held clutched to her chest. Rain ran down her face, dripped off the edges of her black widow's bonnet. Even more than she wanted the beckoning shelter and warmth and safety of that hack, she wanted this man to stay away from her. "Thank you, but no," she said, and kept walking.

His voice came after her, raised above the roar of water. "Goddamn it, madame. Even if there weren't a murderer loose in this city, you could damn well drown simply trying to walk out here. Will you get in the carriage?"

Rain pounded on her head, ran down the inside of her collar to trickle over bare flesh and make her feel cold, but she kept walking. She thought he would get back in his hack and drive away. She listened for the grinding sound of carriage wheels churning through the quagmire of a street. Instead, she heard footsteps on the wooden gunwale behind her. Strong fingers closed around her arm just above the elbow, swinging her around to look up at his dark, set face.

"I couldn't believe it when I arrived at Claire's wake to be told you'd gone off alone, after all that's happened."

Thunder rumbled, distant at first, then again, louder, closer. The rain poured. "I was visiting a sick patient."

He leaned into her, the rain sloshing off the brim of his hat. "So why won't you get in the hack?"

"You know why." She pushed past him, toward the canal. The water in the street was cold and thick with mud. Tucking her shoes under one arm, she lifted her skirts and petticoats higher, painfully aware of her bare, mud-streaked ankles and feet, and the man behind her, watching her. She had just reached the grassy bank of the canal when he said, "I know about Philippe and Claire."

She spun around so quickly, she almost dropped one of her shoes in the canal and had to scramble to catch it, the hem of her gown plopping into the mud when she let it go. "I don't know what you're talking about," she said, her arms crossing in front of her as she hugged her shoes tight.

"Yes, you do." He walked up to her. Lightning

ripped across the sky in great jagged tears of white that showed her the hard planes of his face and the glitter of slow-burning anger in his eyes. Thunder crashed. "You lied to me. Again."

She started to say she hadn't lied, but that was mere quibbling, and she knew it. "What does it matter? Philippe is dead."

"It matters because you wasted my time."

"Time that could have been better employed throwing widows and orphans out of their homes, or confiscating the wealth men have worked their entire lives to build?"

"Don't start on that again." Big and angry and vaguely threatening, he leaned into her. "I asked you who Claire La Touche was fucking, and you said you didn't know."

His words were crude, bare of all embellishment. But then, there had never been any pretense of polite social artifice between them. "What is it you think?" she demanded, the rain falling cold and harsh against her upturned face. "That I killed Claire for *fucking* Philippe?" She gave a low, mirthless huff of what was meant to be derisive laughter. "Half of New Orleans fucked Philippe."

"Is that why you didn't?"

She stared at him through the falling rain. She had said too much, had allowed this conversation to become too explicit, too personal. Turning on her heel, she began to walk along the bank of the canal toward the bridge, the grass wet and cold beneath her bare feet.

"Goddamn it, Emmanuelle," he yelled after her. "If it mattered so little to you, then why the hell did you go at him with a scalpel?"

That stopped her, as he'd surely known it would. She turned slowly this time, her voice kept steady with an effort. "I was angry," she said, then added, "besides, I didn't exactly go after him with it."

She watched, perplexed, as a shadow of amusement deepened the rugged slashes that bracketed his mouth. She wondered if he even realized he'd called her by her first name, and decided he didn't. "What did you do?" he said. "Exactly?"

In spite of herself, in spite of everything, she found herself almost smiling back at him through the driving rain. "I waved the blade in front of him and expressed a desire to cut off a certain relevant portion of his anatomy."

He walked right up to her, the smile fading from his face to be replaced by an intense, probing expression. "Did you know someone informed on Philippe last May? Betrayed his mission?"

She felt a chill run down her spine, steal her breath. "I didn't know for certain," she said, her gaze locking with his, "but I suspected it. It seemed too much a co-incidence, what happened." She paused, trying to read his face, trying to understand this man and what he thought of her. "Are you going to accuse me of that, as well?"

He shook his head. "The scalpel is more your style." He squinted up at the roiling clouds above. Rain ran down his cheeks, turned the dark blue of his uniform to black. "Now, will you get in the carriage?"

"No."

He let out his breath in a puff of exasperation and turned away from her. She thought he would leave her then, leave her to the rain and the dangerous darkness and all the demons of the night, but he swung around again, one hand gripping the hilt of his sword, the other slashing through the rain-filled night between them in a gesture of anger and impatience. "Don't you understand what's happening here?" he demanded, leaning into her. "One by one, the people associated with the Hospital de Santerre are being killed—first Philippe, then Henri Santerre, and now Claire La Touche. That only leaves you and Yardley—unless whoever's doing this plans to start on the nurses, too, in which case Hans Spears and Rudolph and all the others are in danger, as well."

A silence opened up between them, a silence filled with the battering rhythm of the rain and the pounding of her own heart. "I live with the threat of death every day," she said slowly. "Every time I treat a patient who has typhus, or yellow fever, or even the influenza, there's a chance I could sicken from it."

He stared at her, his jaw set, his nostrils flaring as he sucked in a quick breath. "I never questioned your courage. Just your sense."

If Emmanuelle had one vanity, it was her sense—her mind, her intelligence. When the men of her world tried to justify all the laws and customs that kept women un-educated, that curtailed their ability to control their own property, that denied them the right to vote and gave a man the power to beat his wife, it was the sup-posed weakness of the female mind even more than the weakness of the female body that was used as an ex-cuse. Anger flared within her, hot and bright. Blinded by rain and wet hair and rage, she whirled away from him. But she was far closer to the edge of the canal than she'd realized, and the grass beneath her bare feet was slippery with rain and mud. As she came down on it, her right foot shot out from under her, lurching her sideways. She threw out her arms to catch her balance, and one of her shoes went flying through the air like a missile to land far down the steep grassy bank, almost at the water's edge.

"*Mon Dieu,*" she said, twisting around to stare at it as Zach Cooper leaped forward to grab her by the shoulders and keep her from slipping any farther. "My shoe."

His hands ran down her arms to tighten and lift her up, swinging her around to set her higher up the bank. "Stay here," he said, letting her go. "I'll get it."

"No." She touched his arm, stopping him as he turned away. "It's not worth it. You might fall in."

He looked back at her over his shoulder, the creases in his cheeks deepening into a devil-dark smile. "It's not that deep. I can swim, you know."

The wind gusted around them, whipped at the frayed ribbons of her widow's bonnet, snatched at the ends of his officer's cape. "I'm not worried about you drowning, Major." She had to shout to be heard above the roar of the wind, and the rain, and the runoff shooting into the canal. "I am worried about what would be in that water with you. You are familiar with the theory of animalcules, aren't you?"

"Of course I am."

She blinked the water out of her eyes. "Then you understand why you don't want to go swimming in that canal. It's a cesspool of filth and disease. And your wound is still open."

"I won't fall in," he said, and moved away from her.

She stood on the top of the bank, her remaining boot clutched to her chest, and watched as he worked his way down the slope, toward the water's edge. He slipped once, his long, lean body jackknifing sideways as he caught himself on his outflung hand, and she bit her lip. For all his casual talk, he was being careful; she could tell by the way he kept eyeing the water sweeping past, foul with sewage from the city's drains and all the refuse washed into the canal by the storm.

He had reached the water now. He was leaning forward, his hand closing over the heel of her ankle boot, when she saw an uprooted elderberry sapling that had been caught up in the runoff and was now hurtling down the canal. She shouted a warning that was lost in the howl of the wind and the roar of the rain. In the grip of an eddy, the sapling spun around, its outflung branches sweeping the bank to knock the major's legs from beneath him and pitch him headfirst into the canal with a splash that sent water flying up into the air. When it cleared, all she could see was his officer's hat with its crossed golden sabers and cocky ostrich feathers swirling away on the crest of a thick, yellow-brown wave.

CHAPTER SEVENTEEN

The canal was not deep. The major's head disappeared for but an instant, then he shot out of the water, streaming mud and curses.

"*Mon Dieu.*" Emmanuelle scrambled down the bank toward him as he slogged out of the canal and up onto the bank, his boot heels making sucking noises in the mud.

"Be careful," he said, hacking and spitting as if he'd swallowed some of the canal, which he probably had. "Because if you go in, I'm not going in again after you."

She slid to a halt beside him, then took a quick step back. Foul-smelling water dripped off the ends of his dark hair and ran in little rivulets from the hem of his coat. Leaning over, he tried to squeeze out the limp bullion fringe of his sash, lifted his saber on its hook, and swore again.

"You lost your hat," she said, one hand pressed against her lips to hold back the laughter that bubbled inside of her, threatening to erupt.

His head came up. Slowly, he straightened. Lightning flashed, showing her a face so streaked with mud, the whites of his eyes seemed to glow. Then he thrust one slime-coated arm aloft as if in mock triumph, and she saw he still held her muddy ankle boot gripped tight.

"But I have your shoe," he said, and she could control herself no longer.

Laughter gurgled up, warm and wonderful, and she let it come, great ungenteel whoops that mingled with his own rich, deep laughter. She laughed so hard, she had to wrap one arm around her stomach to keep it from hurting, and still she laughed. Then their gazes caught and held, and the laughter quieted as lips parted, and breath hitched.

"Now, will you get in the hack?" he said, his gaze still locked with hers.

She got in the hack.

The door to the bathing room was unlatched, so that it rocked gently on its hinges when she knocked at it some three quarters of an hour later. "Monsieur?" she called, balancing the tray she held on one hip. She'd shown him here, to the room beside Philippe's bedroom, then gone away to get out of her own wet dress, and look in on Dominic, and gather what she needed to rebandage the major's side.

"You can come in," he said, and she pushed open the door to find him standing beside the sink, his sword in his hand. He was naked except for the white swath of the towel he had wrapped around his hips, his bare back and shoulders still gleaming with moisture from the shower. He looked up when she entered, and something leaped in his eyes at the sight of her, something that made her wish she had taken the time to put up her hair again and change into something more proper than a thin summer peignoir.

He eased his saber back into its scabbard, his gaze following her as she went to set the tray on the small painted chest of drawers beside the sink. "Nice room," he said, nodding toward the walls of floor-to-ceiling glazed Portuguese tiles, the deep copper tub, the innovative upright copper and oilcloth shower.

"Philippe had it put in." She picked up the small pad of cloth she'd brought, and soaked it with carbolic acid. Some of the liquid spilled from the dark glass bottle onto the tray, and she realized her hands were shaking. She put the bottle down with a clatter. "You can sit there," she said, nodding toward the high, padded, benchlike table that stood in the center of the room.

"What's it for, exactly?" he said, balancing his hips on the edge.

"Massages."

He looked up at her, his eyes narrowing. "Philippe was somewhat of a hedonist, I take it."

"There were a few of the seven deadly sins he didn't indulge in," she said, bending over his wound. "But not many." The knife slash looked surprisingly healthy, she thought, and had healed far more than she would have expected, in just a few days. "You're lucky you didn't pull out your stitches," she said, laying the pad against the wound. "And you'll be luckier still if this wound doesn't putrefy."

He sucked in a quick, startled breath that shivered the smooth, warm flesh beneath her hand. "Jesus Christ. What is that stuff?"

"An aseptic," she said casually, although it was, in truth, a radical theory, the idea that this acid could kill animalcules and prevent sepsis.

"It feels like you poured raw turpentine on me."

"It has much the same effect. I also want to put a dressing of marshmallow on it." She started to turn away, then paused, swinging back to meet his hard, inquiring glaze. "There's something you should perhaps know, monsieur," she said quickly, before she could change her mind.

"What's that?"

"Someone was in my house last night. I don't know who. I heard a strange sound, and when I went to investigate, I found the front door unbolted."

He sat very still. "You're certain it hadn't been left unlocked?"

She shook her head. "I've been very careful to lock everything since . . . since this all began. Rose has thrown out everything in the kitchen. She thinks someone was trying to poison us."

"You don't?"

"No."

"You don't have any idea who it could have been?"

"No." She went to prepare the dressing for his wound. "Do you believe me?" she asked, her back to him.

"Tell me what happened last spring," he said quietly. "The argument between Claire and Philippe and Yardley."

She turned slowly, the dressing held half-forgotten in her hand, and stared at him.

"Tell me," he said again, his gaze locked with hers, his eyes dark and compelling.

"All right." She went to apply the dressing against his wound, her head bent over her task, his darkly naked leg lying close against her side. She couldn't look at him and say these things to him. "There's a small room at the back of the hospital, beyond the kitchen, where we perform our dissections. I was there, studying the musculature of an upper arm, when I heard them shouting."

"Claire and Yardley?"

"Yes. Hold this," she said. His hand came down over hers. She was aware of the calloused strength of his touch, the warmth of his flesh. Then she eased her fingers away and reached for the roll of bandages. "I didn't pay much attention at first, but they were in Henri's office, and with the windows to the courtyard open, anyone could have heard them." She eased the roll of bandaging around his side, soft white gauze against hard male flesh. "I went to warn them."

"With the scalpel still in your hand?"

"Yes." She glanced up to find his fierce, questioning eyes upon her, then looked away. "But not intentionally." Slowly, she brought the bandage around his leanly muscled ribs a second time. Rain filled the silence of the night around them. The candle flickered, casting golden light and warm shadows over the tiled walls. "Until I got closer I didn't even realize what they were talking about."

"Did you know about Claire before that?" he asked, lifting his arm as she came around his side.

"I didn't know she was involved with Philippe, if that's what you mean. But I knew the way she was with men, yes. She'd had a series of affairs, much as a man might do. All deliberately brief, casual. I'm sure when she began it, she expected her interlude with Philippe to be the same."

"Only it wasn't?"

"No. She fell in love with him." Emmanuelle tied off the bandage and took a step back, her gaze meeting his as she straightened. Thunder rumbled in the distance, a long building crescendo of violence underscored by the pounding of the rain. She wondered when it had happened, when they had reached such a level of intimacy that they could speak so freely of such things, of love and passion between men and women. That she could move so naturally around him, with her hair drying into a tumble of soft, loose curls down her back and the candlelight gleaming warm and golden on his naked flesh.

"You didn't hold that against her?"

"That she loved him?" Emmanuelle sucked in a quick breath that shuddered her chest and startled her, for she hadn't expected it all to still hurt so badly. "How could I?" she said, her lips twisting into an ironic smile. "After all, I fell in love with Philippe myself, when I was her age."

"But you didn't like her sleeping with him."

"No." Her chest burned, her throat closing with emotion, and she turned away to busy herself with tidying the tray and putting the lid back on the jar of salve. "No, I didn't."

His voice came to her, low but insistent. "Why exactly was she arguing with Yardley?"

Emmanuelle stood very still, her back to him, the salve jar gripped in tight panic between her hands. One by one, he was stripping away all the lies she'd lived for so many years, exposing her, leaving her vulnerable. But some secrets were too dangerous to be uncovered, especially to a man who was, she had to keep reminding herself, the provost marshal of a vengeful, conquering army. "He and Philippe were close friends," she said, keeping her voice even. She'd always been so good at it, appearing calm and in control, even when inside she was screaming with fear. "They had similar . . . tastes. Claire had somehow discovered they'd gone together to a certain house on Old Levee Street." She paused, hoping she hadn't said too much. "Have you heard of it?"

"I've heard of it," he said, and from the harshness in his voice, she knew he had.

Her hand was hurting. Looking down, she realized

she'd gripped the jar so tightly, the edge of the lid had
dug deep into her palm. Setting the jar aside, she went
to the sink to wash the salve from her hands. She had
to do something, anything that would occupy her, that
would keep her from having to look at him. "The problem was," she said over her shoulder, "Claire hadn't
only fallen in love with Philippe, she'd also made the
mistake of believing that he was in love with her, that
he was faithful to her. When she found out about his
visit to that house . . . well, she blamed Yardley. I suppose it was easier to blame Yardley than to blame
Philippe."

She was aware of him, quietly listening, behind her,
aware of the softening rhythm of the rain and the
warmth of the night and the raw intimacy of the things
she was telling him, things she had never spoken of to
anyone else.

"When did Philippe move out here, to the *garçonnière?*" he asked.

Emmanuelle leaned against the edge of the sink. It
was becoming more and more of an effort to hide her
feelings, to maintain her usual facade of composure
and sangfroid, but she kept trying. "That was long ago.
Long before Claire. It's been ten—no, eleven—years
now." How could she forget? Dominic was eleven.
"That's when I first discovered Philippe was"—she
swallowed hard—"unfaithful to me."

"It must have hurt."

She turned to face him, surprised by his words, by
the gentleness with which they had been said. "It did.
At first, I actually thought I could change him." She
tried to laugh, but it came out sounding all wrong.
"Then I realized that he would never change, that he
didn't love me enough to change." She was painfully

aware of the tightness in her throat, the huskiness of her voice. "And that hurt more than anything."

"So why go at him with a scalpel after eleven years of knowing he wasn't faithful?"

She pushed away from the sink. "I suppose I lost my temper. Philippe and I had an agreement, of sorts. He was free to do as he wished, as long as he left me alone, and as long as he was discreet."

"I guess he wasn't exactly being discreet anymore."

"No." She went to stand before him, her head held high, her gaze locked with his, challenging him, daring him to mock her, to look down on her. "You're shocked, aren't you? That I would make such a devil's bargain?"

He straightened slowly. In the flickering gaslight, his face looked hard, unreadable. "You could have divorced him. It might not be respectable, but sometimes it's the only way."

She shook her head. "Not for me."

"Because you're a Catholic?"

"Because I would have lost Dominic. You know what the law says: Children belong to their father. They would have taken him, the de Beauvais family. I would put up with anything, do anything, to keep my son." She paused, realizing the implications of what she had just said. "I suppose it's true, isn't it, what they say? That if you go digging for secrets in anyone's life, you're bound to find some." She sucked in a quick breath. "And now you think it gives me a motive, don't you? For killing Claire?"

"Yes."

A gust of wind blew up, rattling the branches of the sweet olives and banana trees in the courtyard below and setting the door to rocking slowly back and forth on its creaking hinges. She went to close it, then simply stood there instead, her hand gripping the edge of the panel, her gaze on the rain sluicing off the edge of the gallery roof. "I was angry with Claire, at first," she said after a moment, "but I couldn't really blame her. She was so very young, just eighteen. And she knew the truth about how Philippe and I lived—Antoine had let it slip to her once, when he was drinking. She thought I wouldn't care."

"But you did?"

She shrugged. "Not as much as I perhaps should have. Certainly not enough to kill her, or Philippe." She looked at him over her shoulder. "That's what you're thinking, isn't it? That I was the one who informed on Philippe? That I arranged to have him killed, and then poisoned Claire myself?"

"It would fit rather neatly, if it weren't for Henri Santerre."

She swung to face him again, one hand creeping up to curl around her bare neck. "Perhaps I had another reason for killing Henri. A reason you haven't discovered yet."

He came toward her, his gaze hard on her face, his body tall and leanly muscled and naked except for the towel riding low on his hips. Even without his uniform, she thought, you could tell he was a fighter, as fierce and dangerous as any savage or warrior of old. "And how did you get the crossbow into the cemetery that night?" he asked, leaning into her, a hint of amusement deepening the creases that bracketed his mouth. "I've heard of Southern ladies hiding silver spoons under their hoops, but somehow I think a crossbow would be rather awkward."

"I could have hidden it somewhere among the tombs, earlier."

"You could have. But why bother? Why not simply poison Henri, too? Or stab him. That would have been easy, for you. You'd know right where to slip your blade."

"If it comes to that," she said, searching his face, "why not simply stab Philippe? I mean, if I were willing and able to kill Henri and Claire, why not kill Philippe myself, as well?"

He surprised her by bringing up his hand to smooth her loose hair from her face with a gentle touch. "He's the reason you never went back to Paris to become a doctor, isn't he?"

His voice was as gentle as his touch, disconcerting her, unnerving her. "Yes," she said, her own voice uncharacteristically shaky. He still had his hand in her hair, the heel of his palm lying warm against her cheek. "My whole life, I dreamed of nothing but becoming a doctor. Then I met Philippe and I could think of nothing but him." A sad smile tugged at her lips. "I couldn't imagine a future that didn't include him."

"And so you gave it all up." He had both his hands in her hair now, lifting it up, letting it cascade through his fingers. He was so close, she could feel the heat of his body, feel the tight wanting that seemed to thrum through him. Through them both. "You gave up everything you'd ever dreamed of, for him. Yet he gave up nothing for you. Nothing."

"Another reason for me to kill him, hmm?" Her gaze locked with his, and the silence between them stretched out, filled with the patter of the rain and the flicker of the lamp and a breathless kind of waiting. Reaching up, she wrapped her fingers around his wrist and brought it down until the knuckles of his hand brushed her right breast through the thin cloth of her peignoir, and a soft sigh escaped her lips. "Tell me, monsieur," she said, her voice a throaty whisper, her gaze still held fast with his, "how can you think me capable of murder, and still want me? Still want me the way a man wants a woman?"

He shifted his hand so that his palm cupped her breast, and the wonder of it, the joy of his touch, was such that she shuddered. "I don't know," he said, his breath warm against her face, his eyes fierce, glittering. "But I do."

She was exquisitely aware of the pounding of her heart, the soughing of her breath in and out. He held her gaze a moment longer, waiting for her to move away from him, waiting for her to stop what was about to happen. When she didn't, he dipped his head, one hand still warm and possessive over her breast, the other coming up to tangle in her hair, his fingers clenching, pulling her up to him as he took her mouth with his.

His kiss was raw and naked in its power, full of hunger and heat and the wild, sharp edge of the forbidden. Her hands flattened against the warm flesh of his naked chest, then slipped up around his neck to drag his head down to her and draw her body hard against the length of him. And still she couldn't seem to get close enough to him.

Squirming, she brought up one leg to wrap around him, and he caught it, his hand sliding along her thigh, slipping beneath the thin cloth of her peignoir with a touch that stole her breath and left her gasping with want. She leaned into him, twirled her tongue with his, sucked his lip between her teeth, and heard him growl, a low animal sound of want that rumbled in his chest.

His hands were everywhere, pushing aside the edges of her peignoir, cupping and kneading her bare breasts, gripping the swell of her hip, stroking her flesh with fire. She was breathless with an aching need, intoxicated by the touch of his hands and the taste of his kisses and the scent of his hard man's body. She wanted to know the weight of him, bearing her down beneath him. She wanted to look up and see him looming over her, his dark face drawn and intense with a man's purpose as he took her, as he filled all the empty, wanting places so deep within her. And so great was her desire, so powerful her need, that a wild kind of fear pulsed through her, sharp and violent enough that she somehow, somehow found the strength to tear her mouth from his.

He raised his head to stare down at her, his chest lifting and falling with the hard, rapid breathing of arousal, his hands coming to rest on her hips. "You're thinking this was a mistake," he said, his voice a hoarse rasp of desire.

"You know it was," she said, her own breath coming so hard and fast, she was shuddering with it.

He reached up, a strange, bittersweet smile twisting his lips as he laid his palm against her cheek. "You're probably right. But I didn't think you always played by the rules." He moved his hand, turning the touch into a caress. And she let him, because it felt so wonderful, and she needed his touch so very badly.

"There are clothes of Philippe's in the bureau in his room, through the side door there," she said, taking a step away from him, then another, away from his dangerous touch and the seductive nearness of his powerful man's body. "You're welcome to anything you need."

The gentle breeze of the dying storm caught at the edges of her wrapper, fluttering it open, so that she had to clutch it to her with clenching fists. She saw the blaze of desire in his eyes, saw his nostrils flare with intent. "Emmanuelle," he said, starting forward.

But she was already running, her bare feet sliding on the wet floorboards of the gallery, the wind streaming her loose hair out behind her.

Zach stood in the open doorway. The mist from the rain felt cool against his hot bare skin, and he drew the storm-cleansed air deep into his lungs. His body still pulsed with need and want and a primitive, instinctively predatory male urge to go after her, to bear her down beneath his hard body and simply take her, the way he knew she wanted to be taken. Instead, he let out his breath in a long, painful sigh, and turned his back on the night.

The two rooms on this level of the *garçonnière* had been linked by an interconnecting door. Taking the bathing room's simple oil lamp in one hand, he went to turn the other door's glass handle and push it open. Philippe de Beauvais had been dead only a few months, and already his room had an air of musty disuse, the distinctive scents of tobacco and leather grown faint and mingling now with the smell of dust.

The room was small and architecturally plain, with wide cypress floorboards covered for the summer with a simple straw mat, and a small fireplace with an inexpensive wooden mantel. In another household, these rooms would have been used by slaves, or growing sons. But here, Philippe had created a world of restrained elegance, filling the room with a fine cedar sleigh bed and tall bookcases stuffed with leatherbound volumes. Tasteful oil paintings in ornately carved and gilded frames adorned the simple whitewashed walls, and a crystal brandy decanter rested on an inlaid, Regency-style table near the window. In the near left corner stood a tall cedar armoire, and it was to this that Zach went, turning the key and opening the doors.

There were no clothes here. The unmistakable scent of hashish wafted toward him, mingled with the muskiness of vetiver and the sweet tang of opium. On an open shelf nearly level with Zach's gaze rested a trio of shrunken human heads from the Pacific Islands, their hair long and black and tangled, their features compressed forever into horrific grimaces. Beside them lay a whip with a lewdly painted handle and leather thongs that looked well-worn, as did the neatly coiled length of red silk cord beneath it. It didn't take much imagination to know what they were used for. What Philippe had used them for.

Zach took a step back, his gaze scanning the shelves before him. Here was a collection that reminded him, in some way, of what he'd seen in Papa John's bayou hut, except that most of these objects had no medicinal value, had been amassed purely for their ability to amuse or to shock, or arouse, if one were so inclined. He glanced over his shoulder at the tall bureau that stood on the far side of the empty fireplace, and knew a fierce urge simply to shut the doors on this armoire and its terrible secrets. He knew she had not intended him to see these things, didn't want him to know these truths about the man to whom she had been married for twelve years. Outside, the wind had almost died, the rain reduced to a gentle patter. After the fury of the storm, the comparative silence seemed eerie, almost unnatural, the room full of flickering shadows and the insistent memories of murdered men.

Systematically, Zach began to search the armoire's contents, his jaw set hard. He wasn't certain exactly what he was looking for, but it wasn't long before he

found it, anyway. On the last shelf, near a quarto con-
taining photographs of nude young girls, rested a rectangular oak box bound with brass and hinged on one
side.

Slowly, he drew the box toward him, releasing the
latches and swinging the case open to reveal a vampire-
killing kit, furnished with a vial of holy water, a large
cross, a pointed wooden stake, and a small crossbow.
Once, the kit had contained four silver-headed bolts,
each nestled in its own niche.

Now there were only three.

CHAPTER
EIGHTEEN

The rain was falling in a gentle, fragrant mist when Zach let himself out the front door of the house on Dumaine and stood, for a moment, on the brick banquette beneath the overhanging front gallery.

The black suit, white linen shirt, and black tie he wore had once belonged to Philippe de Beauvais, as had the low black boots and expensive beaver hat. Zach found it vaguely disconcerting to realize that they had been of much the same size, he and the man who had collected those headhunters' trophies and photographs of nude prepubescent girls and vampire-killing tools. The man who had been Emmanuelle's husband. Under his arm, Zach carried his own wet uniform wrapped in an oil tarp, along with a rectangular, brass-bound oak box.

He wondered how much she knew about her husband's bizarre interests, about the contents of that armoire. And then he decided she must have known it all, for she'd told him she'd gone looking for the crossbow after Santerre's murder. She said she'd found it missing.

He stepped off the banquette, stepped wide to avoid the still-rushing gutter. The rain fell about him in a soft whisper lit by the flicker of the gas streetlamps. He had to resist the urge to look up, to see if she watched him from her room.

For one, gut-wrenching moment, back there in the *garçonnière,* with Henri Santerre's murder weapon in his hands, Zach had actually believed she'd lied to him, believed that his earlier suspicions of her had been well-founded, believed that he, himself, had let his growing desire for this woman cloud his judgment. He knew she could lie, knew she had lied to him, over and over again. But then he'd realized that if she'd known the crossbow was there, she never would have left him, alone, in that room. And he'd remembered, too, what she'd told him, about finding her door unbolted in the night, and he knew that whoever had taken the cross-bow and used it, had now put it back. It made him feel both furious and coldly afraid to think of someone slipping undetected through the rooms of her house, someone capable of murder. And it disturbed him, too, to realize that if he had ordered a search of the house and found that box with its damningly, incriminatingly missing bolt, he might very well have believed her implicated. He might even have ordered her hanged, if he hadn't believed her pleas of innocence. If he hadn't wanted to believe her innocent.

He'd reached the far side of the street now. Just for a moment he allowed himself to glance over his shoulder at the high, fern-draped, wrought-iron balcony where he supposed her room must lie. He felt a painful pressure building in his chest and tried to expel it with a sharp exhalation of breath. It was all wrong, what almost happened between them tonight. She was a woman only recently widowed, a woman fiercely loyal to a nation he had vowed to destroy, a woman deeply implicated in a baffling series of murders he was supposed to be investigating. Yet knowing it was wrong didn't stop the heat of his wanting, didn't stop him from wondering what would have happened if he hadn't let her go so easily tonight, what would have happened if he had followed her to that room where the lace curtains moved gently as if touched by an unseen hand in the darkness of the night.

The big New Yorker turned the crossbow over in his hands, his bushy eyebrows drawing together into a deep frown. "And did you ask her what this nasty little piece of work was doing back in her husband's room, after she told us it'd disappeared?"

Zach stood at the window of his office at headquarters and watched as a young quadroon boy went about setting up a watermelon stand on the sidewalk outside. The morning had dawned clean and sweet. For once the rain seemed to have brought some relief from the oppressive heat of summer bearing down on the city. "Not yet," he said.

Hamish squinted down at the ornate inlay decorating the bow's wooden stock. "I suppose you had your reasons for waiting."

Zach kept his attention fixed on the boy with the watermelons. "Yeah." If he'd followed Emmanuelle de Beauvais to her room last night, it wouldn't have been to talk about miniature crossbows, but he wasn't about to tell Hamish that.

"What you think it means, this expensive little toy turning up again?"

Zach shrugged. "It means that whoever did the killing is looking to pin the blame for it on Emmanuelle de Beauvais."

"Maybe. But then, she's a clever lady, that little Frenchie widow. Maybe she left you alone in that room deliberately, hoping you'd stumble across this wee bow by accident, and knowing you'd be predisposed by the inclinations of your prick to believe it was planted there by someone else. And you can glare at me all you want," Hamish added as Zach swung around to fix his friend with a hard stare. "But that prick of yours is seriously compromising this investigation, and you know it."

"I'm not sleeping with her," said Zach, lifting the crossbow from Hamish's slack grasp.

"No. But you want to. You can't deny you want to."

Zach settled the bow in its velvet-lined box and closed the lid. "I'm going to church," he said, tucking the box in a canvas haversack.

Hamish gave him a blank stare. "Church?"

"Church," Zach said, and left him staring, beagle-eyed and perplexed.

It was a surprisingly large church, the German community's Catholic church of St. Mary's Assumption. Built of brick in a vaguely Gothic style, it had high, mostly clear-paned arched windows interspersed here and there with a few of stained glass. It wasn't until he neared the shallow front steps that Zach could see signs of construction still under way, the pile of sweetly scented new lumber beside the open door, the sound of hammering echoing through the vaulted interior.

He paused just inside the big front doors and breathed in the familiar scents of incense and beeswax. The nave was striking in its simplicity, the walls white-washed and adorned with little more than a series of terra-cotta plaques depicting the stations of the cross. Up near the altar, a man was working at erecting a beautifully turned wooden railing—a tall, thin young man with a shock of light brown hair that tumbled over his forehead when he looked up at the sound of Zach's footsteps. For one tense moment, the young German stared down the length of the nave, his hand tightening around his hammer. Then he straightened. *"Guten Tag,"* he said, and tossed the hammer into the box near his foot.

Zach walked slowly up the central aisle, his gaze hard on the other man's face. "You work here when you're not at the hospital?"

"This is not work," said Spears, swiping one bare arm across his sweaty forehead. He wore neither coat nor vest, only simple trousers and a collarless shirt rolled up at the sleeves. "This I do for God." He drew his hand in a wide arc, taking in the soaring ceiling and delicate apse. "We built this church, all of us, together. My mother and the other women carried the bricks in their aprons. Even the little children helped, the smallest carrying but one brick at a time."

Zach gazed down at the intricately pieced railing the man had been setting in place. "You're a skilled carpenter. I should think you'd find this sort of thing more profitable than working as a nurse at the Hospital de Santerre."

Spears ran his hand along the smooth finish of the top rail in an almost sensual gesture. "I build with wood for joy, and for the love of God," he said, his voice echoing in the hushed atmosphere of the empty church. "But this will not be my life's work." He half-limped, half-hopped over to lift his vest and coat from where he'd tossed them on the edge of the altar steps. "My mother is a widow with four sons, Major. She could afford to educate only the eldest of us, my brother Bertrand. But Bertrand has paid to educate Carl, and when the medical schools open up again after the war, Carl will pay my fees. Then I, in turn, will pay for Joseph."

"You want to be a doctor," said Zach, wondering why the realization surprised him so.

The young man gave a snort and turned his back to thrust his arms through the sleeve holes of his vest. "I will be a doctor. I've already learned much, working at the hospital. And I study on my own. Not just with books, but with those who know things the medical schools don't teach."

"You mean people like Papa John?"

"Yes, Papa John." He gave the cuffs of his coat an unexpectedly fastidious twitch. "Why?"

Zach opened the flap of the haversack he carried over his shoulder and drew out the brass-bound oak box. "Have you ever seen this before?"

Spears swung about slowly, his gaze lifting from the box to Zach's face. "Yes."

Zach found the other man's honesty almost disconcerting. "When?"

Walking with one hand on the screen for support, the German reached out to take the box from Zach's hands and crouched down to set it on the altar steps. "Philippe showed it to me last spring," he said, releasing the catches on the side. "I have a crossbow I built myself, years ago, before we left Bavaria. Of course, it is not so small as this one. But he knew I was interested." He eased open the halves of the box to lay it flat, and stared at it for a moment in silence, his gaze caught by the slot for the missing bolt.

"So you know how to use one?" said Zach.

"Oh, yes." The young German's chest lifted visibly on a deeply indrawn breath as his head fell back, his gaze hard and intense when he looked up at Zach. "But I did not kill Henri Santerre."

"Who else do you know who's familiar with crossbows?"

Spears let out a short, sharp laugh. "What is this? My opportunity to incriminate someone else, and get myself off the hook? You don't think much of me, do you, Major?"

"I don't know you," said Zach simply, wrapping his hands around the railing and leaning into it. "What about Philippe? Could he use it?"

"Of course. We went hunting together once, he and I, on the Bayou Crevé. He took this bow along and tried it out. It is surprisingly accurate, and cunningly made so that it is easy to string. A child could use it."

"Or a woman."

A flicker of some emotion showed in the other man's eyes, only to be hidden by carefully lowered lashes. "I suppose so."

"How about Antoine La Touche? Did he share de Beauvais's interest in crossbows?"

"The gift was from him, wasn't it?"

Zach smiled. "Was it? I didn't know that."

A muscle leaped along the German's tightened jaw. He dropped his gaze to the box and closed it with swift, sure motions, the snap of the clasps sounding abnormally loud in the stillness of the church. "Anyone could have used it."

"With such accuracy? I doubt it." Zach took the box as the other man held it out silently. "How about Dr. Yardley? Is he familiar with crossbows?"

"I wouldn't know," said the German, stumbling as he rose, trying to keep all of his weight on his one good foot. "I do not know him well."

"But you knew Philippe de Beauvais well?"

Spears reached for his crutch where it rested at an angle against the railing. "Philippe was more than a good doctor; he was a born teacher. He knew it was my intention to attend medical school, and he went out of his way to help me."

It didn't quite fit the image Zach had been building

of the brilliant, dissolute, and self-obsessed man who had been Philippe de Beauvais. "Is that why you went with him that night? The night he was killed?"

Spears hooked the crutch under his arm and rested his weight on it with a small sigh. "He needed someone he could trust. He trusted me."

"Who else went with you?"

He looked up and tossed his head to shake the hair back out of his eyes. "A black man named Bubba. He was killed, along with Philippe."

"No one else?"

"No."

"Did you know the mission was betrayed?"

Balancing carefully on his crutch, Spears reached down to grasp the handle of his toolbox. He straightened slowly, his back taut. It was a moment before he spoke. "No, I didn't know. But Philippe thought so. He said as much, after he was shot."

"I was told he died instantly."

"You should know how few men are lucky enough to die instantly, Major," said Spears, swinging about on his crutch. "Even when they are shot in the head."

Zach fell into step beside him as he moved slowly toward the open doors. "What exactly did Philippe say, after he was shot?"

Spears paused for a moment, his high forehead crinkling in thought. "I think he said, 'the bitch.' Yes, that was it, 'the bitch.' He said, 'She gave the game away. She wanted to see me dead, and she always gets what she wants.'"

"And then he died?"

"Soon after."

"You saw him die?"

The tip of the crutch tap-tapped on the bare floorboards as Spears limped up the aisle toward the sunlight. "Yes."

"Do you have any idea who he was talking about?"

The German shook his head, his jaw clenched noticeably tight. "No."

"Do you think he could have been talking about Claire La Touche?"

"I don't know."

"How about his wife?"

"Emmanuelle de Beauvais?" Spears stopped just inside the open double doors, his eyes squinting as he gazed out into the fierce morning light. "No, she would never have done such a thing."

Zach paused beside him. "How can you be so certain?"

Spears swung his head to look at Zach over his shoulder. "It wasn't only Philippe who died that day. Bubba was killed, too. He might have been black, but he was still her friend. And even if he hadn't been, she would never deliberately be the death of any man."

In the street outside, a boy ran past, guiding a hoop with a stick. "She went at Philippe with a scalpel, didn't she?" said Zach.

Spears surprised him by laughing, his head falling back as he stepped outside and stared consideringly up at the clear blue sky. "Ya. She did. But it was his manhood she was threatening, not his life."

"Because of Claire?"

The German dropped his gaze to Zach's face. "Is that what she told you?"

Zach knew a moment of deep disquiet. "Was there another reason?"

Spears shrugged and moved forward to hop

awkwardly down the first step. "What other reason could there be?"

Zach lifted the toolbox from the other man's grasp and carried it until they'd reached the plank sidewalk.

"*Danke schön,*" said Spears, a fierce light glittering in his eyes as he reached to take back the box, although whether his anger was with Zach, or himself, or the injury that had claimed his foot, Zach couldn't have said. The German started to turn away, then paused, his features settling into thoughtful lines as he looked back at Zach. "We have a word in German, *Leidenschaft,*" he said, all trace of his earlier anger now gone. "I think of it sometimes when I watch Emmanuelle de Beauvais. It means passion, ardor."

"And suffering," Zach said quietly.

Spears's eyes widened in surprise. "You speak German?"

Zach shook his head. "I've read Goethe."

"Peculiar reading, surely, for a cavalryman?"

"No more peculiar than carpentry as a hobby for a doctor."

The other man's face broke into a spontaneous smile of pure, delighted amusement. "You're right, of course. We all have our prejudices and preconceptions, don't we, Major?"

The boy sitting in the neat little shay waiting in front of the house on the rue Dumaine didn't see Zach when he first rode up.

Dominic had his head tipped back, his eyes squinting against the brightness of the noonday sun, the reins slack in his hands, when Zach said, "That horse is going to eat those basil plants right off Mrs. Angelo's doorstep, if you're not careful."

The boy's head whipped around, his jaw going slack

with surprise, his narrow chest hitching on a quickly indrawn breath as Zach nudged his big bay cavalry mount in beside the shay. He saw the boy throw a quick glance sideways, toward the banquette, as if he were thinking of making a run for it. But then the neat little black mare between the traces threw up her head, and he was too busy collecting the reins to think about getting away.

"How do you know her name is Mrs. Angelo?" he asked when he was able, fixing Zach with a wide, intensely blue stare.

"The same way I know your name is Dominic de Beauvais."

Dominic swallowed. "You here to talk to my *maman*?"

"Yes," said Zach, shifting the weight of the haversack he wore slung across his shoulder. "But not about you." He cast a glance over the back of the shay, which was loaded with a picnic rug and fishing rods and crab nets.

"We're going out to the lake, crabbing," said Dominic warily. Belligerently. "That's not against your Yankee laws, is it?"

Zach smiled. "Not that I know of. We used to go after lobsters when I was your age. We'd catch them in pots."

"Pots?" repeated the boy, interested in spite of himself. "How can you catch lobsters in pots?" His nose crinkled in disbelief. "You're making that up, aren't you?"

The door opened, and Emmanuelle came out. She was fussing with something she carried in her arms, so that she didn't see Zach until she had walked around to settle it in the back of the shay. "*Alors*, Dominic, I've looked but I can't find it anywhere—"

She broke off, the color draining from her cheeks as her head fell back and she stared up at Zach. She had the most exquisite face, built wide at the cheekbones, with a delicate chin and a full, generous mouth that whispered of passion and sin and lies. Lies. "We were just leaving, monsieur," she said in that low, husky voice of hers.

Zach rested one forearm on his pommel and leaned into it. "I'm afraid I need to talk to you about something. Something important."

"Now?" said Dominic with a wail, all fear of Zach and his uniform temporarily forgotten. "But we're already late. If we don't leave now—"

"Dominic," said his mother in a low, warning voice. She glanced back up at Zach. "Can't it wait, monsieur? I've been promising him this for weeks."

"No, I'm afraid it can't. But I don't mind riding out to the lake. We can talk while your boy here goes fishing."

She held his gaze, her eyes deep and dark. He had come here to confront her with the damning evidence of that brass-bound box, to force her to tell him the truth, to shake it out of her if he had to. Yet when he looked into her eyes, all he could think about was the sweet, hot taste of her lips and the intoxicating smoothness of her bare skin and the way she whimpered when he cupped the swell of her breast in his hand.

"Eh bien," she said after a moment, the breath easing out of her in a long sigh that told him that she, too, had been thinking about last night, and all that had happened. All that hadn't happened. "If you wish. I'll get the picnic hamper."

Striding into the cool, shadowy entrance of the flagged passageway, Emmanuelle was met by Rose, who thrust the picnic hamper into Emmanuelle's arms with enough force to make her go *whuuhhh.*

"*Alors,* what are you doing?" said Rose in a harsh whisper. "Inviting that Yankee to go with you?"

"I didn't invite him." Emmanuelle gripped the wicker basket against her midriff. "It was either this, or give up the trip to the lake entirely. What was I supposed to do?"

"You know what I think?" said Rose, her head poking forward and her eyes narrowing as she stared at Emmanuelle, hard. "I think you've not only taken a fancy to that Yankee, I think you're fixing to lose your heart to him, if you're not careful."

Emmanuelle gave a low laugh that sounded forced, even to her own ears. "Don't be ridiculous."

"Ridiculous?" Rose clamped her hands on her hips as Emmanuelle turned to go. "You've been without a man you really wanted longer than it's natural for any woman, and that's one good-looking man out there. But just don't you go forgetting who he is, you hear?" Rose's voice followed Emmanuelle back down the passage. "That Yankee major, he can toss your pretty little ass in jail quicker than a Confederate parrot can whistle 'Dixie,' and don't you go forgetting that. Hmmm?"

CHAPTER
NINETEEN

"Papère and I used to go out to the lake crabbing and shrimping together all the time," said Dominic in that boastful tone young males tend to use when they're trying to impress a rival. "He knows lots of things you don't know, about the bayous and the swamps and all the animals and plants that live there."

The major held his big cavalry mount to an easy trot beside the shay on the smooth shell road. "Papère?" he said, ducking his head as if hiding a smile.

"Mon grand-père," explained Dominic with a condescending, sideways glance that said clearly, *You don't know?* "It was Papère who taught me to drive. Maman said I was too young, but Papère says we de Beauvaises are born sportsmen." There was a pause, filled with the steady tattoo of the horses' hooves and the jingle of the harness, before Dominic added, his voice suddenly going flat and tight, "Of course, he can't do much anymore. He needs Baptiste to help him now wherever he goes."

Listening to him, Emmanuelle felt a swelling of emotion close her throat. Up until last May, Jean-Lambert de Beauvais had been a vital, energetic man with boundless energy and a long, quick stride and cheery bright eyes that belied his seventy-something years. Even after her marriage to Philippe had soured, she and

Jean-Lambert had managed to maintain an easy friend-ship, spending long hours together fishing for bass on the bayous of Beau Lac, or attending performances at the French Opera House. Then word had reached New Orleans that the old man's only surviving son had died in a hail of Yankee bullets on the Bayou Crevé, and Jean-Lambert had aged twenty years in one night.

"If it wasn't for his leg," Dominic was saying, "he'd be out there shooting Yankees right now."

"Dominic," whispered Emmanuelle with a warning frown, but the man on the horse only laughed, one hand coming up to catch the brim of his black felt hat as a breeze hit them, warm and heavy with steamy moisture from last night's rain. He had a new hat, she noticed, its twin ostrich feathers fluttering rakishly as his gelding cavorted in playful impatience. Then he glanced sideways at her, his eyes flashing with a smile as quick and bright and dangerous as the lightning that had shattered the sky last night, the night she almost gave herself to him, and she looked away.

They were passing through the outer faubourgs now, the houses here more scattered, with long stretches of whitewashed picket fences disappearing beneath tan-gles of hydrangeas and honeysuckle and altheas grow-ing green and rampant in the moist heat. She could feel the sun warm on her shoulders, but the motion of the cart stirred up a breeze that brought with it a sweet measure of coolness and tugged at the brim of her black straw hat, so that she took it off and held it in her lap. Closing her eyes against the brightness of the sun, she lifted her face to the sky. She could feel the rhythmic motion of the cart, hear the murmur of masculine voices, and for one unguarded moment, she allowed herself to imagine what it would be like if the man riding beside them weren't her enemy, if there was no war, no suspicion between them, no secrets and lies. The yearning that flooded her soul was like an ache that hollowed her out and left her feeling empty and sad.

Opening her eyes, she turned her head and found him watching her, his jaw set hard, a look that was both hungry and sleepy narrowing his dark eyes. She felt a warm heat curl low in her belly, steal her breath. She knew she should look away, knew the flame of desire in a man's face when she saw it, knew what she must be telling him by looking back at him like this, with her own need parting her lips and flushing her cheeks, and her hair swirling windblown and abandoned about her face. But in the end, he was the one who swung his head away to stare at the old Creole-style raised cottage they were passing, his hand closing hard around the edge of something he carried in that knapsack with the hated Federal eagle emblazoned boldly on its flap.

At the lake, they gathered driftwood to build a fire in a pit in the sand where they would set a big kettle of water to boil. Then, while Emmanuelle spread out the rug in the shade of a willow and unpacked the hamper, Zach Cooper and Dominic took the pails and nets out onto the old pier that thrust out into the flat, gray-blue waters of Lake Pontchartrain.

She stilled for a moment and watched them. Dominic was luxuriating in his role as the expert, she thought, watching with a smile as he showed the Union major how to tie the chicken necks and backs to the crab nets before lowering them slowly into the murky water of the lake.

There had been a time, years ago, when they all used to come out here together, she and Dominic and Philippe. At first, they had been able to laugh and enjoy themselves like any young family, despite their differences and troubles. But then the anger and resentment between them had grown and festered until it poisoned even the most innocent of pleasures, and they had quit coming to the lake, quit doing anything that required them to be together.

It was a memory she didn't want to have. Pushing it aside, she rose and walked out onto the pier. The salty breeze off the water fluttered her straw hat and cooled her face and blew away the lingering bitterness of her thoughts.

"Maman," said Dominic, slewing around to look at her from where he lay flat out on the pier, his head suspended over the water so he could watch the movement of the lines. "Major Cooper says that where he comes from, they have lobsters as big as dinner plates. Is that true?"

"And exactly where do you come from, monsieur?" she asked, walking to where he crouched at the edge of the pier, his weight on one knee as he tied a net to the dock with quick, sure movements.

"Rhode Island." His attention was all for the net in his hands. "My father's a sea captain." He eased the net down into the water, his eyes narrowing against the glare bouncing off the gentle waves. "Like his father, and his father before him, and his father before him."

"Yet you became a cavalry officer." She went to lean her hips against one of the weathered pilings, her head tilting as she watched him from beneath the brim of her hat. "Don't you like to sail, Major?"

He glanced up at her, the sunlight falling warm and golden across the strong planes of his face. "I like it. But not enough to make it my life." He rose in one lithe, easy motion and came to hunker down over his heels, his thighs spread wide, as he checked the line beside her. "My mother always says the sea is my father's wife; she's just his mistress, the one he sees on the side."

She found herself watching his hands as he began to haul the line up in a smooth, slow motion. He had lean, sure hands, strong enough to wield a saber with deadly effect, yet gentle enough to pleasure a woman with a simple touch. "It must be difficult for her," Emmanuelle said, disquieted by her own thoughts, "having him gone so much. Unless of course she doesn't love him, in which case she would be happy to see him leave."

"She loves him," he said simply. "And she mourns his absence every day he is away from her."

The breeze gusted up suddenly, flapping Emmanuelle's skirts out behind her with an audible snap and tugging at the brim of Zach Cooper's hat in a way that had him grabbing for the crown. She let out a soft laugh. "If you're not careful, Major, you're going to lose another hat."

He swung his head to look at her over his shoulder, his grip shifting to the brim of his hat, the laughter dying on her lips as her words evoked memories of all that had passed between them last night. "Here," he said, and took off his hat to hold it out to her.

She took the hat in her hands. It was made of fine, sun-warmed black wool felt, an officer's hat, with a jaunty brim caught up on one side by an eagle and decorated with ostrich plumes on the other. On the front, he still wore the number of his old cavalry regiment, with a pair of crossed sabers fashioned in gold. It was a symbol of much that she hated, this hat, yet she could not hate the man who wore it, however hard she tried. She turned the hat over in her hands and saw his name embroidered inside the band in gold letters: ZACHARY X. COOPER.

"Tell me, Major," she said, glancing up at him, "what does the X stand for?"

He hauled the net wet and dripping from the water, and Dominic let out a whoop at the sight of the small blue crab caught in its webbing. "Xavier," said the major, disentangling the crab with practiced ease.

She stared down at him, beguiled by the way his dark hair curled over the collar of his coat, by the way she could see the outline of the strong muscles in his sun-warmed back when he moved. "A strange name, surely, for the descendant of all those generations of New England Puritans."

He went to release the crab into one of the buckets. "My maternal grandfather was the Spanish governor of Cuba."

She almost dropped his hat. "Your mother was Spanish?"

His head fell back, the creases in his cheeks deepening with amusement at the expression on her face. "You see, you aren't the only one with mismatched parents." He straightened and walked toward her. "My father used to sail regularly between New England and Havana. Then one trip, the governor made the mistake of inviting my father and the other officers from his ship to a ball being held in celebration of the king's birthday—a ball that my mother, just turned sixteen, was allowed to attend. A week later, when my father set sail, she went with him."

"After one week?"

He came to stand before her, his hands hanging loosely at his sides, his gaze hard on her face. "She says she would have left with him after that first night."

Emmanuelle ran her fingers along the silken edge of

the hat's ostrich feathers, her gaze on the motion of her hand, her whole being vibrantly aware of the man who stood in front of her. "How could she have been so sure?" she said softly, half to herself. "How could she have known after only one night?"

"She says she listened to her heart."

She looked up then to find him still watching her, the fierce, strong bones of his face standing out stark beneath the tanned, taut skin. "And did she never regret it?"

He shook his head. "I asked her once, how she could have left everything like that, for a man she didn't really know and a place she'd never even seen."

"What did she say?"

"She just smiled."

Emmanuelle sucked in a deep, quick breath. "She was lucky. She could have made a terrible mistake. She could have been miserable."

"Like you were?"

She stared at him, at the uncompromising line of his lips and the knowing gleam in his eyes and the subtle sensual awareness that was always there, whenever he looked at her. A silence stretched out between them, a silence filled with the gentle lapping of waves against the pilings, and the warmth of the wind, and a hundred things left unsaid but understood.

Then there came a splash, and the excited laughter of Dominic's voice, saying, "Maman. Look, there's two crabs in this net."

They turned away, the spell between them broken and the moment ended.

Afterward, they sat in the shade of the willow and ate a dinner of boiled crabs, along with the hard-cooked eggs, wilted lettuce salad, and cheeses from the picnic basket. Then Dominic took off his shoes and stockings and went with a pail and shovel to dig for clams along the lakeshore.

Zach leaned his back against the tree trunk, one elbow propped on his bent knee, and watched as the boy jumped on his shovel to drive it deep into the sandy mud. "I thought the clams around here were inedible," he said.

"They are." Reaching out, she took a ripe orange from the basket beside her and began to peel the fruit, turning it easily between her strong, delicately shaped hands. "They're too full of the lake's mud."

"So why's he digging for them?"

"To bait the lake for shrimp," she said, her fingers curling as she pried the peel from the flesh. "He smashes them and throws them into deeper water, where they sink to the bottom. Then he throws his cast net out into the lake, and pulls in the shrimp that come to feed on them."

"Sounds like a nasty thing to do to the clams, if you ask me."

"How is it any different from baiting crab nets with chicken necks?"

He smiled softly. "I don't know, but it is."

She broke the orange into sections, and the sharp, clean tang of it scented the air. "So. Are you going to show me what you have in that knapsack?"

He swung his head to look directly at her. Her gaze locked with his, she brought one of the orange sections up to her mouth, and he found himself watching as she sank her even white teeth into the fruit, her tongue coming out to catch a drop of juice before it fell. He leaned forward slowly, his attention still fixed on her face as he flipped open the cover of the knapsack and eased the brass-trimmed oak box from the canvas.

She drew in a quick breath, her lips parting in a kind of gasp, the half-eaten orange lying forgotten in her slack hand as she stared at the box. "It's Philippe's vampire-killing set," she whispered, raising her wide-eyed gaze to his face. "Where did you find it?"

"In the armoire in his room. Last night."

"But . . ." She shook her head, her throat working as she swallowed. "That's impossible. I looked there myself, the day after Henri was killed. It was gone."

"Then whoever you heard in your house that night must have been there to put it back."

Setting aside the half-eaten orange, she reached to take the box from his grasp. He watched her slide apart the clasps and swing back the cover until it lay open on the grass. She stared at it a moment, one shaky finger reaching out to trace the empty slot of the missing bolt. Then she raised her intent gaze to his face, her brows twitching as if she were looking for something she wasn't sure she was seeing. "You believe me?"

"Shoot it," he said.

"What?"

He lifted the crossbow from its velvet cradle and held it out to her. "I want to watch you shoot it." He nodded to the trunk of a gnarled old cypress standing some twenty-five feet away. "That should make a good target."

She could have claimed she didn't know how to use a crossbow. She could have made a show of trying to shoot, only to fumble it badly. Instead, she stared at him for a long moment. Then, moving with practiced efficiency, she drew the cord up to the notch, set one of the remaining bolts, and released it.

Hissing through the air, the bolt sank into the cypress wood with a softly efficient *thwunk* that seemed to echo and reecho in the sudden stillness.

CHAPTER TWENTY

Zach sat very still, his gaze on the woman beside him. Down near the lakeshore, gulls wheeled, screeching overhead. The breeze gusted up again, cooled by the water, to rustle the slender branches of the willow and flutter the wide brim of her black-banded straw hat.

Standing abruptly, he went to pry the bolt from the tree trunk. Her head fell back as he came to stand over her, so close that the toes of his boots touched the spreading black bombazine of her skirts. "Who taught you?" he asked, his fist tightening around the bolt in his hand. "Philippe?"

"Yes."

He shook his head, his gaze fixed on the smooth, beautiful, lying features of her face. "Uh-uh. Who was it? Antoine La Touche?"

"*No,*" she said quickly, and something in the flash of guilty panic hidden almost immediately by downswept lashes made him believe her.

"Then who?" He crouched beside her and leaned forward until he was but inches from her. "Tell me, damn it."

She searched his face, her smoky green eyes questioning, troubled, her breath easing out in a slow, shaky sigh. "Dominic," she said after a moment, her voice hushed, tight. "Dominic taught me."

230   Candice Proctor

He held up the bolt, its bright squared head flashing in the filtered sunlight. "With this?"

"No." She shook her head once, sharply. "With a similar bow that was Philippe's as a child." She reached out to close her hand around his, the bolt held between them. "You can't imagine Dominic—"

It was a simple touch. But nothing would ever be simple between them. He eased his hand from beneath hers, leaving the bolt in her grasp. "No."

Straightening, he went to stand beside the wispy trailing branches of the willow and watch the boy. Dominic had a bucketful of clams now and had gone to sit at the end of the pier. Zach could see his arm rising and falling, a half-brick clutched in his fist as he smashed the clams and threw them out into the gently undulating waves. "Philippe hunted with a crossbow as a child?" Zach asked, his gaze still on her son.

Reaching over, she carefully returned the bolt to its velvet lined hollow. "Yes," she said, not looking up.

"With his cousin Antoine, I suppose." Zach swung around to pin her with a hard gaze. "Why didn't you tell me the set was a gift from La Touche?"

She rose slowly, her face almost gaunt with her fear. "Antoine would never do such a thing."

"Such a thing as—what? Kill Henri Santerre? Poison his own sister?" Zach walked right up to her, deliberately intimidating her with his size and his uniform and the power of the attraction between them. "*Someone* is doing this. Someone who knew Philippe kept that crossbow in his room."

"Philippe had many friends. He could have shown the crossbow to any of them."

"And how many of them would have known how to use it? Or had a reason to kill Henri Santerre? Or Claire La Touche?"

She turned away, one hand coming up to move restlessly along the opposite arm. "I don't know. You think I haven't asked myself these same questions, over and over again?"

"What about Hans Spears?"

Her skirts swirled around her ankles as she swung to face him again, her eyes widening in alarm. *"Mais, non."*

"Yardley?"

"No!"

"Papa John?"

She took a quick step forward, her hand reaching out to him, as if she would silence him with her touch. "No. You mustn't even suggest such a thing."

Zach stared at her parted lips, her wide, frightened eyes. "Why not?"

"Because he's black. Don't you understand? That makes him an easy target, an easy excuse. It could mean his death."

"All right." He kept his voice even, low. "How about Philippe?"

Her head snapped back as if he had slapped her. "Philippe is dead," she said in a harsh whisper.

"What if he isn't?"

He had expected her to dismiss the suggestion outright. Instead, she walked away to sink to her knees amid the picnic things and begin to slowly, methodically pack them away. A tense silence stretched out between them, filled with the rustling of the wind through the willow branches and the gentle lapping of the lake against its shore. "Philippe would have no reason to kill Henri Santerre," she said at last, her head still bowed over her task.

"Would he have a reason to kill you?"

She settled back on her heels, her head coming up as

she looked at him over her shoulder through narrowed, angry eyes. "You think I betrayed him, don't you? You think I told the Yankees about the Bayou Crevé." Her voice throbbed with emotion. "How can you even imagine I would betray my own son's father?"

"I think you might, if you were desperate enough." He paused. "I saw the contents of that armoire."

He watched her eyes widen, her chest lift on a quickly indrawn breath, although she said nothing. Slowly, he walked over to her, his hand coming down to close around her upper arm and draw her to her feet. "Did he beat you?"

She turned her face away. "No. Never."

Zach caught her chin in his hand and forced her head around until she had no choice but to look at him. "Did he tie you up with those silken cords, and take that whip to you?"

"*No.*"

He could feel her trembling now in his grip, little betraying tremors of all the emotions she was trying to keep bottled up inside her. "Yes, he did."

She pulled against him, but when he refused to let her go she went still in his grasp. "*Eh bien,*" she said, her gaze on his face fierce and proud. "He did. Philippe liked to play games. When we were first married, I . . . played with him."

"What else did he do to you?"

The westering sun cast a golden light through the green leaves of the willow, illuminating her face with a kind of glow. Her lips parted and he waited, his heart pounding, the blood thundering through his veins. "What else?" he said again.

A strange smile curled her lips. "Nothing I didn't agree to. Does that shock you, monsieur? Hmmm? Disgust you?"

"No."

She stared up at him, her chin and cheek still cradled in his hand, her eyes huge as she searched his face. Her hair was coming down, dark heavy locks that lay against the white flesh of her slender neck and curled against her full, high breasts. "What, then?" she asked, her voice husky. "Does it excite you?"

Her body was warm against his, the delicate skin of her face unbelievably soft beneath his touch, her scent sweet and musky and damnably evocative. He could feel his desire for her flaring up hot and bright, pulsing through him until his heart was pounding and his breath coming hard and fast. He had sought to intimidate her, with his size and his strength, and she had responded by seducing him with the essence of her femininity. It was the age-old dance of male advance and female retreat, a game he'd thought to play for his advantage, to use against her. Instead, he'd fallen victim to the power of the attraction between them and the surge of his own desires.

He wanted to bear her down onto the fecund earth and take her with swift, savage lust. He wanted to rip away the discreet high bodice of her plain mourning gown and luxuriate in the sight of sunlight warm and golden on the smooth flesh of her bare, beautiful breasts. He wanted to ruck up her full skirts and dig his fingers into her naked hips and wrap her long, slim legs around his waist. He wanted to touch her, kiss her, everywhere. He wanted her, and so great was the power of that wanting that if her son hadn't been at the end of the pier, his shrimp net unfurling with practiced ease as he sent it spinning out over the water, Zach would have taken her here and now, in the iridescent green light beneath the willow, where anyone might have come along and seen.

"Damn you," he whispered, his grip on her tightening, the urge to cover her soft, full mouth with his almost overwhelming. Instead, he let her go and swung away.

She stopped him by touching her fingertips to the cuff of his uniform, her hand jerking back when he spun to face her again. "I did not betray my husband," she said, her voice calm, and such was the strength of his own passions that it took him a moment to remember that this was, after all, what they had been discussing. "Philippe and I lived separate lives for years. The only things we shared were our work at the hospital, and Dominic. There was unhappiness between us, yes; unhappiness and anger and resentment. Yet as much as I am relieved to be free of my marriage, Philippe was still, in some way I can't even understand myself, a friend. I mourn his death, and I would never, ever have deliberately caused it—even if he had been the only one to die on that night, which he was not."

He took a step that brought him up close to her again, although he was careful, this time, not to touch her. "You're still hiding something," he said, his gaze hard on her face.

She sucked in a quick breath in a way that parted her lips and lifted her breasts and damned near broke the fragile control he had on his raging instincts. "I hide many things, monsieur," she said. "We all do."

"But what you're hiding could get you killed."

She shook her head. "I don't believe that."

"Believe it," he said, and walked away from her to where his horse grazed unconcernedly in the slanting golden light of the fading day.

That night, Zach took a glass and a bottle of brandy out onto the gallery that ran along the second floor of the Uptown house General Butler had appropriated for the use of his officers. The evening was blessedly mild, the air scented with the blossoms of the moon-flowers and angel's trumpets and honeysuckle glowing pale white from out of the darkness. Pouring himself a drink, Zach left the bottle on a weathered wooden table beside the door and went to stand with his fore-arms resting on the cast-iron balustrade, one boot hooked on the lower railing as he stared out over the shadowy garden below.

The night was cool and sweet, but he still had a heat in him, a heat that kept building, hotter and hotter, every time he saw her, every time he touched her. One day soon, he thought, if he wasn't careful, he was going to bear her down and take her the way a man takes a woman he's hungry for, with a desperate intensity just short of violence. The image made him shudder, and he swore softly to himself and drained the brandy in his glass.

He was reaching for the bottle again when a creak of wooden boards in the darkness brought his head up. The open doorway from the hall filled with a tall, broad-shouldered figure silhouetted against the lamp shine behind him.

"Want a drink?" Zach said, splashing brandy into his glass.

"Not unless that's Scotch you've got in that bottle," said Hamish, coming to toss his hat on the table with a sigh that spoke of long hours spent beneath a hot Southern sun. "It was a woman, all right," he said, scrubbing his hands across his face. "A Frenchwoman. I've been out to Bayou Crevé, talking to the lieutenant of the patrol she met with."

Zach paused with his drink suspended halfway to his

lips, his hand gripping the glass so hard, he wondered it didn't shatter. "She?"

"The woman who betrayed Philippe de Beauvais. She was wearing a heavy veil, the lieutenant says, but there was no missing her accent. She drove herself out to their camp in a neat little one-horse shay, told them what they needed to know, then went away without giving her name."

"And he simply let her go without asking any questions?"

Hamish stretched his neck and lifted his chin as he smoothed the line of his mustache with a thumb and forefinger. "I gather she was a haughty one, decked out in taffeta and pearls, with the grand manner of a duchess and a tongue like vinegar, and him nothing but a raw college boy from Philadelphia. He didn't dare try to stop her."

Zach stared out at the rooftops looming dark and silent beneath the stars. "So it could have been Claire La Touche."

"Aye. Or it could have been Madame de Beauvais."

He took a sip of brandy that burned all the way down to the fire within him. "She says she didn't do it."

"Aye," said Hamish again, his eyes glittering with brittle amusement. "Just like she said she didn't know the name of the man who was buggering Claire La Touche, or who gave that nasty little vampire kit to her husband for his birthday. She's no' exactly wed to the truth."

Zach took a longer, slower sip of his drink. "But why not admit this? At least to us."

"Secrets are hard to keep. And long after we're gone, she's still gonna have to live in this place."

Zach swung around to rest his lower back against

the balustrade, his elbows propped on the railing behind him. A palmetto bug buzzed through the air to
flop around in the shadows near the doorway, and
Zach watched it idly, the brandy glass cradled in his
curled palm. "And Philippe de Beauvais? Do we know
for certain he's dead?"

"Weeell . . . not exactly," said Hamish, propping a
shoulder against one of the elegant round columns sup-
porting the gallery's roof. "According to the lieutenant,
they buried two men, one black, one white. Buried
them right there in the swamp, where they fell."

Zach glanced up in surprise. "Why not bring them
back to New Orleans?"

"A couple of dead Confederates?" The palmetto bug
was crawling across the floorboards now, and Hamish
watched it anxiously. "In this heat? What do you
think?"

"And the German?" said Zach. "Hans Spears? How
did he get away from an entire Union patrol with a
minié ball in his foot?"

Hamish shrugged. "Luck, I suppose. That and more
guts than most have got, hiding out with a bloody foot
in a swamp full of hungry alligators."

Zach brought his glass up to his lips. "This lieutenant, what made him think the white man they
buried out there was Philippe de Beauvais?"

"His papers."

Zach swung his head to look at his friend. "No one
actually identified him?"

"No."

"So it could have been someone else."

"Aye." Hamish blinked. "Although I thought Hans
Spears told you there were only the three of them, that
night."

Zach pushed away from the railing, his boot coming down to squash the palmetto bug with an audible crunch that made Hamish wince. "What do you think? That Emmanuelle de Beauvais is the only one lying to us?"

CHAPTER
TWENTY-ONE

On a balmy Monday evening, Zach took the mule car up Esplanade Avenue to the white, two-story Greek Revival house of Jean-Lambert and Marie Thérèse de Beauvais.

He was shown into the front parlor by the same dignified elderly black man he remembered from the night of Claire La Touche's death. Pausing just inside the wide parlor doors, Zach let his gaze drift over the room's linen-draped chairs and polished rosewood tables backed by exquisite falls of lace at the windows. All the disorder and associated unpleasantness he remembered from that night had vanished along with Claire La Touche's corpse. It seemed strange to realize that anyone looking at the room, now, would never know of the violent death this elegant parlor had witnessed.

"I'll tell Madame de Beauvais you're here," said the man, setting Zach's hat on a low table and bowing himself out.

The distant sound of a child's voice drew Zach across the room to one of the long, high windows overlooking the side yard where Dominic lay, flat on his back in the sunlit grass. As Zach watched, the boy disappeared beneath the leap of a liver-colored hound that began to yap in enthusiastic counterpoint to

Dominic's laughter as they rolled over and over, boy and dog, a tangle of paws and torn trousers and close-cropped golden curls. The boy's mother was nowhere in sight.

"My grandson tells me you're a deft hand at crabbing," said a heavily accented voice.

Zach turned to find himself the subject of intense scrutiny by the woman who stood just inside the doorway. Marie Thérèse was unusually tall, taller by far than Emmanuelle de Beauvais, although so fine-boned and thin, the impression was still one of fragile elegance given a severe edge by the unrelieved black of her mourning gown. She was an attractive woman, more handsome than beautiful, her face lean and sharp-featured, her silver hair worn in an elegant chignon beneath a black lace cap. If there was any hostility in the coldly intelligent gray eyes that studied him, Zach thought, it was carefully hidden. She might hate the Union soldiers occupying her city as much as anyone, but she was a shrewd, wealthy woman who knew the power of a provost marshal. She would not deliberately antagonize him.

"Your grandson is a good teacher," Zach said, wondering as he came away from the window just how much Dominic had told his formidable grandmother about that outing to the lake.

She extended her hand in a gracious gesture toward a chair near the parlor's elaborately carved and gilded harp. "Please, have a seat, and tell me how I may be of assistance to you."

"I thought you might be able to help me answer a few questions," Zach said.

The delicately arched eyebrows rose in a polite expression of surprise. "Questions?" she said, sinking with quiet grace to sit at one end of a sofa.

"About the deaths of Claire La Touche and Henri Santerre."

"Claire and Henri? But . . ." She paused. "Surely the two matters aren't related?"

"I think they might be."

She lifted one shoulder in a genteel shrug. "Dr. Santerre was an associate of my son, monsieur. I'm afraid I myself was barely acquainted with the man."

"But you knew Mademoiselle La Touche."

"*Bien sûr.* Her mother is my husband's second cousin."

"Do you know of anyone who might have wanted to kill her?"

The question seemed to trouble her, although she hid it well, her hands clenching together in her lap but an instant before she relaxed them. "No. I can't imagine who would do such a thing. She was a sweet child."

Zach leaned forward in his seat. "Was she?"

The look she gave him was fixed and hard. "You must not believe everything you are told, Major."

He glanced up as a stout, middle-aged black woman appeared in the doorway, a heavy silver tray with a steaming *cafetière* and a pitcher of hot milk in her arms. It was Madame de Beauvais herself who poured the thick, rich coffee together with the milk into porcelain cups so thin and delicate, Zach could see through the rim when he lifted his to the light. He waited until the black woman had withdrawn from the room, then said, "Tell me about your son."

A small, sad smile touched Marie Thérèse's lips. "Which one, Major? I bore four sons."

"Philippe."

"Ah, Philippe," she said on a bittersweet exhalation of breath. "A brilliant, bright star destined to die young."

"Do you know of anyone who might have wanted to see him dead?"

Raising her cup to her lips, Marie Thérèse took a delicate sip of the café au lait. "My son died a hero's death, Major."

"And did you never think that someone might have betrayed him?"

For a moment, she froze, the cup suspended in midair. "I take it you're telling me he was betrayed," she said with admirable sangfroid. She lowered the cup to her lap, her head bowing for a moment. When she looked up again, her face was still carefully wiped of all emotion. "By whom?"

"We don't know exactly."

"It was a woman, wasn't it?" Her cup rattled in its saucer, and she set it aside, rising quickly to go stand and look out the side window, the full black silk skirt of her mourning gown brushing the lace panel so that it swayed lightly back and forth.

"I'd rather not comment."

"You don't need to, Major," she said, her back held straight and taut. "My son was not happy in his marriage. As men will do, he sought consolation elsewhere."

"With whom, exactly?"

"I wouldn't know. That's a question you should ask of his widow."

"She knew?"

"That my son was unfaithful to her?" Marie Thérèse turned from the window, her mouth held in a tight, bitter twist. "Oh, yes. She knew."

Zach rose from his seat, the coffee cup forgotten in his hand. He thrust it aside. "Tell me, madame, what do you think of your daughter-in-law?"

"What do I think of her?" Marie Thérèse sucked her

upper lip behind the lower in an expression that was inimitably French. "She was my son's choice."

"But not one you approved of?"

Her face hardened as if touched by an old, angry memory. "He might have selected from any of New Orleans's oldest and finest families. Instead, he took to wife the daughter of a poor doctor."

"A poor doctor who had married the descendant of a French *comte*," said Zach softly.

"Ah, yes. The mother was well-born enough— although the family lost everything in the Revolution, of course. But the father . . ." Again, that light shrug. "Pure petty bourgeoisie. Did you know he was a revolutionary? It's why they were forced to leave France."

"That scandalizes you, does it?"

Marie Thérèse came to stand in the center of the room, her hands loosely linked to lie against the black skirts she wore in memory of her dead son. "Perhaps it does much to explain some of my daughter-in-law's more . . . shall we say, unorthodox behavior?"

"Such as her ambition to become a doctor herself?"

"That, too."

From outside came the sound of Dominic's voice, raised in a familiar greeting. Zach didn't need to look out the window to know that Emmanuelle de Beauvais had arrived. He could feel her nearness, like a breathless hum in the air. "Do you think she was a good wife to your son?" he asked, although he already knew the answer this woman would give him.

"Men with good wives do not seek consolation elsewhere." Turning, Marie Thérèse went to where the *cafetière* rested on a round table. "May I offer you some more coffee?"

Zach lifted his hat from the table near the door. "Thank you, but no. I was just leaving." He could hear her now, Emmanuelle, on the front gallery outside, her voice light, relaxed, as she spoke in easy French with her son.

"You must be a very busy man, Major," said Marie Thérèse. If she were aware of her daughter-in-law's approach, she gave no sign. "Yet you seem to be devoting a great deal of time to this unpleasantness of ours."

Zach stood with his hat in his hand, every fiber of his being tuned to the woman just out of sight in the entry. He could hear the old butler saying, "She's in the parlor, Miss Emmanuelle, with a visitor."

"Two murders are bad enough." Zach tightened his grip on his hat. "I wouldn't want to see a third."

"If she's with a visitor, I won't disturb her," said that husky female voice in the hall.

"*Mais non,*" came the old man's reply. "She said she wished you to join them."

"Surely that is unlikely?" said Marie Thérèse. "A third death."

Zach shook his head. "As long as the murderer remains undetected, I'm afraid it is very likely. Those who kill once and get away with it often kill again."

A step in the hall brought Zach around to face the door, and it occurred to him as he felt himself tensing in anticipation that Marie Thérèse had deliberately delayed his departure, that she had been as aware as he of her daughter-in-law's approach, that she had wanted them to meet. Wanted to watch them meet.

Emmanuelle de Beauvais appeared in the doorway, her hands gripping the knob of the black umbrella she carried against the threat of coming rain. She had her thick dark hair swept up beneath a black widow's bonnet, its long untied ribbons swirling around her when she drew up short, her lips parting on a quick breath, the pupils of her eyes dilating in the dimness of the

room so that they might have been black, too. She
brought with her the scents of the garden and the
promise of warm rain and that hint of musky spice that
was all her own. And he knew as he stared at her that
everything he felt for her, from intense awareness
through hot-blooded lust to that quiet, almost spiritual
connection he'd known with her from the beginning
but would never understand—all must be writ there, in
every inch of his being, for anyone to read.

"Madame," he said, bowing with a formal politeness
made a mockery by the heat of the blood pulsing
through his veins and an inescapable rush of images,
memories of the swell of her naked breast warm beneath his palm, the sweet taste of her mouth opening
beneath the insistent pressure of his.

She inclined her head with equal formality. "Major."
She threw a quick glance at her dead husband's mother.
"If I am disturbing you, I can simply take Dominic—"

"No," said Zach. "I was just leaving." Turning to
the older woman, he added, "Thank you for your time,
madame."

"I'm sorry I could not have been of more assistance,"
she said, her brows drawing together in a concerned
frown as if she really meant it.

And it occurred to Zach as he settled his hat on his
head and turned to leave that they were all acting, the
three of them, as if each had been assigned parts in
some bizarre play where nothing was as it seemed, and
every line might be a lie.

Emmanuelle went to the parlor's guillotine windows
and watched Zach Cooper walk down the broad front
steps of her in-laws' house, his head tipping back as he
squinted up at the thick banks of clouds building overhead.

"Why was he here?" she asked, glancing over her shoulder at the woman who still stood near the wide doorway, her face set in disapproving lines.

Marie Thérèse stared at her a moment, then shrugged. "He wished to know some details of the evening of Claire's death. I must say, he does seem genuinely intent on catching the person responsible. I wonder if he'll succeed?"

"I don't think he has much to go on," Emmanuelle said, her attention caught once more by the man who now paused with one hand on the gate, the brim of his dark officer's hat lifting as he turned in answer to Dominic's shout.

"Dominic tells me this major accompanied you on your expedition to the lake."

Emmanuelle watched her son race across the lawn toward the front gate, the dog bounding at his heels. That day at the lake, after their tense confrontation about the crossbow, Zach Cooper had gone down to the shore to help Dominic pull in his shrimp net. They'd got into a furious argument then, her son and the Yankee major, about the North and the South, and the war. But it had ended with the major showing Dominic his cavalry saber, and Emmanuelle watching them with her head resting on her bent knees as she tried to understand how the possibility of a grudging friendship between this man and her son could both disquiet her and please her at the same time.

"Dominic hates Yankees," said Marie Thérèse in a voice that brought Emmanuelle around to face her. "They killed his father."

"I am trying to raise my son without prejudice and hatred," Emmanuelle said with deliberate calm. "Without even my own prejudices and hatreds."

A quiver of disdain passed over Marie Thérèse's features. "Is that what this is about? Love thy enemy? Hmmm?" She took a step forward, her voice dropping, her hands coming up to flash through the air in a swift, angry gesture. "It doesn't look good, Emmanuelle. It doesn't look good at all. A Yankee? And you less than three months widowed."

A few days ago, Emmanuelle would have denied the implications. She would have denied, even to herself, the dangerous drift of the tenor of her reaction to this tall, dark-haired man with the deadly cavalry saber and hated Yankee uniform. Now she simply said, "I have never believed in allowing a preoccupation with appearances to dictate how I live my life. You know that."

"Oh, I know." Marie Thérèse gripped the high back of the chair beside her with ringed, claw-like hands. "You admit, then, that you have feelings for this man?"

"I didn't say that."

The older woman shook her head. "You didn't need to. And what of Dominic, hmm? What will become of my grandson and his ties to Beau Lac if you marry a Yankee?"

Emmanuelle let out a sharp laugh. "Do you honestly think I would marry again? After what I went through with Philippe?"

A dangerous flare of anger gleamed in the depths of Marie Thérèse's crystal-gray eyes. "How dare you? How dare you say such a thing, especially to me?"

Emmanuelle held herself very still. "We both know what Philippe was like. Why should we pretend otherwise between ourselves?"

The anger spread, contorting Marie Thérèse's features, pulling at her mouth, making her look older than she was, old and bitter. "You made Philippe into the husband he was. You."

"No." Emmanuelle shook her head, her grip tightening around the umbrella she still held in her hands. From the front of the house came the quick tramp of a boy's feet, racing up the porch steps, and the sharp disappointed yap of a dog. "You might be able to convince yourself of that, but I know the truth. And so do you, deep in your heart."

"I know Philippe's father—"

"Philippe was not his father," said Emmanuelle, turning to go. "He never was."

"He could have been. With the right wife."

"Perhaps. We'll never know, will we?"

She had almost reached the doorway when Marie Thérèse's voice stopped her. "Did you know someone had betrayed Philippe to that Union patrol on the Bayou Crevé?"

Emmanuelle swung slowly back around, conscious of Dominic's nearness, of the happy chatter of his voice as he spoke to Leon, the old black butler. "So that's the reason Major Cooper was here," she said softly. "Because of Philippe."

"Why?" The anger faded from the other woman's face, leaving only strain and a fierce kind of sadness. "What has Philippe to do with Claire's death?"

Maybe nothing, maybe everything, Emmanuelle thought, her own anger draining out of her. She shook her head. "I don't know."

Marie Thérèse kept her fierce gaze on Emmanuelle's face. "Was it you? Did you betray my son to those Yankees?"

There was a pain in Emmanuelle's chest, a pain that had been building and building for days now, beneath all the fear and worries that troubled her. Because while she might not have betrayed Philippe herself, she couldn't help but feel that she was somehow responsible for what had happened to him. She could never have changed what he was, but perhaps if she'd been a better wife she might have saved him, saved him from himself. "And if I said no," she asked his mother softly, "would you believe me?"

The other woman swung away, one hand coming up to shade her face as if the dim light filtering through the lace panels at the windows suddenly hurt her eyes. "Dominic keeps asking when we go to Beau Lac."

"I know." Usually, Dominic spent months there every summer, riding through the fields, fishing the lake and bayous, learning to maneuver a pirogue through the swamps. But this year, Emmanuelle couldn't bear the thought of letting him out of her sight. Too many people in her life were dying.

"It would mean much to Jean-Lambert," Marie Thérèse was saying, "to be able to go there now, and to have the boy with him."

"I don't think it's safe for either you or Dominic to stay at Beau Lac right now. The Bayou Crevé might be under Union control, but the Rangers make constant raids in the area."

Marie Thérèse turned to regard her steadily. "And that's a bad thing?"

"When the Yankee reprisals fall on innocents, yes."

"People are saying our troops may launch an offensive to retake Baton Rouge."

Emmanuelle let out her breath in a long, troubled sigh. Too many people were dying everywhere. "Then pity the women and children of Baton Rouge," she said.

CHAPTER
TWENTY-TWO

Two days later, Emmanuelle stepped out onto the shotgun house's narrow back stoop and stared up at the night sky. Thick clouds hung low over the city, dark thunderheads that shut out the moon and the stars and piled up one on top of the other, holding in the heat of the vanished day and crackling with lightning and promising a downpour that didn't seem to be coming anytime soon. Just like the baby she was here to deliver.

Her legs felt suddenly shaky and she sat down for a moment on the edge of the porch, her head tipping back against a weathered wooden post. In another few hours, it would be morning. Emmanuelle had been here, in this small house in the poor, riverfront part of the city people had taken to calling the Irish Channel, for the better part of twenty-four hours now. And if the woman laboring in there in her narrow iron bed didn't give birth soon, she would die.

As a licensed midwife, delivering babies was one of the few medical activities Emmanuelle could legally do, although these days it was typically only the poor and the more recent immigrants who called in midwives. Those who considered themselves progressive or affluent usually sent their women to the hospitals, where doctors often went straight from handling corpses to examining new mothers, never bothering to wash their own hands in between and then wondering why their female patients sickened and died at such alarming rates. Of course, there were few in New Orleans who could afford such a luxury now, and most of the city's doctors were away in the war, anyway.

An agonized scream rent the air, followed by a child's panicked voice, shouting, "*Dhia*. Miss Emmanuelle! Oh, come quick, do."

Sighing, Emmanuelle drew the hot, still air deep into her lungs, pushed up from the step, and went back inside.

The rising sun was sending pale streaks of orange and gold shooting across the heavy underbelly of the clouds when Emmanuelle left the narrow house in the mean lane near Tchoupitoulas Street and turned toward the rail line and home. Around her, the city still slept, the early morning quiet disturbed only by the clatter of a milk cart rattling through the narrow streets and the dark, distant silhouette of a vendeuse, her body swaying with inimitable grace, a basket balanced on her head as she made her way to market with the produce of some outlying farm. The rain had never come.

It felt good to walk, Emmanuelle thought, good to draw the morning air deep into her being, good to behold the wonder of a newly unfolding day. She hadn't slept for a night and a day, and still she smiled. She'd been part of a miracle tonight, for in the quiet hour just before dawn the child had come at last, big and brawny and screaming with lusty indignation, but healthy, blessedly healthy. And the mother would be all right, too; Emmanuelle had left her trembling with exhaustion, but radiant with joy and triumph as she gazed down at the new son in her arms.

As Emmanuelle walked, the light grew stronger,

showing her the gray threat of clouds still hovering overhead and the boarded-up remnant of a glass window on the side wall of the grocery store at the corner ahead. She found that her heart had begun to beat faster, her skin tingling with a prickle of foreboding. This was a rough neighborhood, but she had walked these streets dozens of times at all hours of the day and night, and never until today had she felt unsafe.

She quickened her step, her gaze scanning the silent shops and sagging houses, every nerve in her body seemingly aquiver. The sound of a step brought her head whipping around, her fear leaping like a live thing within her, but the rutted lane stretched out behind her empty except for a mud-streaked pig rooting about in the slimy mud of the gutter and a skinny calico cat that blinked at her from a nearby stoop and made her feel vaguely foolish.

"Bonjour, ma petite chat," she said with a shaky smile, and kept walking.

She was tired. The sense of elation and the exhilaration it brought had worn off, leaving only a profound exhaustion that went beyond the last twenty-four hours. It wasn't like her, this attack of nerves, this feeling of weakness and vulnerability. Turning the corner by the boarded-up grocery, she tightened her grip on the medical bag she carried in her left hand, an umbrella in her right. Behind her, the pig squealed, and she glanced back again, quickly, before she could stop herself. When she swung around again, a man stood in front of her.

She sucked in a quick, startled gasp of air. He was just above average in height, with a threadbare, stained drab coat and torn, spotted cotton shirt worn open at the neck. Only the bowie knife he held clutched in one grimy fist looked new, its blade gleaming bright and sharp in the cool dawn light.

"You've been following me," Emmanuelle said, her voice coming out raspy, her gaze fixed on the knife.

"Huh," grunted the man. He had a full, untrimmed, reddish-blond beard that covered most of his face and blended into the ragged hair hanging down beneath a beat-up old black slouch hat. The flesh above the beard was slack and grayish with the unhealthy tinge of an opium addict, his eyes wild, the pupils tiny pinpricks in glassy circles of gray. "It's waitin' a night and a day for you, I've been."

"Waiting for me?" Emmanuelle glanced beyond him. Like the lane she had just left, this street was deserted, a churned expanse of drying mud between tumble-down shacks and wretched tenements and weed-choked stoops bathed in a pale, harsh light. "I've a few dollars with me, and there's morphine in the bag. You can take both, but please leave me the medical instruments."

"Oi, I'll take your money, and the morphine, too. But it's no' why I'm here."

From the sagging roof of the boarded-up shop beside them came the call of a starling, pure and sweet in the thin morning air. "And why would that be?" Emmanuelle asked, her terrified gaze fixed on the knife held fast in the man's fist.

"It's no' anythin' personal, you understand?" For an instant, his gaze darted toward the opening of the lane behind her, his nostrils flaring in alarm at the distant sound of a horse's hooves striking softly in the mud.

Emmanuelle's grip tightened convulsively around the leather handles of her bag, the seams biting into her palm.

"I never kilt a Frenchwoman afore," said the Irishman, his gaze coming back to her face, his hand flashing up, lunging toward her breast, the knife cutting through the air, the blade winking wicked and lethal in the light of the rising sun.

Emmanuelle screamed, a full-throated, calculated scream, as she brought her medical bag swinging up between them. The bag was heavy, its impact with the Irishman's wrist hard enough to jar her arm and send the knife spinning out of his grip. He howled in surprise and pain, his head turning as his startled gaze followed the arc made by the knife.

"*Bâtard,*" she shouted, bringing her umbrella down on his head. "*Assassin.*" She hit him again on the side of the head. "*Aidez-moi.* Help me. Someone, please," she called, remembering belatedly to switch to English as she hit him again.

From somewhere up ahead came the sound of a shutter being thrown back. The hoofbeats thundered into a canter that came nearer. A man shouted.

The Irishman hunkered down, one crooked elbow coming up to protect his head from her umbrella as he reached for the knife that lay up against the store wall. Emmanuelle hit him in the face with her medical bag, sending him flying back to land on his rump with his hands splayed out behind him. "Son of a bitch," he swore, staring up at her, a trickle of blood running from one nostril, his eyes widening as his gaze shifted to something behind her.

She tried to hit him again, but he scrabbled backward out of her reach. "You're barmy, lady," he said over his shoulder as he rolled onto his knees and shoved himself, stumbling, up onto his feet. "No wonder they want you dead."

"Who?" she cried. "Who wants me dead?" But he

was already running, the tails of his old drab coat streaming out behind him, his big broken boots clumsy on the rotting boards of the gunwale that served as a sidewalk here.

Emmanuelle stayed where she was, her bag and umbrella gripped tight, her heart pounding in her chest, her entire body quivering with fear and anger and reaction.

She heard running footsteps behind her, but before she could turn, a man brushed past her, a man she realized with a jolt was a Union soldier. Then a warm, strong hand fell on her shoulder, drawing her around, and she found herself staring at a dark blue uniform with twin rows of eagle-faced brass buttons.

"Emmanuelle," said Zach Cooper. "Are you all right?" Beside them, a big bay horse moved restlessly, its reins dragging in the drying mud of the street, its navy saddle blanket emblazoned with bold gold letters that spelled U.S. CAVALRY.

Zach gripped her other shoulder, almost shaking her. "Did he hurt you?"

She felt suddenly as if she hadn't breathed in a year, and sucked the river-scented air deep into her lungs with a gasp. "I'm all right." She gazed up at him, at the fierce angles of cheekbone and jaw, and knew an uncharacteristic surge of weakness, an almost overwhelming urge to throw herself against that hated blue uniform and feel the wonder of his arms tightening around her. Except that she was a widow, and he was a Union officer who half-suspected her of murder, and they were on a public street, a street filling with the banging of doors being thrown open and the sound of men's and women's voices raised in excited inquiry. Holding herself rigidly erect, her teeth set against the uncontrollable shudders starting to rip through her,

Emmanuelle took a step back. "What are you doing here?"

He let his hands fall from her shoulders. "I've had troopers watching you around the clock." He glanced beyond her, toward the end of the street where the Irishman and the soldier chasing him had both disappeared. "I was on my way to the camp out at Carrollton, and thought I'd swing by and see if you were still here. I rode up to the cottage just as you screamed."

"You—" She took another step back, her hand tightening on her medical bag, the urge to swing it at *his* head almost overwhelming. "You've had men watching me? Following me? *Spying* on me?"

Something of her thoughts must have shown on her face, because he took a step back himself, his gaze shifting warily between the bag and her umbrella. "It was for your own protection. Mainly."

"Mainly." The shuddering had stopped. "And if I said thank you but I don't need anyone to protect me, Major?"

She watched, bemused and reluctantly beguiled, as his face relaxed into a slow smile. "I'd say I know of at least one Irishman who would agree with you." His gaze went beyond her, to the narrow, rutted street filling rapidly with men and women and children, all talking at once and mingling in noisy confusion with a motley collection of barking dogs, mewing cats, squawking hens, and one squealing pig. "Actually, make that an entire neighborhood of Irishmen."

"How long?" Emmanuelle de Beauvais demanded, facing Zach across the darkened length of her front parlor. The sun was up now, the streets below coming to life with the rattle of carts bouncing over paving stones and the banging of shutters being thrown open to a new day. But no one had opened the shutters on the windows in here yet, and the clouds were too thick to let through much light, anyway. She was only a dim shadow, rigid with fear and anger. "How long have you had your men following me?"

They had barely spoken as he escorted her here through the awakening streets, to the house on the rue Dumaine. Now he stood just inside the door to the room, his plumed officer's hat dangling from one hand as he stared back at her through the gloom, and it occurred to him that the closeness that had been theirs that day on the sunlit shores of Lake Pontchartrain had vanished as if it had never been. In its place was the old, familiar wariness and mistrust. Her mistrust.

"Since Friday night," he said, and saw her head snap back as if he'd hit her when she realized that it was Friday they'd gone crabbing at the lake, Friday when he'd held her in his arms and told her he believed her. Then he'd come back into town and ordered his men to watch her.

She swung abruptly away to walk over and open the French doors and throw apart the shutters, letting the feeble gray light into the room. "And here I thought you were actually starting to believe me."

"I do believe you," he said, then added, "about most things."

She actually laughed, a low, mirthless laugh that cut him more than he'd have expected it to. "Then why didn't you tell me you'd set your men to watching me?" She turned her head to look at him over her shoulder. "If they were for my protection?"

In the street below, a vendor with a cart rumbled past, shouting, *Calas! Tout chaud!* "I suspected you wouldn't like it."

She suddenly seemed to realize she still wore her

low-crowned mourning hat and gloves, and tore them off with reckless impatience. "You were right." She tossed hat and gloves together onto a nearby chair, then stared at them as if they were some black indictment of all that she had done, and all that she had almost done with him. "I don't like it."

"Exactly why not?" He walked up to her, close enough that he could have touched her, although he didn't. "Because the soldiers wear blue uniforms, like me?"

"I don't like the idea of *anyone* watching me."

"That man today was watching you," he said, deliberately making his voice hard. "Watching you, and waiting for you."

"I know." Sighing, she brought up one hand to rub her forehead in a gesture that was becoming a habit with her.

"Emmanuelle . . ." He paused, searching for some way to reach her, to reach through the defenses she'd been throwing up against him ever since that first night, in the cemetery. "If you have any idea what's happening here, you must tell me. You do see that, don't you? I can't help you if you don't trust me." The problem was, he thought, that she had no reason to trust him, and they both knew it. As much as he might try to deny it, in a very real sense he was still her enemy.

She let her fingers slide down the side of her face to press against her mouth, then curled them into a fist that dropped to her side. "You asked me once if I thought Henri might have been killed by mistake, if I might have been the real target that night." She let out a long, tired sigh. "I did think that, at first. But now, since Claire's death . . . I'm not so sure. Perhaps someone simply wants us all dead. Perhaps you were right all along. Perhaps it's some soldier who lost an arm or a leg at the hospital, and holds us all responsible."

"Perhaps," he said, although he didn't think so. Not anymore. "Who do you know that might want to see you dead?"

She shook her head. "I've thought and thought, but none of it makes any sense."

"Not even if it's Philippe?"

"Philippe is dead," she said, keeping her voice even with obvious effect.

"And if by some chance he isn't?"

The pulse at the base of her throat was beating so hard and fast, it fluttered the narrow white band of lace edging the black collar of her mourning gown. "Philippe was a healer," she said, "not a killer."

"But it has occurred to you that he might be doing this, hasn't it?"

She swung away to go stare out the window again. "I thought at first . . . if he believed I'd betrayed him . . ." She shook her head. "But he wouldn't do this. Not Philippe. Whoever is doing this must be mad." She paused, her gaze still fixed on the awakening street below. "After I knocked him down, that Irishman said I was barmy. Crazy. He said it was no wonder they wanted me dead."

"They," Zach repeated sharply. "Is that exactly what he said?"

"Yes. I don't think he knew exactly who hired him."

"He'll know something." She looked so small and vulnerable and yet fiercely, determinedly brave, standing there in the pale light of another sultry, overcast day, that it was all he could do not to go to her and fold her in his arms. Instead, he tightened his grip on his hat and turned to leave.

"I haven't thanked you," she said, stopping him.

He paused to look back at her from across the room. "For what?"

"For trying to protect me."

Just when he thought he was coming to understand her better, she always seemed to surprise him. "You're a damned hardheaded woman, you know that, don't you?"

She gave him a wry half-smile. "I know that."

"How in the name of all that's holy," demanded Hamish, the finger and thumb of one hand smoothing his mustaches over and over again as he stared out at the muddy expanse of the river. "No, better yet, make that how in the name of everything that's holy and unholy do you think we're going to find one lousy Irish opium addict in a city of close on two hundred thousand people who hate our guts and wouldn't cooperate with us even if the Pope anointed us all?"

He'd come here, to the wharf opposite the cathedral, to inspect the papers of a ship bound for Boston and to approve its sailing. But it was a cursory inspection only, for the ship's cargo was one of cotton and sugar collected by Andrew Butler, the general's rapacious—and increasingly wealthy—brother. It would take more than a query from the provost marshal's office to keep this ship from sailing.

Zach leaned a shoulder against one of the wharf's weathered wooden pilings and squinted up at the ship's tall masts, several of which weren't as straight as they should be. "You tell me. You're the policeman."

"Huh," grunted Hamish. "Besides, how do you know this fellow wasn't just some opium addict after her morphine and a few dollars, and whatever else he could lay his hands on?"

Zach brought his attention back to his friend's heat-flushed face. "She said he told her someone wanted her dead."

Hamish gave Zach a steady, unblinking stare. "*She* said? She *said*? And since when did we start believing anything Madame de Beauvais says?"

"I think she's telling the truth in this."

"Oh you do, do you? Up until now, our killer has been doing his own dirty work, remember?"

Zach turned his gaze back to the ship. It was a clumsily built vessel, too wide at the bow and deep at the stern. If he were Andrew Butler, he'd think twice about entrusting his cargo to this tub. "Maybe," he said slowly. "Maybe not. We don't really know for certain, now do we?"

Hamish leaned forward, his brows drawing together. "What are you trying to tell me? That your hookah-smoking Paddy from this morning somehow managed to send that wee crossbow bolt straight through Henri Santerre's heart?"

Zach shook his head. "No. But if our murderer hired a thug to do his killing for him this time, he could have hired someone else, before."

"*He*, you're saying. And what if it's a *she*? What if that Frenchie widow hired Paddy herself, just to make us think someone was trying to kill her?"

"She didn't know we were having her watched."

"She *says* she didn't know."

"She's not that good of an actress."

"Huh. You know what I say? I say she's looking more like our killer all the time. Think about it. She had the crossbow before Santerre's murder, she had it after, and she knows how to use it." Hamish waggled a stumpy, sunburned finger in front of Zach's face. "And if you believe that shit about someone sneaking into her house to steal that brass-bound box and then sneaking in again to put it back, I'm going to start thinking maybe you're the one who's taken up hookah-smoking."

"Jesus Christ, Hamish." Zach pushed away from the piling to stand easily on the dock's gently rocking planks. "Why would Emmanuelle de Beauvais want to kill Henri Santerre? So she could inherit a hospital building so heavily mortgaged to support the Confederate war effort that she's working herself to exhaustion simply trying to keep it open?"

"Greed isn't the only reason people kill."

"Oh, right. What's she supposed to have wanted revenge for? The fact that he'd been like a father to her ever since her own father died nine years ago?"

"I'm not talking about revenge. I'm talking about self-protection. Maybe Santerre found out she'd betrayed her husband to the Yankees."

Across the square, the cathedral bells had begun to peal, ringing out slow and solemn over the old part of the city. Zach shook his head. "We don't know she's the one who betrayed Philippe. Besides, even if she was, what do you think? That the old man would be likely to rush right out and betray *her*?"

"She might have thought he would."

"No. She wouldn't kill for something like that."

"Ah." Hamish's broad face split into a smile so smug, it practically sent him rocking back on his heels. "So you do still think she could kill."

The cathedral bells tolled on and on, calling the faithful to mass and stirring up the pigeons in the square. "I think most people are capable of killing, given enough provocation," Zach said slowly. "Those who say they couldn't probably aren't being honest with themselves—or they haven't been given a strong enough reason."

"So maybe she had a reason we don't know about." They turned together to walk back toward the levee, Zach's step practiced and sure despite his limp, Hamish wobbling with each lurch of the dock. "You're the one who always said she was hiding something, remember? Even back when I thought she was just a fragile widow."

"I still think she's hiding something. But I don't think she's our killer."

"Well, I do," said Hamish, jumping awkwardly from the edge of the wharf. "And I think I can prove it."

Seagulls wheeled screeching against the heavy gray clouds hovering over the city, mingled with the pigeons from the square. Zach tipped back his head, his eyes narrowing as he stared up at the threatening sky. "You can try. But for now, just find the Irishman, will you?"

Two days later, the clouds still hung gray and low over the city, and it still hadn't rained.

Zach was in the courthouse, dealing with a backlog of petty cases, when he spotted one of Hamish's men, the corporal with the breaking voice and unshaven cheeks. The boy was looking anxious and unsure of himself, but was obviously bursting with news.

"Major, sir," he said, saluting sharply when Zach made his way over to him. It was only about five o'clock, but the heavy cloud cover cast a gloom over the day, making it feel much later. "Captain Fletcher says to tell you he found your Irishman, sir."

Zach knew a satisfying surge of anticipation. Now maybe they would start getting somewhere. "Where is he?"

"The captain? He's at the army hospital on Magazine Street, sir."

"Is he hurt?"

"He's dead—I mean the Irishman, sir," he added quickly when he saw the expression on Zach's face. "Captain Fletcher's had the body taken there for an autopsy."

For a long, tense moment, Zach simply stared at the private, while the boy's face turned white and he started to shake. "Jesus Christ," Zach said at last, his voice low and carefully controlled. "He killed him."

"No, sir." The boy's head shook back and forth like a door swinging in the wind. "The man was dead when we found him. Captain Fletcher wants an autopsy to be sure, but there isn't much doubt about what killed him."

Somehow, Zach had a feeling his hookah-smoking Paddy hadn't been stabbed or shot. "What killed him?"

"Poison, sir."

CHAPTER
TWENTY-THREE

Once, the St. James Army Hospital on Magazine Street had been a hotel, an elegant brick and stucco building with fine high windows and cast-iron railings and plaster detailing. But General Butler had requisitioned the hotel the same way he had so much else in this conquered city. Now it was the scene of shouting and confusion as carts rumbled in and out the cobbled courtyard, although few of the men overflowing the hospital's wards or being trundled off to the city's cemeteries were actual battle casualties. Most suffered from such things as scurvy and dysentery and measles, and the swamp poison that was killing the men sent to garrison the outer regions at the rate of two or three a day. The stench rising from the hospital—and the fouled gutters outside it—was enough to make a man gag. As he passed through the former hotel's lobby with its crystal chandeliers and blood-splattered faux marble–painted pillars and once polished floor now encrusted with drying mud and debris, Zach thought of the scrupulously scrubbed floors and whitewashed walls of the Hospital Santerre, and felt a renewed surge of respect for the woman who was fighting so hard to keep it open.

The small building the army doctors used for autopsies, dissections, and embalmings was a brick-walled chamber with a packed-dirt floor located in what had always struck Zach as unhealthy proximity to the kitchen. "So where'd you find him?" Zach asked Hamish, when they met in the courtyard just outside the brick building's open doorway.

"In a corner of what's left of one of those burned-out storehouses down by the wharves," said Hamish. "According to the doctor who did the autopsy, he probably died soon after his attack on our widow."

"Is he around? The doctor, I mean?"

"Dr. Austin Sinclair," said Hamish, adopting a foppish stance and pretentious Bostonian accent. "He's in there," he added, dropping the pose and the accent and jerking his head toward the building's open doorway, where a shallow flight of steps led downward. "Embalming some dead soldier whose folks want him sent home to Colorado. I told him you'd be wanting to see the Irishman's body, just to be sure we've got the right hookah-smoking Paddy."

"Come on, then," said Zach, pausing just inside the doorway to grin over his shoulder at Hamish when the big New Yorker hung back.

Inside, the air was thick with the smell of chemicals and rank flesh and a dank, overwhelming odor reminiscent of an old crypt, although that came less from the room's use than from the way it had been built, with the lower three feet or so of the walls actually lying below ground. Most buildings in New Orleans weren't built with basements. Every time it rained, Zach thought, this room must run with water. He hoped the rain held off until he was out of here.

"Yes?" said a young man of probably no more than twenty-five who looked up from the body of the soldier laid out before him. Dr. Sinclair was built short and plump, with prematurely thinning brown hair and pudgy, forgettable features and pale, pale skin. The cloth he wore stretched over his drab brown suit might once have been white, but it was now as stained with blood as the apron of any French Market butcher. There was dirt under his fingernails, and he seemed to have a cold or something, because he kept sniffing as he stared at Zach over the rims of the glasses he wore pushed down on the end of his nose.

"This is Major Cooper," mumbled Hamish, his nose and mouth disappearing behind a big white handkerchief he held in front of his face. "He's here to see the poisoning case we brought in."

"Ah, yes." Laying aside his scalpel, the doctor turned to whip a sheet off a body on one of the room's other elevated slabs. "Here he is."

"Jesus," said Zach, involuntarily taking a step back.

The doctor sniffed. "Strychnine poisonings are never pretty. The victim's body essentially becomes overstimulated by the action of the drug, resulting in the sort of convulsions you see frozen here. Rigor mortis sets in almost immediately after death, and the body remains as if in its final agony, eyes wide open, the face twisted into a rather hideous grimace. An important point to remember," he added, "since it affects one's estimate of the time of death."

Zach leaned forward, his eyes narrowing as he stared at the man's contorted face, with its wildly staring pale gray eyes and tangled reddish beard. "What did you do to the top of his head?"

"You don't want to know," said Hamish. What little was visible of his face had taken on a decidedly greenish tinge. "Just decide if it's him."

"It's him."

"Good. Let's get out of here," Hamish said, and bolted for the steps and the rectangle of gray sky above.

"Know what I think?" he said, leaning back against the building's thick brick outer walls, his hands on his knees, his body hunching over as he worked to draw the relatively fresh air of the courtyard into his lungs. "I think any man who can do that to what used to be a human being has got to have something very important left out of his own makeup. And when I think about a *lady* peeling off a body's . . ." His eyes went wide as his voice trailed off, and for a moment Zach thought the captain was going to lose his last meal all over the flagged courtyard. Hamish scrubbed one beefy hand across his face, and swallowed hard. "Well, hell. Let's just say that shooting a crossbow bolt through your old friend's heart or poisoning your husband's lover would be nothing after that."

"Come on," said Zach. "Let's go."

They went for a walk along a nearby grassy neutral ground filled with pink and white flowering oleanders and towering, leafy sycamores and elms. "Look at that," said Hamish, squinting up at the roiling clouds overhead. "How many days have we been putting up with this? If it's going to rain, I wish it would just do it and get it over with."

"Any idea as to exactly who the Irishman was?"

"Not a blessed clue." Shaking out his white handkerchief again, Hamish began to mop his damp face. He'd gone from being green to flushing red. "All the poor sot had in his pockets was a fancy gold watch he probably lifted off some sucker, a broken comb he doesn't appear to have used much, and one hundred dollars in U.S. government currency."

"U.S.?"

"That's right. Oh, and this." Hamish fished in the pockets of his uniform and came up with a small brown glass bottle he tossed toward Zach. "According to Austin Sinclair, it's opium. Liberally laced with strychnine."

Zach caught the bottle out of the air and held it up to the fading light. "Makes you wonder if our murderer doesn't have some ready access to opium and laudanum."

"Hell, you can buy them in any drugstore."

"But you'd need to sign the poison books for the strychnine, wouldn't you?"

Hamish let out a long, pained sigh. "Let me guess. You want me to check the poison books of every drugstore in the city?"

Zach gave him a slow smile. "Good idea."

"Huh."

They walked on in silence for a time as the hot wind kicked up and the clouds grew darker and the evening slid into night. "Where exactly was this warehouse where you found him?" Zach asked.

"Not too far from where your widow says she was attacked."

"She was attacked. I saw it, remember?"

"Yeah, right," said Hamish. "And what are you glowering at me like that for?" he demanded when Zach swung his head to stare at him. "You suspected her even when I didn't. And I tell you, every day she's looking more and more like the one we want."

"Why? Because she's capable of performing an autopsy, and you almost upchuck just at the sight of one?"

The red in Hamish's cheeks deepened to an angry crimson. "She's a *woman,* damn it. It's just not natural, the things she does. Who wants a woman who's capable of cutting up bodies and peering at their innards?"

"I admire her," Zach said quietly.

"Yeah? Well, I'd think twice about taking anything

she offered me to eat or drink, I can tell you that much."

The tolling of the cathedral bell ringing out over the city told Zach it was just on nine o'clock, but the tall, narrow town house on the rue Dumaine was already dark when he got there, the only light a dim glow through the shutters of the front bedroom on the top floor. He thumped the door's brass knocker, anyway, not really expecting anyone to answer, but in a moment he heard the sound of soft footsteps on the stairs. He waited, listening to the harsh squeal of a bolt being drawn back. Then the door swung inward, and he found himself looking at Emmanuelle.

She held a simple brass candlestick in one hand. The bare flame flickered and danced in the warm wind to cast a golden light over the delicate planes of her face and bring out a wine red glow in the cascade of thick dark curls tumbling down her back. She wore a simple peignoir of tucked white linen knotted by a sash at her waist, and he was very, very sure she wore nothing beneath it.

"You shouldn't answer the door looking like that," he said.

"I knew it was you." She gave him an enigmatic smile and turned away, toward the spiral steps at the end of the hallway. After the briefest of hesitations he followed her, the door shutting behind him with a soft catch that echoed seductively in the empty, darkened passage.

"I didn't expect you to have retired so early," he said, following her up the gently curving staircase that led to the house's first-floor living quarters. "I'm sorry if I disturbed you." Her feet were bare, he noticed, her flanks lean and naked and sensuously obvious through the thin cloth of her wrapper. He knew he should look away, but couldn't.

"I wasn't asleep. Dominic is spending the night at his grandparents', and Rose has gone out, so I decided to go to bed early and read."

Impossible to ignore the image her words provoked, of that slim body sprawled naked between crisp white sheets, her hair spreading out silky and sinfully free. In an age when most men and women went to bed wrapped in yards of linen or cotton, and with night-caps on their heads, Emmanuelle de Beauvais obviously slept naked.

At the top of the stairs she turned to face him, the flickering candlelight playing over her delicate features and the loose, sinfully dark fall of her hair. Behind her, the parlor and dining room lay in darkness, but the door to the gallery had been left open to the night air and the sweet scents of the courtyard below. "Did you find him?" she asked. "The Irishman, I mean."

"We found him."

Something in his face, or maybe in his voice, told her the truth. She swung away, one hand coming up to press against her lips. "Oh, God. He's dead, isn't he?"

Anyone seeing her now would think she really cared, that it grieved her to learn of that bedraggled Irishman laid out on Dr. Austin Sinclair's cold slab. "The man tried to kill you," Zach said. "Why should you be bothered by his death?"

She went to stand in the open doorway, the flame of her candle flaring up wildly as the wind hit it, then snuffed it out. She set it aside. "Partially, I suppose, because his death is linked somehow to me. But any death diminishes me."

"You're probably the only person in this city who feels that way about this one. We don't even know his name."

She stepped out onto the gallery, the hot wind snatching at her loose hair to blow it about her face, her bare feet padding lightly on the wooden floorboards as she went to stare out at the darkness below. "Which means you probably have no idea who hired him, either, do you?" she said after a moment.

"No. But we know how he died," Zach said, then added, when she looked back at him in inquiry: "Strychnine-laced opium tablets."

"*Mon Dieu*. What a horrible death."

"Horrible for him, yes, but it just might lead us to his killer. Strychnine's a registerable poison. If the man who hired that dead Irishman bought it in this city, he'll be on some druggist's books."

She wrapped her hands so tightly around the gallery's square wooden railing that the skin glowed white in the night. "He might not have bought it," she said after a moment. "It occurs naturally in some seeds and plants, strychnine—just like the poisonous oil in tansy. If someone knew how to obtain the one, he'd probably know about the other, wouldn't he?"

Zach walked over to stand beside her, close enough that when the wind blew, he was aware of the long, fine skirt of her peignoir billowing against his leg. "So who would know how to extract it? Besides Papa John," he added softly, when she didn't answer.

She lifted her head, and he saw the fear in her eyes before she hid it with a downward sweep of her lashes.

"Jesus," he said, feeling suddenly as if someone had kicked him in the chest, knocking the air out of him. "You know how to do it, don't you?"

She nodded, her face pale and strained in the dim

light of the night. "We worked on it together, the three of us. Henri and Philippe and I. You see, in small doses, strychnine can be used to rid the body of intestinal worms. Like tansy."

"Does anyone else know you experimented with it?" Zach asked, his hands falling hard on her thin shoulders, jerking her around to face him. "Anyone."

Her head fell back, her lips parting as she stared up at him. "I'm not sure. Charles Yardley. Hans, perhaps. Why?"

"Because I have a captain who's convinced himself that you're our killer, and this little piece of information would probably be enough to make him think he's got a solid enough case to put a noose around your neck."

She drew in a quick, hitching breath, but she didn't flinch away from him, didn't flinch from what he'd said. "What about you?" she asked, staring at him, her eyes roving intently over his face. "What do you think, Major?"

He brought up one hand to cup her chin. "I think whoever is behind these killings is more than a bit mad." He rubbed his thumb back and forth across the smooth skin of her cheek. "And you're not mad."

"I could be." A wry smile touched her full lips. "I could be wildly, deviously insane. Maybe you just don't know it."

"I know you." The urge to do more than touch her face was strong; the urge to pull her woman's body warm and close to his, to know again the heady wine of her kiss, to run his fingers through her silken hair and touch the yielding softness of the naked flesh so temptingly obvious beneath thin white linen. Shuddering, he put her away from him and went to stand at the edge of the gallery, one shoulder resting against a wooden post, his gaze fixed on the lightning crackling through the thick, dark clouds above. The night wind blew around them, warm and heavy with damp from the rains that kept threatening and threatening, but never came.

"Three years ago," he said, "at a fort out West, there was a series of killings. They weren't like these in the sense that at Fort McKenna, each death seemed unrelated to the last, but they kept happening. Men, women"—he paused, swamped for one unexpected moment by a remembered tide of rage and grief and irrational but soul-twisting guilt—"even a child. The only thing those people had in common was that they died. Brutally. I wasn't a provost marshal then, just a captain at the fort, but the first man killed was one of my men, and I was young enough—and cocky enough—to think I could catch whoever was doing it."

She came to stand beside him. Lightning split the sky, tearing open the night with startling flashes of brilliant white, but she was watching him, not the storm. "And did you catch him?"

"Eventually." Eventually, but not soon enough, Zach thought; not for Rachel, not for all the others, and he had to tighten his jaw against the urge to say more. "The man doing the killings was one of the lieutenants at the fort. He was even younger than I was, just twenty years old, a West Point graduate, good Maryland family . . . he seemed to have everything going for him."

"Was he insane?"

Zach let out his breath in a long, painful sigh. "I don't know. I'm not a doctor, but he didn't appear to be. That was probably the most frightening part of it. He seemed so lucid, so intelligent, so . . . normal. But he was lacking something. It's taken me a while, but

I've come to believe that what he lacked was a sense of his own fundamental tie to humanity. He had such an all encompassing arrogance that he genuinely believed whatever he wanted was more important than anything else, more important even than another man's life."

"And what did he want? Why was he killing?"

Zach turned toward her, his spine pressing hard against the post behind him as he reached out to her, his hands riding low on her hips to draw her close. "It was just a game," he said, his hands moving in slow circles, her flesh smooth and warm and comforting beneath its thin covering of linen. "A contest of wits. His wits, against mine."

She rested her forearms against his chest, not pushing him away, but not drawing him closer, either. "Why? Did you know him?"

"He wasn't a friend, but yes, I knew him."

"There, you see? You knew him, and still you had no idea of what he was capable."

"I know he wouldn't have been troubled by the death of some unknown opium addict who tried to skewer him with a bowie knife in the Irish Channel." The wind caught at her hair, tangling it across her face, and he brought up one hand to smooth it back, his fingers light as a caress against her cheek. "Sometimes I think you're too aware of the ties that bind you to the rest of humanity."

She gave a soft laugh tinged with a hint of self-mockery. "I don't know about that. Lately I seem to spend less and less time worrying about humanity, and more time worrying about myself."

She would have turned her face away then, but he caught her chin, forcing her to look up at him again. "You're scared, aren't you?" he said, his gaze searching those beautiful, carefully composed features. "You might not show it, but that doesn't mean the fear's not there."

Her breath came out in a keening sigh, as if she'd been holding it forever and found it a relief to finally let it go. "I'm terrified," she said simply, her eyes wide and vulnerable as she stared back at him. "Dominic has already lost his father. I don't want him to lose me, too . . . whether it's to this killer, or to Captain Hamish Fletcher's noose."

He shifted his hand to the nape of her neck, his thumb splayed against the soft white flesh of her throat. "I won't let that happen to you."

She met his gaze unflinchingly. Met it, and held it. "And if it turned out your friend Fletcher was right about me? Hmmm? What would you do then, Major? Would you still stop it from happening?"

He didn't say anything, but then he didn't need to. She read the answer in his eyes, and smiled. If Hamish was right, then Zach would go out of his way to make sure she swung. She knew it, and she didn't care. It had always been there between them, the rivalry and the challenge and the danger, feeding the passion and giving a cutting edge to the hunger.

She was still smiling when he tangled his fist in her hair, tipping her head back and pulling her hard against him. She came up on her bare toes, her arms twining about his neck, her body arching warm and supple as she pressed against him, a soft whimper easing out of her as she opened her mouth to his.

It was a kiss of fire, of need and fear and passion, all too long denied. He was drowning in her kiss, burning in it, his mouth slanting, seeking, demanding, taking, giving. She brought up one bare foot to let the sole slide sensuously, invitingly down the length of his leg, and he caught at her thigh, felt the edges of her peignoir slide open, felt her flesh smooth and bare beneath his searching fingers. She moaned deep in her throat, her hands pulling at the buttons of his coat. The wind gusted hot and wild around them, lightning flashing white and stark and almost instantaneous with a rolling crescendo of thunder that shuddered the gallery and rumbled on and on and on.

"I want you," he whispered, the words slurred by the movement of his mouth against hers. His hand slid up her leg, up over the warm, naked curve of her hip to dig into the soft flesh of her bottom and pull her tight against the throbbing length of his erection. "Here. Now. Nothing held back."

"Nothing," she said simply, and he pushed her through the French doors, into the darkened dining room beyond. There were a dozen or more reasons why he shouldn't be allowing this to happen, but at that moment, he didn't give a damn about any of them.

CHAPTER
TWENTY-FOUR

The dining room was little more than a pattern of shadows on the edge of Zach's consciousness, a darkened unknown where lightning gleamed on polished rosewood and looming sideboards appeared reflected in the flash of a massive mirror suspended high above an empty hearth. He thrust her back from the open doors and the fury of the gathering storm, and they clung to each other, tongues twining, hands seeking, bodies yearning. His hip banged into what felt like the edge of a table. A chair went over as they careened into it, and he tore his mouth from hers long enough to bear her down onto the floor.

The movement pulled apart the edges of her peignoir, baring to his gaze her full, high breasts and the beckoning shadow at the juncture of her thighs. He yanked at the white sash still knotted like a slender binding about her waist. It came free in his hands and he tossed it aside, then looked up to find her staring at him, her eyes intense. He kept his gaze locked with hers as he lowered his head to close his mouth over one rosy peak, and she cried out, her back arching, her shoulders coming off the ground when he sucked the nipple between his lips.

"Oh, God," she whispered, cradling his face between splayed fingers as he made love to her breasts with his tongue and his lips and the heat of his breath. She squirmed beneath him, her voice a frantic whimper, her hands tightening in his hair, holding him to her, willing him to devour her. He'd dreamed of making slow, sweet love to her, of touching her and tasting her everywhere, but already he was near the edge, swirling away in a white heat. No, he was over the edge, and she was there with him, frantic hands sweeping down to pull at his clothes. He reared up to fumble with his sword belt and rip off sash, coat, shirt. She rubbed her palms over his bare chest and arched her hips invitingly beneath him, and he was so hungry for her, he thought he might die.

"Now," she said in a guttural whisper, her long, slim legs wrapping around him as she lifted straining against him. "Please. Now."

Bending forward, he caught her open mouth with his in a deep, wet kiss of shuddering breath and aching need as he fumbled with the buttons of his trousers. Already she was tugging at the waistband to yank them down over his hips. Then her hand closed around his erection, and he gasped into her mouth.

"*Mon Dieu,*" she said with a shaky laugh as her hand moved up the aching, rigid length of him.

"Do you want it?" he whispered, nipping at her ear, slipping his hands beneath her hips to lift her up to him.

She answered by tightening her hand around him and guiding him to where he wanted to be. Her gaze locked with his, her eyes as dark and unknowable as an enchanted sea, and he fell into them, fell into the essence of her being as she took him inside herself.

He drove into her hard and deep, and heard her let out a breathy cry, her hands gripping his upper arms, her body arching up. She was making small, erotic noises deep in her throat, driving him on, faster, harder as he plunged into her again, and again. He was consumed by need and want and a savage pleasure such as he had never known. He took her there, on the floor of her dining room, with the French doors open to the wind and lightning splitting a turbulent sky. She was holding on to him, her hips rising to meet each thrust, her hair a dark tangle that wrapped around them both. He braced himself above her on outstretched arms so that he could watch her face as he pounded into her. And he knew, somewhere deep within him, somewhere far beyond the power of this all-consuming moment of savage pleasure and blinding need, that he could spend the rest of his life making love to this woman and gazing into her sea eyes, and it still wouldn't be enough, that what he wanted from her was more fundamental even than this primal union, more intimate, more demanding, and infinitely more enduring. But then the thought was gone, swirled away on a violent roll of thunder and an all-consuming fever of painful need and fierce pleasure and a hot, frantic climax of soughing breaths and pounding hearts and sweat-slicked bodies straining toward each other.

She clung to him, her fingers digging into the tensed muscles of his upper arms, her neck arching as she screamed and writhed in the grip of a wild rapture ripping through her with such intensity that it pulled him over with her. He flung back his head, his teeth gritting, his voice joining hers. He gave one last, powerful thrust, burying himself in her. But the shuddering went on and on, and he gave himself up to it, surrendered to the onslaught of ecstasy, and to her.

Emmanuelle lay on her back, the floorboards with their thin summer covering of woven straw hard beneath her spine and shoulders, his man's weight heavy at her breast. She could hear the thunder rumbling, far away at first, then closer, wilder, a hot wind gusting up to rustle the fronds of the banana trees in the courtyard below and set the French doors to creaking on their hinges. It had been years since she had truly enjoyed holding a man in her arms like this, since she had reveled in the thrill of running her hands down a man's sweat-slicked bare back and feeling his heart beating hard and fast so close to hers. Years since she had known this trembling moment of enervation and exquisite pleasure and ease mingling with the slow reawakening of a desire too heady and intense to be satisfied with one release.

"I must be crushing you," he said softly, and shifted some of his weight onto his bent elbows, although he kept his face buried in the curve of her neck. "Did I hurt you?" His lips moved against her flesh, trailing warm kisses along her neck.

"I'm not as fragile as I look."

He lifted his head to gaze down at her, and she saw in the depths of his eyes the reflection of her own resurgent passion. "I know that."

In the fierce light of the gathering storm, he was beautiful. Dark and beautiful, his face hard, almost cruel-looking in arousal, yet still tender. He both excited her and frightened her, this man. Even if he didn't half-suspect her of murder, even if he didn't have the power to send her to her death, he would still frighten her. He was too passionate, too intense, that unfathomable, innate connection between them too demanding of a level of intimacy that went far beyond this simple union of their bodies, and terrified her.

He bent his head, his mouth closing over hers in a long, deep kiss that drove away thought and left only sensation and want and a growing, insistent need. She was losing herself again in his kiss, swept away by a swirl of mating tongues and sharp, nipping teeth and a breathless heat. He tangled his fingers in her hair, his thumbs brushing against her cheeks as he lifted his head and stared down at her with eyes that seemed to glow.

"I want you again," he whispered. She watched, bemused, as the edges of his lips quirked up in that bad-boy smile of his that always came so dangerously close to stealing her heart. "Are the rug burns on your backside as bad as the ones on my knees?"

She let out a startled gurgle of laughter, her hands sweeping down his sides to the swell of his wonderfully tight, naked buttocks. "I do own a bed. Although you'll need to promise to take off your boots and spurs."

"My—" He pushed himself up, and she knew by the surprised widening of his eyes and the way he swung around to stare down at the trousers shoved below his hips that it hadn't occurred to him until now that he still wore them. He rolled onto his back, his weight propped on his elbows, his head falling back as a laugh burst out of him, a deep, sensual man's laugh that took her breath and brought a wholly inexplicable sting of tears to her eyes.

Emmanuelle lay beside him, her peignoir ripped open, her body bare to the night air and vaguely sticky between her thighs where he had been. She stared at him, saw lightning flash, gleam blue-white and dangerous on the taut, naked skin of his chest and the corded sinews of his throat. A desperate urge stole over her, the wish that she could reach out and catch this moment and hold it. Afterward, she decided it was his laugh that undid her, that made her want to hold him in her life, forever.

She'd left a light in her bedroom, a hurricane lamp set high on the carved mantel, where it cast a warm flicker over walls papered in faint gold on cream stripes. In the center of the room she stopped to swing suddenly about, her arms creeping up to hug her waist as she stared at the man who paused just inside her door, his coat and sword belt thrown casually over one shoulder. It was an infinitely more frightening thing to be making love to him at leisure here, in the intimacy of her room. Downstairs, with passion running as high and wild as the night wind, she might be able to convince him, convince herself that what she felt for him was raw lust, simple and uncomplicated by feelings or needs or secret wants. But here . . .

"Second thoughts?" he said, his eyes narrowed, his jaw hard as he gazed back at her. He'd fastened his trousers, but his suspenders dangled in wide loops against his thighs. And while he'd pulled on his shirt, he hadn't buttoned it. "Should I be putting this coat on?"

Reaching out, she took the coat from him and turned to drape it over the round-backed chair of her dressing table. It gave her a peculiar sense of dislocation to see it there, that hated dark blue cloth with its double row of eagle-crested brass buttons. Strange, how she could find herself forgetting for hours at a time what uniform he wore, what he was.

"It bothers you, doesn't it?" he said, coming to stand behind her, his gaze meeting hers in the mirror. "Yet less than two years ago, the uniform I wore was the uniform of your country. My country was your country."

"This isn't two years ago."

"No." He put his hands on her shoulders and swung her to face him. "Two years ago, your husband was still alive."

She looked up at him, her heart beginning to thump painfully in her chest as she studied his face. "Tell me, Major; who just said that? General Butler's provost marshal, or my lover?"

He ran his hands in a possessive sweep down her back, his fingers cupping her buttocks to pull her in close. "Your lover."

He kissed her long and hard and deep, his hands roving with sure familiarity over her body. "Now," he said, raising his head. His breathing had deepened, become more rapid; beneath the fine linen of his shirt, she could see the hard rise and fall of his chest. "We're going to do this right." He tugged at the sash she'd knotted again about her waist. "Take this off. I want to see you. Here, in the light. All of you."

She took a step back, a faint smile on her lips as she untied the sash. "I'm beginning to suspect you're a bit of a sensualist yourself, monsieur," she said, watching him watch her as she eased the thin linen peignoir from her shoulders. It slid down her arms to fall in a soft whisper at her feet.

He stared at her, his eyes dark and cruel with a man's desire, and she knew a shiver of delicious apprehension and fierce excitement. "And you like it, don't you?"

She took another step back that brought her to the side of the great rosewood bed with its ornately carved headboard and towering half-tester draped in a film of mosquito netting. With the aid of the steps, she settled on the edge of the high mattress and leaned back on her elbows, her head tipping back so that her hair slid over her shoulders and pooled on the gold and cream brocade of the counterpane beneath her, her legs falling slightly apart as she gazed up at him. It was a blatantly provocative pose, a deliberate taunt that would have frightened many men, but not him.

He came to stand before her, close enough that his thighs touched the inside of her spread knees, dark blue wool pressed against tender flesh, a gentle reminder of who and what he was that brought an unexpected twist of awareness low in her belly, a perverse heightening of arousal. Slowly, he let his gaze rove over her. She could feel the heat of it like a touch, caressing the swell of her bare breasts and sliding down her stomach to the juncture of her thighs, where he had already been. And then he was touching her, a light caress of his fingertips that trailed fire over her breasts and drew an aching line downward, only to stop just short of what she needed.

"You're teasing me, monsieur," she said, curling up toward him.

He cupped the back of her head with one hand, drawing her right up to him, spreading her naked thighs wider as he leaned into her, her tender woman's flesh pressed with exquisite sensitivity against the blue cloth of his uniform and the hardness beneath. "Turn about is fair play," he said, smiling at her with his eyes as he nipped her lower lip with his teeth, and she laughed.

He pressed her down into the feathery softness of the bed, but when he would have bent over her, she stopped him with an upflung hand against his chest. "Your boots and spurs, Major."

He straightened slowly, his eyes dark and almost frightening in their intensity as he took a step back. He kept his gaze on her face as he gathered handfuls of his shirt's soft linen and drew it over his head in one swift, flowing movement of taut sinew and flexing muscle. He tossed the shirt aside, his hands falling to ease open the buttons of his trousers. But then he must have remembered his boots, for he swung around to rest his hips against the edge of her mattress and pull off first one, then the other, their gilded spurs gleaming in the lamplight. As he bent, his trousers gaped open, revealing the ridged, tight plane of his belly and the darkness below. Then he stood and with swift purposefulness peeled the dark blue cloth down over his hips, baring to her gaze the muscled curve of his buttocks. He was naked and he was beautiful, and she couldn't quite stop herself from reaching out to skim her hand over that pale, evocative curve.

He straightened slowly and swung to face her, his trousers still clenched in one fist. As she watched, he flung them aside with a quick, almost angry flick of his wrist, his hands settling on his hips as he stood naked before her, legs straddled in a blatantly masculine pose. "Tell me; am I still your enemy without my uniform?"

A strange pain clutched at her chest. She let out her breath in a long sigh, trying to ease it. "You'll always be my enemy."

He walked up to her and nudged her knees apart so that he stood again between her spread thighs. "Because I am a man?"

She opened her eyes wider, both surprised and dismayed by how well he knew her. "I can handle men," she said, shaking her hair back from her shoulders.

He placed his splayed hands on her bare breasts, cupping their fullness, dark strong fingers against her pale woman's flesh. "So it's something more."

She could have said, You are my enemy because you make me feel the way I haven't felt in ten long years, the way I never wanted to feel again. You are my enemy because I dream of the taste of your lips, because I lay in this bed at night and ache for what I have now, the touch of your hands on my breasts. You are my enemy because I want you with a fierceness that consumes me, and I swore I would never, ever allow any man to have that kind of power in my life again.

Instead, she said, "You frighten me." And even that was perhaps too much.

Another man would have said, *Don't be frightened,* and lavished tender loving kisses upon her. Zach Cooper smiled a rakish smile and slid his hands down her arms to tighten around her wrists and stretch her arms above her hair, pinning her beneath him. "But you like that," he said, leaning into her, and she laughed.

CHAPTER
TWENTY-FIVE

Long, lean, and naked, he slept facedown in her bed, this enemy, this Federal provost marshal who had become her lover.

Lying beside him in the familiar darkness of her room and listening as the first scattered raindrops from the storm began to pound against her shutters, Emmanuelle knew a strange sense of dislocation, of unreality. She had made love to this man more times and in more ways than she could remember. He had explored every inch of her body with his tongue and his lips and his hands, and she had come to know him with the same intimacy. Yet somehow she still could not quite believe that he was here beside her, that she had given herself so openly, so utterly to him. Through all those long, passion-filled hours of the night, she had held nothing back—except, of course, her heart.

She had thought him asleep, but when she touched her hand fleetingly, impulsively, to the smooth, taut curve of his naked shoulder, he turned his head and gave her a lazy, contented smile. "What time is it?" he asked, one arm curling out to wrap around her waist and draw her companionably close.

"Three, I think."

"Hell." He nuzzled his face in the mass of tangled

curls at her throat. "Somewhere out there on the rue Dumaine is a Federal soldier who watched me come in here at nine o'clock."

"Whose reputation are you worried about? Mine, or yours?"

She felt the warm air of his laugh against her shoulder. "Mine."

"Huh." She brought up one hand to run her fingers through the fringe of dark hair at the nape of his neck, the way she might do with Dominic. "I've been thinking, monsieur. Murder isn't always a product of arrogance or selfishness and greed."

He lifted his head to stare down at her. "You've been lying here beside me in the dark and thinking about murder, have you?"

She smiled. "Mmmhmm. For quite some time."

He rolled onto his side, facing her, one wrist resting in negligent familiarity on her naked hip. "All right. When isn't it?"

"Last summer, one of the slave women out at Beau Lac lost her only child, a girl, just eight years old. At first, everyone thought the little girl had fallen from the broad gallery that runs around the house's second floor, and hit her head on a flagged walkway below."

"But she hadn't?"

"No." Emmanuelle glanced toward the connecting door to Dominic's empty room, her voice quavering as she was struck by the swift onslaught of that paralyzing terror that comes to every mother when reminded of how vulnerable any child—her child—really is. "The little girl was already dead when she was thrown over the railing. It turned out that the woman's lover—a slave, as well—had been abusing the child. She'd started to scream, and in the process of trying to shut her up, he smothered her."

"So he killed her to protect himself. How is that not an example of greed and selfishness?"

Emmanuelle shook her head. "I'm not talking about the murder of the child. After she found out the truth, the little girl's mother killed herself by walking into the bayou. But before she did, she fed her lover foxglove leaves mixed in collard greens, and killed him."

"Foxglove leaves?"

"Mmm. They're deadly."

"Does everyone down here count poisoning as one of their specialties, or is it just the people you tend to associate with?" He rolled her onto her back, his weight shifting to pin her beneath his long, naked body. "Hamish warned me to be careful what I eat or drink around you."

She stared up at him. "My point is, monsieur, that that was a murder of neither arrogance nor greed. That murder was born of great grief, and passion."

He went quite still. "Do you think that's what we're dealing with here? Revenge killings?" She would have looked away, but he cupped his hand beneath her chin, forcing her head up so that she had no choice but to meet his fierce, probing gaze. "Revenge for what? What did you and Henri Santerre and Claire La Touche do that has provoked such violent hatred in someone?"

"I don't know." She sucked in a deep breath that did nothing to ease the sudden pressure in her chest. "But what if you were right in the first place? What if Henri was hit by mistake?"

"Then the question becomes, what did you and Claire La Touche do to make someone hate you so much?" He kept his gaze locked with hers, one hand coming up to smooth the tangled hair from her face with a touch so light and gentle, it was an effort to re-mind herself that these hands could kill. Had killed. "If you know," he said softly, "you must tell me. It's the only way I can help protect you."

She shook her head, her eyes closing against the onslaught of frightened tears she refused to let fall. "I don't understand any of this."

"Even if the killer were Philippe?"

She opened her eyes wide. "Philippe is dead."

He sat up suddenly, pulling her with him so that they faced each other amid the crumpled sheets of her bed. "You keep saying that, but how can you be so certain? He was buried on the Bayou Crevé by a Federal patrol that only identified him because of the papers they found in his pocket."

"Hans told me Philippe died in his arms."

"Maybe. Or maybe Hans has his own reasons for not being entirely honest about what happened out there on the bayou. After all, he's the only one who escaped alive, isn't he?"

"What are you saying?"

"I'm saying that you can't take anything for granted. Not when your life is at stake."

"You don't understand." She knelt naked before him, her hands coming up between them, pressed together as if in prayer. "Philippe might have flirted with death and danger—he might even have done things that most people would find shocking and decadent—but he would never deliberately take a life, not like this. I've seen him weep with grief over a patient's death, and suffer another's pain as if it were his own. Besides . . ." She paused, and the silence in the room filled with the drumming of the rain on the roof overhead and the rush of water as the gutters began to overflow. "Philippe would have no reason to kill me."

He gazed at her so long and hard, she felt a shiver of apprehension mingling with a resurgent echo of excitement. "Wouldn't he, Emmanuelle? You're the only one who really knows the answer to that question."

She thought he would ask her then about the other men she'd had in her life, the other men she'd taken between her legs during all those long, angry, frustrating years while Philippe amused himself elsewhere. That other one, Hamish Fletcher, would have asked. But Zach Cooper didn't. He simply reached out to catch her by the shoulders and draw her hard up against his naked body and take her mouth in a kiss full of hunger and passion and a leashed kind of violence that brought her to a state of instant, shivering want.

And afterward, she realized he had asked, in his own way. And she thought she had probably given him an answer, of sorts.

He left her in the pale light of the dying night, slipped softly from her bed to assemble his clothes and begin quietly to dress. She lay unmoving in the darkness, not letting him know she was awake, not letting him know she watched him. She watched him pull on his dark blue trousers, his fine officer's shirt, his coat with its double rows of brass buttons and major's shoulder straps. She watched him, and wondered how they'd come to the easy familiarity of this moment, how he'd come to be here, in the darkened bedroom of a woman he'd once half-suspected of murder. How she'd come to be lying here, naked, watching this enemy buckle his sword belt, and feeling not hatred and revulsion, but a dangerous yearning of the heart.

One hand steadying his scabbard at his side, he bent to kiss her cheek, his lips soft, his breath warm against her skin as he whispered, "I need to go. Don't get up."

Her hand crept around his neck, holding him to her for one brief, heart-wrenching moment. She closed her eyes, her face buried in the warm curve of his shoulder. He smelled of the night and himself and the hot, intimate things they'd done together in her bed, and she felt a welling rush of great sadness, knew again that unwanted urge to hold him close, hold him in her life forever.

"I'm scheduled to meet with General Butler today," he said, his lips traveling over her jaw, her ear, "and I'm not sure when I'll be free. Can I see you on Sunday?"

She turned her head, her lips finding his, her mouth opening beneath his in a long, deep kiss that ended slowly, his lips coming back to hers, again and again, as if reluctant to draw away. She'd already made arrangements to go with Rose and Dominic to Congo Square on Sunday, but even if she hadn't, her answer would have been the same.

"I can't do this again," she whispered, her arm still wrapped around his neck, holding him close.

He knelt on the floor beside her bed, both hands coming up to bracket her face as he stared at her. "We don't need to do this again."

"But we will. You know we will."

He smiled, that lopsided bad-boy smile that clutched treacherously at her heart. "I won't deny I want you." He didn't say it—he didn't say he loved her, but it was there, in the dark warmth of his eyes, in the sensual curve of his smile, in the softness of his touch as he smoothed the tangled hair from her face. And then he did say it, with a calm certainty that took her breath. "I love you."

"No." She pressed her fingers against his lips. "Don't."

He nibbled at her fingers, pressed a kiss to her palm, light kisses, but his eyes had narrowed, his face hardened. "Don't love you, or don't say it?"

She shook her head. "It's not love, what we did tonight."

"What do you think it was? Lust?" He speared his fingers through the hair at the side of her face, holding her head steady when she would have looked away and forcing her to meet his merciless, steady gaze. "It might be lust, what you feel when I do this—" His free hand swept down to close over her bare breast with a fierce suddenness that made her gasp. He leaned into her, his lips almost but not quite touching hers, his eyes flashing with a raw and ragged anger. "But don't you presume to think you know what I feel."

He let her go and stood up with an abruptness that almost made her cry out. Then he turned on his heel and left her there, in the lonely darkness of her room. It was what she wanted, or what she'd thought she wanted. But it didn't stop her from turning her face into her pillow once she heard the front door close behind him.

She wanted to weep, weep like she hadn't wept in years. But all that came was a shuddering sense of loss and a painful, tearing confusion.

The next day, the sun came out scalding hot and golden in a clear blue sky, and the rain-soaked city steamed.

By early afternoon, the heat in General Butler's office was intense, the thick, unmoving air rank with the smell of men's sweat and wet wool mingling with stale smoke and fresh spittle as some half a dozen fidgety men in heavy blue uniforms puffed on cigars or squirted tobacco juice at overflowing brass spittoons.

"Now," said the general, sifting through the pile of papers on his desk, "on the matter of this Mrs. Eugenia Phillips, arrested for laughing at our dead—"

"Sir," interrupted Zach. By now, they'd been going over confiscation orders and arrest orders for four hours, and Zach had been standing the entire time. He was feeling short-tempered and hungry and uncomfortable, with drops of perspiration rolling down his spine and his wet shirt sticking to his skin. "As I understand it, the woman was holding a children's birthday party on her balcony at the time the incident took place. She wasn't even aware that there was a funeral procession passing in the street below."

From his desk beside the open window, the general looked up, a faint flush suffusing his cheeks. "Are you aware, Major, that this woman was arrested in Washington and charged with espionage?"

It was Hamish who answered. "Yes, sir. We looked into that. She was released." The big New Yorker flicked a quick glance at Zach, then away. Hamish was sorely aggrieved about something today, and Zach knew better than to make the mistake of thinking it was just the heat.

"Huh," said the general. Beside him, the little colored boy Butler used to wave his fan dozed. Butler poked the child with the toe of one boot, and the boy straightened with a jerk and began to flap the palmetto fan vigorously back and forth. "The woman is obviously disloyal. When I offered her the opportunity to apologize for this disgraceful incident, she refused. She says since no offense was intended, no apology should be required."

"General," said Zach quietly, "the woman has nine children."

"Whom she is no doubt training to spit on Union

officers. They'll be better off without her." Dipping his pen into the inkwell, Butler signed the document before him with a quick, irritated scratch. "Her status is to be reduced to that of a common woman of the streets."

Zach felt a peculiar, hollow sensation, deep in his gut. "But sir, that means—"

"I know what it means, Major. If these Rebel women wish to act like whores, I am more than ready to oblige by arranging to have them treated as such. She is to be sent to Ship Island until further notice." He looked up, his mismatched eyes somehow managing to focus on Zach for one, angry moment. "Is that clear, Major?"

"Yes, sir." Privately, Zach thought the severity of the woman's sentence had less to do with the imagined insult to the dead lieutenant than with the fact that she was Jewish, and that her husband was well-known around Washington as a better lawyer than the general. But this time Zach kept his opinion to himself.

"What are you, the new, self-appointed defender of Southern womanhood, or what?" demanded Hamish when they left headquarters some half hour later. "First you interrupt the Big Man, then you argue with him. If you're not careful, you're going to find yourself sent back to your old regiment, all right. As a private. Major."

It was never a good sign when Hamish called him by his rank. Zach sighed. "Got something you want to say to me, *Captain*?"

Hamish's mustaches twitched violently back and forth. "Say to you? What would I have to say to you, *Major*? After all, you're the one who had me order a watch on a certain lady who lives in Dumaine Street. It's not like you didn't know the lad was out there. And who am I to question the wisdom or ethics or anything else of what you do. Major."

Zach let out his breath in a long sigh. "How are you coming with those poison books?"

Hamish sniffed. "I didn't see any names that rang a bell, but there were some doctors on the list. I set a couple of soldiers to looking into them, to see what their connections to the Hospital de Santerre might be. But I'm not expecting much."

"I've been thinking about riding out toward Bayou Sauvage," said Zach. "Have another chat with Papa John." He didn't look at Hamish when he said it. He wasn't exactly sure what he was going to do if the big New Yorker took it into his head to come along.

The worry was unneeded. Hamish had had enough of bayous and gators and the old Haitian's uncanny prescience. "You do that," he said, jerking the kelpi hat he always wore down lower on his forehead. "Maybe that old voodoo king can give you something that'll help you keep that prick of yours in your trousers, where it belongs."

"Jesus," said Zach, the muscles in his jaw tightening as he worked hard to bite down on his anger. "I'm not going out there to discuss my prick."

"Yeah, well, maybe you ought to think about it. That lady is bad news, and don't you be forgetting it. *Major.*"

It was late in the afternoon by the time Zach reined in his big bay in the shadow of an old cypress tree that grew with its roots reaching up like gnarled knees from out of the heavy black waters at the edge of the bayou. The waning of the day had brought no relief from either the heat or the humidity. It was like trying to breathe through a wet towel, just being out in the moist, hot air. Sometimes he felt as if the air here were smothering him, that he was drawing more water than oxygen into his lungs. A man could drown just trying to breathe out here.

Around him, the swamp was alive with sound, the whirl of insects and the croak of frogs so big, the Creoles used hounds to hunt the old wararrons and ate their legs with no more thought than a New Englander might give to feasting on a turkey. Zach thought for a moment he could hear a dog howling, way off in the woods, but it might have been some bird. He swung out of the saddle, his leg stiff from the ride and the long day and the lack of sleep the night before. It took all his concentration to minimize his limp as he crossed the clearing to the mushroom-shaped hut with the thatched roof and ladderlike steps and tall black man in a frilled white dress shirt who smiled as Zach drew closer and said, "I was wonderin' when you'd be back."

CHAPTER
TWENTY-SIX

"You know why I've come?" said Zach, his head falling back as he stared up at the tattooed face of the man who stood in the hut's open doorway.

"Mmm. I know. But do you?"

Until now, Zach would have said he was here to talk about poisons. Instead, he found himself saying, "Tell me about Philippe de Beauvais."

"Every man is a complicated set of virtues and weaknesses, inconsistencies and contradictions," said Papa John. "What do you want me to tell you about Philippe?"

"Was he capable of killing?"

The old man came down the steps, his movements still as graceful and effortless as a hunter on the prowl. "Why? Because he was fascinated by pain and death? Or because he kept shrunken heads, and liked to tie up his lovers with silken cords and titillate them with little leather whips?" At the base of the steps, he stopped, his head cocking to one side as he studied Zach with an intensity Zach found disconcerting. "What if I told you Philippe de Beauvais freed every slave on the small plantation given him by his grandfather, and would have tried to do the same at Beau Lac if he'd lived to inherit it? What would you say then?"

"I'd say the war will free all the slaves."

Papa John waved one weathered hand through the air in a gesture vaguely reminiscent of a conjurer. "So everyone keeps saying. But the war's been going on for a long time now, and the woman who washed that shirt you're wearing is still a slave, isn't she? Only difference is, now she's slaving for the Yankees."

Taking off his hat, Zach swiped one forearm across his hot forehead. It bothered him that Butler had taken over the slaves of the houses he'd seized with the same predatory attitude he'd shown toward items of fine furniture—or silverware. But Zach was still wearing the shirt. "From what I understand," he said, carefully readjusting his plumed officer's hat, "de Beauvais was shot in the head. If he did survive, the wound could have deranged him."

Papa John opened his eyes in a meaningless stare. "I have heard of men so altered by head wounds that they could kill. Kill even their best friends and their loving wives."

"I didn't know de Beauvais had a loving wife," Zach said dryly. He was beginning to realize that whatever he was looking for, it didn't seem very probable that he was going to find it here. Like an enigma out of a child's fairy tale, Papa John just kept answering a question with a question.

"Tell me this, Major," said the black man, walking over to a sunny patch of ground where a scattering of herbs grew in a wild confusion of parsley and rue, oregano and fleabane. "Have you found the woman who betrayed him to your Yankee patrol?"

Zach stayed where he was, at the base of the steep steps leading up to the hut. Papa John hadn't invited him in today, and Zach found himself wondering why. "You know we haven't."

Stooping, the old man began to gather handfuls of

some pale, sharply serrated leaves that released a pungent, vaguely unpleasant odor into the air. "You think with blinders on," he said, his attention all for the plants at his feet. "Blinders formed by your own preconceived notions and prejudices."

"What's that supposed to mean?"

Straightening slowly, Papa John looked over at Zach, and laughed. "I think maybe you need to figure that out for yourself."

Zach drew in a slow, even breath. "Who in this city might be capable of extracting strychnine from plants? Antoine La Touche? Or how about Charles Yardley?"

The handfuls of leaves dangling at his side, Papa John walked back to where Zach still stood at the base of the steps. "I see you didn't bring your friend Captain Fletcher with you this time. Is it because you didn't want him to hear what I might have to say?"

Zach met the man's gaze, and smiled his meanest smile. "You aren't exactly saying much." He started to turn away, then stopped. A breeze had come up, blowing hot and heavy with moisture from off the bayou. "You know," he said, glancing back at the man who still stood at the base of the ladderlike steps, "from what I hear, most people would have considered Henri Santerre your friend. Yet instead of helping me find whoever was responsible for his death, you act as if I were your enemy."

A hard, brittle light shone in the old man's eyes. "There are black men fighting and dying on both sides of this war, Major. Both sides. Why you assume I'm on your side? Because now your president is talking about freeing all black men? And then what, hmmm? What will become of them, all those ex-slaves, with no jobs, and no one to look after them when they're old and sick?"

"At least they'll be free."

"Will they? I don't think so. Someday, maybe. But not for a long, long time. And the longer this war lasts, the more that's destroyed, the more people are hurt, the more hatred that's stirred up, the worse things are going to be."

"Sometimes things need to get worse before they can get better."

From the open door above them came the barest whisper of a sound, like an involuntary movement quickly stilled. It might have been the white cat, except that Zach could see the cat stalking a lizard or some such thing over near the edge of the clearing.

Papa John didn't even bother to look up. "Tell me, Major," he said, fixing Zach with a hard, challenging stare, "how you think those Yankee shippers up North got to be so rich, hmmm? Running the triangular trade between New England and Africa and the Caribbean, trading in sugar and rum and slaves, that's how. Why, up until a few years ago, they still had slaves in New York, and in Connecticut, too. Yet you think that because the people down here in Louisiana own slaves now, and you Yankees no longer do, that you're somehow better than them? More moral, more righteous?" He leaned in closer, close enough that Zach could see the yellow of his eyes and each faded blue tattoo line on his face. "This war might seem like an easy answer to your guilt, but don't make the mistake of thinking I'm on your side."

"I get your point," Zach said, and swung away. He was gathering his horse's reins when the old man's deep, melodic voice stopped him.

"Hey, Major."

Zach looked over to see Papa John standing once more in the open doorway of his house.

"Watch your back," he said. "You hear?"

"Why?" Zach asked, his eyes narrowing as he squinted into the lowering sun. "Why warn me?"

The old man's lined, tattooed face broke into an unexpectedly broad smile. "Emmanuelle's a friend of mine."

"Are you going to tell me why we're here?" demanded Hamish. Doing a quick sidestep, he managed to avoid being trampled by a handful of Negro boys practicing *raquettes,* only to almost crash headlong into a rickety wooden stall selling gumbo filé, instead.

"We're taking off our blinders," said Zach, his gaze drifting slowly over the sweating, sun-dappled, multi-hued crowd that surged in and around this place known popularly as Congo Square.

It was a Sunday afternoon and they had come here, to this dusty parcel of scraggly grass and spreading sycamore trees, where the city's slaves gathered once a week in their Sunday best to dance and play and make quick, furtive love. Not everyone here was a slave, of course. Many were *gens de couleur libres,* free people of color. And there were white people, too, drawn by the food and the music and the general relaxed air of gaiety.

Hamish had stopped to gape at a wooden rooster on a pole, its bright ribbons fluttering in the breeze. Now he turned his head to give Zach a blank stare. "Come again?"

"Think about it," said Zach. "This is a city of some one hundred and seventy thousand people. Of those, something like eleven thousand are free people of color, and about as many more are black or colored slaves."

"Yeah." Hamish made a little rolling motion through the air with his hands. "And?"

"The gatekeeper at the St. Louis Cemetery tells us about two black men, and all we can think about is maybe asking them if they saw anything. We're told a woman with a heavy French accent drives herself out to the Bayou Crevé and betrays Philippe de Beauvais, and we immediately ask, who was it, his wife, or his aristocratic lover?"

"If you're thinking what I think you're thinking, then all I got to say is, that lieutenant out on the Bayou Crevé, he might not be the brightest lad out of Philadelphia, but even he would have noticed if the lady in question had been black. Blinders or no blinders."

"Would he? He said she was wearing a veil, and you know she'd have had on gloves. Hell, this city is full of quadroons and octaroons with skin no darker than mine, and more than enough money to afford silken gowns and stylish carriages. And most of them speak French."

Hamish put up a hand to smooth his mustaches, his expression quietly thoughtful. Around them, the crowd surged suddenly, for at the far end of the Square, drums had begun to beat in time to the rattle of jawbones and the thump of a tambourine, sending out a rhythm that seemed to pulse through the mass of people. There would be dancing soon, strange, savage gyrations of half-naked, leanly muscled black bodies. They weren't all black, the onlookers already forming a circle, their hands clapping, shoulders swaying in time to that primitive tempo. But white, black, or colored, there was no denying that most of the people here had at least this one thing in common: They were all speaking French. Yankees were tolerated because they must be, but it was well-known that *nègres américains,* American blacks, were not welcome here.

"Take a good look sometime at the people you see living in those little Creole cottages on the edges of the Vieux Carré, or along the streets of the inner faubourgs like Tremé and Marigny," said Zach, his voice barely audible above the weirdly exotic call of a wooden horn. "Take a good look, and notice how many are dusky women with pale-skinned children. They call it *plaçage*. White men, keeping colored women, having children by them. It's a venerable institution here. Old, and venerable."

"What are you suggesting?" said Hamish, his face suddenly, oddly flushed. "That de Beauvais had a French-speaking colored mistress stashed away in some Tremé cottage—a colored mistress he somehow made very, very angry?"

"It's possible."

"You could always try asking his wife." A lingering spark of malice glittered in the big New Yorker's eyes as he leaned in close to whisper, "It's called pillow talk."

With effort, Zach just managed to keep a tight rein on his temper. There was no denying Hamish had a damned good reason to be nursing a grievance. "She might not know."

"Huh," scoffed Hamish. "That woman? If her husband was keeping a colored bit on the side, she'd have known." Beside them, a dark-skinned woman in a plaid tignon had set up a table against the Square's rusting iron fence and was selling bottles of *bière du pays* from a bucket of cold water. Hamish stopped to buy a couple, then lingered under the stand's fluttering canopy of gaily colored cotton and pressed one dripping bottle to his face. "So why exactly are we here?" he said, handing the second bottle to Zach. "Seems to me maybe we'd do better checking out the balls at the

Salle d'Orleans. See what dusky beauties are looking for new protectors."

Across the Square, near the swaying, cheering crowd of spectators, a woman turned. A tall, handsome woman with a swanlike neck and graceful carriage and skin the color of café au lait.

"Here, hold this," said Zach, thrusting his dripping bottle of apple ginger beer into the New Yorker's free hand.

"Hey!" yelled Hamish, his beer bottle–filled hands spreading wide. "Where you going?"

Zach was already pushing his way through the crowd. "Go have some jambalaya or *estomac mulâtre*," he called back. "I'll find you."

By the time Zach reached the far side of the Square, Rose had disappeared.

Frustrated and hot, with beads of perspiration rolling down his spine and his shirt sticking to his skin, Zach stood at the edge of the stomping, clapping circle and listened to the jungle beat of the tam-tam and the ghostly rattle of the jawbones. He could feel the rhythm begin to vibrate through him, stirring his soul, awakening the primitive, lingering vestiges of a jungle past that live in all men.

"Got to be some kind of a fool," said a woman's melodic voice from behind him, "wearing a heavy blue wool uniform in heat like this."

Zach swung about to find Rose staring at him with a closed, unsmiling face. It was at least ninety-five degrees in the sun, the air full of dust, even the breeze hot. Yet she looked serene and unruffled and enviably, unbelievably cool. "You knew I was looking for you," he said.

"I knew."

He wondered why, having avoided him, she'd decided instead to approach him. He let his gaze drift over the swaying crowd, men and women and children of all ages. Some were coarse and ungainly, common and plain, as at any gathering. But there was a beauty here, too, a breath-catching beauty clad in dusky or golden skin, with exquisitely molded bone structure and a feline grace intensified by the lure of the exotic, that same inescapable sensuality that was there in the beat of the drums and the wild gyrations of the dancers.

"I understand a lot of rich white men down here keep colored mistresses," Zach said, almost casually.

Rose gave him a long, hard look. "Lots of white men do. But Michie Philippe wasn't one of them, if that's what you're asking."

"Why not? He was hardly faithful to his wife."

"See that child over there?" Rose nodded toward a little girl of about six who stood wide-eyed and mesmerized at the fringe of the crowd. She was as delicate and beautiful as a Dresden figurine, small of bone and pale of skin, with eyes of the brightest blue and a riot of golden curls that tumbled down the back of her expensive, lace and ribbon trimmed gown. "You look at her, and what do you see?"

"I see a pretty little girl."

"A pretty little white girl?"

"Of course."

Rose sniffed. "That's because you from up North. You haven't been taught what to look for, like folks from around here. People here, they look at that girl, and they don't see her white skin, or those pretty blue eyes. They see the particular way her blond hair curls, and how full her lips are, and what a long, thin neck she's got on her, the way she holds herself when she walks, and they don't need anyone to tell them, they *know*. They know that she's not really white."

"But she is white," said Zach, knowing what Rose meant, yet unable to accept it. "Her skin is whiter than mine."

"Sure it is. Four grandparents that child had, and three of them were white. But one of them was black. That's all that matters. Even if it was just one great-grandmother, or even a great-great-grandmother, it'd be enough. That child might have blond hair and blue eyes and skin paler than yours, but she'd still be colored."

As Zach watched, the little girl tossed back her head in a quick laugh and began to run. A man knelt down to sweep her up into his arms, a white man with the high black boots and unmistakably patrician air of a successful planter. The woman at his side was as fine-boned and beautiful as the child, although the woman's skin and hair were both perceptibly darker. They were a family, of sorts, this rich white man with his colored lady mistress and their pale-skinned, golden-haired, *colored* child. But somewhere, whether in the city or out on a plantation, this man would have another family, a white, *legitimate* family, untainted by African slave blood.

"And you know what the worst part of it is?" Rose was saying. "That little girl thinks she's colored, too. She might look in the mirror and see white, but inside, she knows she's colored. All that white blood flowing through her? It might as well not even be there."

Zach stood very still, staring down at the proud, beautiful woman beside him. White blood flowed in her veins, too. He wondered how she reconciled these two disparate heritages that had joined and become one within her, the slaver, and the enslaved. And then he realized she hadn't reconciled them. Rose's father might have been white, but as far as Rose and the rest of the world were concerned, she was colored.

"Not many whites understand that," she said more quietly, her voice losing some of its vehemence, "understand what it means. But Philippe de Beauvais, he understood. A man goes around poking his thing into colored women, and sooner or later, he's going to have a child like that little girl over there. A child that don't belong nowhere. Too black to be white, and too white to be black. Michie Philippe, he wasn't going to do that to no child of his."

Zach let out a long, surprisingly painful sigh. "So can you think of a French-speaking colored woman who might have had a reason for wanting to see Philippe de Beauvais dead?"

Rose breathed a harsh laugh. "Maybe it was me, mmm? That what you thinking? That maybe it was me who drove out to the Bayou Crevé and had that little talk with your Yankee patrol?"

"Did you?"

She was no longer laughing. Eyes hard and glassy, she leaned into him, one dusky hand coming up to close around the silver amulet she wore at her neck. "If I was going to start killing, Michie Philippe's name wouldn't have been on my list."

"So who would be?" he asked, holding himself quite still.

"Who?" She laughed, a real laugh this time, before she turned away. "Maybe you."

He couldn't find Hamish.

Zach wandered through the crowd, his gaze scanning the lines of booths selling chicory-flavored coffee and sweet cakes and *sagamité*. He stood for a time watching the boys playing *raquettes,* then he made another round of the throng near the dancers, all without success. He had just about decided that Hamish must have gone off chasing a pickpocket or some other malefactor who'd offended his New York policeman's soul, when a dark-skinned little boy with tightly curled hair and a bare, rib-thin chest careened into Zach's bad leg with enough force to send him staggering.

"Steady, lad," said Zach, grasping the boy's skinny shoulders as the two of them almost toppled into a stand selling roasted peanuts. "You all right there?"

The boy looked up at Zach with vivid, scared green eyes. Then he snatched the Colt pistol from Zach's belt and took off at a run.

"Hey!" Zach shouted as the boy slid around the corner of the next booth. "Come back here with that."

The boy dove into the crowd, Zach hard on his heels. He was little and thin, sliding easily under a big man's spread elbows and darting through a group of tignon-headed women who had to step back, mouths gaping, to let Zach through. But Zach had the authority of his blue uniform and his white, privileged skin. The crowd parted before him.

He chased the boy out the Square and across the dusty street, the little boy's bare feet flying, his skinny brown arms pumping as he worked to suck air into his heaving chest. By now, Zach was beginning to notice that while people might be moving out of his way, they were always just a shade slow and a bit awkward in doing it. Their sympathy was all for the little boy with the woolly hair, and they were doing the best they could to help him get away.

The boy wasn't exactly getting away, but Zach wasn't gaining on him, either. Zach was starting to suck in air by now himself, the blue wool of his uniform hot and damp and uncomfortable. He followed the boy down a sun-blasted block of narrow shotgun houses and around a corner into a short lane lined with boarded-up old warehouses and brick outbuildings that rose straight up from the banquette and closed in around him like a trap. The boy skidded to a halt and swung about, his eyes darting everywhere, his entire body shuddering with fear and exhaustion.

"Give me the pistol," said Zach, his own breath soughing painfully in and out, the sweat running into his eyes. "Give it to me now, and I'll let you go."

The little boy backed away, the pistol clutched to his skinny, heaving chest, his eyes so wide, Zach thought it a wonder they didn't pop right out of his head.

"I won't hurt you," Zach said. "Just give me the gun."

The boy was no longer looking at Zach but at something beyond him. Something, or someone. Zach turned slowly, one hand going by habit to the hilt of his saber.

There were some eight men behind him, maybe ten. Black men, men with skin of ebony or chocolate and stony, enigmatic faces. Zach brought his saber singing from its scabbard, but he already knew it was useless. He could kill six, maybe more of these men. But the one who was going to kill him was the one who stood near the back, calmly lifting a Choctaw blowgun to his lips. If Zach had still had his Colt, he could have shot the man easily. But whoever planned this, whoever had sent that little black boy to steal Zach's gun and lure him here, had already thought of that.

Only, whoever wanted Zach dead had reckoned without a bottle of *bière du pays,* and a black-gloved lady who knew exactly which part of a man's head to aim for.

CHAPTER
TWENTY-SEVEN

The bottle didn't break when Emmanuelle de Beauvais brought it down on the back of the black man's head. But the impact stunned him enough to knock the blowgun from his hands and send him staggering, and that was all Zach needed. He leaped forward, saber swinging, and heard Emmanuelle cry, "*Elas!* Don't kill them all."

Zach's sword caught the man nearest him in the throat. "Why"—he jerked the bloodied blade free, his teeth gritting, eyes narrowing with fury as he swung again—"not?" He kicked the second man off the saber, and lunged at a third. "They're trying to—" His sword caught the third man in the arm, but he was already running away. They were all running, feet scrabbling, eyes wide as they threw quick, frightened glances over their shoulders. Zach let them go, his bloodred blade dripping as he lowered the point. "—kill me."

He twisted slowly to gaze back at the woman who still stood near the entrance to the cul-de-sac, the fraying black ribbons of her mourning bonnet fluttering in the hot breeze as she stared at the dead men sprawled around her. "What are you doing here?" he demanded, his voice coming out harsh, cold.

She raised her head to look at him, her face as composed and emotionless as if they'd been mere acquaintances discussing a balloon ascension, or a performance of one of the circuses that used to set up in the Square. Yet the last time he'd seen her, she'd been naked in her bed. She'd been naked, and he'd told her he loved her, and she'd effectively kicked him in the balls with her response. Now she said simply, "I saw you chase that little colored boy down the street, and then I noticed these men. I thought you might need help."

The wind gusted up, harder, rustling the leaves of a stand of live oaks nearby and setting their dripping swags of moss to swaying back and forth against the sun-leached sky. "Did Papa John tell you someone was planning to kill me?"

She shook her head.

He walked up to her, his saber dripping blood into the sun-dried mud at her feet. "But you were there, weren't you? That afternoon."

Dropping her gaze, she stooped to pick up the furze-tipped dart the black man had dropped. Wary of its sharp end, she held it carefully beneath her nose and sniffed.

"Don't tell me," Zach said, driving his saber back into its scabbard with a vicious hiss. "It's poisoned, right?"

Her breath came in a long, shuddering sigh, as if she'd been holding it. "I'm afraid so."

Reaching out, he touched his hand to her cheek, turning her face up to him. "You saved my life," he said, his voice softening as the blood lust thrumming through him began to drain away. "Just saying *thank you* doesn't seem very adequate."

He saw her lips tremble, then stretch into a smile that would have stolen his heart, if he hadn't lost it to her long ago. "I guess you could buy me a new bottle of ginger beer."

• • •

Zach never did get the chance to buy her that ginger beer.

He had two dead bodies and a growing crowd to deal with. The arrival of Hamish, breathing hard and dripping with sweat and looking dangerously red in the face, helped in some ways, but not in others.

"Everybody clear the area," he barked in his loud, New York policeman's voice, his arms sweeping back and forth like someone trying to herd a reluctant gaggle of geese. "Back, back, back." He leveled a fierce, suspicious stare at Emmanuelle, and said, "It'd be best if you left, too, ma'am."

"Of course, Captain." The serenity of her expression never slipped. "Although I suggest you consider having something to drink and sitting down to rest for a few minutes. A man of your size and habits shouldn't rush about in this heat." She turned to go, leaving Hamish sputtering and gulping, his mustaches twitching alarmingly.

Zach stopped her with a hand on her arm. "Are you sure you're all right?"

Looking up, she met his gaze and gave him a shaky half-smile. He had held this woman naked and hungry in his arms. He had joined his body to hers, lost himself with her in a night of dark passion and wild ecstasy and quiet communion. Yet she was still a mystery to him. A part of her was still hidden from him, kept inaccessible to him. "Yes," she said simply.

"I'd like to stop by your house this evening. See how you're doing," he said quietly, and heard Hamish snort behind him.

For a heartbeat, he thought she meant to refuse him. Instead, she sucked in a quick breath that lifted her high breasts and betrayed, for one brief moment, a degree of agitation he'd never have imagined she was suffering. "I'd like that," she said, and slipped from beneath his grasp.

It wasn't until considerably later, after the bloody mess near Congo Square had been cleaned up and a search instituted for the black men who'd survived Zach's sword, and their little boy accomplice, that Hamish finally consented to sit down and have a beer. Not a ginger beer this time, but a hearty pint of ale from a dockside tavern that sold boiled crabs and crawfish and shrimp by the dozen, and served them on big round enameled tin platters.

"You must be getting close to learning something about this killer," said Hamish, wrenching the claws off a crab with swift, practiced strokes. "If you're his new target."

"Then why don't I feel like I'm getting close?" Zach sat with one hand wrapped around a cold, sweating glass, his fingers swiping restlessly up and down, up and down. "The way I see it, we're looking for someone who knows how to shoot a crossbow and is intimately familiar with poisons, and the only person we've found so far who both fits that description and has anything to do with our victims is supposed to be dead."

"Or female," said Hamish.

"Jesus." Zach brought his glass down on the ring-marked wooden table in front of him hard enough to make an audible *thump*. "She could have strangled me in my sleep, if she'd wanted me dead."

"Yeah." Hamish poked an empty claw shell at him. "But then she'd have needed to get rid of that big body of yours, and that wouldn't be easy, not with only a black woman and a little boy to help her."

Zach stared out the tavern's grimy window at the street of rutted, half-dried mud slowly beginning to fill with a rollicky waterfront crowd. The sun was still bright and fiercely hot, but there was a golden quality to the light that told of the coming of evening. "I wish we could have found that boy who stole my Colt," he said, half to himself.

"He probably couldn't have told us much," said Hamish, shoving crabmeat in his mouth.

"No. But I'm afraid he might know enough to get himself killed."

Hamish reached for another crab. "The kid almost got *you* killed. Why should you care what happens to him?"

A memory reasserted itself, a memory of wide, frightened green eyes and a skinny, heaving chest. Zach pushed back his chair and stood up. "I care."

"Sweet mercy." Hamish paused with the crab half-cracked in one hand, and stared up at him. "Not again."

Picking up his glass, Zach took a long, deep drink of his beer, then set it back down with slow, ominous control. "Don't push your luck, Captain," he said, and left.

Emmanuelle sat on her front gallery, a book lying open in her lap, a palmetto palm waving gently to and fro in one hand. She was alone in the house. Sundays were Rose's day off, and Dominic had gone to spend the night, once more, with his grandparents on Esplanade. She'd come out here, hoping for a breath of fresh air, but instead of focusing on her book she found her gaze wandering again and again to the street below. He'd said he'd come. She wanted him to come. But she was afraid he wouldn't.

She kept remembering the things she'd said to him that night, the night she'd given herself to him with a passionate abandon that would have scared most men. Only, her uninhibited sensuality hadn't scared Zach Cooper, hadn't driven him from her. She had driven him away, by the way she'd reacted when he'd told her he loved her.

For some men, the words came easy. She knew that, knew it all too well. Some men simply loved women, all women, loved the siren call of silken hair sliding over a bare feminine shoulder, loved the soft smoothness of a woman's flesh beneath their seeking hands. For such men, the words were not so much a lie as an exaggeration, or perhaps a trivialization, a confusion of something that was supposed to be eternal and profound with the fleeting and casual intoxication of a moment. For others, of course, the words simply were a lie, a calculated device to soothe the qualms of the virtuous and timid—a vague, hollow promise that the attraction and devotion would endure beyond the passionate embrace and hot breathless release of driving need.

But sometimes, she knew, sometimes men and women said the words and meant them. Sometimes, they actually believed in love, believed it could last, believed that the magic and the joy and the sweet contentment would go on and on, forever.

Once, Emmanuelle had believed in love and happily-ever-afters. Once, she had loved with a violence and intensity that had overwhelmed her being and subsumed her life and lifted her up in the bright white light of the sublime. No one could have loved more than Emmanuelle had loved. Yet that love had still died. It had bled to death slowly, brutally, hideously, one awful, disillusioning day at a time. And with her love had died, too, her belief in love. Not only her belief in her own ability to love, but her belief that any love ever truly endured for a lifetime. And if even the most intense love didn't always last, then what was love, really, but an illusion, a delusion? A confusion thrown up by passion and hunger and the human need to believe oneself above the baser promptings of such a thing as primitive lust.

Her book forgotten, Emmanuelle flicked her fan back and forth, back and forth, her gaze fixed on the end of the street. The heat of the day lingered still, the air heavy and oppressive despite the setting sun that had already thrown the street below into shadow. Surely, she thought, he must have finished at Congo Square by now. She glanced anxiously at the watch she had pinned to her bodice, and knew it again, that shameful, unwanted dread, that worry that for some reason, any reason, he wouldn't come. And she knew, too, that piercing sweet yearning, that desperate need to see him, to watch his lips quirk up in the smile she loved, to hear the soft murmur of his voice, to hold his hard man's body close to hers.

It was both humiliating and frightening, to realize that one didn't need to believe in love in order to experience its symptoms. One could believe love an illusion, a passing obsession, a kind of mental sickness even, and still suffer from it, anyway.

He came in the first hush of twilight, when she was in the front parlor lighting a candle, and the air was beginning to sweeten with the scent of night-blooming jasmine and mock orange carried by the river breeze from the high-walled courtyards and secret gardens of the old city. By then, she'd half convinced herself that someone had tried to kill him again and succeeded, a fear that struck her now as both highly fanciful and un-characteristically, shamefully *female*.

She took her time walking down the curving stair-case, her hand gripping the polished wooden railing tightly to keep herself from hurrying in answer to the jingle of the bell. She told herself she shouldn't read too much into his being here, for he would have come in any case to thank her for what she had done. She slid back the bolt with the same studied casualness, al-though inside, her heart was thumping so loudly, she wondered he didn't hear it.

He stood on her doorstep, a tall, darkly uniformed man with gilded spurs on his boots and the long deadly arc of a saber worn close to his side. The glow from the gaslamps on the banquette highlighted the hard planes of his face, but his eyes were in shadow.

"You're all right," she said, before she could stop herself.

"Did you think I wouldn't be?" He took off his plumed hat and she saw he was smiling, a wry, teasing kind of smile that melted something inside her. "With-out you there to protect me with your bottle of ginger beer?"

The need to touch him suddenly became overwhelm-ing. She slipped one hand behind his neck, saw the flare of surprise in his eyes before she pressed her face against his chest. His arms closed around her, warm and hard and wonderful, holding her close, and she felt a small shudder rip through her before she could stop it.

"Don't tell me you really were worried?" he said, his breath warm against her cheek as he nuzzled her hair. "A man's pride is a tender thing, you know, and I think mine's just been grievously wounded."

She laughed softly into his chest, but sobered all too quickly. "I know how easily death can come."

He seized her by the shoulders, drawing her back so that he could stare down at her with eyes dark and compelling with a man's hunger, a man's need. "And are you telling me you'd care, Madame de Beauvais?"

She answered him by raising herself up on her tiptoes and kissing him, pushing his lips apart with her tongue. His lips moved with hers, hungry, seeking. His hand clenched in her hair, once, then relaxed, sweeping down her back to cup her bottom and pull her hard up against the cradle of his hips as he braced his legs wide. She was drowning in his kiss, drowning in him, lost to the world around her. She was only dimly aware of the door slamming shut behind him as he kicked out with one booted foot, then staggered slightly as she leaned into him and he took their weight on his bad leg.

"I thought you didn't want to do this again," he said, breathing softly against her ear, nipping at her jawline, laying a trail of kisses that burned like fire down her throat. His breath was coming harsh and fast, as fast as her own, his hands already working at the row of jet buttons that marched in prim correctness down the bodice of her mourning gown.

"I lied," she whispered, her hand in his, pulling him with her toward the back of the passage, stopping halfway up the steps to wrap her arms around his neck and drag his head down to her kiss.

In the end, he took her there, on the winding staircase, her back up against the whitewashed wall, her skirts bunched around her waist, his breath hot and urgent against her neck. But he didn't say he loved her, and it was only then, when his breathing stilled into silence, that she realized how badly she wanted to hear those words, even if she didn't believe in them.

Lukewarm and gently scented with lavender and rose, the bathwater caressed her body, the water and his dark, strong man's hands, moving in slow, luxurious circles over the bare white flesh of her breasts. She half-sat, half-lay cradled between his spread legs, her shoulders against his chest, so that she had to tilt back her head, the ends of her hair dipping into the water as her mouth sought his kiss, and found it.

They were in the big copper tub in the tiled bathing room on the second floor of the *garçonnière,* a bottle of wine and two glasses on a table beside them, a single flickering candle casting a small circle of golden warmth that left the corners of the room in shadow. It was big enough for two, that tub, six feet long and three feet wide and three feet high, although Emmanuelle had never shared it with anyone, until now.

"Emmanuelle," he said, his voice rough with an undercurrent of hunger, and she eased herself around so that she was lying along the top of him, her breasts pressed against his chest, his sex hard up against her. She ran her hands over his shoulders and up his neck. She loved the feel of him beneath her spreading palms, warm silken skin, hard powerful muscle. He was dark and he was beautiful and he was young, so young, and she was a fool, surely, to be wishing that any of this could last, to be thinking that she wanted this to last. To be wishing that what he thought he felt for her would last.

"How old do you think I am?" she asked suddenly, resting her forearms on his chest, her chin propped on her crossed wrists.

Reaching for his glass, he brought the wine to his lips and sipped it slowly, his gaze steady on her face. "Is it supposed to make a difference?"

"It should. I'm thirty years old. What are you? Twenty-six? Twenty-seven?"

He looked neither surprised nor shocked, but only gave her a slow smile. "Twenty-five as of last November."

She felt her heart sink, although somehow she managed a light laugh, pushing herself up to rake the fingernails of one hand across the exquisitely defined muscles of his chest. *"Alors, un enfant."*

He caught her wrist in his strong grip and jerked her back down so that she landed hard against him, bare wet flesh smacking against bare wet flesh with a splash that sent bathwater rolling in a crested cascade against the tub's high copper edge. "That's me, all right," he said, a wicked gleam in his eyes, his voice a husky, sensual whisper as he brought his face close to hers. "A real hell-born babe." She thought he would kiss her then. She wanted him to kiss her. Instead, his gaze locked still with hers, he tilted back his head and drained his wine.

She arched her spine, putting more space between them, her hand reaching out to grasp her own wineglass. Only she was shaking so badly, she almost sent the dark red liquid sloshing over the edge, and she drank more deeply and more quickly than she should have, the wine warming her belly and steadying her nerves, so that she sounded almost casual when she said, "Have you ever been in love before?"

She felt his chest lift beneath her as if on a sigh, watched the teasing light die out of his eyes to be replaced by something darker, something cold and fierce and dangerous. "No. Although I came close to it, once."

Emmanuelle held herself very still. "What happened?"

"She died."

"How?"

"She was murdered."

Emmanuelle set aside her wine. He wasn't looking at her anymore. His gaze had fixed on the flickering flame of the candle beside them, and whatever his thoughts, she knew they brought him great pain. "It was at that fort you were telling me about, wasn't it," she said softly, suddenly understanding. "Fort McKenna."

He nodded, reaching out to her then, his arm sliding around her neck to draw her close up against him again. She laid her head on his wet shoulder, felt his heart beat hard and strong beneath her. "Her father was the commanding officer at the fort. He wanted her to go to his family back East, find herself some solid, respectably settled pillar of society for a husband. Only Rachel had other ideas."

"She loved you," Emmanuelle said, knowing it, and ashamed of the swift rush of irrational jealousy that surged through her at the realization that some woman had loved him before her.

"It's why she died." His voice had gone oddly flat. He set aside the wineglass, his free hand coming up to stroke the wet tangle of her hair, although he kept his gaze fixed on the far wall. "It was the only thing they had in common, you see, the people that lieutenant killed. They were all close to me, or at least they mattered to me in some way . . . a young corporal from my outfit . . . an old Mexican woman who did my laundry . . . a little girl I was teaching to play chess." He paused. "The last one was Rachel."

Emmanuelle turned her face into his shoulder,

one hand creeping up to touch his cheek in mute comfort.

He took her hand in his, his fingers gripping hers hard. "The lieutenant was simply playing a game with me. I'd humiliated him at chess one night, and he wanted to show me he was smarter than I was—that he could hurt me, hurt those around me, and that I couldn't catch him, I couldn't figure it out."

"Yet you did catch him."

"Eventually. He used to leave these notes, taunting me, asking if I needed another body to help me figure it out." He paused, and she thought they must haunt him, those notes, those jeering challenges, forever burned into the core of who he was. "And then he'd deliver one."

"So he wanted to be caught?"

"No. He was due to be shipped out to California. If I hadn't figured it out when I did, he'd have been gone."

"What did you do to him?" she asked, her voice hollow, hushed. "Did you kill him?"

"No. I wanted to. I could have. And for one, terrible moment, I almost did."

"I didn't think you had any trouble killing."

He cupped his hand beneath her chin, urging her head back so that she had no choice but to look up and meet his steady gaze. "You're thinking about this afternoon, aren't you, and that night on the rue Conti?" He shook his head. "I'm a soldier, Emmanuelle. I learned a long time ago that if someone has shown he's willing to kill you, you don't let up until you're damned sure you've got him in a position where he can't do it. I've seen too many men ease off too soon, and die for it."

"And the lieutenant at Fort McKenna?"

"If I'd killed him, it would have been cold, calculated murder. I'm not an executioner."

She laced her fingers with his and brought their entwined hands up to her lips. She'd always thought of him as a killer, a remorseless bringer of pain and death and destruction. Yet she thought she must somehow have also known this truth about him, that he fought only to protect himself and others, that he maintained always a profound respect for human life. She'd simply shut her eyes and refused to see it.

"Those men who tried to kill you tonight," she said softly, "do you think they were sent by the same person who set the Irishman on me?"

"Hamish thinks so. He thinks I'm getting close to something."

"But you don't?"

He surprised her with a low laugh. "I think there are about two hundred thousand people out there who hate me, who'd like nothing better than to see me laid out as a cold cadaver on Dr. Austin Sinclair's embalming slab."

The image sent a shudder through her. "Don't say it," she whispered before she could stop herself. "Don't even think it."

He wrapped his hands around her arms, hauling her up so that she rose wet and naked and dripping above him. "Why, Madame de Beauvais," he said, a wicked smile curling his lips. "You surprise me. Are you so sure you don't love me?"

"No. It's just lust," she said. But she clung to him as if terrified she might lose him. And when he took her lips in a long, lingering kiss, she felt the sting of tears rare and hot in her eyes.

He made love to her then, slow and sweet, a gentle giving and taking of pleasure. And this time he did say it, those three hushed words whispered hoarsely in her ear. *I love you.* And God help her, she almost said it back. Almost.

In the pale light of early morning, the big house on Esplanade Avenue was a thing of fancy, white Doric pillars soaring toward the sky, high front steps reaching out with elaborately cast-iron railings flaring wide as if in welcome. But Emmanuelle didn't climb them. Skirting the side of the house, she made her way down the narrow brick alley edged with rosemary to a small side garden hidden away near the stables.

Jean-Lambert was there, where she knew he would be at this time of day. By nine o'clock, the sun would have risen golden bright and savage in the sky, and it would have become too hot for an old man to tend his garden. It was a labor of love, this garden, with its neat hedging of dark green dwarf box backed by silver catmint blooming purple and exuberant, its swags of climbing roses festooned above a riot of lilies and zinnias and carefully tended parterres of herbs. He rose early every morning, just for the sheer joy of being in it.

Her step on the path brought his head around for, crippled as he was, there was nothing wrong with either his sight or his hearing. He straightened slowly, a pair of secateurs in one hand, a basket filled with baby pink roses hanging by its handle over the arm that also gripped his cane.

"Papère," she said, standing on tiptoe to brush a kiss against his cheek, for he was tall, almost as tall as Philippe had been. "I need to talk to you."

His vivid blue eyes narrowed as he searched her face. "What is it, child?"

"I want you to take Dominic to Beau Lac."

"And you come all the way out here so early, for this?" He swung back to snip off a lily and lay it carefully in his basket. "Two months now, I've been wanting to take Dominic to Beau Lac. You said it was too dangerous."

"I still think it's dangerous."

He selected another lily, then cast her a sideways glance. "So what changed your mind?"

Emmanuelle let out her breath in a long, trembling sigh. "I'm afraid someone might try to kill him."

CHAPTER TWENTY-EIGHT

"Dominic?" Jean-Lambert's voice was sharp, his eyes haunted with a fear she'd never seen in him before. Most people thought of him as an astute businessman, a successful planter, but the truth was, Jean-Lambert's world began and ended in the small person of his grandson. "Who? Who would want to hurt Dominic? And why?"

"I don't know." For a moment, Emmanuelle wondered if she'd made a mistake, mentioning her fears, for Jean-Lambert was old, and not well. Yet if she were to trust him to keep Dominic safe, Jean-Lambert needed to be told. "I don't even know for certain that he is in danger." She ran her hand along the feathery tops of the catmint at her side, the soft leaves tickling her palm. "I don't understand why any of this is happening."

"Hmmm." He shifted awkwardly, his weight on his cane, and stooped to cut a spray of Queen Anne's lace. "You didn't tell me someone tried to kill you the other day," he said, his attention all for the flowers beneath his hand. "In the Irish Channel."

Her hand tightened over the catmint, then released it. "How did you know about that?"

He glanced at her over his shoulder, and she saw a faint sparkle of amusement mingling with the concern in those intense blue eyes. "This is still a very small town, at heart."

She wondered what else he'd heard, if he'd heard about the incident near Congo Square, or the many hours a certain Yankee major had spent in the darkened house on the rue Dumaine. She'd often wondered, in the past, how much Jean-Lambert knew about the things his son, Philippe, did. The things she did.

He snipped another zinnia. "What makes you think Dominic is threatened?"

"It's just . . ." She ran one hand up and down her other arm, feeling oddly chilled, although the sun was already up bright and hot. It was as if she could feel a cordon of darkness and danger, wrapping around her, tighter and tighter, threatening everyone she loved. "Too many people around me are dying."

"That Union major—the provost marshal—he doesn't have any ideas as to what's behind it all?"

"No."

"Does he think Dominic might be threatened?"

"I don't know—he hasn't said. But I need to know my son is safe."

Jean-Lambert rested his secateurs in the basket on his arm and turned slowly to face her. "And what about you, my child? Will you come to Beau Lac with us?"

"You know I can't. My work is here."

"You can't help people if you're dead."

Emmanuelle returned his gaze steadily. "As long as I can keep the Hospital de Santerre open, I will. I must. Besides, they've detailed a soldier to watch me. I'll be all right."

"Hmmm." He lifted his head, his eyes narrowing as he stared toward the lower gallery where their black woman, Celeste, was setting a table for breakfast. "I still think it would be better if you came with us."

"I promise I'll be careful."

He cast her a speculative sideways glance. "I can't change your mind?"

Emmanuelle smiled. "You know you can't."

Jean-Lambert let out a low laugh. "Oh, I know it. Come," he said, motioning her closer. "I see my breakfast is ready. You can help me up the stairs." He paused to glance around in some confusion. "I just need to find my secateurs."

"They're in your basket, Papère."

"Ah." He glanced down, a faint flush touching his weathered cheeks. "So they are. It's hell to get old."

Emmanuelle looped her arm through his and gave it an affectionate squeeze. "The alternative isn't so attractive, either."

He let out a short, startled bark of laughter. "It isn't, is it?" He took an unsteady step, his weight leaning heavily against her. "Come, my child. Come have some café au lait, and tell me all about this Irishman you bested with a medical bag and an umbrella."

That afternoon, Emmanuelle was in the storeroom, checking the hospital's dwindling supplies, when Charles Yardley threw open the door with enough force to send it banging against the wall.

"What the bloody hell have you done with my patient?" he demanded, standing on the threshold, a dark, disheveled figure silhouetted against the harsh midday sun.

Emmanuelle spun about so fast, she almost dropped the tray of lint she'd been holding. "Oh. You startled me."

"The woman with the ulcerated leg," he said, taking

two steps into the room. "What have you done with her?"

Now that she was no longer staring into the bright light, Emmanuelle could see him better, and what she saw took her breath. Charles Yardley had always cultivated a rakish air of nonchalance in his appearance, but the effect had been deliberate, controlled. Never had she seen him looking like this, his shirt collar stained yellow with sweat, his coat rumpled, his normally slicked-back blond hair sticking out at odd angles around a pale, haggard face. "*Mon Dieu,* Charles. You look terrible. When was the last time you slept?"

He passed a distracted hand across his eyes. "A couple of days ago, I think. I don't know." He fixed her with a hard, belligerent stare. "But the woman with the—"

"You discharged her," Emmanuelle said gently, setting aside the tray. "Saturday night. You came in late and you looked at her. She told you she wanted to go home, and you said she could. Don't you remember?"

He leaned back against the nearest wall, his eyes squeezing shut. "Oh, God," he said on a harsh expulsion of breath, both hands coming up to cover his face. "How could I forget?"

She touched her fingers to his coat sleeve, a brief contact gone almost before it happened. "Charles? What is it?"

He dragged his hands down his face until they covered only his nose and mouth, and stared at her with wild, bloodshot eyes. "Have I ever struck you as fanciful? Overimaginative? Delusional?"

"Hardly. You're probably the most prosaic, cynical person I've ever met." She gave him a wry smile. "Why? What is it?"

"It's just that lately . . ." He pushed away from the

wall, his hands dropping, and gave his shoulders a shake, as if to wake himself. "No. Never mind."

"Tell me. Something's obviously bothering you."

He fixed her with an intense, challenging stare. "I keep thinking someone's watching me. There. Now you can laugh."

Emmanuelle felt a cold whisper of fear touch her heart. "Have you actually seen someone?"

"No. If I had, I wouldn't feel like such a bloody idiot, now would I?" He took a quick turn around the room. "It's just this . . . feeling I keep getting. It . . . it raises the hair on the back of my neck." He let out a sharp laugh. "I always thought that was a ridiculous expression, but it does happen, you know." He shot her a quick, defensive look.

"I know."

"Lately, I find myself looking over my shoulder every time I walk down the bloody street. And when I'm home alone, I spend all night getting up to check that the door is locked, and peering out the windows. It's like I *know* someone is out there. I can't see him, but he's there." He went to stare out the open door, his face tense, strained. "I've even taken to leaving a light burning all night, like some bloody woman."

"Have you done anything about it?"

He swung his head to look at her over his shoulder. "Aside from not closing my eyes, and spending very little time at home alone, what can I do?"

"You could talk to the provost marshal."

"Ha." The laugh was hollow, derisive. "And have him think I've gone bloody bonkers? Not bloody likely."

"Listen, Charles." She took a step toward him, then stopped, her hands twisting together before her. "Henri and Claire are already dead, and someone tried to kill me the other day, in the Irish Channel. If you really are being watched, you can't just try to pretend it isn't happening."

In the unforgiving glare of the sun, his face looked white, drawn. "What are you saying?" he whispered. "That someone is *targeting* us? Trying to kill us *all*? Who?"

"I don't know."

His hands fell on her shoulders, almost shaking her. "You must have some idea."

She held herself very still. "Zachary Cooper thinks it might be Philippe."

He dropped his hands and took a step back, almost staggering, a strange twist of terror contorting his features. "Philippe? But . . . Philippe is dead."

"Charles, please." She started to reach out to him, then stopped. Too much lay between them, too many bad memories, too many hard feelings, for her to touch him, comfort him, now. "Go see Cooper. Talk to him."

He raked his hands through his hair, combing it back from his face, a strange kind of shudder quivering through him. "All right," he said, his head falling back as he met her gaze. "I'll do it. I'll do it this afternoon." A wan ghost of a smile touched his lips. "Now, would you tell me what patients I do still have?"

She did reach out to him, then, her hand closing over his in a quick squeeze. "Go see Cooper. And then go home and get some sleep."

"I've made a list," said General Benjamin Butler, tossing a sheet of paper across the desk at Zach. "I want one of your men stationed in each of these churches next Sunday. If these preachers"—the general stabbed an angry finger down on his list, causing the paper to skitter across the polished mahogany—"fail to

follow my orders and include the President of the
United States in their weekly blessings, then I want the
churches closed and the clergymen arrested."

"They're claiming freedom of conscience, sir," said
Zach, picking up the list. "Instead of the required
prayer, the congregations are being given a few minutes
of silence to pray for whomever and whatever they
wish."

"Including the triumph of the Confederacy,"
snapped Butler.

"Well, they're not allowed to do it out loud."

"Huh. Once they're arrested," continued Butler,
puffing on his cigar as he shuffled through his pile of
papers again, "I want them sent to the military prison
in New York. That ought to keep them out of trouble
for the rest of the war."

And teach them not to try to defy the Beast of New
Orleans, thought Zach, scanning the names in his
hand, although he didn't say it. "I don't see Father
Mullen on this list," he did say, looking up in surprise.
The seventy-year-old priest of St. Patrick's had probably defied Butler with more fire and gumption than
anyone in the city.

Butler glanced up, his back teeth chomped down on
his cigar, holding it in place as he smiled around it. "I
like the Irish. Now . . ." He lifted another long list of
names, the smile gone. "The editors of these newspa-
pers . . ."

It was close onto five o'clock by the time Zach left
the general's office. He was walking down the broad
stone steps of headquarters when a soldier came running up behind him. "Major Cooper, sir."

Zach swung around.

"There was a man here to see you while you were
with the general, sir. He said it was important, but you

know how the general doesn't like to be interrupted. . . ." The soldier fidgeted and looked sideways.

Zach hid a smile. "What'd this man want?"

"I don't know, sir. He wouldn't say. He was a queer-
looking fellow. An Englishman, from the sound of him.
He said he was a doctor, but he didn't look—"

"Dr. Charles Yardley?" Zach said sharply.

"Yes, sir. That's what he said his name was, sir."

"What time was this?"

"About two or three hours ago. He said to tell you
he was going home. Mumbled something about taking
a nap."

That morning, the sky had been a brilliant, fairy-
land blue, but by the time Zach left headquarters, the
afternoon storm was already starting to roll in, massive
black thunderheads pushed by a hot wind that scuttled
dry magnolia leaves across brick paving and rattled the
fronds of the banana trees.

Dr. Charles Yardley rented a small Creole cottage in
the Fauberg Tremé, a square house that fronted directly
onto the banquette and was raised only two steps
above it. They were much of a type, these Creole cottages one saw scattered throughout the old city, a com-
monsense, straightforward kind of building with stucco
walls and high end gables and four square, symmetri-
cal rooms arranged so that one led into the other without any need for a hall. The front entrance was a
French door with glass above and solid panels below,
flanked by vertical board shutters. There were strap-
hinged shutters on all the front windows, and except
for the ones on the entry door, they were all closed, although this was the time of day when most homeown-
ers threw them open in search of a cooling river breeze.

Knocking on the front door, Zach was surprised to

find the panel swinging inward three or four inches beneath his touch. "Dr. Yardley?" he called, the hinges creaking as he pushed the door open another foot or two into shadowy darkness.

The silence in the house was complete. From the street outside came the high-pitched chant of a child, *Five o'clock, six o'clock, seven o'clock, ho,* and the *clip-clop* of a tired horse pulling a rattling wagon down the rutted lane. Someone, somewhere, was playing a fiddle. But inside the cottage, there was no movement, no life, only the fluttering of a piece of paper as the breeze from the open door caught its edge and sent it spinning to the floor.

CHAPTER
TWENTY-NINE

The front door opened directly into a small square room with high glass-fronted bookcases covering most of the walls and a round Regency table littered with more books and scattered piles of papers. Stooping to pick up the fallen sheet, Zach found himself staring at a half-written letter bearing today's date and beginning, *Dear Mother and Agnes* . . . Zach tucked the letter beneath the bottle of brandy that stood with an empty glass near a chair pulled back and left partly askew. It struck Zach as both unexpected and strangely touching, the image it provoked, of Charles Yardley sitting here in the gathering dusk, dutifully penning a letter to the family he'd left behind in England.

"Dr. Yardley?" Zach called again. Beyond the light thrown by the open door, the house lay in near darkness, the closed shutters excluding all but thin slats of daylight. In the doorway leading into the adjoining front room, Zach paused to let his eyes adjust to the gloom and found himself looking at a parlor. Unlike most of the parlors in New Orleans, this one wore no "summer dress." The heavy velvet drapes still hung at the windows, no cool cotton covers hid the dark satin of the room's sofa and chairs, no gossamer balloons of tulle swathed the gilt gasoliers overhead.

At first, Zach thought he was asleep, the man who

lay stretched out on the burgundy and navy striped sofa that stood at a right angle to the empty hearth. He lay quite still, one hand flopped over the edge of the sofa to curl against a plush velvet pillow that had slipped onto the Turkey carpet, his head tipped back at an odd angle against another pillow, this one of embroidered silk.

The heat in the house was oppressive. Zach could feel his wet shirt sticking to his back, a trickle of sweat beginning to bead and roll down one cheek. He walked over to one of the front windows and opened it to throw back the shutters, letting a gust of wind and the scent of coming rain into the room. He stood there for a moment, one hand gripping the open window, his breath coming hard and fast with an old fear. Then he turned back into the room to go crouch beside Dr. Charles Yardley, and try to decide what had killed him.

"Damned if I know," said Hamish, squatting down beside the dead Englishman an hour or so later. By then, the rain had come and gone, a quick cloudburst that did nothing to ease the heat and only left the city steaming. "Could be poison, although it does't exactly look like he suffered, does it?" The big New Yorker leaned forward to sniff experimentally "He's been drinking."

"French brandy," said Zach, one shoulder propped against the wall beside the empty fireplace, his thumbs hooked on the leather of his sword belt. It was almost dark by now. The drapes at the windows had been closed against the prying gaze of the curious, leaving the room lit only by the intersecting circles of light thrown by a couple of oil lamps. "It's on the table in the other room," he said by way of explanation when Hamish glanced up.

"Ah." Hamish straightened with a creaking of stiff knees and a half-smothered groan. "We'll have to send the body over to the army hospital. See if they can figure it out."

"Yardley came to see me this afternoon, at headquarters." Zach pushed away from the wall. "When I was with the Old Man."

Hamish looked around in surprise. "What the hell for?"

"That's what I came here to ask him."

Hamish stooped to pick up the velvet pillow at his feet and toss it onto a nearby chair. "Have you looked around?"

Zach shook his head. "Not much. I was waiting for you. This is your profession, not mine." He had read the letter Yardley was writing to his mother, a caustic, dry-witted observation on the heat and the humidity and the Yankee occupation of the city that had told Zach nothing.

He left Hamish leafing through the papers in the front room and went back into the bedroom. Beneath its film of mosquito netting, the bed was made, although a vague depression in the center suggested someone had lain down on the counterpane. Lighting the brass lamp on the bedside chest, Zach let his gaze drift around the room. It was like the other rooms in the cottage, small but elegantly appointed, the furniture expensive without being ostentatious, everything carefully, artistically arranged, then ignored and allowed to slip into a lazy kind of disarray that suggested the man himself.

Zach pulled open the top drawer and began a methodical search of the room. He knew a vague, uneasy sense of intrusion, of poking into things that were private, things that Yardley, in life, would have objected violently to letting Zach see. He didn't really expect to find anything here. If Charles Yardley's death was linked to anything, Zach thought, it was to that tall, whitewashed building on the rue Bienville and the people who worked there—or who had been treated there.

Straightening, he moved to run his gaze over the litter of objects decorating the mantel. He was an unsentimental man, Charles Yardley. There was little of the personal or intimate even here, in his bedroom. Things of beauty, yes: intricately carved small ivory chests, tastefully framed architectural renderings of the churches of Christopher Wren, a silver flute lying on an end table atop a pile of sheet music. But nothing to suggest the passions that lived within the man—except, perhaps, that fondness for beauty and music.

Lifting the flute, Zach studied the score that lay beneath it, *Le Rossignol-en-Amour.* "I think of you whenever I hear this," someone had written across the top in a delicate black script. "Now, when you play it, perhaps you'll think of me."

Zach held the flute lightly, thoughtfully, in one hand. Then he set it aside and went over the room again, looking for something he might have missed. Ten minutes later he found it, a wedge of paper lying forgotten in the pocket of a heavy winter overcoat.

It was only a small piece of paper, folded over twice. "You must come to me tonight," someone had written in a hasty scrawl. "You make me burn as no man has ever done. Ever. Don't fail me." The script was the same as that on the music. Only, this time, the writer had signed a name, of sorts. *de B.*

De Beauvais.

"Finding anything in there?" called Hamish, his tread heavy as he crossed the parlor to stand in the open doorway, his hands braced against the frame at his side.

"No. Nothing." Zach turned, the sweat on his face drying into a thin, cold film, the folded paper with its damning signature already in his pocket.

A haze veiled the waning moon and stars, leaving only a faint glimmer to light the night. Zach walked the top of the levee, his gaze fixed on the dark and thickly rushing mass of the river, a fierce and building anger mingling with a sick kind of dread within him.

It was happening again. One death, and then another, and another, and there didn't seem to be anything he could do to stop it. So far, his best suspect was a dead man who could just as easily be a victim himself. And beyond that, what did he have? A voodoo king living in an African hut out toward the Bayou Sauvage, a man with an extensive knowledge of poisons and an eerie way of knowing what was going on deep in the guts of a man? An enigmatic German emigrant with a fierce ambition to become a doctor and a tragically maimed foot, legacy of someone's betrayal—some *woman's* betrayal? A high-strung, crippled brother with enough reason to kill his sister and her lover, and perhaps, by some twisted extension of logic, the old doctor who had allowed it all to happen under his nose? But not Charles Yardley—unless, of course, Yardley had been Claire's lover, too. Yet even then, Zach could see no reason for Antoine La Touche to send someone to kill Emmanuelle.

And then, of course, there was Emmanuelle de Beauvais herself.

Zach turned his back on the river, the cool wind blowing hard enough now to buffet his back and rattle the saber at his side. One by one, the lights in the city below were winking out. They were his responsibility, the people in those houses down there. He was doing his best to protect them from the depredations of yellow fever and the unsettled, desperate refugees flowing into the city, and even the sticky fingers of the Brothers Butler. But in this, he was failing them.

Burying his hands deep in the pockets of his coat, Zach fingered that small, telltale wedge of paper. If the old man had in fact been killed by mistake, then that left the four of them, Philippe and Emmanuelle, Claire and Yardley. Two men, two women, bound together in a twisted web of passion and betrayal and death. Someone was killing them, methodically, ruthlessly. Someone who thought he—or she—had a damn good reason to kill. Someone who wouldn't stop until they were all dead.

Standing at the crest of the levee, the wind almost cold against his back, Zach knew it again, that sick clenching deep in his belly. It could so easily have been Emmanuelle who'd died tonight. And he was so afraid, so terribly afraid, that he might not be able to protect her, that he might not catch the killer in time. That she might die, too.

She'd said she didn't believe in love. Not a love that went beyond the sweet intoxication of attraction, beyond the desperate, possessive need of the moment, beyond the scalding hot rush of lust. But he believed. He believed in a love that could be not only all-consuming and passionate, but noble and enduring. A love that could last into eternity. Perhaps it's a kind of luck, he thought, what happens to love. Perhaps the endurance of love says more about the honesty of the man and woman who love than about the quality of their love. Because when two people are honest with each other, when they love the person who is really there and not some false image that has been created for them—or that they've created for themselves—when they're open about who and what they are, about what they want, then the chance of disillusionment is surely lessened, the chance of growing apart reduced.

Well, Emmanuelle de Beauvais wasn't being very honest with him. From the beginning, he'd known that, known she was hiding parts of herself from him, important parts. He'd known, but it hadn't stopped him from desiring her, hadn't stopped him from falling in love with her—or at least, with the parts of her she'd let him see. But he couldn't help wondering what it was she was hiding. And a part of him—the part of him that was Ben Butler's provost marshal—acknowledged that it might be something terrible indeed.

He found her in the chapel on the second floor of the Hospital de Santerre. She was kneeling at the rail before the altar, her head bowed, her hands clasped in prayer, her face bathed golden by the morning light streaming in the tall, clear windows beyond her. His uneven step on the tiled floor brought her head around, and she made a quick sign of the cross and rose to her feet. She looked pale and shaken and very, very afraid.

"You've heard?" he said, stopping before her.

He saw the surge of rampant fear in her eyes, her chest lifting as she sucked in a quick, shuddering breath. "Not long ago." She brought up one hand to rub her forehead, then let her hand drop. *Mon Dieu. Who is doing this?*

He knew a swift, powerful urge to take her in his arms and comfort her. Instead, he said, his voice cold and hard, "Why didn't you tell me you'd slept with him?"

Her head snapped back as if he had slapped her, her nostrils flaring, her eyes widening as she stared up at him. Her eyes were the blue-green of a coral sea, deep and hurting. As he watched, the hurt faded, subsumed by anger and a fierce, icy control. "I didn't think it was any of your business. I don't recall asking you for a list of who you've slept with in the last ten years."

"The people around me aren't dying."

"I see." She drew in a deep, shaky breath. "It's not my lover who wants to know, but Ben Butler's provost marshal. My mistake."

She would have pushed past him, but he grabbed her arm, his fingers digging into the stiff black cloth above her elbow, jerking her around to face him again. "Why didn't you tell me?"

She held herself very still in his grasp, her voice even, controlled. The voice of a stranger. "I didn't think it was relevant. I still don't."

"What about Henri Santerre? Did you sleep with him, too?"

At that, she jerked her arm from his grasp, and he let her go. "How can you even suggest such a thing?" Anger flashed, then disappeared again behind cold scorn. "Next you'll be asking if Claire La Touche and I were lovers."

"Were you?"

She simply stared at him, her breath coming hard and fast, her face a frozen mask. "How did you find out?" she demanded. "About Charles and me?"

"From this." He held the crumpled wedge of paper out to her, and after a moment's hesitation, she took it. In the hush of the chapel, the rustle of the paper as she unfolded it sounded unnaturally loud. She stared at it in silence for a long moment, then said softly, "How unlike him, to keep such a thing."

"I doubt he meant to. It was in one of his pockets." From the distance came the peal of the cathedral bell, ringing out over the city. "Were you still seeing him?"

"Who wants to know? Ben Butler's provost marshal, or my lover?"

"I want to know."

Turning away, she went to stand beside one of the tall, narrow windows overlooking the street below. "No," she said after a moment. "I wasn't still seeing him."

Zach stayed where he was, one hand gripping the pommel of his sword. "Why not? What happened?"

She lifted one shoulder in a shrug. "Nothing dramatic or unusual. He found someone who interested him more."

Zach knew her better now. Knew when she wasn't being quite honest with him, knew when she was holding something back. "And you?" he said, pressing her, wanting to hurt her, wanting to make her hurt like he was hurting. "Did you still *burn* for him?"

He saw her stiffen, although she kept her face turned away from him. "I didn't kill him in a jealous passion, if that's what you're asking." A silence fell between them, a silence broken only by the rumble of a wagon from the street below. Then she said, "How did he die? Do you know?"

"According to the autopsy, he was smothered. Someone probably found him on the sofa, asleep, and held a pillow over his face."

"Poor Charles." In one brief display of weakness, she hugged her arms over her stomach, her shoulders hunching forward as if around some inner pain. Then she straightened, visibly struggling to hide all the hurting, frightened bits away before she turned to face him. "He said he was going to see you yesterday. Did he?"

Zach shook his head, aware once again of that urge to take her in his arms and comfort her, to tell her it was all right sometimes to give way to pain and weakness and fear, to tell her she didn't always need to be so damned in control of her emotions. The only time this woman let herself go, it seemed, was in bed.

"He tried," Zach said, his voice as impersonal as he could make it. "I was in a meeting. By the time I got to his house, it was too late." He kept his gaze on her face. "Did he tell you what he wanted?"

"He was afraid. He thought someone was following him, watching him."

"He didn't know who?"

"No. He never actually saw anyone. It was just a feeling he had." A sad smile touched the edges of her lips, then faded. "Charles didn't put much stock in such things as feelings, intuitions. He was badly rattled by it."

"He was a good friend of Philippe's," Zach said, strolling over to stare at the chapel's simple altar, "wasn't he?"

"Yes."

Zach glanced back at her over his shoulder. "Did he know? Did your husband know you were sleeping with his good friend and colleague?"

Her gaze fixed with his, she slowly nodded her head.

"How?" he demanded, walking right up to her again. "How did Philippe find out?"

"Charles told him."

Jesus, Zach thought. What kind of a marriage did she have? "And was he angry? Philippe, I mean."

"No."

"Why not?"

She let out her breath in a long, tired sigh. "Because Philippe was in love with someone else."

He leaned into her. "Who?"

She met his gaze squarely, her beautiful eyes wide and frightened and lying, lying. "I don't know."

"You know," he said, and turned away and left her there, in the golden light of the deserted chapel.

CHAPTER
THIRTY

An afternoon breeze stirred the drying berries of the Chinaball tree in the courtyard and brought down a drift of crepe myrtle blossoms that scuttled across the paving stones in a shimmer of soft pink and white. Emmanuelle leaned her head back against the worn green leather of Henri Santerre's old office chair and let her breath out in a long sigh, her gaze on the scene outside the window, her hands falling idle in her lap.

It was over. They had dedicated their lives to building up this hospital—she and her father, Henri Santerre, and Philippe. Endless hours and sleepless nights, so much sacrificed over the years. And now it was over.

She heard the thump of a crutch on the wooden floor behind her. A man's cold, bony hands descended on her shoulders, gripping her tightly. "*Alors,*" said Antoine La Touche, swinging her chair around so that she faced him. He looked thinner, more unwell than ever, his eyes bloodshot, his mouth drawn down with worry. "I've just heard. What is wrong with these Yankees? Why can't they stop this?"

Emmanuelle laid her hand over one of his and tried to smile reassuringly up at him, although she doubted she succeeded very well. "They're doing everything they can, Antoine. I honestly believe that."

Hitching his crutches around, he sat on the edge of the desk and leaned forward to fix her with a scrutinizing gaze. "And you, *bébé*? How are you holding up?"

She let her own gaze drift around the high-ceiling, book-lined room. "It's not easy, closing this place down."

He took her hand again and held it between both of his. "There is no way around it?"

She shook her head. "I've been fighting a losing battle for weeks now. I've known that. But I can't fight this. You can't have a hospital without a licensed physician." They'd looked into trying to find someone to help them, before, she and Charles Yardley. But with virtually every able-bodied doctor in the city gone to join the Confederate war effort, only the very old and the very young were left, and they were all—even the interns—already overwhelmed.

"What will you do with your patients?" Antoine asked, his gaze still fixed on her face.

"I've spoken to the sisters at the Hôtel de Dieu. They can take some. And Lewis over at Charity Hospital said he'd take the rest."

"It's not your fault," Antoine said suddenly, his grip on her hand tightening. "You've done everything you could."

She squeezed his hand, a wry smile tugging at her lips. "I know that rationally. And yet . . ." She paused. "I'm not always rational."

"Huh." He flicked her cheek with his fingertips. "You're one of the most rational, levelheaded, competent people I've ever known. When this is all over, when the war is over, you can reopen."

A painful lump of emotion swelled Emmanuelle's throat, forcing her to swallow, hard. "This building was mortgaged to pay the fines Butler levied on everyone who had contributed to the Confederate war effort. By the time the war is over . . ." She shook her head again, unable to continue.

"Emmanuelle." Antoine leaned forward, his face pinched, intense. "I don't understand what's been happening around here, but I do know one thing: You are in grave danger. Now that you no longer have the hospital holding you here, please . . . will you leave New Orleans?"

She let out her breath in a long, shaky sigh. "Philippe's parents are taking Dominic to Beau Lac, at the end of the week."

"Then go with them. You must. For Dominic's sake. You know that. He needs you alive."

"I know, but . . . how can I? There's so much to be done."

Sliding off the edge of the desk, he tucked his crutches under his arms and gave her a cocky smile. "Tell me what to do first."

It was late by the time Emmanuelle took the mule car out Esplanade Avenue, the towering oaks and magnolias mere black silhouettes against a mellowing turquoise sky streaked by the setting sun with high, fluffy stripes of orange and violet tinted clouds. Lately, she'd taken to encouraging Dominic to spend his days and even many of his nights here, on the outskirts of the city, where bullfrogs croaked in the nearby bayous and fireflies flitted through the live oaks. It seemed healthier, surely, than letting him roam the old quarter with its crowded streets and seedy cabarets, its burned-out warehouses and busy wharves. Healthier, and safer. Yet as she approached that big white house with its classical pediment and double galleries wrapped with cast iron, she was conscious of a sadness deep within her, a profound sense of loss and guilt that went beyond the closure of the Hospital de Santerre.

Dominic was her dearly beloved son, her firstborn and only child, the center of her existence and the light of her life, yet she'd seen him so little these last months, since Philippe's death, and then Henri's. She tried. She tried, always, to be there to take breakfast with him, to share his dinner and talk with him about his day. She tried to find the time to walk with him along the levee, to go blackberry picking, to picnic in the park. But it never felt as if it were enough. And she had, always, always, this sense of being pulled apart, of neglecting one responsibility for the other, of failing him, failing the hospital, failing herself.

Perhaps, she thought, letting herself in the garden gate, perhaps in some ways it was better that the hospital was closing. She couldn't keep it going on her own. And a boy needed his mother, especially a boy who'd already lost his father.

"Maman." At the foot of the steps, Emmanuelle paused, her head turning toward the stables. "Maman," Dominic called again, racing across the lawn, a string of catfish dangling from one raised arm. "Look. I caught the biggest, and the most."

"You always catch the biggest and the most," she said, laughing, as he skidded to a halt before her.

"Only when you're not there," said Jean-Lambert, limping up, his weight resting heavily on Baptiste's arm. *"Bonsoir, ma petite."* He leaned forward to let her reach up and brush a kiss against his cheek. "You're looking tired."

"I am tired, Papère," she said, linking her arm through the old man's and nodding to Baptiste, who turned away.

"Come, Michie Dominic," said the big black man, lifting the string of fish from the boy's hand. "Let's go show these to Celeste and see if she can't fry some up for your supper, hmmm?"

"I heard about that English doctor," said Jean-Lambert, his voice hushed as he watched Dominic take off at a run toward the kitchen. "That Charles Yardley. It's troubling, very troubling." He brought his gaze back to Emmanuelle's face. "Come to Beau Lac with us, child. You must."

There was a weathered old swing at one end of the porch, and they sat there, sharing an unvoiced reluctance to leave the freshening breeze and sweet smell of moonflowers and honeysuckle. Emmanuelle leaned her head back, her eyes wide as she stared up at the stars beginning to wink at them from out of the purpling sky. "The people here still need medical attention," she said, feeling guilty, torn. And yet without the hospital behind her, she wondered, how many would call on her, a woman, with no official medical certification?

"The fighting in the area has lessened, which means fewer military casualties to fill the wards at Charity and the Hôtel de Dieu," Jean-Lambert said gently. "Besides, doctors are scarce in the river parishes, too, you know. You could do much good there."

The chains holding the swing creaked gently in the stillness of the evening. A lazy, peaceful image beckoned, an image of moss-draped oaks and still black waters, of a hip-roofed French plantation house with thick brick piers and wide, shady galleries. Her gaze still fixed on the distant stars, Emmanuelle sucked in a deep, painful breath and let it out again in a long sigh. The urge to go was strong, to leave behind the terror of the Yankee-occupied, heat-festering, suddenly dangerous city and lose herself in the safe, healing rhythms of the countryside. She thought of quiet, undemanding days spent riding the fields or fishing for bass with Dominic and Jean-Lambert on the lake, and she knew a gentle yearning mingled with a fierce sadness that was like a grieving for something lost.

There could be no peace for her at Beau Lac, not now, but it offered her a sanctuary of sorts, and she wasn't too proud to admit how badly she needed that, how badly she needed a place of refuge, a haven, far from the reach of an unknown but ruthless killer. Far from Zach Cooper with his darkly stirring eyes and hard-driving body and whispered words of a love that could last forever.

She felt it keenly, the sense of emptiness, of desolation that had been riding her all day, ever since that cold, brief confrontation in the chapel. It was there, deep inside, a kind of protective numbness beneath the tide of fear and grief that had come with the news of Charles Yardley's death, with the acknowledgment of the heartbreaking inevitability of the hospital's closure. She supposed, in some way, this inner deadness was a blessing. Because she wasn't sure she could bear the pain she knew lurked beneath it.

She never should have allowed them to happen, those breathless nights of endless passion. She knew that now, had always known it so surely that she wondered how it had ever come about. How had it happened, she wondered, that they had come to this? She a widow of less than three months, fiercely loyal to the South however critical she might be of its *peculiar institution,* a woman who hated violence and this killing business of war. And he, this man who had made war his business, who strode her city as a conquering enemy, who had begun by believing her capable of murder, and who now thought—what?

She could hear the croaking of bullfrogs in the distance, the stirring of the banana trees in the warm
breeze, the melodic laughter of an African voice carrying from the back of the house. This was her world,
this the life she had made for herself twelve years ago.
And if she had dared to hope, in the warm embrace of
the night, that she might know some other future than
this narrow, lonely existence, that she might know love
and grasp at an eternity of joy and laughter, then what
she had seen in those hard, dark eyes this morning had
warned her, surely, of the dangerous, seductive lure of
hopes and dreams.

"Emmanuelle," said Jean-Lambert, the swing creaking softly as he shifted toward her. "Come to Beau Lac
with us."

"I'll come," she said, and knew an inner pain so
sharp and piercing, it took her breath. But it faded
quickly, submerged beneath that rising tide of numbness and an overwhelming, quite sudden sensation of
exhaustion.

They called them shotguns, these narrow houses one
found concentrated in the poorer sections of the city,
the idea being that if someone fired a shotgun in the
front door, the blast would pass through each room in
succession and then out the back. There were a lot of
shotgun houses in the Irish Channel, most built of gun-
wales from barges that had come down the Mississippi
and then been broken up for their lumber. But some
were more substantial structures, built of milled wood,
still only one room wide but with high front gables and
cast-iron railings and slender Italianate or neo-Grecian
columns embellishing their tiny facades.

As soon as Zach turned into the narrow street off
Tchoupitoulas, he knew which house belonged to Fra

Spears and her four sons. He could see it, halfway down the block, the shutters freshly painted, the front stoop scrubbed, the shallow front yard free of all traces of the trash and weeds that disfigured so many of the shacks and tenements that surrounded it. And as he drew closer to the tiny, painstakingly maintained house, Zach found himself wondering what had driven her so far, this widowed German woman and her four boys, and why she had chosen to come here, to New Orleans, with its fierce storms and killing heat, its yellow-fever epidemics and endemic swamp sickness.

A man sat on the house's narrow front porch, a tall, slim young man idly strumming a guitar and watching Zach's approach with a narrowed, steady gaze. "*Guten Morgen,* Major," said Hans Spears, his hands stilling for a moment on the strings as Zach drew nearer.

"Good morning." Zach paused with one foot propped on the bottom step as he stared up at the young German. A neat stack of books and papers lay on the wicker table beside him, untouched.

"You've come to talk about Charles Yardley," said Hans, his fingers moving again to pick out a sweet, sad melody. It wasn't a question.

"May I come up?"

Hans nodded, his attention all for the music he coaxed from his guitar.

"Did you know him well?" Zach asked, his gaze hard on the other man's face.

"Not as well as I knew Philippe, if that's what you are asking." The words were calm, cool, but Zach could see a muscle ticking nervously in the other man's cheek.

"Tell me," said Zach, propping one hip on the edge of the porch's iron railing to take the pressure off his aching leg. "Are you afraid?"

Hans brought his hand down on the strings in a loud, discordant crash. "You mean, am I afraid I might be next?" He swung his head to look over one shoulder at Zach, his thin face drawn and held tight. "Of course. Wouldn't you be?"

"Yes."

He put the guitar away from him and lurched up to go stand at the top of the steps, his hands tucked up beneath his arms, his gaze fixed on some distant, unknown point. The sun was fierce today, the sky a brilliant blue, the air so humid, the world seemed to drip. "Who's doing this?" he said, his voice shaken, yet still controlled. "Who, and why?"

"I don't know." They had a lot in common, Zach thought, Emmanuelle and this self-possessed, self-disciplined young German. "I thought maybe you could help me figure that out. Maybe think of someone who was treated at the Hospital de Santerre recently, someone who might have a grudge against the people who worked there? Someone who might have threatened them." Hamish was still plowing his way through a long list of patients, looking for someone with a grudge, but it had always struck Zach as an unlikely way of finding their killer.

The boy looked thoughtful for a moment, then shook his head, the muscles in his throat working as he swallowed. "I can think of no one."

"What about that day at the hospital last May, before Philippe de Beauvais was killed? The day of the quarrel between Claire La Touche and Charles Yardley. You were there, weren't you?"

"Not at first. I came in near the end, with Santerre." That clear, steady gray gaze swung around to fix on Zach's face. "Why?"

"Everyone involved in or even present at that quarrel is now dead. Everyone except you and Emmanuelle de Beauvais."

"You think I don't know that? You think I don't lie awake and think about that?" He flung out one hand in a swift, savage gesture. "I try to read, to study, and the words simply blur before my eyes."

Zach stared down at that neat pile of books, and the open notebook beside it. The notebook was a common enough one, bound in black cloth worn rusty by time and use. But it was the delicate, slanting script that drew Zach's attention, and held it.

"What exactly is this?" he said, reaching to slip the notebook from beneath the volume holding it open.

"Some notes Philippe gave me, from when he was in medical school. He thought I might find them useful." The German's eyes narrowed in sudden interest. "Why?"

"Philippe?" Zach's fingers tightened around the notebook, almost crushing it. "This is Philippe's writing?"

"Yes."

Sweet mercy, thought Zach, as all the events of the recent past spun about in his head and realigned themselves in a new pattern of sudden, startling clarity. Sweet, sweet mercy.

CHAPTER
THIRTY-ONE

He thought he might find her at the Hospital de Santerre, but she wasn't there. No one was there except the
big Senegalese nurse who answered Zach's shout with
slow, ponderous steps and said, "Ain't nobody here no
more. They gone. All gone. She closin' this place down,
didn't you know that? Now Dr. Yardley done got his-
self kilt, cain't have no hospital without no doctor,
uh-uh."

Leaving the tall, whitewashed building on Bienville,
Zach stood on the sunbaked banquette and listened to
the dull clank of the cathedral bell in the distance, ringing the Angelus. She hadn't told him, that morning he'd
found her in the chapel. She hadn't told him she would
be closing the hospital, just as she hadn't told him the
truth about that folded slip of paper he'd found in
Charles Yardley's coat. Emmanuelle might very well
have slept with Yardley herself; the more Zach thought
about it, the more he decided she probably had. But the
de Beauvais who had written that desperate, passionate
note, who had burned for the Englishman as for no
other, had been not Emmanuelle, but her husband.

Philippe de Beauvais.

He found the door to the dark, narrow passageway
of the house on the rue Dumaine open, and followed

the sound of a woman singing to the courtyard. There, all was confusion, the paving stones littered with trunks and cases, some closed, some half-packed. He paused in the arched opening to the yard and the singing stopped abruptly as Rose looked up from where she knelt before an open trunk and saw him.

"What you doing here?" she said, her face closed and unfriendly, her French accent unusually pronounced. "We're busy. Leaving for Beau Lac, we are, come Friday."

"Where is Madame de Beauvais?"

Rose bent over the trunk and busied herself with rearranging the contents. "She doesn't want to see you."

How much, Zach wondered, staring at that regally inclined neck and rich café au lait skin; how much did this tall, beautiful mulatto know about the people whose lives she'd shared for so many years? How much did she know about him? "She doesn't exactly have a choice," he said quietly.

"Ah." Rose tilted her head, an unfriendly, humorless smile touching her lips as she stared at him across the sunny yard. "So you're here as a Yankee and not as a lover, hmmm?"

"You can take me to her, or I'll announce myself," Zach said, his jaw hardening. "The choice is yours."

He expected her to stand then, and lead the way up the curving flight of steps. Instead, she simply shrugged and bent over her packing again. "Announce yourself. She's up in Dominic's room. You know where it is."

She had the French doors and shutters of the bedroom at the back of the house thrown open wide, although the sun was high in the clear blue sky and dazzlingly hot. He knew she must have heard his uneven step on the stairs, the scrape of his spurs, but she didn't look up when he paused in the doorway from the hall. She stood beside a case that lay open on the bed amid a jumble of boy's clothes, her back to him, a shirt in her hands.

"You should have told me you were leaving," he said quietly.

"Because I'm still a suspect?" She did look around then, although her hands continued the work of folding the shirt with quick, sure movements. "All I can think about is getting my son away from here. Going someplace where he can be safe. Where I'll be safe."

"Is that the only reason you're leaving?"

She bent to place the folded shirt in the case. "It's the main one."

Zach glanced around the room, at its shelves jammed with books and all the clutter of a boy's life. "Where is he? Dominic, I mean."

"He has a friend who lives over near Rampart Street. He's there." She reached for another shirt. "Why?"

"Because you lied to me. Again." She went quite still, and he saw it, that brief flash of guilt and fear before she hid it behind her habitual mask of sangfroid. He walked right up to her, close enough that when he leaned into her, his face was only a hand's span from hers. "I can see you thinking, *now, which of my many, many lies has he discovered?*" She didn't say anything, and he turned away, one open palm slapping at the high bedpost in frustration. "You know, I might be a lot closer to catching this killer you're so afraid of if every other word out of your mouth wasn't a lie."

"Are you going to tell me what you're talking about?"

Zach went to stand beside the open French doors overlooking the courtyard below, "I saw Hans Spears this morning. He's a bit nervous, too. So nervous, he's been having a hard time bringing himself to look over the medical notebooks your husband so kindly lent him."

"What exactly are you saying?"

He swung to face her again, his gaze hard on her white, drawn face. "That note I found in Charles Yardley's house. You didn't write it. Philippe did."

She stared at him, unblinking, for a moment. Then she let out her breath in a long, pent-up sigh, her hands coming up to brush her hair off her forehead. "I didn't exactly lie to you." She brought her gaze back to his face, her chin lifting. "I slept with Charles, too."

"What, the three of you, together?"

"No!"

He gave her a mean smile. "My apologies. I'm reaching the point where I'll believe almost anything." The sound of running feet, pounding up the stairs, drew Zach's attention to the hall. A boy's shout echoed up the stairwell, followed by Dominic's unmistakable laughter, and Emmanuelle lost whatever color she'd had left in her face.

"Get your hat and gloves," Zach said. "We're going for a walk."

They turned toward the river and the cathedral, a tense silence between them. The heat in the streets was thick and oppressive, the high stucco walls of the Spanish-style houses sun-drenched and close and echoing with the booming clatter from a ship unloading down at the wharves.

"Tell me about Philippe," Zach said, his gaze hard on the profile of the small, fine-boned woman who walked beside him.

She said nothing for a moment, her eyes downcast, one hand fisted tight around the sunshade she carried.

Like her clothes and her hat and her gloves, the sunshade was black. "I was seventeen when I met him," she said at last, her voice coming out strained, hoarse. "You must understand that until then, even back in France, books and medicine had been my entire life." She paused, and he had the sense that she was lost in the past, trying to recapture the girl she once had been. "There aren't very many men who are comfortable with a woman like that. It didn't take me long to come to the conclusion that if I wanted to be a woman—a desirable woman—then I couldn't be a doctor, too. And I was determined to be a doctor."

He tried to imagine her as she must once have been, young, eager, easily hurt. "So you resigned yourself to being a woman men found undesirable."

She let out a short, startled laugh. "Yes, I suppose you could say that." Her gaze lifted, her eyes narrowing as she squinted up at the high tiled roofs of the surrounding houses. "And then I met Philippe."

"He was different?"

She nodded, her face still turned away from his. "Philippe told me I was both beautiful and brilliant." A sweet, sad smile touched her lips. "I think I would have loved him for that alone. He saw me as both a woman and a man." She glanced sideways at him. "If that makes sense?"

"I think so. He admired your intelligence and strength, and still found you desirable."

Her eyes widened, as if she were surprised he understood. Surprised anyone understood. "Yes, that's it. The other men I'd met had all been intimidated by my knowledge, or laughed at my desire to learn medicine, but Philippe encouraged me. He admired me. Liked me. It was a heady experience. He was so handsome, so brilliant, so intense and passionate. Not just about medicine, but about art . . . music . . . life."

"And the sins of the flesh," Zach added dryly.

"Yes." Again she smiled, a secret, naughty smile this time that sent a startling and unpleasant wave of jealousy coursing through him.

"And so, for love of him, you gave up your dream of going back to Paris and becoming a doctor. It seems ironic."

The smile faded. "He filled my world. I couldn't see anything beyond him. I was afraid his parents would oppose our marriage, but they didn't."

They crossed St. Anne Street, passing a billiard hall through whose open doors could be glimpsed white men, and colored ones, too, wearing black coats and brilliantly colored silk vests draped with gold watch chains that gleamed out of the shadowy interior. "Were you happy?" Zach asked, bringing his attention back to her face.

"At first, yes. He introduced me to a world I'd never dreamed existed."

"The world of the senses," Zach said. "Hashish and silken bonds and the erotic thrill of that fine line between pleasure and pain."

They had reached Jackson Square now, with its rows of sycamores and elms moving gently in the river breeze. She turned to face him, her parasol slipping back so that the sun fell full on her face. "Yes." She tilted her head, that defiant smile curling her lips, the small gold hoops in her ears moving against the dark thickness of her hair. "I enjoyed it. Does that shock you?"

"No."

She took a deep breath, her chest rising as the breath

caught and the smile faded, leaving her expression intense. "Because it's in you, too, isn't it?" she said suddenly, her gaze hard on his face. "That wildness, that need to push the bounds of what's expected, what's allowed."

He didn't deny it. How could he, given what had passed between them? "So what happened with Philippe?"

They turned to walk together along the rusting iron fence that bordered the square. "Dominic happened." She threw him a quick, sideways glance. "Don't get me wrong. Philippe was thrilled at the thought of having a child. But he . . ." She swallowed. "He lost interest in me, as his wife. At first I thought it was because he was afraid he might hurt the child I carried, or because he found my rounded body unattractive." She fell silent for a moment, lost in the past. "Philippe liked women who were thin. Boyishly thin."

Women like Claire La Touche, Zach thought; young women, built narrow of hip and small of breast, like a boy. The birth of a child would change that.

"I convinced myself that once I had Dominic," she said, "things would go back to the way they had been."

"But they didn't?"

She shook her head, her chin lifting, her eyes narrowing as she gazed toward the forest of bare masts just visible above the levee. "Philippe started spending more and more time away from home. He was teaching at the medical school as well as working with my father and Henri at the hospital, so I didn't think too much of it. He had his room in the *garçonnière* by then. He set it up when I was carrying Dominic—to keep from disturbing my sleep, he said, and then, later, because the baby's crying at night disturbed him."

She paused, the slim muscles in her throat working

visibly as she swallowed. The heat had driven most of the people indoors by now. For a moment, there was no sound but the breeze, mingling with the raucous cries of the seagulls circling overhead. "One night, I woke up and couldn't get back to sleep. I wanted him so badly." A faint touch of color brushed her cheeks, as if she somehow found it shameful, that a young wife should desire her errant husband. "I decided to go to him. He'd had one of the students from the medical school there with him, earlier, but I thought the boy had gone home by then, it was so late."

"He hadn't?"

"No. I found them. Together." Her hands twisted and turned on the handle of her sunshade, sending it spinning back and forth in quick, angry jerks. "After the boy left, Philippe told me he'd always been more interested in men than in women. He said he would never have married, except that he was his father's only heir and he needed a son. He said he liked and admired me as a person—he even said that for a time he had desired me. He'd hoped marriage to me might 'cure' him. But of course it hadn't, and he'd realized he didn't want to be cured, anyway."

She stared off into the distance, that bitter smile touching her lips again, although he could see the glint of unshed tears, too, in her eyes. "I felt so betrayed. And such a fool, for not having known the truth, for believing everything he'd told me. I think that's what hurt more than anything, that betrayal of my trust, that lack of honesty. He should have told me before. He shouldn't have let me think I was marrying one kind of man when I was actually marrying someone I didn't even know. I remember telling him, that night, that I would never be happy again, and I think that, in a very real sense, I never have been." In anyone else, the words might have been dismissed as melodrama. Only, there had never been anything the least bit melodramatic about this woman. "You don't get over it easily," she said, her voice hushed, "that kind of shattering disappointment in someone you love. Someone you've given up everything for."

"So what happened?" Zach asked quietly.

She shrugged, a vague twitching of one shoulder that was so quintessentially French. "He promised it wouldn't happen again. And I was so besotted with him, even then, that I believed him." A fierceness came over her expression, a fierceness that was anger at herself as much as at Philippe. "I wanted to believe him. I wanted the life I'd dreamed of."

She kept her face half-averted from him, her gaze on some distant point. Zach looked at the smooth skin of her cheek, the sparkling intelligence of those narrowed eyes. He wanted so desperately to touch her, to ease the misery within her, to ease the ache that burned within himself. Instead, he said, his voice hard, "He didn't keep his promise, did he?"

She shook her head. "Less than a year later, I found him again, with a woman this time. And then I discovered there'd been others I hadn't known about, men and women, both."

"A lot of women would have left him, then."

"I couldn't. I'd have lost Dominic. The de Beauvaises would never have let him go."

"Even if the truth had become known?"

She swung to face him, her eyes wide and a little wild as she searched his face. "Do you think I would do that to Dominic? You know how people are, what they would have said, how they would have treated him, how they would have treated Philippe. I couldn't do that."

"So you still cared about him? About Philippe?"

"Does that surprise you?" They turned into the square itself, passing through the high, open gates. "I don't believe that love just . . . disappears. It dies slowly, one day at a time, one hurt, one betrayal. Even up to the end, Philippe and I were still friends, of a sort. We had our shared interest in medicine, the work at the hospital, Dominic. I don't want you to think my life was miserable, because it wasn't. It's just . . . there was so much missing. And as time passed, we became more impatient with each other, more resentful."

Clouds were building in the sky, to the north. Thick, high white clouds turned a breathtaking gold by the light of the sun. "That day at Congo Square," Zach said, his eyes narrowing as he stared at the distant storm, piling up fast, "Rose told me Philippe would never take a colored mistress because he didn't want any child of his to suffer the way a child of mixed parentage suffers. She said he understood what it was like, not to be accepted for what you are, not to feel as if you belong anywhere." He glanced down at the woman beside him. "That's what she meant, wasn't it? He never felt he belonged, did he?"

"I don't believe it's something he chose." Emmanuelle met his gaze, her expression open, vulnerable in a way he'd never seen it. "We can't choose whom we desire, whom we love."

"We can choose whether or not we act on those desires." Yet even as Zach said it, he was aware of his own choice, in defiance of all logic and discipline, to act on his desire for this woman.

She shook her head, that sweet, sad smile touching her lips again. "Philippe was a hedonist. He didn't believe in denying himself physical pleasures of any kind."

They walked along in silence, the growing wind sending big dried magnolia leaves scuttling across the pavement before them. After a moment, Zach said, "Tell me what happened that day at the hospital, last spring."

She blinked, as if she'd forgotten, for a moment, where this was all leading, and it disconcerted her to realize that he had not. "All right," she said softly, although it was a moment before she was able to go on. "After I found Philippe that second time, we came to an agreement. We would continue to share the same house, to appear to others as man and wife. But he moved permanently into the *garçonnière,* and we agreed that as long as we were discreet, we would both be free to live our lives as we chose." She tilted her head, her gaze hard on his face as she stared up at him, as if daring him to be shocked, to condemn her.

When he said nothing, she continued, her voice low, her words carefully chosen. "I never thought I would actually do anything. But as time passed . . ." She wrapped both her fists around the handle of her sunshade, gripping it so tightly, he wondered it didn't crack. "I used to lie in bed at night and ache, simply ache for a man to hold me, to touch me, to join with me. It was an agony. Eventually I started thinking, If Philippe can take pleasure with others so easily, why can't I? So I tried it. But it never really satisfied me."

How many? Zach wondered. How many men had she taken, as she had taken him? The thought twisted his stomach, tore at something deep inside him. "Is that what happened with Charles Yardley?" he asked, his voice coming out harsher than he'd intended.

The wind fluttered the brim of her hat, loosened a lock of hair to send it across her cheek. She nodded, her face pale, one hand coming up to catch the stray curl and tuck it behind her ear in a gesture that struck him as oddly innocent and childlike.

"Did you know he was like Philippe?" Zach asked. "That he found pleasure in both men and women?"

"No. Not until that day at the hospital. Philippe really was in love with him, you know. Violently, passionately in love. We tend to think of those kinds of feelings as existing only between a man and a woman, but it isn't always so."

"And Claire? Did she know Philippe also . . . liked men?"

"She knew. She was far wiser about such things than I was at her age."

It was so simply said, he wondered at her, this woman who could speak calmly of her husband's infidelities and unorthodox carnal impulses. But then, he supposed she'd had years to accustom herself to it. "So exactly what was the quarrel about?" he asked, knowing that what he'd heard before had contained part, but only part of the truth.

"Claire knew of Philippe's tastes, but she didn't care. She loved him, anyway. It was when she found out he was in love with Charles Yardley that she threw the scene."

Zach thought about that thin, cynical Englishman with his long, straight blond hair and negligent good looks. "What about Hans Spears?" he asked suddenly. "Was Philippe involved with him, as well?"

Reaching up, she collapsed her sunshade in one quick motion, her expression thoughtful. "I honestly don't know."

A silence opened up between them, a silence filled with the mournful cries of the gulls and the buffeting of a rising wind that sent the black ribbons of her widow's hat streaming out before them. The sun had disappeared, overrun by the fast scuttling clouds that had turned darker, more threatening as they piled up. It always surprised him, how quickly it could come on to rain in this city.

"So that's why you stopped believing in love?" he said after a moment. "Because one man was less than honest with you?"

"That's not why." She stared at the gathering storm, her head falling back, her slim neck arching in a way that made her look fragile, vulnerable. "When I first met Philippe, I was so in love with him, I believed it could never end." A sad smile curled her lips. "How could something so intense, so violent, so all consuming simply . . . go away? But it did."

"It doesn't always."

She brought her gaze back to his face. Her eyes were dark and troubled and a little wild. "Yet it can. No one can really promise forever. They can promise faithfulness, but they can't promise their love won't someday die. We can't choose whom we love, and we can't control when love dies."

"So you do believe in love."

Her breath caught, then eased out in a soft laugh. "Perhaps. Perhaps it's simply the endurance of love I don't believe in."

A spattering of rain hit the pavement, big drops that filled the air with the smell of dust and damp stone. "Tell me something," he said suddenly. "All those other men you slept with—"

"There were only three of them, including Charles."

"—you said they didn't satisfy your ache. Did you ever think it was because you didn't love them?"

She swung to face him. He was surprised to see she was trembling all over, her face pale, her lips pressed together as if she were afraid of what she might accidentally say. The wind gusted around them, wet, wild, billowing out the skirts of her severe black gown and sending a heavy lock of hair across her face again. Reaching out, he tucked the windbown hair behind her ear, his fingertips brushing her cheeks. "And those nights you spent with me?" he said softly. "Did they satisfy you?"

"You know they did," she whispered.

It was raining harder now. He could feel it, canted by the wind, striking his face. He put his hands on her shoulders. She was so fine boned and delicate, so damned vulnerable. He wanted to take her in his arms and hold her close, hold her safe, and never let her go. And he was so afraid, so terribly afraid that he would never be able to hold her again. "Love is a leap of faith, Emmanuelle," he said, his thumbs brushing back and forth against the soft, rain-wet flesh of her throat. "It always has been. Yet men and women have been making that leap for longer than anyone remembers."

Fragrant and soft, the warm rain fell between them. He watched her throat convulse, watched the tears form in her eyes, although he knew she would never let them fall. "I can't. Not again. I haven't the courage."

"You have more courage than anyone I've ever known, man or woman."

She shook her head, a strange smile of sadness and pain touching her full, sensual lips. "Not for this."

He wanted to dip his head and turn the sweet sadness of that beautiful, beloved mouth to wondrous joy. He wanted to crush her hard against him and hold her forever and *make* her love him. Instead, he let his hands slide down her arms in one last, desperate caress, and let her go. "When do you leave for Beau Lac?" he asked as they turned together to walk through the rain. They walked side by side, not touching, the gulf between them suddenly seeming so vast and unconquerable, he found it a wonder they'd ever managed to reach across it.

"Friday, early." She could have put up her sunshade, used it as an umbrella, but she didn't. "We stay until the end of September, when the weather breaks."

September, he thought. By September, he would be gone. "I've decided to go over Butler's head and put in a request to Washington that I be returned to my old unit. But I promise you this: I won't go until I find this killer."

She glanced up at him, her eyes bruised-looking, shadowed by a myriad of emotions he could only guess at. Rain streamed down her cheeks, dripped from the ends of her black bonnet ribbons. And he thought, this is how I first saw you, that fateful night, in the cemetery. It was raining, and you were so wet. So wet and mysterious and eternally, seductively alluring.

"And if you don't find him?" she said.

"I'll find him."

CHAPTER
THIRTY-TWO

Battered, smudged, and warped, as if it had got wet at some point and then dried, the file landed on Zach's desktop with a loud clap, a sheaf of loose papers spilling partway out of it.

"What's this?" Zach asked, looking up into Hamish Fletcher's florid, unsmiling face.

The splendid, red-blond mustaches twitched violently back and forth as Hamish worked his jaw muscles. "The file on the families of everyone who died or underwent an amputation at the Hospital de Santerre in the last two years."

"Anything?"

"Not a blessed thing"

Another file hit Zach's desk. "And this?"

"The report on the pharmacy poison books." The big New Yorker took out a handkerchief and wiped his sweat-dampened forehead.

"Nothing?" said Zach.

"Nothing."

Pushing back his chair, Zach stood and went to stare out the office's window. It faced north, so that the sun never hit it, with the result that the glass in the lower panes had taken on a greenish tinge. Algae, he supposed. It seemed that what couldn't rust or rot or mold in this town could still grow algae.

"So where do we go from here?" Zach asked, one shoulder resting against the frame, his gaze on the busy street outside. The light was so bright that for a moment it made his eyes hurt. The sun had come up hot that morning, glinting off the puddles left in the streets and baking the city with an intense, ferocious brilliance.

"Damned if I know. It ain't easy, when your best suspects keep dying on you." Hamish stuffed his handkerchief back in his pocket and sank into the wooden armchair beside Zach's desk. "I knew there was something off about that Englishman, from the first time I saw him." It hadn't sat well with Hamish, what Zach had told him about Yardley and de Beauvais. The gritty truth about Emmanuelle's marriage, and her involvement with Yardley, Zach had kept to himself.

"Oh, Lord." Hamish's heat-flushed face suddenly turned an even darker red, his eyes widening as if a thought had only just occurred to him. "Don't tell me that German lad, Spears, is one of those, too?"

One of those. Zach found the expression both disturbing and distasteful, and linked in some way he couldn't quite define with the memory of a blue-eyed, blond-haired, half-caste little girl whose father could never marry her mother because the woman was colored. He remembered the expression on Ben Butler's face as he sent a Jewish mother of nine off to prison for laughing at a child's birthday party, and the condescension in Charles Yardley's voice when he'd said of Emmanuelle, "She would have made a fine doctor, if she'd been a man."

The more Zach thought about it, the more he understood why she had been so adamant about keeping this truth a secret. The effect on a young boy like Dominic, should such damning information about his father become widespread knowledge, could be both painful and catastrophic. "Maybe. Maybe not," Zach said slowly. "I think we should put a couple of men onto watching him."

"You reckon he's our killer?" Hamish said, nodding.

"I don't know. But if he's not, he could very well be our next victim." Zach leaned his spine against the window frame. "It's strange, isn't it, that this didn't come up before, when we were checking into de Beauvais's background and friends?"

Hamish smoothed his mustache with a slow, thoughtful motion of one thumb and forefinger. "It's the kinda thing he'd be likely to try to keep quiet, now isn't it? Him being a Catholic and a doctor and from such an important family and all."

"Secrets can be dangerous things." Zach pushed away from the window. "Sometimes, people will kill to keep them."

Hamish's forehead puckered in a heavy frown. "What are you saying now?"

Zach shook his head. "I'm not sure. Send someone out to the Bayou Crevé, would you?" He reached for his hat. "I want the lieutenant who led that patrol brought into town so I can talk to him."

"What do you think he's gonna tell you we haven't already heard?"

"Maybe we've been hearing it." Zach settled his plumed black officer's hat low on his forehead, and reached for the door handle. "Maybe we just haven't been listening."

"Jesus. Don't you start doing it," said Hamish, shaking one thick finger at him.

Zach paused in the doorway to look back. "Doing what?"

"Talking in riddles, like some Bayou Sauvage voodoo king."

By Thursday afternoon, the shutters on the town house on the rue Dumaine had all been closed and latched, the bell taken off the front door, the trunks and cases loaded on a wagon. They would be setting out for Beau Lac early in the morning, and so it had been decided that they would all spend this last night in the big house on Esplanade.

Emmanuelle stood alone in the center of the darkened parlor, her hat and gloves in one hand. She could think of no reason to put off their departure any longer, and yet the uneven tread on the stairs she'd been waiting for, hoping for, had never come.

"Did you really think he would come, that Yankee?" Rose said from the door.

Emmanuelle looked up. She wanted to deny it, but couldn't.

Rose pursed her lips and let out a long, tired sigh. "He told you he loved you, and you told him you didn't believe in love and that you didn't have the courage to try again. What did you think he was going to do? Come here and try to change your mind?"

A faint smile touched Emmanuelle's lips. "I thought he might try."

"Huh." Rose went to give one of the lace panels at the front windows a twitch, as if to straighten it. "For a smart woman, you sure can be dumb sometimes."

Emmanuelle tried to laugh. She really tried to laugh, only it came out sounding something like a sob.

Rose turned to fix her with a hard, steady gaze. "And were you ready to change your mind, then?"

Emmanuelle put on her black straw hat and recklessly tied the ribbons. "I honestly don't know."

Rose nodded. "Then I reckon that's why he didn't come."

Friday morning, the lamplighters were still making their rounds with their stepladders, putting out the gas streetlights when Zach left the Garden District and turned his horse's head downriver. By the time he reached Esplanade Avenue, with its grassy median planted with sycamores and elms and graceful crepe myrtles blooming now in drifts of white and pink and red, the sun had crested the horizon, spilling golden light across the city. Zach nudged his big bay gelding into a trot. It was already hot. Anyone with a long journey ahead would make an early start.

Not far from the de Beauvaises' white, double-galleried house, he reined in beneath the moss-draped shadows of a spreading old live oak. Two carts piled high with trunks were pulled up in front of the house and, as Zach watched, a well-sprung, shiny black and yellow carriage swung out of the drive.

He couldn't say exactly why he had paused here. It certainly hadn't been to speak with her, or even in hopes of catching a last glimpse of her. But he stayed until the dust raised by the carriage's passing had disappeared into the hot morning air. Then he turned his horse's head toward the Bayou Sauvage, and rode on.

He found Papa John in that small patch of herbs that grew to one side of the round African hut. He was bent over, pinching back some low-growing plant, but as Zach reined in, the black man straightened and slowly turned.

"So you've learned a few things, have you?" he said, the edges of his eyes crinkling in amusement.

"You could have told me," Zach said, and swung out of the saddle.

"I could have."

Zach looked up from tying the big bay to a nearby cypress limb. "Some men tried to kill me a few days ago. Some black men."

Papa John snorted. "I did warn you, didn't I?"

Zach came to stand before him, the sun pouring down hot and golden on his back. "Who hired them?"

The old Haitian shook his head slowly. "Can't tell you that."

"At least you're not going to try to claim you don't know."

Papa John showed his teeth in a wide smile. "That wouldn't be very good for business, now would it? I'm supposed to know everything."

"I could haul you in. You know that."

"I know it. But I still wouldn't tell you anything."

Zach let out short laugh, and started to turn away. "No. I don't suppose you would."

Papa John stayed where he was, his feet planted wide, the sun gleaming on the frilled front of his white dress shirt. "Then why'd you come out here, Major?"

Zach untied the bay and reached for his stirrup. "You said Emmanuelle's a friend of yours."

"That's right."

Zach swung into his saddle. "I wonder if you know she's gone to Beau Lac?"

The big black man didn't say anything, but Zach rather thought from the sudden slackening in the old man's face that here was something Papa John hadn't known.

Zach kneed the bay forward, then reined in hard when Papa John started after him suddenly, calling, "Major!" Sweat glistened on the old man's ebony face, and his eyes were round, almost afraid as he tilted back his head to stare up at Zach. "You find the name of the woman who betrayed Michie Philippe to that Yankee patrol, and you'll know who sent those men to kill you last Sunday."

Zach's fist tightened involuntarily on the reins, causing the big bay to sidle nervously. "A woman? I'm looking for a woman?"

"I didn't say that." Papa John stepped back, his gaze still hard on Zach's face. "Miss Emmanuelle, she claims you're different from most folks. She says you see things more as they are, and not as you want them to be. I hope for her sake, she's right."

It was early on Monday morning by the time the lieutenant from the Bayou Crevé made it into the city. He was a gangly, punctiliously dressed young man with a thick shock of blond hair and a weak, receding chin he had a habit of drawing back even further into his neck when he grew thoughtful or felt challenged in any way.

"What do you mean, how do I know the man we buried in the swamps was Philippe de Beauvais?" said the young lieutenant, his gray eyes bulging out as he pulled his chin down and back. "He had his papers on him, sir."

Zach had been down near the wharves, looking over a burned-out warehouse Butler wanted rebuilt to store Brother Andrew's growing accumulation of cotton, when the lieutenant had tracked him down and saluted with a flourish and a sharp, "Lieutenant Presley reporting, sir."

"Can you remember what this man you buried looked like?" Zach asked now, turning to walk with the lieutenant along the levee.

Lieutenant Presley had to stop and think about it a moment, his chin puckering as it flattened against his chest. "He was tall, I think. Tall and thin, with blond, curly hair and blue eyes. Unusually vivid blue eyes." The chin lifted. "I remember that because one of the soldiers closed them after we already had the Rebel in the hole we'd dug for him. Said it wasn't right, putting the dirt on top of those open eyes."

Dominic had eyes like that, Zach thought. Startlingly blue eyes, and thickly curling pale hair. "Are you sure he was dead?" Zach asked. He'd heard of men, left for dead and buried hastily in shallow graves, who later revived and somehow managed to claw their way to the surface.

The lieutenant laughed. "Of course he was dead. Half his head was blown away."

The man was starting to grate on Zach's nerves. A steamboat appeared around the wide bend in the river, sun glistening on fancifully intricate, white-painted gingerbread, smoke belching from high smokestack, giant paddle wheel churning up foamy brown waves as it chugged its way upstream. He watched it for a moment, and somehow managed to rein in his mounting irritation. "Who else was with this man you buried?"

"That we killed?" The lieutenant shrugged. "Some nigger. I don't know who he was. There was a third man, but he got away."

Hans Spears, thought Zach. With one foot mangled beyond repair, the German couldn't have gone very far very fast, but looking at the young lieutenant before him, Zach wasn't too surprised the patrol let the third member of that small smuggling party slip away. "I understand it was a woman who told you to expect the smugglers," Zach said, turning to walk along the river again.

"Yes, sir."

Zach brought his gaze back to Lieutenant Presley's face. "Do you remember what she looked like?"

The other man shook his head. "She was veiled, sir. I never saw her face."

"Could she have been colored?"

"A nigger?" The lieutenant laughed. "I don't think so, sir."

Zach felt it swell within him again, the irritation, mingling this time with anger. "How can you be so sure," he said, keeping his voice even with effort, "if she was veiled, and wearing gloves?"

"She was a lady, sir."

Zach nodded toward the narrow streets below. "Stand on any corner in the old quarter, and you'll see them: colored women, dressed like ladies, *raised* as ladies, well educated, speaking French, wearing silks and satins, and owning black slaves of their own."

The lieutenant's chin was starting to disappear into his neck again. "Well, I suppose she could have been colored, sir," he said slowly. "They do come tall like that, don't they?"

Zach swung abruptly to face him. "She was tall?" Rose was tall.

"Yes, sir. Unusually so. Especially for a woman that age."

Zach held himself very still. The sun was beating down fierce and hot on his shoulders, but he suddenly felt cold inside, as if all the blood were draining from him. *Blinders,* Papa John had said. "What do you mean by that?"

"Just that she was old, sir. At least, she sounded it. You can hear it, can't you, in a woman's voice?"

It was all Zach could do to keep from grabbing the

front of the lieutenant's unusually well-tailored uniform, and shaking him. "How old?"

Lieutenant Presley shrugged. "I don't know. Fifty. Maybe sixty."

"You're sure?" said Zach, his voice like a whiplash. Two images played themselves across his mind. Marie Thérèse de Beauvais sitting tall and straight in the parlor of her Esplanade Avenue house, her lips pressing into a thin, angry line as she said, "Men with good wives do not seek consolation elsewhere." And a newer, sharper memory of windblown dust raised by the well-sprung chaise carrying the woman Zach loved away from him, to Beau Lac, and death.

"She wasn't young," said Lieutenant Presley, "I know that, sir. Sir?"

But Zach was already running.

CHAPTER
THIRTY-THREE

Almost as old as the city of New Orleans itself, the vast and wealthy sugar plantation known as Beau Lac lay on the banks of the Bayou Crevé. Here was no Grecian temple with tall white columns stretching to a pedimented roof, such as the American planters had built up and down the banks of the Mississippi. The house at Beau Lac was French colonial in style, with its main floor on the second story, high above a stuccoed *briquette-entre-poteaux* first floor given over to storage. The de Beauvaises could have replaced it long ago with something far larger and more splendid, but they hadn't, preferring the simplicity of the steep-roofed white house with its dormered attic windows, its elegant allée of moss-draped live oaks, its broad sweeps of wooden-railed galleries entwined with creepers. Yet as he urged his tired horse down that long, shady allée, Zach was only dimly aware of the quiet beauty of the big white house that rose before him. It was a good day's hard ride from the city, and he had practically killed his big cavalry bay, getting here.

A child's laughter drew Zach's attention to a side garden of orange trees and roses, where Dominic was trying to haul the liver-colored, joyfully barking hound out of an octagonal-shaped fishpond with high sides and a weathered statue of a naked woman holding an urn that poured water in a gentle trickle.

"Napoléon," shrieked the boy as the dog leaped from his grasp to land back in the pond with a soggy splash that sent silver fans of water spraying up into the air and a swell of waves decorated with shredded green lilies and golden flickers of hapless fish washing over the sides of the pond. "Napoléon," Dominic screamed again, abandoning the dog in favor of scrambling about the brick paving to scoop up the wriggling goldfish and fling them back into the pond.

The sight of the boy brought a measure of relief to the constriction of terror that had held Zach in its grip ever since he'd left the city. She must be all right, he thought, his eyes squeezing shut in a quiet moment of thankfulness. No child who had just lost his mother could laugh and play so heedlessly.

"May I take your horse, Michie?"

Zach opened his eyes to find a slim young black man in a blue workshirt and a straw hat smiling up at him. "Yes, thank you." Swinging out of the saddle, Zach ran one hand down the bay's sweat-darkened neck. "Take good care of him, will you? I rode him hard."

"I'll cool him down good, Michie, never you fear."

"Major," called Dominic, the glistening white shells of the drive crunching beneath his feet as he came running up, one hand fisted around the collar of the dripping, panting hound at his side. "*Qu'est-ce vous faites ici?*"

Zach swung to face him. An early evening breeze had come up, stirring the broad leaves of the oak trees and carrying to him the sweet scents of lemons and roses and jasmine, and the light trickle of water from the dog-ravaged fountain. The sun shone warm and golden on the house's stuccoed walls and the wide, slightly worn flight of steps that led from the shell drive up to the front gallery with its ladder-backed rockers and open double doors. For one, intense moment, Zach felt the quiet beauty and idyllic serenity of this place envelop him, so that he found himself wondering if he might not be mistaken after all. How could someone who lived amid such peace commit such a violent string of murders?

"Is your mother inside?" he asked Dominic.

"*Non.*" The boy shook his head. He was breathing heavily, and had to pause to suck in a quick gulp of air. "She and Papère took the pirogue out on the lake."

"The lake?"

"*Oui.* She's a very good fisherman, *ma mère,*" said Dominic, dropping to one knee to throw an arm around the dripping, panting dog. "I would have gone with them, but Napoléon was missing."

"I see you found him."

"*Il est très méchant.*" Napoleon happily endured another fierce hug. "He'd got himself locked in a stall in the old stables."

Something stirred on the broad gallery above, a shimmer of black satin that detached itself from the shadows and came forward. Marie Thérèse de Beauvais, tall, thin, meticulously groomed, lethal.

Zach kept his gaze on the woman above. "Make sure that stable hand is taking good care of my horse, would you, Dominic?"

"*Mais oui, monsieur,*" said the boy, one hand coming up to grab his wide-brimmed hat as he took off around the side of the house, the dog at his heels.

"Major Cooper," said Marie Thérèse de Beauvais, coming to stand beside one of the slender round wooden colonnettes of the second level. "Is something wrong?"

"As a matter of fact, yes." Zach mounted the wooden steps slowly, his gaze hard on her face. The sound of Napoleon's enthusiastic barking faded into the distance as boy and dog followed the big cavalry mount toward the stables. "I don't take kindly to people's attempts to kill me."

Gray brows lifted in a parody of consternation. "Did someone try to kill you, monsieur?"

"You did." Zach paused at the top of the stairs. "Last Sunday, at Congo Square."

"I'm sorry, Major, but I have never been near the place."

"No. The eight black men and one small mulatto boy who attacked me there were hired. By you."

She tilted her head slightly, her expression serene and faintly contemptuous. "They said I was responsible, did they, these black men? And you believed them?"

He had no proof, of course, and she knew it. Even if he could find the men responsible, it would still be only their word against hers, and they were black, while she was white, and a de Beauvais. "Tell me, madame," Zach said, going to stand at the railing beside her, his gaze not on her but on the vast fields of sugarcane stretching out beyond the gardens below, "does your husband know you killed your own son?"

"I killed no one, Major."

"No. You get others to do your killing for you."

"My son was killed by Yankees," she said in that same calm, even tone. "His life might have been a shame, an abomination, even, but he died a hero's death."

Zach swung his head to look at her. "That's why you betrayed him, was it? So that he would die honorably in war, rather than disgrace the family name with his unorthodox behavior?"

Her nostrils flared on a quick intake of breath that fluttered the black lace at her throat. It suddenly struck him as the greatest abomination of all, that she should be wearing mourning for a son whose death she had deliberately caused. "You think I don't grieve for my son's death?" she said, her voice throbbing. "I do. Four sons I bore, and not one remains. All I have left in this world now is a little boy who isn't even mine to raise."

"You have your husband."

She surprised him by smiling, a tight smile that curved her lips but brought no warmth to those hard gray eyes. "Let's say you're right, Major. Let's say I was the one who betrayed Philippe. What would you arrest me for, hmmm?"

"The murders of Henri Santerre, Claire La Touche, and Charles Yardley."

She shook her head, the smile still firmly in place. "I told you, Major, I killed no one." A quiver of distaste passed over the aged, aristocratic features. "Although I will not pretend to any sadness over their deaths. Claire La Touche might have been born and raised a lady, but she had the instincts of an alley cat."

"Her family mourn her," Zach said quietly.

"Only because they don't know what she was. If they knew, they'd be more than happy to be rid of her, believe me."

"And Charles Yardley?"

Again, that flash of disdain. "The world is better off without him. He was another such as my son."

"He was also a dedicated doctor. As was Henri Santerre." Zach pushed away from the railing in an almost violent gesture that brought him right up close to her. "All those people you killed, trying to keep the secret of your son's life from becoming known, and all you succeeded in doing was calling attention to the very thing you were trying to hide."

She held herself very still, only her head tipping back as she stared up at him. "Do you think me such a fool, Major? I keep telling you I have killed no one, and you simply refuse to believe me."

She was too arrogant, too proud of a woman to lie. He saw that now. She might not have admitted setting those men at Congo Square to kill him, but she hadn't denied it, either. And he knew quite suddenly and with awful, terrifying clarity, that he'd been wrong. Whether or not she set those men on him, she had certainly betrayed her own son. But Marie Thérèse de Beauvais hadn't killed Henri Santerre or Claire La Touche or Charles Yardley, and she hadn't tried to kill Emmanuelle.

He thought of Emmanuelle telling him about how Dominic had learned to shoot a crossbow from his grandfather, and about Dominic saying proudly, *My papère knows lots of things you don't know, about the bayous and the swamps and all the animals and plants that live there.*

Dominic saying, *She and Papère took the pirogue out on the bayou.*

Sweet mercy. Zach's fingers closed on the older woman's shoulders, shaking her hard. "Where are they? Where has Jean-Lambert taken her?"

Her composure never slipped. "You're too late, Major."

He thrust her away from him almost violently, his breath coming hard and fast, shuddering his chest, turning his voice into something raspy, savage. "Jean-Lambert didn't know, did he? He didn't know you were the one who betrayed Philippe. He thought it was Emmanuelle. He found out about the argument at the hospital and he blamed her for Philippe's death. He blamed them all, and so he killed them all, one by one. Not to silence them, but to punish them. And you . . . you let him do it. You let him kill them. Even your own grandson's mother."

The arrogant complacency was gone now. Something ugly twisted the older woman's features, brought a throb of hatred to her voice. "I blame her more than anyone for what happened. She was a nobody, a poor doctor's daughter, yet I allowed her to marry my son. I thought she could control him, the way I have controlled his father all these years. Oh, yes," she said, when Zach's eyes widened in surprise. "His father has the same tendencies. But never has there been one breath of scandal. If I could do it, she should have been able to do the same."

"Where are they?" He couldn't be too late. Couldn't be, couldn't be . . .

"Do you think I fish the bayous? How would I know?"

"Dominic," said Zach suddenly, his head lifting as the sound of a dog's barking carried on the warm breeze.

"You can't mean to involve the child in this," she said, starting forward as if she would stop him. But Zach was already running down the stairs, his spurs and saber jingling.

"You're too late, Major," she called after him from the top of the stairs as his feet crunched the shell drive. "Too late."

CHAPTER
THIRTY-FOUR

Emmanuelle had always loved fishing on Beau Lac. It was said that once, the mighty Mississippi had rushed through here on its way to the Gulf. But the river had long ago changed its course, so that now the sweeping oxbow was only a quiet lake of willow and cypress-shaded dark water draining off through the tangled swamps and waterways of the Bayou Crevé toward the Gulf Coast and Biloxi beyond.

They had come here often through the years, she and Jean-Lambert, fishing for bass from an old pirogue. In the past, she'd always found a measure of peace and contentment adrift on the still black waters, but this time, that comfortable sense of serenity eluded her. Again and again, she found her gaze lifting to the thickly growing stands of creeper-draped cypress that marked the entrance to the wilderness stretching away to the east. Somewhere in there, Philippe lay buried, his grave lost, unmarked and untended.

"I think of it often, as well," said Jean-Lambert, his gaze following hers. "He shouldn't have been left out there, alone."

Emmanuelle reached to close her fingers about his gnarled old hand in a quick spasm of shared grief. "When the war is over, we can send people in there, to look for him."

"It will be too late, by then," said Jean-Lambert, and she knew he was right. She'd seen potato vines and elephants ears and angel's trumpet completely obscure the foundations of a burned-out house in one hot, humid season of luxuriant growth. In another two or three years, no one would ever find those graves.

Slim and beautiful, a snowy egret rose from the edge of the marsh. Emmanuelle watched it take to the sky, her head falling back, her eyes narrowing as she squinted against the dazzle of the hot afternoon sun. She felt oddly close to Philippe, on this lake. And she decided that perhaps it was good that she had come to Beau Lac, after all, even if she couldn't find peace here. Perhaps, here, she could eventually make some sense of her life. Make sense of herself.

"Why did you do it, Emmanuelle?" Jean-Lambert asked softly. "Why did you tell the Yankees about him?"

She brought her gaze back to the old man's sad, drawn face, and knew a strange chill that seized her heart and made her blood run cold. "It wasn't me, Papère."

He sighed, the tired sigh of an old, sick man. "It was Claire, then. I knew it had to be one of you." Setting aside his fishing rod, he began to push the pirogue away from the shallows near the shore. "Philippe told me about what happened, that day at the hospital," he said, his attention all for his work with the paddle. "You, Claire, the Englishman. Because of it, he decided he was going to join the army." He glanced up at her suddenly. "Did you know that? After he took the Confederate gold to Biloxi, he planned to just keep going. He told me he was hoping to get killed. He was tired of living a lie, he said, tired of pretending to be something he wasn't." He paused, and the silence filled with the rustle of the breeze through the tops of the cypress trees and the slap of the thick dark water against the pirogue's narrow bow. "My only surviving son, and he wanted to die."

Emmanuelle stared at the familiar, beloved face of the man before her. "Papère," she said slowly, still not quite believing it, not wanting to believe it. "Was it you? Was it you who killed all those people?"

"Santerre was an accident," he said, as calmly as if they'd been discussing the best bait for bass, or which of their favorite snags to try. "You tripped. I regret the mistake. I really do."

"Papère," she said again, her voice low, intense. "I didn't betray Philippe."

He shrugged. "It doesn't matter. You were all to blame. The three of you. It was because of you Philippe left New Orleans. And because of you he was killed."

She stared at the ever-widening expanse of duckweed-coated water. They never came out this far. "Where are we going?" she asked, keeping her voice level.

"The lake's quite deep in the middle. Did you know?"

She threw a quick glance toward the shore, where Baptiste sat with his back against the trunk of an oak, his hat tilted forward over his face as if he were asleep. She was thinking about calling out to him, when Jean-Lambert said, "He won't help you."

And she understood, then, how he'd done it—how *they* had done it. "Those two black workmen the gatekeeper at the cemetery saw," she said. "It was you, wasn't it? You and Baptiste."

A faint smile played around the old man's lips. There was nothing even faintly suggestive of the African about his features, but years of riding through the cane fields had tanned the skin of his face and hands to a sunwarmed brown that was darker than that of more than a few quadroons. "No one ever pays attention to the comings and goings of slaves," he said, his blue eyes shining. "All I needed was some old clothes, and a broad-brimmed hat to pull low over my face. That gatekeeper saw Baptiste's black skin, and never gave us another thought."

"And Charles Yardley? Did you have Baptiste kill him?"

"Baptiste watched him, and put the opium in his brandy to deepen his sleep. But I was the one who held the pillow over his face. I wouldn't ask Baptiste to do that."

"Why not? What's the difference?"

"There's a difference," Jean-Lambert insisted, but she knew from the vague tightening of his lips that it bothered him, having to use Baptiste, and she wondered at the big black man. Had he done nothing to try to stop his master? Nothing at all? "I wouldn't have involved Baptiste if I hadn't had to," Jean-Lambert was saying. "But I couldn't do it by myself. Not anymore."

Emmanuelle glanced back at the silent figure waiting so patiently, so faithfully, on the shore. It would have been easy for Baptiste to have slipped the vampire-killing kit from Philippe's room. Easy. Easy for him, too, to have put it back.

"I didn't need his help with Claire, though," Jean-Lambert was saying, almost proudly. "She actually came to me, complaining of sick headaches and how hard it had become to find laudanum since the war. She knew I'd be able to get her some. I even told her I'd mixed in a few extra herbs, to help her headaches, just in case she noticed the taste."

For as long as Emmanuelle had known him,

Jean-Lambert had had an interest in plants and their uses. He kept an extensive herb garden here, at Beau Lac, in addition to his small plot in the city; foxglove and rosemary, henbane and tansy, and she'd never given it a thought. Not a thought.

"So why hire an Irishman to kill me?" she asked, watching him dip the paddle into the dark water. "Why not just try to shoot me again? Or poison me, like Claire?"

Jean-Lambert shook his head. "After what happened with Santerre, I was afraid to try something like that again. And I couldn't use poison. Not with Dominic in the house."

Dominic, Emmanuelle thought, her stomach clenching with fear and panic and despair. Dominic, waiting for them, back at the house. Dominic, unable to come fishing because his dog was missing.

Overhead, a red-tailed hawk soared high above the gap in the trees that was Beau Lac. All around her, the buzz and whirr of insects was like a constant, high-pitched, warning hum. They would be in the middle of the lake soon. She'd thought, at first, that he meant to take her into the swamps on the far side. Now she wasn't so sure. "What are you planning, Papère?"

"We will drown, my child. Together. Here."

"Papère . . ." Emmanuelle leaned forward, her gaze hard on his aged, beloved face, her heart thumping so wildly in her chest that she could barely catch her breath. "Think of Dominic. What is this going to do to him?"

"It will be hard on him, losing us both. I know that. But he'll still have Marie Thérèse. It's odd, isn't it? She loves him far more than she ever loved any of her own sons. She even tried to have that Union major killed, because she was afraid you'd marry him and take

Dominic away from here. She thinks I don't know. But I know."

"Papère, listen to me." They would be in the middle of the lake soon. Dangerous currents were there, Philippe had told her; strange eddies that alternately sucked you down and tossed you around like a cork. Long, long ago, in the halcyon days of their first summer together, he had taught her to swim, but the thought of trying to swim in petticoats and hoops brought a tight twist of fear to her stomach, and stole whatever breath she had left. "Papère," she said again, her hands gripping the edges of the pirogue beside her. "This is something you never would have done before you became sick. You have always been one of the kindest, gentlest people I know. Please, don't do this."

"They say drowning is a peaceful death, if you don't struggle and simply give yourself up to it." He was no longer looking at her but at the tangled mass of cypress and hackberry and willow that marked the edge of the swamps where Philippe had died. And she knew, then, that Jean-Lambert was ready to die, that he'd made up his mind to die, and that unless she acted quickly, he was going to take her with him.

As hard as she could, she threw her weight sideways. The pirogue rocked down and back, once, violently. She saw Jean-Lambert's startled face, heard his enraged cry. Then the near edge tipped beneath the surface of the lake, and the boat flipped.

She felt her side smack against the water with an impact that jolted her. Then she plunged fast and deep as a thick, dark wave closed over her head to steal sun and sky and air.

CHAPTER THIRTY-FIVE

The ridge that Zach Cooper followed had once been a riverbank. *Cheniers*, the Creoles called them, these winding spits of high land dotted with oaks and pecans. It was the quickest, surest route, Dominic had told him, to that bend in the lake where the bass grew big and fat and Jean-Lambert had kept a pirogue since the days when Spain ruled Louisiana and the Indians who had made this trail were still a force to be reckoned with.

Zach sent his borrowed chestnut at a reckless gallop down the narrow, shadowed path, heedless of the hackberry branches that occasionally slapped his face. It was like a live thing, the fear in his gut, the fear that tore at his insides and stole his breath, so that he had to keep reminding himself to breathe.

Up ahead, a broad expanse of sun-shimmered water appeared through a break in the high green wall of moss-draped cypress. Zach urged the chestnut on harder, faster, its hooves sliding in the deep, damp humus of the bank as he hurtled down the slight slope to the lake's edge. He could see them now, Emmanuelle and her dead husband's father, their pirogue riding low in the water and unexpectedly far out toward the center of the lake.

Then the pirogue pitched sharply sideways.

"Emmanuelle," Zach screamed, driving the terrified chestnut snorting and splashing right into the lake itself. He heard Jean-Lambert's cry, saw Emmanuelle plunge deep. And then all he could see was the pirogue's smooth wooden bottom and a high, wide wash of dark water spreading out into emptiness.

She was surprised at how cold the water was. She felt it first on her hands and face, and through the thin lisle of her stockings, the shock of the sensation opening her eyes on a strange green watery world. Then the wide hooped skirts of her mourning dress must have acted like a kind of buoy, bobbing her up. Her head broke the surface, and she sucked in a deep gasp of air, her hands flailing. She banged her knuckles on something smooth and realized it was the pirogue's paddle. Grabbing it, she looked about wildly, searching for the near shore. She saw a blur of green trees rising above the water and kicked out toward it, the paddle clutched to her.

She knew she had a minute or two, surely no more, before the waterlogged weight of her clothes would drag her down again, and she was afraid the slender paddle wouldn't be enough to keep her up. She could taste her fear, cold and thick as bayou water in her mouth. She kicked again, and felt something bony and grasping wrap around one ankle.

She twisted about, the paddle gripped in both hands, and saw Jean-Lambert's hand gripping her leg. For a moment she thought he'd latched on to her in a desperate attempt to save himself. Then she saw the smile on his face, and she knew he still wanted to die. Wanted her to die with him. And unless she could loosen his grasp, now, he was going to kill her.

Her fist tightening on the paddle, she swung it at his

face, hard, hard enough that she felt the impact of it all the way up to her shoulders. His fingers slipped off her ankle, and she kicked out again toward the shore.

But already her skirts were growing heavier. She kicked harder, harder, the air tearing in and out of her lungs as she fought to keep her head above water. She went under, once, managed to fight her way back up, only to sink again. And then she knew rage, a rage so infinite, it left no room for fear, because she wasn't ready to die, she refused to die, not like this. She struggled up, up to the air. She couldn't even see it now, the sky, except as a dim light that shone through the darkness.

She felt something close about her chest, something strong and hard that hauled her tight up against a warm body. She struck out, blindly, weakly, thinking it was Jean-Lambert again, taking her with him, killing her. She heard a grunt, and a Yankee voice saying, "Do that again and I'm liable to drop you back in the lake."

Then she closed her eyes, because it was a voice she loved, and she was safe.

They told Dominic his grandfather had drowned when the pirogue overturned, which was true enough, in its way. But one day, Emmanuelle swore, she would tell her son the whole truth, because secrets and lies could be dangerous things.

It wasn't until they'd found Jean-Lambert's body wrapped in the arms of his dead black slave, Baptiste, that Emmanuelle even remembered the big African who had been waiting onshore. But whether he had drowned trying to save Jean-Lambert, or had simply decided to join his master in death, Emmanuelle would never know. Looking at the African's death-smoothed features, she found herself remembering what Marie

Thérèse had told Zach about Jean-Lambert and the "tendencies" he had in common with his son, and Emmanuelle thought she understood.

Later that evening, when Emmanuelle was helping Rose repack their trunks, Marie Thérèse came to stand in the open doorway and said, "Will you allow me to see my grandson again?"

"Occasionally, yes," said Emmanuelle, looking up. "But for his sake, not yours."

For one, intense moment, the two women's gazes caught and held. And Emmanuelle thought, *You have been a part of my life for more than twelve years now. You are the mother of my dead husband, my son's grandmother, and yet I neither know nor understand you.* This woman had caused the death of her own son, sought to kill the man Emmanuelle loved, and stood by, silently, while Jean-Lambert tried to kill Emmanuelle herself. And yet all Emmanuelle could feel when she looked into the other woman's pale, set face was pity, and a vague and disturbing uneasiness.

When they left Beau Lac, riding in one of the estate's wagons with Zach Cooper at the reins, Emmanuelle looked back at the old, high white house to see Marie Thérèse standing at the top of the broad steps and watching them drive away.

They spent what was left of the night at an old inn not far from the Bayou Crevé. After the others had fallen asleep, they wandered out onto the wide gallery that wrapped the inn's upper floor. The evening was mild, the sky starless and promising a rain Emmanuelle could smell on the warm, jasmine-scented breeze. From the railing she could see only a faint gleam of dull water that was the bayou, away to the right. The trees were black twisted shapes, silent against the thickening clouds. They were infinitely familiar to her, these things, the sight of moss dripping from giant spreading oaks, the primeval scent of the swamp, the high-pitched, ceaseless hum of a thousand locusts on a hot summer night, and yet it all seemed strange to her, and oddly new, and she wasn't sure that was a bad thing.

"I still can't believe it was Jean-Lambert killing all those people," she said, leaning her back against Zach's chest as he came to stand behind her. "I keep telling myself the seizure he had last May when he found out about Philippe must have affected his mind somehow." His arms came around her, drawing her hard up against him, and she held on to him, her hands gripping his. "I have to believe that. The Jean-Lambert I knew and loved would never have done those things."

"Huh," said Zach, his breath warm against her ear. "What's his wife's excuse?"

She turned in his arms, her gaze searching his shadowed face. "What will you do to her?"

"Nothing. As far as the United States government is concerned, she's a hero. After all, the information she gave led to the capture of five hundred thousand dollars in Confederate gold."

"She tried to have you killed."

"I have no proof of that."

Emmanuelle pressed her cheek against his chest, her arms slipping around his waist. She could feel his heart beating, strong and steady. "Jean-Lambert knew. But he didn't know she was the one who had betrayed Philippe."

He brought up one hand to stroke her hair, his gaze fixed on the impenetrable wall of cypress swamp in the distance. "It's a terrible thing," he said softly, "to think that a woman could love her family's name more than she loved her own child."

"I always knew appearances were everything to Marie Thérèse. But I never thought even she could go so far."

He closed his fingers gently on her shoulders, holding her away from him so that he could see her face. "What will you do now?"

She felt a sad smile curl her lips as she stared up at him. "Go back to Paris. Be certified as a doctor."

"And then what?"

"Come back here. Everything Jean-Lambert owned is Dominic's now. Besides, New Orleans is our home. I can't imagine living anyplace else."

"They won't let you practice here."

"Not at first. But someone has to fight them. Someone has to be the one to make them change."

A silence opened up between them, a silence filled with the song of the locusts and the whisper of warm night air moving gently through the shadowy branches of the oaks. "My French isn't very good," he said after a moment, his voice oddly husky. "But I'm willing to learn. This war can't last forever."

Emmanuelle let her head fall back, her breath catching in her chest as she searched his face. "You would do that? Move to Paris, and then come back here to live? You would do that for me?"

"I would do that," he said simply. A muscle bunched and hollowed in one lean cheek. "I love you, Emmanuelle, whether you believe in it or not. And I swear—"

"Don't." She touched her fingers to his lips, stopping him. "What's the worst thing about yourself that you've never told me?"

His eyes widened in surprise, then narrowed down as he thought about it. "You know how I told you my father is a sea captain?" he said after a moment, his lips moving against her fingers.

"Yes."

"What I didn't tell you is that he owns his own ship." Zach paused. "Actually, my family owns the entire shipping company."

"And how is this a bad thing?"

He kissed her fingers. "The shipping company was begun by my great-great-grandfather. He made a fortune running slaves from Africa to the Caribbean."

"The sin was your forefather's, not yours."

"I still thought you should know, before you agreed to marry me."

She shook her head. "You haven't asked what's the worst thing about myself that I've never told you."

The edges of his eyes crinkled, as if he were thinking about smiling. "All right. What is it?"

"I lied to you," she said, settling her arms around his neck.

"You lied to me about a lot of things." His hands spanned her waist, gripping her tightly. "Which particular one are you referring to?"

"When I told you I didn't love you. I lied. I do love you. Desperately. I don't know if it will last, but I want it to. I've never wanted anything so much in my life."

He crushed her to him, his words a soft murmur against her ear. "That's all I can ask for," he said. Then he held her face in his hands, and kissed her mouth so softly and sweetly, she felt a sting of tears start in her eyes.

She supposed there would be times when his ways would anger her, just as there would be times when she would frustrate or perplex him. He was a man of war, hard and violent and not at all the kind of man she would ever have thought she might love. Yet no matter what the future might bring, she knew she would never regret this moment, this decision.

Sometimes . . . sometimes, she thought, a woman needs to take a chance on love.

EPILOGUE

The steps to the attic of the house on St. Charles Avenue were narrow and winding, but the little girl clambered up them two at a time, the rubber soles of her untied sneakers making soft squishing noises on the worn old wooden boards. Behind her, her grandmother came more slowly, one gnarled hand braced against the roughly plastered wall for support.

At the top of the steps, the little girl threw open the door, then paused, going uncharacteristically still as she stared in awed silence at the half-forgotten jumble of broken chairs and shadeless lamps and old leather suitcases only vaguely discernible in the dim, dusty light.

"There," said her grandmother, nodding toward the big, camelback trunk that stood in an embrasure created by one of the old house's high gables. "That was hers."

The little girl, whose name was Emmanuelle, ran across the floor to fall to her knees before the arched, wood-banded lid. "It looks like a treasure chest." She glanced up, her eyes wide with excitement. "Did it used to belong to pirates?"

"No. Only my grandmother." The climb had been hard on the woman's knees, and she sighed as she sank down onto the fraying seat of a nearby caned stool. "Go on. Open it."

Hinges squealed as the little girl carefully lifted the lid and peered inside. "What's this?" she asked, lifting the worn and cracked black leather bag that rested on top of a jumble of ribbon-tied papers and faded, sepia-colored photographs.

The elderly woman leaned forward to take the heavy bag, and smiled. "This was my grandmother's medical bag. She was one of the first women to be licensed as a doctor in the state of Louisiana, you know."

The little girl nodded solemnly, for she'd heard the stories many times, although she never seemed to tire of them. "She's the one who went to jail for fighting for women's suf . . . suf . . ."

"Women's suffrage. She was determined to live long enough to see women win the right to vote in this country, and she did."

The little girl was rummaging again in the trunk. This time she came up with a large, cardboard-mounted photograph. "Look, Grandma. This must have been taken on the front steps of your house." Squinting, she turned so that the light streaming through the dusty panes of the gabled window fell on the faded image. "Who are all these people?"

The elderly woman leaned forward, her cheek pressing against her granddaughter's long dark hair. "That's my grandmother and grandfather in the middle. I think it was taken on their fiftieth wedding anniversary. Those are their children and grandchildren and great-grandchildren around them."

Eight-year-old Emmanuelle, who was an only child, sat back on her heels, her voice a stunned whisper. "They had a lot."

Her grandmother smiled. "They were very much in love."

Emmanuelle pointed to the thin, white-haired man

who stood near the edge of the crowd, his weight balanced negligently on a crutch. "Who's that man? He only has one leg."

"That's Uncle Antoine. We called him *uncle,* but he was actually a distant cousin of my grandmother's first husband. He lost his leg in the war. My grandmother always used to say his wounds should have killed him, but he was just too stubborn to die."

"Which war was that?"

"The one between the States, child." Stooping, the elderly woman pushed aside a bundle of old letters with Parisian addresses, and carefully lifted a faded black felt hat, its ostrich plumes limp, the golden crossed swords on its crown now tarnished and threadbare. "This was my grandfather's cavalry hat."

Evidently, this was one story Emmanuelle hadn't heard before. She sucked in her breath in a quick gasp. "He was a *Yankee?*"

"Mmmhmmm. Beast Butler's provost marshal." There was no need for the elderly woman to explain who the Beast was. Even a hundred years after the war, every schoolchild in New Orleans still knew—and reviled—the name of Spoons Butler. "After he married your great-great-grandmother, he rejoined his cavalry regiment."

"And fought for the North?"

"Yes. But he left the army as soon as the war was over, and came back down here to set up a branch of his family's shipping company in New Orleans."

The little girl fell silent for a moment as she stared at the photograph of the proud, straight-backed woman who stood surrounded by her descendants, her husband's hand resting lightly on her shoulder. "I'm glad I'm named after her," Emmanuelle said suddenly. "She looks . . ."

The little girl paused while the elderly woman thought of all the words that could be used to describe the strong-willed, awe-inspiring woman who had been born Emmanuelle Maret. "How does she look, Emmanuelle?" prompted the little girl's grandmother.

"Like she lived happily ever after." Emmanuelle's head fell back, her forehead crinkling as she stared questioningly up at her grandmother. "Did she?"

Her grandmother laughed. "Yes. Yes, I think you could say she did."

AUTHOR'S
NOTE

Until the beginning of the twentieth century, New Orleans was one of the unhealthiest places in North America to live. Yellow fever, typhoid, and malaria carried off thousands every year, which perhaps explains why the city became known, early, for its medical facilities. In fact, before the war, Louisiana was one of the few states that even bothered to license physicians.

Its unhealthy situation and climate notwithstanding, New Orleans at the outbreak of the Civil War was one of the nation's largest and wealthiest cities, and four times larger than any other city in the South. It was a city with a rich mixture of cultures, the old Spanish and French elite having been joined in recent decades by a flood of immigrants from both Europe and the northern United States. Out of a population of almost 170,000, only 4,169 people in New Orleans—among them, Creoles, Yankees, immigrants, and even freemen of color—owned slaves in 1860. Almost half of the city's 25,000 blacks were free, while Irish and German immigrants outnumbered those of African descent by almost two to one. This large population of immigrants formed a cheap—and expendable—workforce: At one point, over eight thousand Italians and Germans lost their lives digging the short, six-mile stretch of the New Basin Canal.

Perhaps it was this ever-present awareness of death that combined with a unique cultural blend to produce a city like no other. When General Benjamin Butler officially took control of New Orleans on May 1, 1862, he had little understanding of its people, and no idea of how to handle them. By the time he was recalled eight months later, his rapacity and venality had made him a rich man, but he never came close to subduing the spirit of the people of New Orleans.